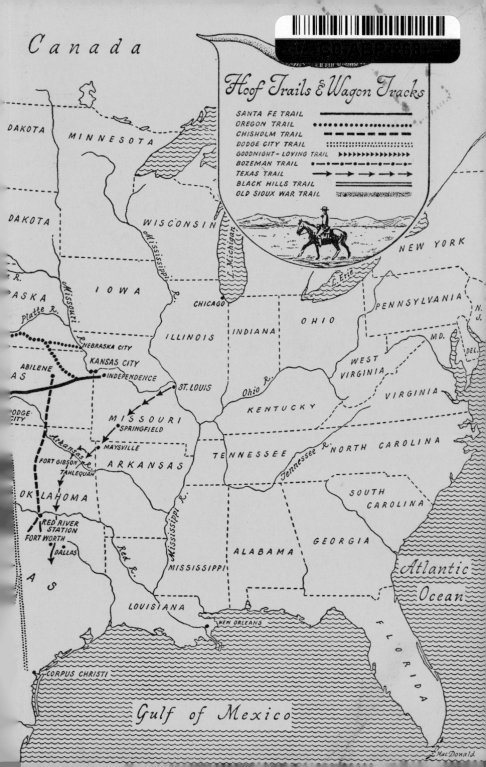

Hoof Trails & Wagon Tracks

SANTA FE TRAIL
OREGON TRAIL
CHISHOLM TRAIL
DODGE CITY TRAIL
GOODNIGHT-LOVING TRAIL
BOZEMAN TRAIL
TEXAS TRAIL
BLACK HILLS TRAIL
OLD SIOUX WAR TRAIL

HOOF TRAILS AND WAGON TRACKS

HOOF TRAILS and

WAGON TRACKS

STORIES OF THE WESTERN TRAILS BY
MEMBERS OF WESTERN WRITERS OF AMERICA

Edited with an
Introduction by Don Ward

DODD, MEAD & COMPANY · New York · 1957

Note

The Western Writers of America is an organization of professional authors, whose aims are to promote their common interests, encourage the writing of better quality Westerns, and bring them more effectively to the attention of the reading public. One part of WWA's extensive program has been the publication of an annual collection of stories by its members. There have been four such volumes prior to this one: *Bad Men and Good; Holsters and Heroes; The Fall Roundup;* and *Branded West.*

Introduction

ONE WAY OF TELLING THE STORY OF OUR WESTERN FRONTIER IS TO present it in terms of its great trails, the arteries along which flowed the surging humanity which was the lifeblood of the new land. Every American has heard of the Oregon and Santa Fe Trails; probably of the Chisholm Trail, too. He may have a vague idea that the land-seeking emigrant settlers used the Oregon Trail, a shaky notion that the Forty-Niners poured westward over the Santa Fe, and the too-simple conception that the Texans drove their stockyard-bound longhorns up the Chisholm. And that would be about as far as the average American's knowledge goes. There were, of course, a good many other trails besides those; many of them were of relatively minor importance, but the three widely known ones just mentioned were rivaled by others as main east-west and north-south routes, which, pictured on a map of the trans-Mississippi region, make a huge irregular grid. These east-west trails (after 1800, at least) were for the most part wheel-made; the north-south ones were hoof-made.

Stanley Vestal says that in the old days there were three main routes by which the Easterner could go West: the Missouri River-Columbia River route, the Oregon Trail, and the Santa Fe Trail. The first of these, the river route, was the pathway used by Meriwether Lewis and William Clark in their 1804-1805 expedition. They followed the Missouri up to its headwaters, went through Lolo Pass, across present northern Idaho to the Snake, down that stream to the Columbia, and thence to the Coast. It was then territory almost, but not quite, virgin to white men—the Frenchman Vérendrye, with a small party from Ontario, was in the Dakotas and perhaps in parts of Nebraska, Montana, and Wyoming in 1740-1743 (Vérendrye, believing that he was west of the continental divide, thought that somewhere farther down its course the Missouri must turn west or southwest and find its way to the Pacific!).

The Missouri-Columbia route had the advantage of following the river valleys, with relatively easy going, but it swung far north and made a long journey, afoot or horseback. A more southerly path, approximating what was eventually to become famed as the Oregon Trail, was laid out by John Jacob Astor's Pacific Fur Company group, led by W. P. Hunt and Ramsay Crooks, in 1811. Leaving St. Louis, the Hunt-Crooks party went by boat up the Missouri to the Aricara villages, some 1325 miles above the river's mouth, thence overland by horse and on foot, through Union Pass and along the Snake, and reached newly established Astoria in January, 1812. A returning group, led by Crooks and Robert Stuart, followed more closely the route later established as the Oregon Trail, missing the still unknown South Pass by a narrow margin. Historic South Pass was discovered in 1823 by an advance party of the Rocky Mountain Fur Company expedition under Andrew Henry.

Nathaniel Wyeth led a party of Massachusetts emigrant-settlers over the Trail to Fort Vancouver in 1832; they had the good fortune to be accompanied and guided from St. Louis to the Snake by a number of veteran trappers under the Sublette brothers, Bill and Milt. In 1836 Marcus and Narcissa Whitman's God-fearing flock made the long trip; they were guided by another mountain man, Tom Fitzpatrick. Fremont's much-publicized expedition

was made in 1842; and in 1846 the great historian Francis Park-
man covered part of the route at the height of the great migra-
tion and collected material for his colorful book *The Oregon Trail.*

As finally established, the eastern terminus of the Oregon Trail
was at Independence—later, because of the vagaries of the shifting Missouri River, it was changed to Westport. Thence it cut
northwestward to the Platte River, followed the Platte to Fort
Laramie and beyond, swung southwest through the valley of the
Sweetwater and South Pass to Fort Bridger, turned sharply northwest to Fort Hall on the Snake, and then followed the Snake,
short-cutting its big bend, to the Columbia.

Emigrants—both land-hungry farmers and treasure-mad gold
seekers—who were bound for California turned off the Oregon
Trail some fifty miles west of Fort Hall, taking a route which lay
north of Great Salt Lake and along the Humboldt River, and
southwest to Sutter's Fort: the old California Trail. To many of
these the necessity of making the long trek northwest from
Bridger's Fort to Fort Hall and then angling back sharply southwest to the Humboldt seemed long and gallingly roundabout, but
Hastings's vaunted "cut-off" from Bridger's place to the Humboldt,
going south of Great Salt Lake, was murderously difficult for
wagon trains, as the Donner party found out so tragically.

Most of the early Oregon immigrants finally settled in the
Willamette Valley, which involved another trek south from
Astoria; in 1847, Applegate's Cut-Off—which led from the Humboldt section of the old California Trail direct to the Willamette,
avoiding the Columbia and the troublesome Blue Mountains—
became the standard route to Oregon. For the California-bound,
the Overland Trail, leaving the Oregon at Ogallala to follow the
South Platte River and reach Fort Bridger by a more southerly
route, thence going by way of Great Salt Lake and Carson City,
became another popular roadway. Other thousands of emigrants
heading for the gold fields followed the so-called Southern Route

to California; starting at Fort Smith, Arkansas, this followed the Canadian River to Santa Fe, turned south to Donna Anna, southern New Mexico Territory, went west along the Gila to Fort Yuma, on to San Diego, and then north to the diggin's. Credit for blazing this trail is generally given to Captain Randolph B. Marcy, USA.

It was another east-west trail, however, that had the longest history of them all. The Spanish conquerors, persisting in their stubborn search for the fabulous "Seven Cities of Cibola," made their eager explorations in the Southwest in the sixteenth century. Coronado's 1540-1542 expedition met disappointment and made bitter enemies of the Indians, and only later did the excitement of gold and silver discoveries again impel the Spaniards into "Coronado country" and beyond. The first expedition covering the entire distance from Santa Fe to the Missouri River was made by a Spanish military force in 1720. In 1739, the Mallet brothers journeyed from the French settlements on the Mississippi to the Spanish towns in New Mexico, and in the early 1760's French traders from the upper Mississippi reached the vicinity of present-day Pueblo, Colorado, *via* the Arkansas River. William Morrison, merchant of Kaskaskia, Illinois, sent Baptiste La Lande, in 1804, to find his way to Santa Fe and look over the trade possibilities there; La Lande ascended the Platte to the mountains and turned south to reach Santa Fe—and once there liked the place so well he didn't go back. In 1805, James Purcell of Kentucky, trading with the Indians in the Platte valley, obtained permission from the authorities to enter Santa Fe; and he, also, stayed on for many years. Lieutenant Zebulon Pike, the first U. S. government officer to journey to Santa Fe, in 1806-1807, had his troubles with the authorities. The title, "Father of the Santa Fe Trail," was eventually given to William Becknell, founder of the Santa Fe trade, and deservedly so—Becknell, in 1821, was the first to use the route generally followed afterward, and the first to take wagons over it.

Independence served as the eastern terminus for the Santa Fe Trail, as it did also for the Oregon; the two trails split at Round Grove, about 35 miles west of the Missouri town. Caravans for Santa Fe generally organized for the trip at Council Grove, well over 100 miles west of Independence, single wagons or small parties going this far on their own. Here wagons were readied, loads repacked for the long haul, a train captain was chosen, and guard duty assigned. From Council Grove, the regular wagon route went southwestward, across the Arkansas River, Sand Creek, and the Cimarron, where the crossing was usually made at the Willow Bar. Some caravans went on farther west before crossing— indeed, it was the habit for earlier travelers to proceed up the Arkansas as far as Bent's Fort before turning south.

Generally speaking, the east-west trails were made by wheels. Of course the early trail blazers—the French and Spanish explorers, the Lewis-and-Clark party, Ashley's and Astor's trappers (not to mention the Indians who preceded them all)—trudged or rode horseback; but the great roadways which they later became were made by turning wheels and served mainly as highways for pulled vehicles carrying cargoes of human beings and chattels.

Not so the north-south trails. Originally made, in some cases at least, by the herds of migrating buffalo, they remained essentially highways for hoofs: the pounding hoofs of the longhorns being driven north from Texas. Of all the great cattle trails, though, the earliest followed paths which had been formerly used by Americans heading southwest. One which was later called the Sedalia Route ran from St. Louis west to Sedalia, then south and west to Fort Smith, down across part of the Choctaw Nation over a road which Jesse Chisholm helped lay out (this was *not* the Chisholm Trail, however) to Fort Towson, where, at Fort Towson Landing, it crossed the Red River into Texas. As early as 1858, Oliver Loving brought a herd of cattle north from Texas over this

Sedalia route to Quincy, Illinois. It was not until after the Civil War, however, that it was much used as a cattle trail; quite a few herds came north this way in 1866, one of which was bossed by dependable Jim Daugherty, who was all of nineteen years old.

Another of these early routes was the so-called Texas Road, which had been a main highway for Americans migrating to Texas in the 1820's and 1830's. From St. Louis, this proceeded more directly south than the Sedalia route, through Springfield, Missouri, to Maysville, Arkansas, Tahlequah and Fort Gibson, in Indian Territory, on to Colbert's Ferry on the Red River and into Texas. Northbound cattle herds starting from the Fort Worth-Dallas region, from Austin and San Antonio, and even from the Gulf Coast, traveled up this trail. This Texas Trail, the first of the main cattle roads, brought only a relatively small number of beeves north, however, and a large percentage of these were stockers bound for the new ranges in Nebraska and Wyoming rather than for the stockyard markets. Losses on the trail were high, because of stampedes, dangerous crossings and deserting drovers.

It had other problems, too: there was too much timber land, not well suited to driving herds of cattle; there were the grangers who feared the Texas-fever ticks borne by the plodding longhorns and who opposed the influx by quarantine lines, backed by gunpowder; and also the "Jayhawkers"—freebooters who preyed on the northbound beef-on-the-hoof. So the trailsmen began to swing farther west, aiming successively, after St. Louis, at Sedalia, Kansas City, Junction City—and finally at Abilene. It was this town, Abilene, where the farsighted Joseph G. McCoy built his pens and persuaded the Hannibal & St. Joe to load steers for the Chicago 'yards, that became the first great railhead terminus for the bound-for-market Texas beeves. The cattle route, having shifted considerably farther west, followed one used in 1865 by Jesse Chisholm for his trade wagons, bound from Wichita for the

Washita River market in the Nations. Chisholm was merely using a path made by Union garrison troops under Lt. Colonel William H. Emory, retreating from posts in Indian Territory into Kansas, in 1861. Chisholm's trade wagons used it four years later; two years after that, in 1867, the longhorn herds were pushing along "Chisholm's trail"; two of the leading drovers in that first year were Jesse L. Driskill and H. M. Childress. From the Washita River south, the Chisholm Trail ran eighty miles to Red River Station—about 100 miles west of Colbert's Ferry, on the Texas Trail—and feeder lines led into it from pretty much all of east and central Texas.

But the Chisholm Trail developed its own troubles. The Chickasaws and Choctaws, through whose lands it ran, levied a tax of ten cents a head on stock going through; and there were fences and nesters to contend with. Many of the trail outfits began to swing even farther west, to join with herds from West Texas— and the Dodge City Trail was born. It started north at Fort Griffin, crossed the Red at Doan's Crossing into Indian Territory, hit Cedar Springs and Buffalo Springs, crossed the Cimarron and the Kansas line to Deep Hole Crossing and thence led to Dodge on the Arkansas. The Dodge City Trail had its own problems: it traversed country held by Comanches, Kiowas, Cheyennes and Arapahoes—somewhat more belligerent characters than the civilized Five Nations tribes farther east. But by and large, the drovers got through with their herds and their scalps; and the railroads obligingly kept on shifting their cattle terminals westward, away from farmers and fences. The Dodge City Trail was eventually extended north from Dodge, *via* Ogallala, to Fort Buford in northern Dakota Territory; the extension has been called the Western Trail, but it should be noted that the original Fort Griffin-Dodge City route itself was sometimes called by this name, too.

Taking off in another direction, Charles Goodnight and Oliver Loving, in 1866, drove a herd of 2,000 longhorns from the upper Brazos southwest to Horsehead Crossing on the Pecos, thence up the Pecos to Fort Sumner, New Mexico, where part of the herd was sold. Loving then took the balance north to Denver while Goodnight went back to Texas to collect another herd, which he brought through the same year. This drive was a brutal test of endurance for men and animals, as it included a ninety-mile waterless stretch on the Horsehead route before the Pecos was reached. This became known as the Goodnight-Loving Trail; it was later extended north from Denver to Cheyenne, and eventually on as far as Fort Keogh (Miles City) on the Yellowstone.

The same year that Loving and Goodnight made their historic drive to Fort Sumner, 1866, Nelson Story showed up in Fort Worth, Texas, with his pockets full of gold he had dug out of Alder Gulch. He bought a thousand head of longhorns, hired a crew, and started north for Kansas City. Blocked by irate grangers and thieving jayhawkers, he detoured to Fort Leavenworth, took the Oregon Trail to Fort Laramie, and against everyone's advice drove his herd up the recently established Bozeman Trail toward the Montana gold fields. At Fort Phil Kearny, Colonel Carrington forbade him to go farther without orders from headquarters in St. Louis, but after a few days' delay Story set out anyhow. He got through in spite of Red Cloud's raiding hostiles—partly because he'd armed his riders with new breech-loading Remingtons —and delivered plenty of welcome beef to the hungry miners of Virginia City. Story's exploit stood in unemulated splendor, however, the Bozeman remaining primarily what it had been set up to be—a road for the military and for the miners bound for the Montana diggin's, and closed even to them for a few years after 1868 when a triumphant Red Cloud forced its abandonment. Another gold-seeker trail, not as well known as the Bozeman but still important, was the Black Hills Trail from Sidney, Nebraska, to

Deadwood; it is the setting for the story, "Miss Morissa," in this book. The Cheyenne-Deadwood gold trail was also very active for a short time. The main route to the Colorado gold boom was the Smoky Hill Trail from Fort Leavenworth to Denver, named from the Smoky Hill River along which much of it ran.

Before the white man's roads came the Indian trails, many of them long established and heavily used. "Warpath," another story included in this volume, tells of action on one of them: the old Sioux War Trail up the Yellowstone and into Crow country. By the way, all the incidents in "Warpath" actually happened to Indians whom the author knew and interviewed, the combination alone being fictional.

But these are only the bare bones. The West's great trails served as highways to adventure as well as paths to a new world. The deeds of the venturesome men and women who used them made colorful chapters of frontier history and, happily for our purposes, afforded the raw material for many an exciting fiction story. Here was the stuff of men-in-motion adventure, of hardship and peril, of stark challenge and the raw courage that rose to meet it. Members of Western Writers of America have, time after time, used it to produce prime entertainment.

DON WARD

Contents

CONTENTS

CHISHOLM TRAIL

DODGE CITY TRAIL

GOODNIGHT-LOVING TRAIL

TRAIL'S END

HOOF TRAILS AND WAGON TRACKS

SANTA FE TRAIL

Bridge Crossing

by VERNE ATHANAS

THERE WAS NO HIRED WAGONMASTER AT THE BEGINNING. OLD AARON
Courtney led off, as a matter of course, full of years and dignity
as head of the family, riding his spring wagon behind the two
matched bay mares.

The Courtney train was a family train. Old Aaron and his wife;
his two sons and their wives and families; the six hired men—
Jonathan Free and Dai Evan and the rest.

Jonny Free hired on because he was young and handy with
tools and stock, and it was a chance to move West, and be paid
for it; Dai was a Welshman with a rover's itchy foot. The Courtneys—well, the Courtneys were quite a family. They had means
among them to make up the family train, three big Conestogas
with their arching bows taut under new canvas, a couple of wood
and bed wagons and Aaron's spring wagon; some three hundred

1

head of spare oxen and meat cattle and loose horses; a pious, proper and provident train moving West to Oregon.

Providence went with them. Jonathan Free thought it should; old Aaron said the Words each morning before he mounted to the seat of the spring wagon—he read from the Book each night before they rolled in. Jonathan sometimes thought a little more night guard would have reinforced the prayer, but during the reading of the Book and the saying of the Words he could stand in the circle close to Charity Courtney, and that was about all the chance he got.

They went well enough until they hit Sand Creek. Old Aaron led off, splashing into it with his wagon. About midway, one of the mares got nervous and spooked the other, and the upshot of it was the wagon turned over, and Dai Evan had a bit of a time getting the old man ashore on the far bank. The Conestoga next behind the wagon stopped and began to settle, and bogged until even its four-yoke ox team couldn't handle it, and it was deep dark before they got the last of the train across that hundred-foot stretch of shallow water.

Aaron stood on the shore wrapped in a blanket and with his long white whiskers still streaming water, gave devout thanks that God, in His Infinite Mercy, had seen fit to spare his life in this, the Winter of his years. The next day, it was the eldest son, Provider, who lined them out and set the wheels rolling.

Thereafter, though he stood merely at the right of the splint-bottomed chair that was unloaded at each stop for the patriarch to sit, it was Provider who usually had the last word to say about the next day's drive, and by and by the rest of them looked to him for the word as to who should do what in their work.

A tall, wide, humorless man was Provider Courtney. But there was horse sense in him, and not a lazy bone. His two sons, almost men grown, were quick and obedient, and his two daughters were neat, mousy and ladylike. When a couple of ragamuffin Kiowa

bucks rode in one evening to beg sugar and then tried to steal a
couple of horses, it was Provider who smartened up their back-
sides with a load of fine shot from his fowling gun and sent them
howling over the hill. Thereafter, Malachi, the second son, as well
as the boys, went on guard duty half the night on odd nights, and
so did Provider.

Provider straightened out Jonny Free, too. That was across the
Missouri. An Iowa train was camped a mile away, and they were
not in good shape. Two wagons were broken down and the best
of their stock lamed. Provider sold one yoke of oxen to them, after
much dickering, for $150. They were small steers, not well-broken.
Jonny drove them over, visited around, and came back. Aaron
sat in his splint-bottomed chair, and Provider was hunkered down
at his right.

Jon went to Aaron and said, "Mr. Courtney, I'd like to draw a
bit on my pay."

Old Aaron looked up at him keenly, plucking and teasing at his
white chin whiskers, and he said slowly, "Well, now, Free . . ."

Provider said, "You were engaged for the emigration, Free. All
the way."

"Yes," said Jon, "but I've a chance to buy a yoke of oxen at a
good price, over yonder, and I want to draw no more than is
fair . . ."

"Why, now," said old Aaron, and Provider said, "There's right
and wrong, Free. You engaged to travel all the way at a set sum,
and it would not be right to pay before the job of work is done.
Besides, we've no time or labor to spare with sick and lamed
oxen."

"But I've looked at them," said Jonathan Free. "All they need
is . . ."

"No," said Provider Courtney.

Jon stopped and looked hard at Provider. "Right and wrong,"
he said. "Let's understand it. When I engaged to your father, I

was told I could throw any stock of my own in on the common drive."

"Right," said Provider quickly. "And you were engaged from Ohio to Oregon. Nothing was said of drawing against pay before Oregon."

"Right," said Jon through his teeth. He turned away and walked to the last bed wagon, where his kit and possibles were. He got a slim hide pouch out of his stuff and thrust it under his belt. He mounted his horse and rode out without looking back at the Courtneys. At deep dusk he came driving two shambling oxen ahead, and turned them in with the grazing stock. He silently took his place at the fire by Aaron's wagon, where Malachi's daughter, Charity, did the cooking.

Charity was a remarkably pretty girl, particularly here among the rest of the Courtney women, who tended to have a uniformly subdued look about them. She gave Jon a smile and got up to go to the big kettle to serve him. There was hog jowl in with the beans, and she found a piece, well streaked with the lean, to go on his heaped plate. She got him a bit of short-bread from the reflector and tea from the bucket, and when she went back to her own place by the rear wheel of the wagon, she moved over a bit so that there was space beside her. Jonny walked over to sit there.

Old Aaron finished his plate, laid it aside, separated his beautiful white beard from his beautiful white mustache with two fingers to drink off his tea and said gently, "Some water, Charity?"

The girl got up, took his cup, rinsed it, and brought it to him filled with warmed water from the bucket. He parted beard and mustache again, swished water through his teeth, dampened his red bandanna and carefully cleaned a little dribble on his beard. He said, "You bought the oxen, then?"

"Yes," said Jon.

"We'll not be able to hold back for them," Aaron said regretfully, "in case they cannot keep up."

"They'll keep up," said Jon.

"Fine," said Aaron. "You have the first guard, I believe?"

"That's right," said Jon. He finished his plate of beans and took the plate and cup over to the washing tub. He cut across the camp to where his horse was tied, thumbing tobacco into his pipe as he went. He stopped by Provider's fire to pick up a coal to light it, and Provider looked across the fire at him.

"You bought them," said Provider.

"Yes," said Jonny. He got his pipe going.

"Maybe you'll spend more time tending them, then, and less lollygagging."

Jonny took the pipe out of his mouth and said directly, "You'll have to make it plainer than that. I'm doing my work."

One of the girls giggled, and a flush of color came up Provider's face, spreading up from his dark beard.

"There's right and wrong," he said in his steady, unhurried voice. "You were hired to perform your task and not to lollygag about, making sheep's eyes at young females."

"I'm a hired man," Jon said evenly. "Hired to your father, not you."

"We are all one, in this family," said Provider.

"That I can believe," said Jon through his teeth. He clamped down hard on the pipe stem and walked on around the fire to his horse. It started to rain about midnight.

It rained all of the two days before the murder. That brought them up to the creek that never had a name before, unless the Indians had a name for it. After that it went down as Murderer's Creek.

They made scarcely ten miles a day through the rain. Twice they had to double-team through low places where the water tended to gather and soak, and they used up most of the precious

hoarded wood they'd brought in the wagons. Wet buffalo chips
just won't burn.

The morning of the second day they came to the bridge. Jonny
hunched miserably in a wet saddle and sucked at his empty pipe,
wishing he could make it smoke. The wagons pulled up, and
Dai and Jonny slacked back and let the herd drift to a halt.

Jonny, cold, wet and restless, waited for something to happen
up ahead, finally waved at Dai and walked his horse around the
herd and toward the wagons. As he passed Aaron's Conestoga,
Charity looked out at the sound of the horse and called, "What
is it?"

"Don't know," he replied. "I'm going to have a look."

The lead wagon was stopped a hundred yards short of the
creek. Three men sat horses in a group ahead, and the Courtney
men were gathered in a knot by the lead ox team. Aaron and
Malachi stood like two great wet roosters, uncomfortable but
bent on retaining their dignity. Provider stamped to and fro,
shaking water off his beard. His face was dark and raw in color.

"Fifty damned dollars," he shouted as Jon rode up within hearing. "Fifty dollars! It's robbery, I tell you!"

"Swearing will not make it better," said old Aaron pontifically.
"Perhaps if you talked to them again . . ."

"I've talked enough," Provider shouted. "I'll see them in hell
first!"

"My son," Aaron started sternly, and then he vented a pro-
digious sneeze and rainwater flew from his beautiful white
mustache.

"I won't do it," roared Provider. "I'll swim and carry every
damned wagon across before I'll pay fifty dollars toll to these
robbers!" He wheeled and stalked around his father and brother,
and whipped a sweeping arm through the air.

"Circle in," he bellowed. "Swing 'em in to park!" He did not wait to see the order carried out, but stamped over to his horse and swung up, turned his back on the men by the bridge and the train alike, and started off down the banks of the swollen creek. The rain was tapering off when he got back, but Provider was still growling with anger. The bridge men had gone back to their fire and a couple of canvas flies that made their camp.

"We'll swim the stock across," said Provider. "You can see how these thieves have done it. Held up the trains till they've et off the grass and had to pay to get across. There's grass on the other side."

So they drove the loose stock a mile down the stream to where the miry banks shelved, and drove into the water. They lost Provider's Durham bull and two of the milch cows.

Dai Evan had privately nicknamed that bull A'd Aaron, and there was some justification for the Welshman's wry humor. A'd Aaron the bull, was like Old Aaron the man; full of years and an impenetrable, unthinking dignity, bland of face and slow and ponderous of stride. A'd Aaron the bull wallowed out into the fast muddy water, swam half of the distance, decided he didn't like it, and turned back. The hurrying water took him away downstream, along with two of his harem who had followed him these many hundred miles now.

Provider thought a lot of his bull. He cursed and roared when the water took the bull, but had to stick with the job of getting the rest of the herd across, or lose more; but when he got ashore finally, he laced into his hired man, one George Stringer. Stringer had put in as wet and tiring a time as any of them, and being a silent and brooding man, hadn't said much about it. He said nothing now, until Provider rode his horse up alongside and laid a heavy shaking hand on him, and then George Stringer pulled a new Colt's Patent revolver out of his waistband and shot Provider through the belly at about two-feet range.

Provider fell out of the saddle in a helpless sprawl and landed on his head and shoulders in the muddy grass. George Stringer stared at him for a long moment, as if he were as surprised as anybody, as if now he wished he could take it back, and then he yanked his mount around and spurred him into a run.

Jon had been circling the loose herd to hold them from spreading, and he ran his horse at the sound of the shot. He met Stringer, who leveled the pistol at him and yelled, "Stay clear, there!" and Jon, who had no weapon, and whose mother hadn't raised any simple children, pulled up and let the man run on past. Stringer was out of sight by the time someone came with a gun, and there was nothing but to carry Provider back to the train.

Provider died a little after sunup the next day. The clouds drifted away reluctantly, and the sun came through, to make the earth steam as it dried. Jon and Dai rode back to where they'd seen an abandoned wagon and brought in boards and built a coffin.

There was no preacher. Old Aaron read from the Book and the women sang a song, and then Aaron walked with his slow unheeding stride back to the wagons while the younger men filled in the grave and put up a board.

Old Aaron spent the rest of the day reading to himself out of the Book and writing in his journal, which he had kept up every day since the train had left Ohio. The hired men stood around waiting for someone to tell them what was next, but no one did, and finally they took up among themselves and split the work. Jon and Dai rode down the creek and dragged back a huge bundle of willows for firewood, and Charity and her mother made shift to feed the lot of them. After dark, Jon and Dai went out to guard the stock across the river. It didn't do much good, though.

A little mob of screaming, whooping Indians rode through and stampeded the whole shebang a little before midnight. Jonny and

Dai each fired a shot at shapes in the dark which they hoped were Indians, and then very prudently flattened on their horses and rode north while the cattle and Indians stampeded south. Then they swam back above the bridge and shook out the camp, and spent the rest of the night on their bellies by the wagon wheels with every gun in the train loaded and close at hand.

Breakfast was pretty dismal, though the sun was out bright and warm. Jon sat on an ox yoke and watched old Aaron and Malachi. The old man sat in his splint-bottomed chair and Malachi squatted beside him, and they didn't seem to be talking much. Charity worked silently at cleaning up after the meal, and he spoke to her, but even she was depressed. All he got was a wan smile and a murmur that said nothing. Finally Jon knocked out his pipe and went over to the two men. "Hadn't we better be taking a look about the stock?" he asked.

Malachi looked up at him almost furtively and said viciously, "Those red devils!" Old Aaron thumbed reflectively through the thin leaves of his Book, and finally looked up. "It is the Lord's will," he said with his bland, unshaken dignity.

Jon waited. Aaron went back to his Book and Malachi squatted and tore grass apart with his fingers and muttered about the accursed things that had happened since they left home. Jon said as patiently as he could, "The Indians won't have any use for the cows and oxen. We can't move without them anyway. We've got to try to find them."

Old Aaron muttered, "It is the Lord's will. It is a judgment."

Jon jammed the empty pipe between his teeth and slapped his thigh with one hard hand. "That may be," he said around the pipe stem, "but I don't think He's going to hold it ag'in me if I go out and see can I find 'em." He tramped across the encampment, chewing vigorously on the pipe stem.

Dai wanted to go. They had their horses, and two others they'd kept in camp for emergencies, and one of Provider's boys went along.

It took them all that day to round up what was left of the stock, and that was most of the cattle and oxen. The Indians had killed half a dozen and butchered out the tongues, and of course, had taken all the horses in the bunch, but Indians knew the white man's *wohaws* couldn't compare to buffalo meat, and they'd just chased them till they were tired of it. Jon recovered both of his oxen. One had just been starved and worked down, and the other was coming along nicely since he'd lanced the swelling on its left foreleg. Grass or no grass, they swam them back across the creek and herded them close to the wagons for the night. One of the bridge men rode over in the evening. He sought out Aaron and Malachi and demanded bluntly, "You goin' to cross the bridge tomorrow?"

Jon thought there was just a touch of uncertainty in the way old Aaron looked up, but the old man said, "We have had a great loss in our camp here. We mourn our dead. I will decide later."

"Well, be thinkin', gramp," the bridge man said. "It might go to seventy-five tomorrow."

"It is unseemly," said the old man with lofty dignity, "to dicker and bicker when our son lies newly buried yonder."

The man said something short under his breath and then aloud: "You'll still cross our bridge if you cross, so think on it."

Jon drifted closer and said suddenly, "You never built that bridge."

The man looked down at him from the saddle. He was a big man, rough and bearded and his coat skirts were ragged across his thighs where his rifle was balanced. "No?" he said.

"Stands to reason," said Jon. "Look at your outfit. A horse apiece and a couple of ragged tarps and your blankets. You never skidded timber thirty mile to throw in a bridge when you had no wagons to cross. It's not your bridge."

The man grinned unpleasantly. "Try crossin' it and see," he invited.

Jon crossed the encampment a little after sunup and watched while old Aaron clambered stiffly down from his wagon. The old man grumbled and rubbed at his legs and clumped around to pull his chair out from under the wagon bed. Jon said, "Mister Courtney, are we going to cross today?"

Malachi came down from his wagon and walked over to squat by his father's chair. The old man mumbled something and opened the Book across his knees.

Jon said, a little more sharply, "Are we crossing today?"

The old man looked up. His mustache bristled out and fell back as he worked his lips under it. "Young man," he said severely, "your ways are most unseemly. Our business can wait for Prayers and meditation."

Jon said shortly, "Unseemly!" He looked almost wonderingly at Malachi, but the man did not look up. Jon got his horse and rode out and cut his two oxen out of the herd. He drove them in close, dragged a spare yoke out of one of the wagons and with Dai's help, got them yoked. He balanced his tool box across the saddle bow. Then, without asking permission or saying any other word, he drove the yoked team ahead of him, back the way they had come. He heard Charity call once, but he did not look back.

It was after noon when he came back, driving his weird rig. It was the two good wheels and an axle from the abandoned wagon they had used to make Provider's coffin. He'd cut the bed in two and balanced half of it on the axle and patched the broken tongue with dowels and a strap of iron from the rest of the wreck. The hubs squealed dryly, and the wheels wabbled a bit, but it moved. He drove it into the circle of the camp, and again tramped across to the Courtneys, father and son.

"Are we going to cross?" he demanded again.

There was a steady tremor to old Aaron's white beard as he tipped his head back, almost as if he couldn't stop the shaking of his chin. He looked out sternly under his frosty brows, and then his eyes went aside, out and above the wagons to the little knoll where the board stood up out of the prairie grass. He cleared his throat harshly and his hand shook as it went back to the Book on his knee. "I will think on it," he said finally. He looked away from Jon. Jon switched his eyes to Malachi. The man fidgeted, and looked almost imploringly at his father, but he said nothing, and he said it sullenly, almost frightenedly, with just the flickering shift of his eyes and the hunching of his shoulders. He was a rudderless ship, with Provider dead.

"Mr. Courtney," said Jon quietly, "it has to be done. I know how you feel about . . . well anyway, we can't just sit here. One way or another, we've got to cross."

The old man read from the Book, apparently not hearing, clear on down the page, and then he looked up absently. "Provider will . . ." he said, and then his faded blue eyes came sharply into focus and the tremor started in his beard again. He stared fixedly at something midway between him and Jon. "I will think on it," he said finally in a vague voice.

Malachi got to his feet suddenly and his voice cracked. "My brother Provider was slain. God will send a judgment on the thieves who have slain him!"

"Fine," said Jon, not following the reasoning, entirely, but hopeful that something was finally going to happen.

But Malachi slowly squatted down again. He looked at his father, and then at Jon's boots, without raising his eyes higher. "There is time," he said. "The Lord will provide."

"Now that," said Jon, "I aim to find out."

He found Dai, and said, "I'm going across. Are you with me?"

"Tha'll pay 'em?" asked the Welshman.

"I'm going across," repeated Jon. "Are you with me?"

The Welshman grinned a slow grin. "A'm tired i' the hunkers, lad," he said. "Reckon a'm wi'tha."

"Fine," said Jon, and told him what he wanted done. Then he went and got his kit and blankets out of the bed wagon and loaded them into the cart. He drove down toward the bridge. As he pulled around the wagons, Charity's brother Tobias came running, swinging his short old caplock rifle at the end of his arm and said, "I'll go with you, Jonny."

"Better stand clear, button," said Jon. The oxen slouched over the shoulder of the bank and started toward the timbered bridge. Across the bridge a rifle boomed and the slug slapped into the mud not six feet ahead of Jon. "That's far enough," called the bridge man. Tobias fell flat on his belly and thrust his caplock's muzzle ahead. "Stop that, you tarnal fool," snapped Jon, and then he yelled back at the bridge man, "I'm coming across."

"You are like hell," the man retorted. He handed back his fired gun and took another from the man behind him. Tobias said a bad word and eared back the hammer of his gun, and Jon said, "Wait," and then he heard the light pattering of feet running behind him, and Charity Courtney came around the cart, holding up her skirts to clear her hurrying feet.

Her face was flushed and one end of the braids about her head had come loose and bobbed to her running like a limber little horn. Jonny groaned under his breath. "Get back," he said.

Charity's eyes snapped. "I will not!" she said. She dropped her skirts and clenched her fists, and her small mouth compressed firmly. "Those bullies," she said, and the words fairly crackled, "those great bullying boobies! Just let them shoot at *me!*"

Jonny grabbed, but she was past him, and stamping her small feet into the mud approaching the bridge. Jonny groaned again and then tipped his head back and roared despairingly, "Dai!" He wheeled aside and snatched his double-barreled gun out of the cart.

The man on the bridge yelled at the girl, "Now, stop, dammit." Jonny took three running steps and cocked his gun. Then, across the creek, from behind the flied tarps of the bridge men's camp, Dai Evan rose up like a drowned Lazarus. His clothing still dripped from his swim across upstream, but the long dragoon's pistol he pulled out of its oilskin wrapping was dry. He trained it on the bridge men and said dryly, "Tha'll be smart to stay put." The bridge men stayed put.

Jonny hurried, but he didn't catch Charity until she was completely across. She was still marching on the fuddled bridge men with her fists clenched when he caught her arm and held her. He kept the butt of his cocked gun under his arm pit and let them look into the double muzzles. "It's not your bridge any more," he said. "Pack up and git."

And while Dai watched them carefully with the dragoon's pistol carelessly in his hand, they packed and got.

Jonny laid his gun down so he could use both hands at the job, and he put them on Charity's shoulders and shook her. He shook her rather severely so that her head snapped forth and back and the limber end of the detached braid bobbed briskly. Then he saw that her eyes were wide and her lips were trembling as if she were about to cry, and he stopped and put his arms around her. He really hadn't meant to hurt her, he said, and somehow his arms got all the way around her. He saw the way her mouth trembled, and he didn't really remember kissing her, but he must have, because she was kissing him back, and it was all very confusing.

"Well," said Jonny, and from behind him, Dai Evan said dryly, "A'd say that do't verra well," and Jonny turned loose quickly.

Old Aaron wrote in his slow, careful hand:

July 20. Clear morning, fine warm day. Today traversed 21 miles.
    Our wagonmaster, Jonathan Free, has proved out most
    capable, though inclined to impulsiveness.
    We are now .....

Jon waited for the old man to look up from his writing. When
he did, Jon said carefully, "Mr. Courtney, I understand there is a
preacher with the train camped over there. I've spoken to Charity's father, but she wanted me to speak to you too. We plan—
well, we plan on getting married this evening."

For a moment, the old man seemed almost to hesitate. Then
he said, "Yes, of course. You have my blessing." He looked down
at his pen, stuck it in the ink bottle and offered his hand. "It is
the Lord's will, I suppose," he said, almost resignedly.

"I wouldn't be a bit surprised," said Jon soberly. He shook the
old man's hand vigorously, and turned back across the encampment to where Charity waited.

But just the same, he thought rebelliously, *I don't think it frets*
Him too much if a man puts his back into it and keeps things roll-
ing when He's busy someplace else ...

"I think he's coming," Charity said with a queer breathlessness
as he came up. Jon grinned and took her hand and held it tightly
as they walked together across the encampment to await the
preacher riding toward them from the other train.

Buckskin Empire

by HARRY SINCLAIR DRAGO

TALL, SOBER-FACED GIDEON SKENE RANGED AHEAD OF HIS FAST-traveling wagons in the predawn chill. They were nine days out of La Paz and well into Kansas. It was his intention to be in Pawnee and the railhead before darkness fell again. Kiowa Smith, a grizzled, pint-size little man, rode at his side. Kiowa fancied he knew the reason for Skene's haste this morning, for in that country a man had few secrets.

"Yo're shore breakin' a gusset to git there," he said. "We better drop back a bit; we're drawin' purty far ahead. It's been a wet spring; the Kiowas like to raid this far north when there's water in the *charcos*."

Skene swung around in his saddle, measuring the distance back to the wagons by the faint rumble that reached his ears. "You're right. We'll pull up."

Where Indians were concerned, the little man was seldom wrong. From somewhere along the upper Arkansas he had been carried off as a child by a war party and raised among the Kiowas. He bore them no ill will. He had given himself the name of Smith, not having the least idea who he was.

"You know how them steam trains is," he said as they waited. "They're allus late—or later. I don't expect to see Miss Lavinia in Pawnee before tomorrow mornin'. It's shore goin' to be nice

havin' her back. By Jasper, Gid, we'll have to be careful how we
step, I reckon, when she begins usin' all them manners and education she's been learnin' back there in St. Louie."

Gideon recognized Kiowa's right to speak so personally. Lavinia
had been only a very young girl when the little man had gone to
work for her father. In the years between, Jeptha Marr had pros-
pered. His sheep and cattle in the thousands roamed the great
Rancho Santa Magdalena, and his freighting business had grown
so that wherever a wheel turned between La Paz and the Kansas
towns it oftener than not belonged to him—the finest oxen for
the heavy loads and the best Chihuahua mules for the lighter
work. Even old La Paz itself had lost some of its identity in his
success. In speaking of it, it was common practice for his enemies
to refer to it as Marr's Castle, a slurring reference to the great
house he had built, with its service of solid silver and its tapestries
and crystal chandeliers.

"I don't expect to find her changed very much," Gideon said.
It was something that had often been in his mind of late. He spoke
confidently, but there was a shadow of doubt in his blue eyes.
He had been in St. Louis several times. Life was easy back there.
Young men like himself had airs and graces that he did not pos-
sess. Kiowa seemed to read his thought.

He said, "She won't come back thinkin' she's too good for us.
This is her country, and when she picks her man it wa'n't be none
of them Eastern dudes."

A smile touched Gideon Skene's strong, generous mouth and
gave his lean tanned face a youthful look that was in keeping with
his years. "You sound as though you could name the very man."

"Wal!" Kiowa grunted. "Mebbe I could if I was the presumin'
kind. But there ain't no accountin' fer what a young fella will—"
He stopped abruptly, and his ears were suddenly cocked and
alert.

Gideon had caught that faint sound, too. It was like wind rushing through the tall grass. But he knew it was not the wind. Not a leaf was stirring. The distant murmur swelled, receded, and was gone, and the world was still and empty again. Behind him he could hear the teams coming up. In a quick glance over his shoulder he caught a glimpse of the swaying wagons, piled high with wool and hides, as they moved ghostlike through the mist that hung close to the ground. He glanced back at Kiowa, sitting with his rifle across his saddlebow.

"Ponies?" he queried.

"I dunno," the little man muttered. "Jest as well we hauled up before we rode through that plum thicket at the bottom of this draw."

It was growing lighter every second. He stood up in his stirrups and peered ahead. Down there at the bottom of gently rolling slope nothing moved, but Kiowa did not relax his attention even when the first of the teams came abreast of him. Gideon rode back along the wagons shouting, "Bunch up! Look sharp!"

He didn't have to tell his skinners why; they were experienced men, Missourians to a man. Jeptha Marr paid them their wages, but it was their boast that they worked for Gideon Skene. He not only held the record between La Paz and the Missouri River towns, but his wagons got through, come hell or high water.

The hoarse cries of the teamsters and the cracking of whips quickly had the wagons bunched. Past the plum thicket they rolled and up the far slope. Kiowa had a quick look at the bottoms.

"Injuns," he reported when he rejoined Gideon at the head of the train. "Fifteen to twenty of 'em. Tracks everywhere."

The sun began to lick up the mist. The country opened up, and they traveled fast for an hour. Ahead of them a thin spiral of smoke wafted up from the prairie. It put a question in the eyes of both men that remained there until they topped a slight rise. Black against the horizon stood the still-smoldering remains of the Washburn and Sublette stage for Santa Fe.

A savage curse forced its way out of little Kiowa Smith's locked lips. He knew at a glance what had happened here. Skene, his jaw set at a hard, grim angle, said nothing. This moment was not new to them; they had encountered it before. But their blood ran cold as they spurred ahead.

A few minutes brought them to the stage. The still, huddled mounds on the ground told their own story.

"Got 'em all," Kiowa growled as he slipped out of his saddle. One horse had been killed. It lay where it had fallen. The others had been run off. The driver and his three passengers had obviously been dragged from the stage before it was fired. Gideon pointed to the driver.

"Bill Parrott."

"Yeah— And Bill allus said they'd never lift his hair." The little man shook his gnarled head. "Wal, I don't suppose he figgered he had to look fer anythin' like this within fifty miles of Pawnee. This was civilized country to Bill."

He picked up a blood-smeared arrow and examined the wind funneling on the shaft. "Kiowa," he pronounced. "Reckon it was the same bunch that did all that burnin' and killin' down at Streeter's Station last fall." He glanced up to find Gideon staring with slitted eyes at the body of a young girl in her early twenties.

"That's awful!" Kiowa groaned. "The murderin' young devils! I know I'm jest a white Injun, but this makes my blood boil! I'd like to go after 'em and run a knife around their insides. Why, Gid, do you realize that if she'd been a day earlier Miss Lavinia would have been on this stage?"

"Yes," Skene muttered, his face grim. Lavinia had been his first thought. "She won't be on tonight's stage unless it has a cavalry escort."

The wagons had come up. The skinners got down and stood around. They were hard men, but they were touched.

"Get your shovels," Gideon told them. "We'll bury these people."

He got his blanket and wrapped the girl's body in it. An hour later the wagons rolled over the shallow graves. Gideon spoke to Kiowa. There was a troop of cavalry stationed at Old Fort Hibben, just outside of Pawnee. It was imperative that word be got there at once. The little man offered to go.

"I won't run into no trouble," he said. "Them devils is a piece west of here by now. But it ain't Injun nature for 'em to be satisfied with what they done; they'll have a try at sumthin' else—most likely the eastbound stage—before they head back for the Llano. If that's it the cavalry won't be able to do nuthin' about it. It'll be all over 'fore they git there."

Gideon nodded. "The stages pass each other in Gallatin. When Bill doesn't show up the agent will know something is wrong. He may hold up the eastbound a few hours—though there's no accounting for what a stage agent will do. But you make the ride; that's the least we can do."

"Shore," Kiowa said. "When do you figger you'll be rollin' into Pawnee? You've lost more'n an hour here."

"I know it," Skene answered. "If the train happens to be on time we'll just about make it. After you've talked to Captain Macgruder you go into town and find out about the train. If I'm not there when it pulls in, and an escort isn't possible, you see that Miss Lavinia doesn't take the night stage. She may be hard to convince —being anxious to get home—but don't take no for an answer."

Kiowa pulled away at once. Gideon watched him until he was not even a bobbing speck on the undulating prairie. Whenever the pace of the teams slowed even momentarily he dropped back to learn the cause, shouting, "Watch your leaders, Wash!" or "Your wheelers are doing all your pulling, Slick! Straighten out!"

Impatience in him seldom boiled to the surface, but he was driving himself as hard as the mules this morning.

He cut the nooning short. By two o'clock he was scanning the horizon for sight of the blue-clad troop from Hibben. Time ran

on, however, and another forty minutes passed before he saw a
detail of a dozen men, guidon whipping flat in the rising wind,
dash across the shallow crossing of La Bonta Creek. To his surprise he saw that Kiowa rode with them. They were spattered
with mud.

Young Lieutenant Daniels, fresh from the Point, pulled up
briefly. "Captain Macgruder's respects to you, sir," he said with
a formality strange to the frontier. "He says he will be pleased to
provide an escort for the night stage as far as the Little Sandy."

Learning that Gideon had no information to give him that
Kiowa had not already imparted, the lieutenant ordered his men
to ride on.

"I didn't expect to see you here," Gideon said to the little man.

"The train's three hours late," the latter explained. "So I borrowed a hoss and came back. Macgruder says it's Kiowas all right
—young Hueco. They burned out that little cow ranch on the
Sweetwater yestiddy and ran off some stock. You been comin' right
along."

Skene nodded in his tight-lipped way. "Been raining east of
here, eh?"

"Yes—two, three days. A real sod soaker."

They began to find pools of water in the trails, and before long
the wagons were wallowing in deep mud. The mules stood up to
it, however, and an hour before sunset Pawnee was in sight, its
sprawling, broken sky line dwarfed by the immensity of the
prairie.

Since the early days of the trail, long before Fort Hibben was
established, men had bivouacked there where crystal-clear Pawnee Creek crossed the long and little-known trace to La Paz and
Santa Fe. They called it the Crossing. Seven years back the finan-
cially uncertain Kansas Central Railroad had come trundling over
the prairie with the knockdown stores and houses that formerly

had been Cimarron City, sixty miles to the east, and overnight
the Crossing had become the town of Pawnee.

Some of those jerry-built houses were still there. But Pawnee
was firmly on its feet, its population doubling and redoubling as
it became apparent that the railroad was not going to leave it
behind. From time to time the Pawnee *Enterprise* still printed
stories to the effect that the Kansas Central was about to build
on to Denver; another time it was swinging south for El Paso.
After seven years no one took those tales seriously, for though
the town was prosperous, the Kansas Central was seldom able to
meet its obligations on time. It had been built on a shoestring,
and its debts were many. Only the beef herds driving up from
Texas and the business it garnered from the shortened trail to
the Southwest kept the wheels turning. Therefore, it was with a
sharp grunt of surprise that Skene saw the freshly graded road-
bed that extended several miles west of town. It had not been
there on his last trip east. No work was being done at the moment,
but some track had been laid and equipment was piled about.

"I wonder what that means," he said with vague concern.
Jeptha Marr had always scoffed at the idea of a railroad building
down into the Territory. Gideon had been skeptical, too. The
Kansas Central had never cast more than a faint shadow across
their minds, but though they had been careful to say very little
about it at the time, he could remember their relief at learning
that the railroad had bogged down at Pawnee. "Did you notice
this before, Ki?"

"Yeh," the other acknowledged lightly. "Don't let it worry you.
Ain't a spadeful of earth been turned in two weeks. The men ain't
been paid. The town's full of 'em, and they're gittin' ugly. From
the little I heard, I gathered that if some money wa'n't forthcomin'
purty soon they'd tear the K.C. loose from its hind legs."

They found Pawnee's main street a sea of mud. The eleven
wagons, piled high with freight, seemed to be of particular inter-

est to the men standing around in little knots on the plank sidewalk. By the look of them they were St. Louis Irish, brought out
by the Kansas Central. A dozen or more of them followed the
wagons to the freight platform beside the track.

"They're spoilin' fer a fight," Kiowa muttered. "It looks like we
might have trouble with 'em."

"Their quarrel is with the railroad," Skene said. "I'm not takin'
sides. Tell the boys to keep an eye open."

The men came down the platform until they were only a few
feet away. There they stopped, and their spokesman, a barrel-
chested man with a thatch of unruly red hair, stepped up to Skene.

"Brannigan's the name," he announced. "Matt Brannigan. I'm
runnin' things fer the lads. You git thim wagons away from here.
There ain't no freight bein' shipped till we git our wages."

Gideon's face thinned and his wide shoulders seemed to become
even wider. "Brannigan, your fight is with the railroad, not with
me. I've got freight to ship, and I aim to ship it." His tone was
deceivingly quiet. "If the Kansas Central needs money, freight is
a good way to get it. You better step aside now."

"Not so fast with that step-aside stuff, me bucko," the red-
haired man growled. "I'm tellin' you to git your wagons outa here.
You can ship when this little matter has been settled—and not
before! Am I right, lads?"

"Right!" was the booming answer.

Kiowa had sounded a shrill trail yell. It brought the bearded
Missourians to the platform on the run. Their methods were un-
orthodox, but in a rough-and-tumble fight Gideon had seen them
lick their weight in human wildcats. A fight was the last thing he
wanted, however. And yet, believing that the right was all on his
side, he didn't propose to back down.

"You're asking for trouble, Brannigan." His tone was tight and
tense. "I'm not moving my wagons."

"Then we'll move 'em for you!" was the bullying response.

Little Kiowa saw the corners of Gideon's mouth twitch. It was a danger signal that he recognized. He expected to see him drive his whistling right into the man's jaw. Instead, Skene caught Brannigan by the belt and collar, swung him high over his head, and tossed him face down into the oozing mud.

Seeing their leader manhandled in that fashion made the others hesitate. Brannigan lay where he had fallen for a minute, the wind knocked out of him. When he scrambled to his feet, dripping mud and water, he cursed them for cowards, but even his bitter tirade failed to whip his followers to action. Growling and muttering among themselves, they beat a retreat, and Brannigan went with them.

"Yuh shore spoiled the fun, Gid," big Wash Clemmons protested. "I was all sot to start crackin' haids."

"You'll git another chance, I reckon," Kiowa said darkly. "This ain't the end of it. If we turn our backs fer a minute they'll tip over every last one of these wagons."

"You wait here," Gideon told them. "I'll step inside and see if the railroad can't give us some protection."

Starting down the platform toward the tiny building that housed the passenger and freight offices of the Kansas Central, he was aware of faces drawing back from the window. But though it told him that the agent was not alone, he was surprised on entering the office to find Phineas Tull, the president of the company, there, and even more surprised to see Vin Sandusky, the town marshal, occupying a chair in the corner. They had been interested spectators of what had just occurred.

"Good afternoon, Mr. Skene," Tull said, continuing to pace the floor. "Good afternoon!" He was a perpetually nervous little man with a pious-looking face who had worried himself bald. "You gave that ruffian exactly what he deserved," he cackled, rubbing his hands behind his back. "I—I don't know when I've enjoyed anything so much."

Gideon's attention went beyond him to Vin Sandusky, and his face was hard and flat. The marshal, grown fat and soft with easy living, shifted his legs uncomfortably.

"I see you're still wearing your badge," Skene said, a cold insinuation riding the words that Sandusky could not misunderstand.

"Gid, what can I do?" he protested. "There's more'n a hundred of 'em. I could deputize a few men, but that wouldn't do no good."

"No, I'm afraid it wouldn't—not if you can sit there and ask me what you ought to do. I know what I'd do if I was policing this town." He turned to Tull and the agent. "Well, what about it?" he demanded. "Do you want Jeptha Marr's business?"

"Of course we want it, Mr. Skene," Tull hastened to assure him. "We are delighted to have it."

"Get my wagons unloaded then," Gideon told him. "We'll give your men a hand—"

"But, Mr. Skene, I—I don't know that it would be wise to unload them."

"We couldn't put a man on that platform," the agent put in. "Brannigan's gang has got everyone scared out of their wits."

"Gid, why don't you drive out to the bed grounds with your wagons for the night?" the marshal suggested. "Tull says that Steve Bent, his general manager, is comin' in this evenin' on Number One with some cash. Things may be different in the mornin'. You'll find a Texas outfit holdin' some beef out there on the flat. They drove in this mornin', but they turned back when they saw how things was."

"Texas?" Skene took him up sharply. "Don't sound like Texas to me." He turned to the agent. "Heflin, open up the freight shed. I'll unload my wagons."

Heflin glanced questioningly at Phineas Tull.

"Oh, very well, if he insists," the latter sputtered. "But I warn you, Mr. Skene, the railroad company is not assuming any responsibility. These hoodlums have threatened to set a match to the shed."

"I'll take care of that," Skene said flatly. "You just look the other way, Vin. If there isn't any law in this town I'll make a little of my own."

The Hunter

by RICHARD WORMSER

THROUGH THE SHORT GRASS COUNTRY AND THE POST-OAK COUNTRY, the trail was pretty well travelled. Parties of west bound homesteaders followed each other as close as dust and grass let them; and passing them with greater speed were little bunches of bachelors, horseback men going to the new gold strikes in Colorado and Nevada.

This was not tough country; everyone was cheerful, yelling greetings as the horsebackers overtook the wagons and passed them; where some family group included a reasonably pretty girl, the gold-strike men would pull up alongside and chat awhile, maybe swapping fresh-shot game for camp cooked bread or biscuits or cookies.

But one man rode alone, and any greetings the wagoners might have given him died on their lips.

Not that he was a bad-looking man, though gaunt. He was tall, about thirty, and his horse was pure Kentucky. His saddle was old but well-spread, and there were no holes in his black hat, or his buckskin jacket and homespun pants.

Maybe it was his arming that shook off friendly folks. Under his left leg he carried a rifle, nose down in a saddle boot. Under his right leg there was a two-barrelled shotgun of the kind called a Roper.

But he had no belt-gun, and those were common enough and just about required uniform for a killer; the tall Kentuckian—he

27

had to be that from the cut of the saddle and the blood of the horse—was no badman. Nor a gambler, for they dressed better.

Thoughtful people, of whom there were not many in that westward heave, would probably have concluded it was his eyes and the shadow that lay on his face that turned the greeting off. That and another thing: thirty was not too young for an outdoorman to have gotten his face creased so that even when he was serious, a stranger could tell which way the line would fall when he smiled.

This man had no smile creases. Not a sign of them.

His name was Loyd Craike.

Where the Arkansas River dipped south, he left the trail, crossed the river, and went off by himself, or nearly so. This southwest trail had few attractions for the homesteaders full of the fables of Oregon and Idaho and eastern Colorado; and none for the miners. No gold had been struck down in the Texas country and land was rumored to be pretty solidly taken up by big cattle companies who looked grimly on homesteaders.

Still, a few wagon tracks, a few hoofprints stretched ahead of Loyd Craike. Maybe traders, he thought; maybe folks going to join relatives. It was no wool off his saddle blanket, in any case; he had his business down in the southwest, and a trail that was not used much would give him easier hunting.

He had forked south at noon; and at five, or thereabouts, he pulled off the trail, unsaddled, and spread grain on his saddle blanket for the Kentucky horse. When the animal had snuffed up the last seed, he picketed him in a patch of bunch grass and took the shotgun from its boot.

This was a dry camp; it was not his custom to stop by water. But they had crossed Ragglesnake Creek a half an hour before, and the horse had drunk his fill; Loyd Craike had two full canteens.

He washed out his mouth from one of them, broke the shotgun

and looked carefully down both barrels, holding a patch of linen at the mouth of each to give him better light. The left barrel was up to his standards, but the other one showed dust; he used his cleaning rod, and then put the chokes back on and took off in the brush.

There was no noise from his passing, though sage brush twigs littered these sandy hills. His feet went over the twigs or around them, apparently without help from his eyes. Certainly, Loyd Craike was not thinking about his boots.

A hundred yards from camp he heard quail talking to each other, discussing the end of the day, quail-fashion. He swung that way, stopped, and loaded the shotgun.

A few long, sliding steps farther, and he saw them. He stopped dead, and brought the gun up to his shoulder; his eye went down to the sight quietly, and he waited.

A Roper could put most of its shot into a 30-inch circle at fifty yards or more; but he waited and waited. Satisfied, he fired the right barrel.

Four quail went tumbling and the rest of the covey took whirring flight.

Careless now, Loyd Craike went forward and picked up his booty. He had made a good lineup, he thought, grunting. All four of the birds had lost their heads, and hardly any shot had gotten into the bodies to chip a man's teeth.

Two for supper, one for breakfast. He tossed the fourth bird away, broke his shotgun and put the unspent shell in one pocket, the spent in another, for reloading.

No longer hunting, he let the shotgun trail from his left hand as he went back to camp. But his feet still made no noise.

The next day, still trailing southwest, he saw dust ahead. He tightened his hold on the reins, and put the horse into a noiseless fox-trot, safe enough in sandy country. Loyd Craike rode now with his legs straight, getting every inch of good his height would give him.

But when he heard the creak of wagon wheels, he relaxed, much as he had after his dinner was secure the night before. Like most solitary riders, he sometimes spent a word or two on his horse. Now he told the sorrel: "Indians don't use wagons," and the red ears twitched in acknowledgment.

When he came up behind the wagon, it looked at first as though the teams were driving themselves. That was strange enough to send him off the trail, and around a sandhill until he was ahead of the wagon, and so placed that he could watch its passing without being seen.

As it passed his dune, the driver became visible; a boy, not more than seven or eight, hunched over on the bracket-seat, holding the lines tight and hunched against the noon sun. The floppy brown hat on the kid's head came down almost to his ears.

Loyd Craike rode out from behind the sand-mound and said: "Hi."

That kid was jumpy. He had whipped the lines under one skinny haunch and snatched up the pistol from behind him almost before Loyd Craike had finished talking.

It was a big Navy Colt's, and it looked bigger than ever in that grimy fist.

Loyd Craike said: "You better cock that afore you throw down on anyone."

The kid let the Navy muzzle droop. "Thought you was Injun."

Loyd Craike said: "Too soon for them. They stay further south, cattle-raiding."

"You live around here?"

Loyd Craike shook his head. "Passing through," he said. There was a grating sound to his voice, as though he used it little, and wanted to use it less. But the kid's eyes were sardonic and untrusting on him, and Loyd Craike added: "But I got good instructions for what's along the way. You ain't likely to see another human for mebbe two days."

The kid said: "Oh, my God!"

Loyd Craike's thin lips got tighter. "Ain't fitten for child'un to swear!"

They had been moving along as they talked, the four wagon horses at a steady walk, the saddle-bred at a light amble. But now the boy brought his lines down hard on the wheelers' broad backs and, as they picked up to a trot, said to Loyd Craike: "You go to hell!"

Loyd Craike carried no quirt or crop; anything like that would have been ridiculous on that well trained Kentucky-bred. But his reins were long and split for ground tying and he gathered the slack up in his right hand now, pulled back as though to lash the kid.

But just then a scream came from the jolting wagon that wiped out all memory. Loyd Craike sat down hard in his saddle and said: "What you got in there, boy?"

The kid looked like he hadn't used up all his profanity. But he was too busy to spend any more of it just then; he sawed the horses down to a walk and then stopped them, dallied the lines around the whip socket quickly, and dived back into the body of the wagon, under the canvas hood.

The off leader stamped as though he were about to take off; Loyd Craike rode to the front and grabbed the leader's headstall. He sat his saddle, impassive, grim-lipped. It was not his trouble, not his woman who had screamed, he told himself; and curiosity was for women and old men. But he had a right to stay and finish bawling that kid out for talking the way he had; Loyd Craike's hard-shell bringing up demanded it.

But when the kid came back through the opening in the wagon-cover, all the vinegar was out of him. Tears were streaking through the grit on his face. He said: "It's my sister, an' I dunno what to do." Then he sat on the wagon seat, hunched up under his foolish-looking hat and let himself cry.

Loyd Craike stared. He said: "I got a hurry to be in Texas." He said: "Ain't none of my concern."

Then he finally rode around to the boy's side, and dismounted, leaving the reins trailing to ground-tie his good horse, and climbed over the wheel and past the boy and into the wagon-bed.

He didn't have to be a doctor or a married man to know what was wrong. He hardly had to glance at the girl's figure, muffled in heavy quilts, though the heat of the sandhill day was mounting up. Just her face would have told him.

Loyd Craike took off his hat, and said: "Where's your husband, ma'am?"

The girl said: "He died. Took sick, and died. We were three weeks along the Osage River ford, waitin' for him to do it."

Loyd Craike nodded. The trail he'd left yesterday was thick planted with wooden crosses. It was a thing that happened. He said: "You should have turned back."

Another pain had gripped the girl; he could tell from the way her teeth gripped down on an upper lip almost as pale as the white teeth. But when she could, she said: "Nothing back home. We worked for a farmer, him in the field and me in the house, and when we got married, farmer threw us off the place. Nothing to go back to."

"I mought know how that is," Loyd Craike said, and surprised himself with a memory of a hill-country cabin, afire and spitting in the rain, and the bank's men out hunting the kid who had burnt his birthplace down sooner than give it to them; burnt the cabin and taken his father's rifle and become long gone.

"We were going to Colorado," the girl said again. "Thomas an' me and my little brother, Jem. But that's no good for a woman alone, except for a little kid; so I headed south. They say woman-cooks fetch high on the cattle ranches."

Loyd Craike nodded. He said: "That would sound right. . . . Lady, there's no ranches for two days' driving. And I'm just plain no use to you. . . . I was my Ma's only, and she the only woman I ever have lived with. . . . Maybe-so I had better ride hard down the trail and send someone back."

It was a woman's answer she gave him: "I'm sorry I screamed so before. No use sending help back, from that far away. It'll be over by then, and I thank you for stopping."

Loyd Craike made a gesture. He'd have given the Roper chokes off his shotgun, the front sight off his rifle, to be out of there and riding on. He owed these people nothing! They ate spoiled meat, and drank soiled water and died of it; they took trails that were longer than they knew and gave birth in the middle of them; they were fools, and—and the God of the hard-shells said: "Call no man Thou Fool."

He sat down on a keg of something—nails, most likely, for the house in Colorado that would now never be built—and said: "Nothing I can do."

The girl said: "It eases me to talk. What do you do, mister?"

Loyd Craike said, stonily: "I am a hunter. Hunted passenger pigeons for the Eastern market. Before too many others took it up, I have shipped a hundred barrels a day; I had two boys plucking and cleaning. I have hunted elk in the mountains to feed Army camps, and buffalo on the prairie to feed railroad builders."

The brown-haired head moved uneasily on the pillow. "It's a strange trade."

"It's mine," Loyd Craike said. "My father left me a rifle, and no more."

She said: "A farmer would know how to help me."

He said again: "I am a hunter, going southwest. I hear that the ranchers pay fifty dollars a head for every Indian cleared off their range."

Her hand came out of the covers, knuckled at her mouth; her

eyes got wide. She started to speak, but the pain gripped her again; this time the little, even teeth drew blood from her knuckles.

But when she could speak, she had not forgotten what she wanted to say: "People! You'd kill human souls for money?"

Loyd Craike picked his hat up from the floor of the wagon-bed. He said: "Those who have souls, nothing can kill those souls. Injuns have none: Comanches, heathen. They live by cattle marauding and stealing."

She looked at him, and it was the look he had gotten from the people on the trail; those who had had a smile and a greeting and a slice of bread for everyone but him.

He said: "Mought as well ride my road. I'm not a doctor; there is nothing I can do for you."

She nodded. "Yes. I seemed to get comfort from you but— Thanks for stopping, mister."

He took his hat and got out of there. The little boy was down on the ground, building a twig fire. It caught, and Loyd Craike said: "You know how to cook?"

The kid said: "Sure," and hunched over his little blaze.

Loyd Craike got on his horse and rode.

But it was time for his evening hunting. He watered where a clay field among the sandhills held a little pond; then he rode down the trail, tethered the horse and went back to the water, carrying his shotgun. He'd been gone long enough and far enough for the ducks to re-settle; one shot got three of them, and chunks of sage root thrown in the water brought them near enough to pick up without soaking himself above the knees.

He started down to his horse again when the ducks were cleaned. Just as his silent walk had not bothered the waterfowl, the people around the tethered saddle-bred didn't hear him coming; and as he had done for the wagon, he got behind a sandhill and looked them over.

Indians! His information had been wrong; they did come this far north.

There were about a dozen of them; three men, the rest women, children, a couple of babies strapped to the squaws' backs. They stood around the horse, and chattered in some outlandish tongue.

Loyd Craike moved a little, and saw that his rifle was still in its boot. That was a strange and wonderful thing to him; it seemed that Indians would steal a gun first thing. Only two of the men carried firearms, and these looked like old smooth bore muskets to him.

A choked shotgun could carry farther and straighter than any smooth bore of that age. Loyd Craike broke his gun and loaded both barrels with buckshot; he would rather have had the rifle, but he could make it do. . . .

He waited to line up at least two Indians to a shot. He'd want to get the two armed men first; but they wouldn't get in a line. . . . But now, one of the women was moving, right alongside a musketman.

She was one of the squaws who carried a baby. She turned her back, and the man put down his musket and unslung the baby for her; took it in her arms and started to unfasten her buckskin shirt.

The Kentucky horse blew then, impatient for his oats, and the Indians all laughed, even the papoose who was about to get his supper. His mother held him out so he could finger the horse's smooth nose, and the baby crowed again.

That seemed even funnier to the Indians than the horse's noise had been. They all laughed a second time, louder than before, and the mother tried to make the baby do it again. But he was tired of horses; he dug into his vittles, hard.

Loyd Craike lowered the shotgun and came forward.

Laughter died on the dark faces, in the dark eyes. Everybody moved a little away from the horse, and the man who had laid his musket down got between the nursing squaw and the hunter.

"Did you figure to steal the horse?" Loyd Craike asked.

There was a murmur among them, and then moved and shoved forward the oldest man Loyd Craike had ever seen. This one said: "I speak English, but I no hear so good. Old, I'm old."

As though he had to say so. Wrinkles covered his face till it was like a mud flat drying out; his eyelids had drooped until they nearly covered the black beads that peered at Loyd Craike.

"I said," Loyd Craike started. He had meant to repeat that about the horse and the stealing; instead he started again. "I said, who are you? Comanches?"

"We are Dika," the old man said. "We call us Dika. That is a good horse."

"I thank you," Loyd Craike said. "Where are your horses?"

"We got no horses," the old man said. His voice was so low Loyd Craike had to lean forward to hear him. "When we had land, we had horses, good horses. Now we got nothing. We hear if we go North, Washington will give us beef."

They were run out by the ranchers, that was it. Well, they had been smart; they got out alive. With the bounty on, they wouldn't have gotten away. Twelve scalps was six hundred dollars, a powerful amount of money.

The old man said: "It is good to see a horse again. When I was young, I rode all day. Good, no?"

Loyd Craike swallowed a couple of times. "Dika, huh?" he asked. He'd never heard of any such Indians before. "Here," he said. "Take these ducks. You can't hit anything with those blunderbusses. . . . Give me five minutes' start, come up to the water, I'll have some more for you."

He broke his gun, reloaded with birdshot.

But the ducks lay at the old man's feet, where Loyd Craike had thrown them. Except for the baby who was still eating, they all had their eyes on Loyd Craike's shotgun.

They thought he was going to kill them. Well, they couldn't be expected to know buckshot from birdshot, even if they'd seen it.

He said: "You were thrown off your land. Once, that happened to me. Take the birds."

The old man muttered in his awful language to his people. One of the girls scuttled forward and scooped up the ducks and got behind the men again.

Loyd Craike said: "You like that horse. One of your women could ride it for me."

That was too much for them. They just stared back. There'd been plenty of expression in their faces when they didn't know he was watching them; but now they looked like hill-people back home when the spring hail had beat their crops down.

Loyd Craike said: "I need a woman to ride an errand for me. A woman who knows about babies and how they come. Up the trail, a short ride on a good horse."

But they still just stared.

He raised his voice in exasperation. "I'll feed you, and then we'll all walk up after her. Nothing'll happen to her; she's needed to bring a baby."

They talked again, in their Dika talk, whatever that was.

The old man said: "My daughter will go. She has had babies; she'll do good."

"All right," Loyd Craike said. "All right. Tell her to eat and go."

"She eats today. She don't need eat again."

It was not the woman with the laughing baby who stepped forward; Loyd Craike had thought it would be, somehow. This one was older, but not as old as the spokesman; maybe nobody in the world was.

He helped hoist her to the saddle, and something about the way he did it started them laughing again. Loyd Craike growled; he couldn't see anything in their way of life to keep them laughing all the time.

The woman leaned from her saddle—Loyd Craike's saddle—and

said some Dika words to her father, if he was her father. The old
man turned: "She says she'll get your baby good for you. Maybe
a boy, like you."

"Tell her to get going."

The old man flapped a hand at the saddle-bred's rump, and the
woman went up the trail, the horse whickering at having to leave
Loyd Craike.

"Let's go," Loyd Craike said. "I will wait for you at the little
pond. I'll have more ducks, we'll eat hearty."

The old man put that into Dika talk, and Loyd Craike started
up the trail after the horse.

The woman's passing would have scared the ducks. He'd have
to shoot several times to get a feed for all those Dika. Well, there
was a time to spend, and a time to save . . .

Lord, lord, he'd left his rifle in the scabbard on the saddle. Getting mighty careless, for a hunter. . . .

Lord, he thought again, and this time it was not just a word.
Lord, maybe they do have souls after all. . . . Maybe he'd better
go north again, cross the Arkansas and take the Colorado trail.

He'd ask the old man to ask the woman how soon a girl could
travel after she had a baby. Maybe pretty soon, with a man
driving . . .

Bet you, after she's well again, she's a powerful cook, a mighty
bread baker. She could sit beside him on the wagon seat, and
when they passed people or were passed by them, they could
hold out a sandwich to a bachelor.

With him to hunt, and her to bake, there'd be no better sand-
wiches on the trail.

Loyd Craike knelt by the little pond, and got ready to shoot
down the biggest feed those Dikas had ever seen. It was too bad
that little one couldn't eat duck yet; but from the way he'd been
going, he couldn't be hungry, anyhow.

OREGON TRAIL

The Way West

by A. B. GUTHRIE, JR.

The Evans family—Lije, his wife Rebecca, and seventeen-year-old son Brownie—of Missouri make last-minute preparations before setting out on the long journey to Oregon...

THE WAGON, BACKED UP TO THE BACK DOOR, WAS NEARLY FULL, BUT not so full it wouldn't take what was left in the house. The pots and pans had been boxed and loaded, the bedding rolled up, the good dishes, such as they were, buried safe in the barreled flour, the clothing packed away, the few pieces of furniture they would try to take along mostly stowed beneath the wagon cover.

There wasn't much to do, not much before they closed the door and rolled away and left the Evans home to be somebody else's. Doing the last-minute things, finding a forgotten towel or stirring spoon, sweeping up so's to leave the cabin tidy, Rebecca Evans tried to match the cheerful hurry of the men. They had got the second wagon loaded, with bought food, plows and harness, the grinding stone and anvil, tools, the heavy stuff that Lije thought might be scarce in Oregon. Afterwards they'd tramped from the barn to start emptying out the house, Brownie asking, "What's next, Ma? What's next?" Lije saying, "It don't matter much now how we load. We'll straighten up at rendezvous."

It was like men, she thought, to be excited and not to feel with their excitement such a sadness as a woman did at saying goodbye to home. To a woman a house long-lived-in remembered the touch of hands and the tread of feet and the sound of voices speaking low at night. It remembered deaths and bornings and the young, gay talk of people newly married.

"You can take the walnut chest," she said and watched Lije and Brownie heave it up and saw the torn emptiness it left.

Each stick and splinter of this place was built by Lije, each little touch of prettiness put there by her or him. Everything had something of them in it. They had come here young and sure and seen the years pass and known trouble and happiness. It was, she thought again as she worked her broom, as if the house had shared their times and feelings, as if, quiet in the walls, sad in the empty rooms, was the memory of their doings, was the dread of strangers coming.

Outside, her menfolks talked, thinking out loud how to place things in the wagon. Lije's voice came to her strong, full of a sort of forward feeling she hadn't heard in years. And so it was all right, she told herself. The moving was all right, hard as it was. Oregon was all right. What Lije needed—and what Brownie would need later—was a better chance than in Missouri. What he needed was a dare. What he needed was to find out what he amounted to. A slow-going, extra-easy-tempered man, said people, not understanding it was his self-belittlement that made him so, not knowing that, without it, there wasn't much he couldn't do.

That was one thing she was sure of. Except for giving up the house she could be almost glad that Lije had got one of his rare and sudden notions and signed up for Oregon.

She swept the dirt out the door and took off her dustcloth. Everything was in the wagon. Everything. Nothing in the house but space, space and the broom and the flecks of dust she'd raised and the unspoken loneliness.

"Old Rock's ready, Ma. How about you?" Brownie's voice echoed in the dead rooms, in the room where he'd been born, where he'd lain as a baby in the cherry cradle Lije had built.

Lije walked from the wagon and came in and had a look around. "Seems you got everything, 'less you want to load up the house, too."

"Wish I could."

"Me, too, Becky," he said and patted her shoulder and went back out, asking, "Ready?" on the way.

"Soon's I get this poke bonnet on." She stepped outside, into the unbearable bright cheeriness of the early sun.

"Pa says I can herd the loose critters along, and him and you'll poke the teams," Brownie told her.

She said, "All right," and added, "Wait a shake," and turned back in, for it occurred to her, as if she had been slighting and forgetful of one who's served them well, that she hadn't taken the last long look that would be her goodbye. For a long minute or two she breathed the deserted air and in imagination put back into their places the fittings that had been torn away.

"Hurry up, Ma!"

She lifted her head and walked out, making sure the latch they'd used so many times was closed behind her.

*   *   *

The Evanses, with the rest of the emigrant party, are on the Ore-
gon Trail west of Fort Hall, many weeks later. Lije Evans has

*replaced one Tadlock as the captain of the train, and Tadlock
and a part of the original company have turned off the Trail to
head for California. Brownie Evans has married Mercy McBee to
take her along to Oregon with him, Mercy's parents having thrown
their lot in with Tadlock . . .*

It seemed to Evans now that one day was like another and
that all were bad. They were all work and worry and weariness,
and dust and sun and wind and night and sun again and work
again. He tried to whistle up the old, bold hope, but it had disappeared. It had ground out under the grind of wheels. It had
lost itself in crazy heights and depths. It had thinned away in
distance. Trying for it, the eye misted. Listening, the ear filled with
the dry complainings of wheels and wagon boxes. Eight miles,
fifteen, eight, twenty-three. It didn't matter. This sorry land was
endless.

Day on day, dust on dust, pitch and climb and circle while the
sand rasped under the worn tires and the rocks clattered and the
wounded sage oozed out its smell. Where's grass? Where's water?
Critters gant and hard to keep together overnight. Faces lank and
eyes empty, or pointed suddenly, thinking forward to the ford
across the Snake. Women cross, and young ones too, and men
sharp-worded through their dusted lips, quick with whip and
goad on teams too tired to care.

Violent country. Land of fracture and of fire, boiled up and
broken when God first made the world. Range of rattlesnake and
jackass rabbit and cactus hot as any hornet. Homeland of the poor
and poisonous, and did Oregon really lie beyond? Mountains
near and others far, sliding in and out of sight, plaguing people
for their brashness. The great gorge of the Snake, the very gut
of earth, the churning gut so steep below a horseman couldn't
ride to it, so far a walker wore out climbing down and back. Eight
miles, twenty, twelve. And still it didn't matter.

Evans knew this time would pass. He was right to try for
Oregon. He had been all along. It was just that the country over-
powered the mind. It was just that a man spent his hope in sweat.
It was just that he couldn't think ahead for watching out against
the here. It was partly that old Rock was dead and the place
empty where he would have trotted. And partly it was Brownie's
marriage, though not so much as once, and the manner of the
man and wife, as if they had to take their state dead serious.
Why, Evans thought, when he had first hooked on to Becky
he was all laugh and prank and couldn't always keep his hands
off her no matter if they weren't alone. No cause to take the thing
so solemn even though the dog was gone. This was a time for
frolic. For frolic, but for work for all.

He couldn't believe, back there at the fort, that the road would
be so hard. For two days afterwards he couldn't believe it yet,
while the train rolled to the Portneuf crossing and on to American
Falls. There were springs above the falls and a river island that
gave good grazing to the stock. But already, he remembered, the
grassy bottoms of the fort had grown to sandy, sagy plains, and
the Snake was scouring deep. The next day and the days that
followed showed him what his mind's eye couldn't see.

No one day tired the outfit out, and no one thing. Day on day
did it, and sand on rock on sage on drought. The sense of getting
nowhere did it, the feeling that the train stood still in spite of
straining wheels. The stingy treats of green and water, although
welcome, served to make the gray miles worse. A man's mind
turned back to them afterwards, as Evans' mind had turned back
to the Raft. Here the California trail veered left, up a shallow
valley toward a ragged peak a million miles away. Here Green-
wood and Tadlock and their men would start the journey south.
But it wasn't the thought of them that kept coming to him later,
while grasshoppers clattered off on dusty wings. It was the

thought of water and of grass. It was the remembered munching
of the stock. It was the fresh wetness on the tongue.

He put the Raft with the marsh they'd bedded by one night,
when he had heard the tear of grass to hungry mouths, far into
dreams. He put it with a campsite that the Snake made, rising
from its cut. He put it with Rock Creek and with Salmon Falls.
They put a cheerless hunger in him while the sunken-sided teams
dragged on to the crossing of the Snake.

A river out of hell, the Snake, or a river still in hell! A river
making hell for burning souls who couldn't get down to it. Summers had called him off one day, and they had teetered on the
great lip of its gorge and peered below and seen it like a frothy
ribbon, so lessened by its depth away that Evans had to tell himself that here was such tormented water as he had never seen.
A fair-sized falls and fair-sized water running white, sending up
a fair-sized rumble—and what it was was sweep and plunge and
thunder like nothing that he quite could believe.

He had pulled back, dizzy, and the question inside him must
have shown, for Dick had said, "We'll ford her just the same."

Evans had asked, "We could go round the loop, like someone
said at Hall, and so dodge both the crossings?"

"Could," Dick said while his eyes answered no. "Just as well
drown as starve, though, I'm thinkin'. You want to lose your last
damn head of stock?" He smiled. "The river calms down some.
We'll make it, hoss."

It was hard to think so, though, remembering how they'd had
to bed above. Once they'd pushed the stock away from camp a
mile or more and found a way down to the river more fit for
goats than cattle. But here was water and a little grass, and they'd
left the livestock there, just lightly guarded, and had packed back
water for the camp. And once, late starting after hunting wandered cows, they had camped entirely dry and found the stock
more scattered in the morning.

That was a thing that bothered a man—the thirst and growing weakness and most of all the hunger of cattle and horses and teams. Driving, a teamster saw the sagging pockets beyond the hipbones of his oxen and the chained knuckles of their backs. When he unyoked, they looked at him softly, their eyes reproachful, as if to ask how he could treat them so. And sometimes under yoke they just lay down, and no goad or whip or fork could get them up again, and a man trying felt more brutish than his brutes. They left them where they lay, with what life remained in them, thinking they had earned the slim chance of a miracle, and sometimes put plunder from the wagons with them—a chest or favorite chair or grinding stone—for every pound now counted. Leaving such, Daugherty had scratched a sign and posted it close by for travelers coming later. It said, "Help yourself." It also said weariness and the sour humor growing out of it. It said help yourself, only you can't, you poor devil like me, and so the joke's on you.

Coming on to good campsites, on to grass and easy water, men and women always tried to believe the hardest miles were rolled. For a little while—until they pulled again into the waste of sand and stone—their spirits lifted and their voices rang out full. That was the way of them at Salmon Falls Creek, where everything was plenty, and at Salmon Falls. Though grass and fuel were scanty at the falls, the Indians had fresh salmon and cakes of pounded berries to trade for clothing, powder, knives and fishhooks. Most of all for fishhooks, which Dick had thought to bring aplenty of. Fresh meat tasted good, even salmon, after days of chewing on dried stuff, eaten stiff or mushed up in a pot, though Evans came to feel he'd just as soon not see a fish again if he could have red meat. And the berry cakes were better yet.

Seeing the Salmon Falls Indians, Evans knew why Summers spoke so low of the fish-eating tribes. They were friendly and talkative and sometimes funny, but childish-minded and dirty and naked except maybe for a lousy rabbit skin, and they ate any-

thing—lizards and grasshoppers and pursy crickets that would gag
a man. They lived in huts of grass and willow that were just half-
circles, open to the south. The huts reminded him of swallows'
nests, niched around the way they were, except that birds were
better builders.

The camp had been a good camp anyhow, or not so bad as
some, no matter if grass and wood were scarce and the Indians
pretty sorry. A change of victuals helped the train, as did the
proof that human life of sorts could live in such a country. And
the great springs that burst out of the solid north wall of the
Snake gave the people something new to talk about. Spring after
spring, there was, like sunken rivers pouring out, which Summers
called the Chutes.

More sand came afterwards, more sage, more rocks, more no-
grass, more no-water, more worn-out stock, more of the hell of
the Snake though they had borne out from it to cut across a bend
it made.

Now when they were about to come to it again, to lower down
the bluff and try the ford, Evans told himself that if any train
could get to Oregon, this one could. It had the best pilot that he
knew of, best man and pilot both. Its stock was poor but no
poorer than would come behind. Its wagons were as good as
others would be by the time they reached the ford. But it was
the men he counted on, the men and women and spirit of the
company. They had their faults, he knew. They had their differ-
ences and sometimes spoke severe, what with sand in their teeth
and worries in their heads, but they wished well for one another
and they hung together. Here where sometimes he'd heard the
trains split up, old On-to-Oregon stayed one. Looking down
the line from head to tail after the long drop to the Snake came
into sight, he felt a kind of wrathy pride. Damn the Snake and
all its sorry kin of sage and sand! Damn the crossing! They'd make
it—he and Summers and Patch and Mack and Daugherty and

Shields and Gorham and all the rest, clear down to Byrd. They'd
make it or go down trying and still damn the Snake to do its
damnedest.

Once he'd wondered if they'd keep him captain. That was
when he'd outfought Tadlock and dared the other men to try to
hang the Indian, but nothing came of it except they showed in
little ways they didn't hold a grievance, maybe knowing without
saying that they had been wrong. Only Daugherty had spoken
open, saying, "I'm hopin' you'll forget it, Captain. It was the
divil in us, temptin' us to mortal sin." He had grinned and added,
as if to give warning that he was his own man yet, "An' let us
hope them Injuns quit their thievin' ways, or else to hell I'll
maybe travel still."

They were for him, Evans told himself while he watched Dick
coming into sight from below the brow of the bluff. They were
for him and he was for them and each was for each other, and
they'd get across the Snake and pull up safe in Oregon.

Summers rode alongside to say, "We can make it, I'm thinkin',
without hold-back ropes or anything. Steep but not too bad."

"Hold up!" Evans called to Patch, whose two wagons were in
the lead ahead of him. He lifted his hand for a stop behind. The
rearward wagons closed up slow and came to rest, the oxen dragging to a halt without command and sagging afterwards as if
from the little weight of yoke. He said to Summers, "Maybe we
better hitch a rope to the first wagon and some of us walk along,
just in case."

Summers gave a nod.

Evans faced down the line and yelled through his hands, "All
out!" though nearly everybody was. The call was relayed to the
rear by other voices. He waited, watching, until the last of them
was down. The last was Mrs. Byrd, moving heavy with the child
in her, and it occurred to Evans, seeing her, that he might as
well have let the people sit until their turns came up. He stepped

down the line, motioning to the nearest men. "Mack! Fairman! Carpenter!" Brother Weatherby came up with them, gray as a desert grasshopper from marching in the dust to save his horse. "Summers thinks we can drive down all right, but let's the bunch of us walk down with the lead wagon and see how it goes. We can stop her if she wants to run."

They followed him back to the head of the column, where Patch stood with his lead team and Summers waited to show the way. One of them had tied a rope to the rear axle. Mrs. Patch stood back with the second team, quiet as always and as always somehow noticeable. Evans thought while he spoke that you couldn't throw off on these two Yankees. They were cool and heady customers. He said, "All right, Dick. You ne'en to help, Brother Weatherby."

Weatherby said, "Why not?" as if there wasn't any answer, not even his sixty-four years.

Patch popped his whip and the oxen leaned into the yoke and the wheels turned and the front ones headed down.

The way was long and steep, but not so steep by Dick's meandering that two or three men, depending on the load and team, couldn't manage trouble if it came. Patch's outfit reached the bottom without real need of help. Still, it seemed wise to send men with each wagon.

The plan took time and wind but worked out safe. The loose stock came behind, footing careful down the pitch and breaking to a heavy, stumbling run for water. Evans saw, before he went to look across the ford, that grass was scant here too. It added to his maybe-foolish load of worry to think that poor teams would make a poor out at getting through the Snake.

The crossing didn't look so risky, though, being broken by two islands that sat like low rafts in the stream.

"It's far across and swift," he said to Summers and the other men who'd lined up along the bank, "but it don't look so deep."

"Deeper'n you'd think," Summers answered. "Water's so clear it makes the bed look close."

"How deep?" Evans glanced up at Summers, sitting thoughtful on his horse.

Summers shrugged. "Not too deep. Way to look at it is, it ain't easy, but it ain't beyond doin', either. We'll make it."

Evans tilted his head and saw the white sun veering down. "Dick," he said, "there's grass aplenty on them islands."

"Plenty."

Evans spoke to the others as well as to Summers. "Let's push the livestock to 'em and let 'em get their bellies full and then line out in the morning. They'll be rested and fed both."

It was Byrd who answered first, saying, "Amen to that." In his fair, ungrown-up face Evans caught the shadow of alarm, and he wondered, as before, how the man had raised the spunk to start out in the first place. He belonged in town.

Summers was saying, "Good idee," and the rest were nodding.

"Let's circle up, though maybe there's no need of it, and git the work stock over."

While he and Brownie freed their teams, Evans thought again of Byrd, thought of him with a little of embarrassment, as if Byrd's weaknesses rested on him. Like some other unmanly men he'd known, Byrd must be a clever man in bed, judging by the flock he'd fathered. It was vexatious to feel responsible for him, and yet he did and more so maybe than with most, remembering the words that Mack had overheard and told him. Back there at Fort Hall Tadlock was working on Byrd, arguing for California. Byrd had answered, "I'll stay with Evans and Summers. If any can, those two will see the train through."

To Evans there was a kind of womanish faith in that answer that, right or wrong, seemed to put an extra burden on him.

He laid the yoke down and let the team step out and saw his

in-law daughter looking at him. "Wore out?" he asked, making himself smile.

She gave him just the ghost of an answering smile. "I'm all right."

Evans was up early. The dark still hung here in the bottom though overhead the sky was lightening. He stopped outside his tent and looked off to the water, seeing it as just a fluid dullness, without the shine of sun or moon or stars. The voice of it came to him, the whishing mutter of its strength. All night he'd heard it, even through his dreams.

He shook himself against the chill, against the inward funkiness of early morning, wishing with a sudden impatience that all the camp was up, ready for a try that weighed heavier with waiting. Right now, with the blood flowing weak in him after sleep and the dark cast of dawn lying on his spirit, damn if he wasn't as bad as Byrd, empty-chested before a danger built up in the mind. They'd get across, down to the last setting hen and chick. It was his being head rooster that put the foolish fidgets in him.

He walked down toward the water, flushing up a ground bird that rustled out of sight. Close up, the river still ran black. He couldn't see the bottom of it. Out in the stream the islands floated like clouds made out at night. The shapeless movement that he saw might be the livestock, getting up to graze.

They'd got the stock out there all right and afterwards, after food and coffee, had made light of the crossing, saying shoo, it wasn't anything. Critters now and then had had to swim and the current sure enough was swift, but still it wasn't anything. And, with grass and rest, the teams would be still stronger.

They'd soon see how it was, Evans thought, while there slipped into his mind the way the river reared against the horse he'd used to drive the loose stock over. The eastward sky was showing red. An hour or so, and they would see. There was just breakfast to get and eat and clean up after, and tents to strike and loads to load and the stock to push back and hitch. Then they'd see.

Except for being unloaded, the wagons were ready, or as ready as the place allowed. By Dick's advice the men had gone wood hunting yesterday and had found a little, mostly smallish-sized. Evans had thought it next to nothing, not much more than good enough for fires, and had said to Summers, "Them poles wouldn't float a cart."

"Don't aim to float the wagons, Lije. Not here."

"Don't?"

"Tide's too stiff. A floatin' wagon might draw the teams along with it."

"So what?"

"What we want is for the wheels to set solid on the bottom. We'll lay the wood on top the wagon boxes—that'll give us extry weight—and h'ist the flour and such on top of it, so's to keep it dry."

There wasn't wood enough to help out much. Here and there the men had found a small and lonesome tree and here and there a piece of punky drift. They laid their pickings over the wagon beds and, to piece them out and get the spoilables above the waterline, used plows and pack saddles and boxes emptied into others.

Evans turned away from the river, hearing sounds in camp, and saw Summers riding up. Behind him the arches of the wagons had divided from the dark.

"Got 'er figgered out, Lije?" Summers asked.

"Sure. All we have to do is cross and then think about the second crossing."

"Second ain't so bad. Close to Boise, too, where there's help if need be." Summers smiled while his eyes studied Evans' face. "You sleep any?"

"Sure."

"Ain't no sartain-sure way against accidents, Lije. If'n one happens, no one'll fault you 'less you do yourself."

"I know that."

"Know it but can't feel it," Summers answered, gazing off beyond the river. "That's what makes you a good captain, I reckon, but it's hard on the gizzard." His eyes came back to Evans. "I swear, Lije, back in Missouri I never thought to see you playin' mother hen."

"Me neither."

"Best put four yoke, anyhow, to a wagon, an' up to six to some."

"That'll mean usin' some teams twicet."

Summers bobbed his head. "With a long string of critters. enough will have footin' if others has to swim."

"I see."

"An', Lije, I'm thinkin' we need a rider at each side, upstream and down. Up man could have a hold-rope on the lead ox nearest him."

"Down man would have a poke, I reckon. Which side is dangerest?"

"Down, I figger. Yonder there's a ripple it would be bad to sag below. Let swimmers do the ridin', Lije."

"That's a job for me then."

"You're a fish," Summers answered, nodding. "Hig's hard to beat, I seen down on the Bear."

"I'll ask him."

Summers clucked to his horse. "Thought I'd scout acrost and find out how to go."

Evans watched the horse take to the river. He saw it splash in, unwilling but helpless under Dick's strong hand, and brace against the sweep and feel ahead for footholds while the water rose. At one place it had to swim, and Dick lifted himself to keep from getting any wetter than he had to. They came out, streaming, on the nearer island.

Evans faced around and made for camp. There was other work to do while Dick did his.

The sun was above the hills by the time the train was ready. Evans had put his own wagons first in line, six yoke to the big one, four to the small, thinking it his duty to try the danger first. The other wagons curled behind his, some prepared to go, some waiting for ox teams to come back. People stood by them or perched inside or watched from on the bank, their talk littled by the thought of things to come.

Sitting his horse by the lead yoke, Evans squirmed around. His eyes met those of Brownie, who sat in the big wagon with Mercy by his side. He rode back toward them and pulled up and said, "I still don't like it. Let's have a try at her, with me up there, before you young'uns launch."

"We argued that out once, Pa," Brownie answered. "Lemme take the first team over. Me and Mercy ain't afraid. We got to go over sometime."

"Later's better, after we see."

"If all was to wait, you'd have to bring the wagons back to carry 'em across. Three crossings, that'ud make."

Evans flicked the end of the bridle reins against his opened palm, weighing one thing against another though he knew the choice was made. Young ones were hard to scare, believing they would live forever. Danger was a tonic to them. Why, right now, this minute ahead of risk, there was a looking-forward in their faces, a keen excitement more fit for new-joined man and wife than the sober manner that he'd wondered at. His gaze traveled back to the second wagon, where Becky sat, anxious but contained, as if she told herself here was a thing they had to meet.

"Never won an argument in my life," he said to the couple while he grinned at them. "Keep on Dick's tail now."

He remembered then he had put aside his goad. He rode to the second wagon and picked it from the wheel it slanted against. "Goin' to make it, Becky," he said. "Goin' to get to Oregon."

Her eyes were solemn. "You be careful, Lije. I'm as scared for you as anybody."

He raised the goad, saying with it that he would, and reined around.

They were waiting for him, Hig mounted yon side of the string, the rope from the near leader's horns dangling in his hand, and Dick ready to lead away.

"Reckon we're set," he said to Dick and saw that Dick's gaze was fixed behind. Turning, he saw Byrd hurrying up.

"Evans," Byrd said, "I'm nervous—about the children."

"They'll be all right."

"I know, but do you suppose you could take them?"

"First trip?"

"Your wagons are better and your teams stronger."

"You kin use my oxen."

"I just have the one wagon, too."

"Makes a big load all right," Evans answered, remembering how Byrd's light and flimsy second wagon had gone to pieces on the Green.

"And I'm not much of a teamster." Byrd spoke as if he'd like to think there were other things he was pretty much of.

"Don't take a teamster. Just takes a setter."

"Still—"

"Whyn't you wait until we try her out?"

"I'd like for the children to go in your wagons," Byrd said simply.

There it was again, Evans thought, the womanish faith in him, the clinging confidence that made him feel half sheepish but somehow answerable. "Bring 'em up if you're bound to," he said.

There were nine Byrd children, not counting the one unborn. Byrd herded them up. The oldest in the bunch was Jeff, who was maybe twelve and fair and open-faced like his father. He climbed into Brownie's wagon and took the toddler that Byrd lifted up. Three others climbed in after him. The rest would wait for Becky's wagon.

"Ready," Evans said.

"Here we go, hoss," Summers said to Brownie. He kicked his horse and reined around. Brownie hollered at the team.

The oxen took to the water slowly, staring out across it as if to calculate their chances. Already the current was bucking against Dick's horse.

Here was the deepest part, from shore to nearer island, the deepest but not the swiftest or the riskiest. The water climbed fast, up the legs of the leaders, to their bellies, up their bellies, streaming around the little dams that their bodies made. Evans wrenched his horse close, so as to be able to use the poke.

The lead yoke sank into a hole and lined out, swimming, giving to the current, their chins flattened on the surface. Evans punched at them, shouting, "Gee! Gee!" above the washing of the water. He felt the cold climb up his legs and felt his horse change gait, from jolt to fluid action, and knew that it was swimming. He held it short-reined, angled against the stream, while he worked the goad. Across the swimming backs he saw Hig's rope tighten like a fiddle string.

The leaders caught a foothold and staggered on and drew the next yoke over, and Evans looked behind him and saw the wagon lurching and Brownie grinning wide and Mercy holding the Byrd baby like the mother of it.

The island neared. In the wide and busy water it was as if the island swam to them. The oxen pulled up on it and drew the wagon after.

"How's that?" Evans yelled to Brownie while the team held up to blow.

The answer had the tone of spirit in it. "Ought to be hitched to a duck."

"Watch them wheelers do their part."

Summers led them across the island and angled upstream, and the water bore on them again and the oxen leaned into it, pitching on the tricky bottom, fighting upward step by step while the wagon balked behind. The second island was close at hand before Dick made a leftward turn and led them out where wheel tracks scarred the banks.

They stopped again to let the oxen catch their wind. Summers said to Hig and Evans, "Next one's hardest, you kin see." He raised his voice to reach to Brownie. "We head well up for two rod or so and then quarter a little down for six or eight and then turn up again for fifteen or twenty. Then point for where the tracks come out. Heavy water, but not so deep as some we've crossed. Watch out for that there ripple. We got to keep above her." The lined face grinned at Brownie. "What skeers me is your pa will git hisself washed off. Can't swim no better'n a salmon."

Fighting the current, seeing the lunge and sway of the wagon and the oxen half falling in the holes, Evans thought that only mountain men would have called this place a crossing. Only they would have found it and, finding, thought it possible to get a wagon through. This wasn't a ford, this wild, deep, uneven-bottomed water. It was an invitation to drown. Let a team be pulled over the muscled ripple to his left, let even a saddle horse pass over! Go it, critters! Again it was as if the solid land swam to them while the current banked against teams and wheels and wagon boxes and boiled off white at front and back. It swam to them, and the oxen lifted to it, and wheels ground in the gravel of the shore.

"We done it!" Evans yelled across at Hig as the leaders found the bank. "By godalmighty, yes!"

Hig didn't answer. He didn't need to. His thin grin answered for him.

"Dick, we done it!"

" 'Lowed we would."

"Fun," Brownie put in from the wagon seat. "Man, it was fun."

"Take the outfit up a ways, Brownie, and you and Mercy mind the young'uns. Don't want 'em underfoot."

"Want to take the team back?" Brownie asked.

"Unhitch and leave 'em rest awhile. We'll git some more across, I reckon, before usin' 'em again."

Later, with Becky across, and Mack and Shields and Carpenter, Evans told himself the talk last night was right: there wasn't anything to it. The crossing had the looks of danger; it sure enough was danger, close-sweeping in the stout and angry tide; but with Dick to lead and him and Hig to ride, there wasn't anything to it, not if a man took care. They'd be across, the whole set of them, by noon or maybe sooner.

Back on the southern shore Evans changed his blown horse, taking Nellie in its stead. "You ready, Byrd?"

"Ready."

"Ain't much to do except set, you and your missus."

"I'm grateful to you. I felt the children would be safest with you."

"Wasn't nothin'. Say you're ready?"

Byrd nodded, sober and watchful as a cornered coon. His woman was the same. Summers had said once she put him in mind of a pigeon, but, looking at her now, Evans figured she'd swelled out to a duck.

Behind them were more wagons. The Patches weren't over yet, or the Daughertys. After the last of them had made the crossing, Insko and Gorham and Holdridge and Botter would push the loose stock over. The herd wasn't so big now that Tadlock had quit the train.

Evans rode to the head of the line. "Good for another trip?"
he joked at Hig, who sat like a bent stick on his horse. A knobby
skeleton of a man, Hig was, with a face like an old white potato,
but he could ride a horse or swim a stream or mend a rifle, and,
what was more, he had a think-piece behind that withered skin.

"Good as gravy," Hig answered.

"Lead away, Dick."

They had hitched six yokes to Byrd's wagon, for it was medium
heavy and the oxen either partly spent or smallish for so hard
a chore.

They took the first stretch fine, barely swimming here and there,
for, after all the trips across, the best course had been learnt.
Glancing back as the leaders pulled up the bank of the first island,
Evans thought Byrd looked like a churchman facing sin, a proper
banker-churchman for the first time meeting evil in the flesh.

The next stretch went fine, too, the critters slanting up the
stream and bending left and coming out like other teams before
them.

While the oxen caught their wind, Evans made his horse step
back. "Just one more hitch," he said to Byrd.

"I honestly believe it looks worse than it is."

"It ain't so bad. Scare you, Mrs. Byrd?"

She said it didn't.

"Just hang on."

Evans walked his horse back and nodded at Dick, and Dick
led off again.

It happened suddenly, close to shore. It happened all at once,
without warning or good reason, like something bursting into an
easy dream. The team was going all right, the wagon rolling safe
above the muscled ripple, and then a leader slipped and thrashed
for footing, and the hungry current took it and wrenched its mate
along.

They descended on Evans, their legs scrambling the water into spray, the weight of them dragging the second yoke out of line. "Gee!" he hollered out of habit and poked with his stick and beyond the tangle of them saw Hig and the hold-rope taut and Hig's horse floundering with the pull on it. "Gee."

Nellie wouldn't hold. She broke before the thrashing push of them, frightened now and unsteady in the tear of water. The line clear back to the wheel yoke skewed to the pull, slanting the wagon below the come-out trail, slanting toward the ripple, slanting off to wicked depths.

The wagon began to skid, half sailing, half grinding over gravel. It was swinging like the tail of crack-the-whip, dragging the wheelers with it, bending the yokes into an arc that it yanked to a straight line, angled up into the tide. The swing squeezed Nellie toward the lower shore, into swimming water she couldn't swim against.

Too late the leaders found their feet. Every yoke was off the course, some trying to swim, some trying to set themselves, and all of them wild and all being beaten back. The landing place was drawing off.

Evans heard Hig shouting and Byrd crying out, in words that lost shape in the rush of water. His eye glimpsed people on the shore and Dick moving with his horse. And then the swinging wagon caught on an unseen boulder and the current tore at it and the upstream wheels lifted. Wrenched between the rock and wash, the wagon flopped over on its side.

For a flash, it seemed to Evans, things happened slow and sharp to see—Byrd grabbing for his woman and missing and she pitching out and he climbing like a squirrel up the side and she floating feathery as a hen tossed into a pond.

It wasn't a pond, this water. It was power and muscle to shame the power and muscle of a man. It was fury. It was the cold fury of the offended land. It rushed at arms and legs and tried to wrench the body over—and ahead of him was just the opened mouth of Mrs. Byrd, the hen's beak opened for a final squawk above the dragging feathers.

The beak went down, but underneath his hand, underneath the rippled water, he saw the blinking blue of cloth. He struck for it and caught a hold and squared around and tried for shore. It wasn't far away. It was a hop, skip and jump without an anvil in one hand. It was the stroke of an oar on peaceful water. It was here. It was streaming here, almost where he could reach it, and he never could. He hadn't strength enough, or wind. He hadn't legs and arms enough to take him over. Beyond, above the waves that lapped his face, he saw the people huddled, watching, and the wagon washed close to the bank and the oxen struggling and one yoke safe on land and Nellie standing near.

He lost them as a wave washed up. There was the water around him and the near-far shore and the sunshine dazzling to wet eyes and heaviness in arms and legs and strangles in the throat. There was the water and the power of water and the voice of it and over it another voice, over it, "Lije! Lije!"

The voice of Summers and the person of him, busy with his horse, and his arm swinging and a rope looping out, and his own arm catching for it and missing and catching it lower down.

Summers pulled him in, easy so as not to break his holds, and slid from his horse and drew Mrs. Byrd farther up the bank. The folks came running, Byrd in the lead, crying, "Ruth! Ruth!"

"She can't be dead," Evans panted at him. "Aint had long enough to drown."

"Ruth!"

Dick said, "Easy," and turned Mrs. Byrd over on her stomach and lifted her at the middle to get the water out.

"You all right, Lije?" It was Becky, scolding him with her eyes for he didn't know what.

"Winded, is all."

They stood by, mostly quiet, while Summers worked on Mrs.

Byrd. "She's comin' round," he said. "I kin feel the life in her."

He turned her over, and she opened her eyes, and Byrd leaned down and pulled her dress so it wouldn't show her leg. "Are you all right, Ruth?"

She didn't answer right away. Her eyes looked big and washed-out, and they traveled from face to face as if to ask what she was doing on the ground with people looking down on her. Of a sudden her eyes filled and her face twisted, and Evans switched his gaze.

She was all right, though, except for the crying. Directly she got up, helped by Byrd and Weatherby, and let them lead her toward the wagons.

"She'd best lay down awhile," Becky said, and followed them to spread a blanket. The women trailed off with her.

"Poor way you picked to git to Oregon," Summers said to Evans then. His smile said something different.

"What's the loss?"

"Ain't had time to count."

Hig shook his head, as if still unbelieving. "I don't think there's a thing except a cracked tongue and some plunder wet."

"Not a critter?"

"Don't seem reasonable, but that wagon kind of coasted into shore. I hung to the rope and the team done the best it could, and she kind of coasted."

"What did Byrd do?"

"Just rode 'er out."

"I swear! What's holdin' the wagon now?"

"Team's still hitched."

Byrd was coming back from the wagons.

"Anything wrong?" Evans asked as he came into hearing.

"No. I think she's all right. I forgot to thank you. I just came to thank you."

"Fergit it! Just happens I can swim."

"I can't forget it, ever. I want you to know that." When Evans couldn't think of more to say, Byrd faced around and walked away.

"Funny nigger," Summers said, watching him. "But still I reckon you got thanks comin', Lije."

"Owe some myself." He turned away from the faces fastened on him. Across the river the other wagons waited. "We'll camp here. There's more outfits to bring across and Byrd's wagon to haul out and fix, and the wood we put in the boxes'll give us fires. You all think that's best?"

Their heads said they did.

"And it'll give the stock another fill of grass," Summers added. "There's more hard goin' ahead."

Call This Land Home

by ERNEST HAYCOX

ONE AT A TIME, THE EMIGRANT FAMILIES FELL OUT WHERE THE LAND most pleased them, and at last only two wagons of the overland caravan moved southward along the great green valley of Oregon; then the Potters discovered their fair place and John Mercy drove on with his lone wagon, his wife in unhappy silence beside him, and Caroline and young Tom under the canvas cover behind. Through the puckered opening at the wagon's rear young Tom saw the Potters grow dim in the steaming haze of this wet day. Rain lightly drummed on the canvas; he listened to the talk of his people.

"Have we got to live so far from everybody?" his mother asked.

In his father's voice was that fixed mildness which young Tom knew so well. "The heart of a valley's always better than foot or head. I want two things—the falls of a creek for my mill and plenty of open land roundabout."

She said, "Rough riding won't do for me much longer."

"I know," he said, and drove on.

In middle afternoon two days later, the wagon stopped and his father said, "I believe we're here." Crawling over the tail gate, young Tom—Thomas Jackson Mercy, age eight—saw the place on which he was to spend the rest of his long life. In three directions the fall-cast green earth ran away in gentle meadow vistas, here and there interrupted by low knobs and little islands of timber, and cross-hatched by the brushy willow borders of creeks. On the fourth side a hill covered by fir and cedar ran down upon the wagon. A stream smaller than a river but bigger than a branch came across the meadows, dropped over a two-foot rock ledge like a bent sheet of glittering glass, and sharply curved to avoid the foot of the hill, running on toward some larger stream beyond view.

John Mercy turned toward the wagon to give his wife a hand, and young Tom noted that she came down with a careful awkwardness. Then his father stamped the spongy earth with his feet and bent over and plunged his tough fingers into the soil and brought up a sample, squeezing and crumbling it and considering it closely. He was a very tall man, a very powerful man, and all his motions were governed by a willful regularity. A short curly beard covered his face as far as the cheekbones; a big nose, scarred white at the bridge, stood over a mouth held firm by constant habit. He seemed to be smiling, but it was less a smile than a moment of keen interest which forced little creases around mouth and eyes. To young Tom, his father, at twenty-eight, was an old man.

John Mercy said, "It will take a week of clear weather to dry this ground for plowing." He turned, looking at the timber close by, and at the rising slope of the hill; he put his hands on his hips, and young Tom knew his father was searching out a place for the cabin. A moment later Mercy swung to face his wife with a slightly changed expression. She had not moved since leaving the wagon; she stood round-shouldered and dejected in the soft rain, reflecting on her face the effect of the gray day, the dampness and the emptiness which lay all around them. Young Tom had never seen her so long idle, for she was brisk in everything she did, always moving from chore to chore.

Mercy said, "In another two years you'll see neighbors wherever you look."

"That's not now," she said.

"The Willamette's beyond this hill somewhere. There's settlers on it."

She said, "I long for back home," and turned from him and stood still again, facing the blind distance.

John Mercy stepped to the wagon and lifted the ax from its bracket. He said to young Tom, "Go cut a small saplin' for a pole, and some uprights," and handed over the ax. Then he got into the wagon and swung it around to drive it under the trees. When young Tom came out of the deeper timber with his saplings, the oxen were unyoked and a fire burned beneath the massive spread of a cedar. The tail gate was down and his father had reversed an empty tub to make a step from wagon to ground. Between them, they made a frame for the extra tarpaulin to rest on, thereby creating a shelter. His mother stood by, still with her unusual helplessness on her and he knew, from his father's silence, that there was trouble between them.

His father said, "Water, Tom," and went on working. When Tom came back with the big camp kettle filled, his father had driven uprights at either side of the fire, connected by a crosspiece on which the hook hung. He lifted the camp kettle to the hook and listened a moment to the fire hissing against the kettle's wet bottom. The grub box was let down from the wagon box, but his mother was idle at the fire, one arm around Caroline, who stood by her. His father was at the edge of the timber, facing the meadow; he went over.

"Now, then," his father said, "it's sickly weather and we've got to get up a cabin. It'll go here. We'll cut the small trees yonder, for that's where the good house will stand someday. So we'll be doing two things at the same time—making the cabin and clearing the yard." His eyes, gray to their bottommost depths, swung around, and their effect was like heavy weight on young Tom. It was seldom that he gave young Tom this undivided attention. "We've got everything to do here, and nothing to do it with but our hands. Never waste a lick, and make every lick work twice for you if you can. No man lives long enough to get done all he wants to do, but if he works slipshod and has got to do it over, then he wastes his life. I'll start on that tree. You trim and cut."

The blows of the ax went through the woods in dull echoing, not hurried—for his father never hurried—but with the even tempo of a clock's ticking. His mother worked around the grub box with her disheartened slowness. First shadows were sooty in the timber and mist moved in from the meadows. He listened to the sounds of the empty land with tight fascination; he watched the corridors of the timber for moving things, and he waited for the tree to fall.

The rains quit. Warmed by a mild winter sun, the meadows exhaled fleecy wisps of steam which in young Tom's imagination became the smoke of underground fires breaking through. They dropped trees of matched size, cut and notched and fitted them. When the walls were waist high, Mercy rigged an incline and a block and tackle, but even with that aid his body took the weight of each log, his boots sank deep into the spongy soil and his teeth showed in white flashes when hard effort pulled back his lips.

After supper, with a fire blazing by the cabin, Mercy adzed out the rough boards for window and doorframe and inner furniture, and late at night young Tom woke to hear his father's froe and mallet splitting the cedar roof shakes, and sometimes heard his mother fretfully calling, "Mercy, come now! It's late enough!" Lying awake, he listened to his father come into the wagon and settle down upon the mattress with a groaning sigh and fall at once asleep. The dying yellow of the firelight flickered against the wagon canvas; strange sounds rustled in the windy woods,

and far off was the baying of timber wolves. Caroline, disturbed
by that wild sound, stirred against him.

The rains held off and the meadows dried before the roof of the
cabin was on. John Mercy said, "It might be the last clear spell
all winter. I have got to stop the cabin and break that meadow
and get the wheat in." He looked at his wife. "Maybe you won't
mind living in the wagon a week longer."

"I mind nothing," she said, "except being here."

John Mercy turned to his son. "Go round up the animals."

The two brindled oxen were deep in the meadow. Driving
them back to the cabin, Tom saw his people at the campfire; they
were saying things not meant for him, his mother with her arms
tight across her breast and her head flung up. Presently his father
turned away to yoke the oxen, hitch on the breaking plow and go
into the meadow.

The ancient turf became coiled, gloss-brown strips. John Mercy
watched the sky as he plowed and worked until the furrows grew
ragged in the fading day; and ate and built his fire and hewed out
the cabin rafters, and by morning's first twilight shadows he was
at work again, harrowing the meadow into rough clods, into
pebbled smoothness. The gray clouds thickened in the southwest
and the wind broke and whirled them on. With the wheat sack
strapped before him like an apron, John Mercy sowed his grain,
reaching for the seed, casting with an even sweep, pacing on, and
reaching and casting again. Young Tom sawed out the top logs,
shortening and angling each cut meant for the cabin's peak; and
at night, by the bonfire's swaying glow, he laid his weight against
the block-and-tackle rope while his father heaved the logs up the
incline into place.

On Sunday his father said, "Take the gun, Tom, and go over
this hill and keep on till you find the Willamette. See what you
can see. Come back around the side of the hill and tell me which
is the short way."

Within a hundred yards the cabin vanished behind the great bark-ribbed firs whose trunks were thicker through than the new cabin. They ran far to the sky and an easy cry came out of them as they swayed to the wind. Pearly shafts of light slanted into this fragrant wilderness place, like the shafts of judgment light shining from heaven to earth in Redway's old geography book. Fern and hazel stood head high to him, and giant deadfalls lay with their red-brown rotted wood crumbling away.

He climbed steadily, now and then crossing short ravines in whose black marsh bottom the devil stock stiffly grew, and stung him as he passed; and down a long vista he saw a buck deer poised alertly at a pool. His gun rose, but then he remembered the cool voice of his father saying, "Never kill meat far from home," and he slapped his hand against the gun stock and watched the deer go bounding into the deeper forest gloom.

A long two miles brought him to the crest of the hill, from which he saw the surface of a big river showing between the lower trees. Another half mile, very rough, brought him down to the river's margin; he turned to the right and presently the timber and the hill rolled out into the meadowlands. Directly over the river he saw a cabin in a clearing, and saw a girl at the break of the bluff watching him. He looked at her and suffered his short shock of disappointment to find a house and people here, for he had been until this moment a lone explorer pushing through a wild and empty place.

At such a distance he would not clearly see her face; she was about his size, and she stared at him with a motionless interest. He stirred his feet in the soft earth and he raised his hand and waved it, but she continued to look at him, not answering, and in a little while he turned and followed the open meadows as they bent around the toe of the dark hill and reached home before noon.

His father said, "What did you see?"

"The river's on the other side of the hill, but it's easier to go around the hill. I saw a deer."

"That's all?"

"And a cabin across the river," said Tom. "There was a girl in the yard."

John Mercy looked to his wife. "Now," he said quietly, "there's one neighbor," and waited for her answer.

She looked at him, reluctant to be pleased. "How far away?"

Young Tom said, "More than an hour, I guess."

His mother said, "If they saw you, they'll come to visit . . . and it's a terrible camp they'll see . . . Caroline, go scrub and change your dress. I've got to fix your hair." Suddenly she was irritably energetic, moving around to put away the scattered pans and the loose things lying under the canvas shelter.

John Mercy went toward a pile of saplings roughly cut into rafters; he cast a secret glance of benevolence at young Tom. Something had pleased him. He said, "We'll get these on in short order."

The saplings went up and crosspoles were set across them. The first row of shakes was laid when a man's strong halloo came ringing in from the meadow and a family moved through the trees, man and wife, two tall boys carrying sacks, and the girl young Tom noticed across the river.

The man said in a great, grumbling voice, "Neighbor, by the Lord, we could of saved you sweat on that cabin if we'd known you were here. Teal is my name. Iowa."

Talk broke through this quiet like a sudden storm. The two women moved beyond the wagon, and young Tom heard their voices rush back and forth in tumbling eagerness. The men were at the cabin.

Teal said, "Boys, you're idle. This man needs shakes for his roof. Go split 'em. It's a-going to rain, Mercy, and when it rains here, it's the world drowned out. The drops are big as banty eggs. They bust like ripe watermelons, they splatter, they splash. You're soaked, your shoes squash, you steam like a kettle on a fire. Boys, don't stand there. Mercy and me will lay on what shakes that's cut."

The Teal girl stood in front of young Tom and stared at him with direct curiosity. She was not quite his height; she was berry brown, with small freckles on her nose, and her hair hung down behind in one single braid. Caroline cautiously moved forward and looked up to the Teal girl, and suddenly put out a hand and touched her dress. The Teal girl took Caroline's hand, but she kept her eyes on young Tom.

"I saw you," she said.

"What's your name?"

"Mary," said the Teal girl, and turned with the quickest motion and walked toward the older women.

The Teal boys worked on shakes, one splitting, one drawing the cedar panels down with the knife. The wind lifted and the roar of it was the dashing of giant cataracts all through the deep places in the forest; the men talked steadily as they worked. The smell of frying steak—brought by the Teals—was in the air to tantalize young Tom. He leaned against a tree and watched Mary Teal from the corner of his eye, then turned and walked away from the trees to the falls of the creek and squatted at the edge of the pool, his shadow sending the loafing trout into violent criss-cross flight. Gray clouds ran low over the land and a deepening haze crawled forward. He hunched himself together, like a savage over a fire; he listened into the wind and waited for the scurrying shapes of the enemy to come trotting in war file out of the misty willow clumps. He sat there a long while, the day growing dull around him. The wind increased and the pool's silver surface showed the pocking of rain. His mother's voice called him back to mealtime.

He ate by the fire, listening to the voices of the older people go on and on. His mother's face was red from the heat of the fire, and her eyes were bright and she was smiling; his father sat comfortably under the cedar tree, thawed by the company. It was suddenly half dark, the rain increasing, and the Teals rose and spoke their farewells and filed off through the trees, Mr. Teal's last cheerful call returning to them.

Silence returned; loneliness deepened.

His mother said, "It was good to see people."

"They'll be fine neighbors," his father said.

His mother's face tightened. She looked over the flames and suddenly seemed to remember her fears. "Four miles away," she said, and turned to the dishes on the camp table. She grew brisk. "Tom, I want water. Stack these dishes, Caroline, and come out of the rain."

John Mercy went into the darkness beyond the cabin and built his work fire; lying awake in bed, young Tom heard his father's mallet steadily splitting out shakes, and he continued to hear the sound in his sleep.

By morning a great wind cried across the world. John Mercy lighted the campfire and cooked breakfast for the women within the wagon. He laid on heavy logs for the fire's long burning and took up a piece of rope and the ax and hammer and nails. "We have got a chore to do at the river," he said to young Tom. "You pack the gun." They skirted the foot of the hill, trailing beside a creek stained muddy by the storm. The meadow turf was spongy underfoot and the southwest wind roughly shoved them forward through sheets of fat raindrops sparkling in the mealy light. When they reached the river they saw a lamp burning in the window of the Teal house, but John Mercy swung to a place where the hill's timber met the bluff of the stream.

"There will come a time," he said, "when I'll have to send you to the Teals' for help. You'll need a raft to cross."

They cut down and trimmed six saplings for a raft bed, bound them with two crosspieces nailed in. A pole, chipped flat at one end, made an oar. Then John Mercy tied the rope to the raft and towed it upstream a hundred yards beyond the Teal house. He drew it half from the water and secured the rope to an overhanging tree and laid the oar in the brush. "You'll drift as you paddle," he said.

Homeward-bound, the wind came at them face on. Young Tom bent against it, hearing his father's half-shouted words, "It ought to be a month or more before the baby's due. But we're alone out here, and accidents come along. We've got to expect those things. No sensible man watches his feet hit ground. He looks ahead to see what kind of ground they'll hit next."

They came around a bend of the creek and heard a massive cannon crack of sound in the hills above them, and the ripping fall of a tree; its jarring collision with the earth ran out to them. They pressed on, John Mercy's pace quickening as though a new thought disturbed him. High in the air was an echo like the crying of a bird, lasting only a moment and afterward shredded apart by the storm, but it rose again thinner and wilder and became a woman's voice screaming.

John Mercy's body broke from its channeled steadiness and he rushed around the last bend of the hill, past the pool of the falls and into the cabin clearing. Young Tom followed, the gun across his chest. Through the trees he saw a figure by the campfire, not his mother's figure, but a dark head and a dark face standing above some kind of cloak. His father stopped at the fire before the stranger; reaching the scene, young Tom discovered that the stranger was an Indian. His mother stood back against the wagon with a butcher knife in her hand; her face shocked him, white and strange-stretched as it was.

He lifted the gun, waiting. The Indian was old and his cheeks were round holes rimmed by jawbone and temple. His eyes were sick. His hand, stretched through the blanket, was like the foot of a bird, nothing but bone and wrinkled dark flesh. He spoke something, he pointed at the food locker. For a moment—for a time-stopped space in which the acid clarity of this scene ate its way so deeply into young Tom's memory that ninety years of living neither changed nor dimmed a detail of it—he watched the latent danger rise around his father's mouth and flash his eyes; then, with complete unexpectedness, his father turned to the grub box and found half a loaf of bread. He laid it in the Indian's fingers—those fingers closing down until they almost disappeared in the bread. His father pointed at the gun in young Tom's hand and pointed back to the Indian, snapping down his thumb as though firing; he seized the Indian at the hips, lifting him like a half-emptied sack, walked a few steps and dropped him and gave him an onward push. The Indian went away without looking behind him, his shoulders bent.

His mother's voice, high-pitched and breathless, drew young Tom's attention. She was shaking, and in her eyes was a great wildness. "I don't want to be here! I didn't want to come! Mercy, you've got to take me home! I want my old house back! I want my people! I'll die here!"

John Mercy said, "Tom, take your sister for a walk."

Caroline stood in the doorway of the cabin, frightened by the scene. Young Tom went over to catch her hand. The half-covered roof kept Caroline dry, and he stood indecisively under this shelter disliking to leave it, yet compelled by his father's order.

John Mercy lifted his wife into his arms, speaking, "The creature was harmless. There are no bad Indians around here. I know the weather's poor and there's no comfort, but I'll have the roof on the cabin by tonight." He carried her into the wagon, still talking.

Young Tom heard his mother's voice rising again, and his father's patient answering. He clung to Caroline's hand and watched the rain-swept world beyond the cabin and saw no other shelter to which he might go. He was hard pressed to make up his mind, and when his father came out of the wagon, he said in self-defense, "Caroline would get awfully wet if I took her for a walk."

John Mercy said, "You did right. Caroline, go keep your mother company." He looked to the unfinished roof, he drew a hand down across his water-crusted beard, and for a moment he remained stone-still, his whole body sagged down with its accumulation of weariness. He drew a long breath and straightened. "Soon as I finish the roof, Tom, we'll line the fireplace with clay. I'll need some straw to mix with the clay. You go along the creek where the old hay's rotted down. Bring me several swatches of it."

The rain walked over the earth in constant sheets, beating down grass and weeds and running vines; the creek grew violent between its banks and the increased falls dropped roaring into its pool. Bearing his loads of dead grass to the cabin, young Tom watched his father lay the last rows of shakes on the roof and cap the ridge with boards hewn out earlier by the late firelight; afterward John Mercy, working faster against the fading day, went beside the creek to an undercut bank and shoveled out its clay soil, carrying it back to the cabin by bucket. He cooked a quick supper and returned to the cabin, mixing clay and dead grass stems, and coated the wood fireplace and its chimney with this mortar. He built a small fire, which, by drying the mud, would slowly season it to a brick-hard lining.

Throughout the night, fitfully waking, young Tom heard the dull thumping of a hammer, and twice heard his mother call out, "Mercy, come to bed!" At daybreak young Tom found a canvas door at the cabin; inside, a fire burned on the dirt hearth and a kettle steamed from the crane. The crevices between logs were mud-sealed, the table and grub box and benches had been brought in. Standing before the fire, young Tom heard the wind search the outer wall and fall away, and suddenly the warmth of the place thawed the coldness which lay beneath his skin. He heard his mother come in, and he turned to see his parents standing face to face, almost like strangers.

His mother said, "Mercy, did you sleep at all?"

His father's answer was somehow embarrassed. "I had to keep the fire alive, so the mud would dry right. Today I'll get the puncheons on the floor and we can move the beds in." In a still gentler voice, the uncertainness of apology in it, his father added, "Maybe, if you shut your eyes and think how all this will look five years from now—"

She cut him off with the curt swing of her body, and walked to the fire. Stooping with a slowness so unlike her, she laid the Dutch oven against the flame and went to the grub box. She put her yellow mixing bowl on the table, she got her flour and her shortening and her salt. She stood a moment over the mixing bowl, not looking at John Mercy. "As long as I can do my share, I'll do it. Tom, fetch me the pail of water."

He stood with his father at the break of the trees, viewing the yellow-gray turf of the meadow, and the plowed ground beyond it, and the valley floor running away to the great condensed wall of mist. He knew, from the dead gentleness of tone, that his father was very tired; it was not like him to waste time speaking of the future. "The orchard will go right in front of this spot," his father said. "That will be pretty to look at from the house. The house will stand where we're standing. These firs will go down." He was silent, drawing the future forward and finding comfort in it. "All this is free—all this land. But it's up to a man to make something out of it. So there's nothing free. There never is. We'll earn every acre we get. Don't trust that word 'free.' Don't believe it. You'll never own anything you didn't pay for. But what you pay for is yours. You've got it while other men wait around for something free, and die with nothing. Now, then, we have got to cut down some small firs, about eight inches through. We'll split them in half for floor puncheons."

He turned, walking slower than usual; he searched the trees, nodding at one or the other, and stopped at a thin fir starved by the greater firs around it; its trunk ran twenty feet without a branch. "That one," he said, and went to the cabin wall for his ax. "Tom," he said, "I want you to go up in the hills and see how close you can find a ledge of rock. That's for the fireplace floor." He faced the tree, watching the wind whip its top; he made an undercut on the side toward which he wished the tree to fall, and squared himself away to a steady chopping.

Young Tom passed the cabin, upward bound into the semi-darkness of the hill; the great trees groaned in their swaying and their shaken branches let down ropy spirals of rain. It was like walking into a tunnel full of sound. His overcoat grew heavy with water which, dripping on his trousers legs, turned them into ice-cold bands; his shoes were mushy. Behind him he heard the first crackling of the tree going down, and he turned and saw his father running. The tree, caught by the wind, was falling the wrong way. He shouted against the wind; his father looked behind, saw the danger and jumped aside. The tree, striking a larger fir, bounced off, and young Tom saw its top branches whip out and strike his father to the ground. His father shouted, buried somewhere beneath that green covering.

His mother came crying out of the cabin. "Mercy! Mercy!" She stumbled and caught herself, and rushed on, fighting the branches away as she reached the tree.

When he got there, he saw his father lying with both legs beneath the trunk. The branches, first striking, had broken the force of the trunk's fall; and then they had shattered, to let the trunk down upon his father who lay on an elbow with his lips the color

of gray flour paste. Young Tom never knew until then how pierc-
ing a gray his father's eyes were.

His mother cried, "Your legs! Oh, God, Mercy!" She bent over
him, she seized the trunk of the tree and she stiffened under her
straining. John Mercy's voice was a vast shout of warning, "Nancy,
don't do that!" His arm reached out and struck her on the hip.
"Let go!" She drew back and laid both arms over her stomach,
a shock of pain pressing her face into its sharp angles. "Oh,
Mercy," she said, "it's too late!" and stared down at him in terror.

Young Tom raced to the cabin wall, got the shovel and rushed
back; a branch interfered with his digging. He found the ax,
thrown ten yards away by Mercy in his flight; he returned to cut
the limb away. Mercy lay still, as though he were listening. He
watched his wife, and he put a hand over his eyes and seemed to
be thinking; the impact of the ax on the trunk threw twinges of
pain through him, but he said nothing until young Tom had
finished.

"Give me the shovel," he said. "Now go get Mrs. Teal."

Young Tom stood irresolute. "You got to get out of there."

"Those legs," said John Mercy, and spoke of them as though
they didn't belong to him, "are pinched. If they were broken, I'd
know it . . . and they're not." He paused and a dead gray curtain
of pain came down on his face; he suffered it and waited for it
to pass. "Do as I tell you." Young Tom whirled and started away
at a hard run, and was almost instantly checked and swung by
his father's command, "You've got a long way to go, and you'll not
do it starting that fast. Steady now. I've told you before. Think
ahead."

Young Tom began again, trotting out upon the meadow; he
looked back and saw his father awkwardly working with the
shovel, sheltered by the outstretched apron of his mother. But
even before young Tom ceased to look, she dropped the apron,
put both hands before her face and walked toward the wagon.

The scene frightened him, and he broke into a dead run along the margin of the creek, and began to draw deep into his lungs for wind; he ran with his fists doubled, his arms lunging back and forth across his chest. A pain caught him in the side, and he remembered his father's advice and slowed to a dogtrot. He grew hot and stopped once to crawl down the bank of a creek for a drink, and was soon chilled by the wet ground against his stomach and the rain beating on his back.

After a rest of a minute he went on, stiffened by that short pause. The river willows at last broke through the rain mist forward, and the low shape of the Teal cabin. He crossed the last meadow and came to the bank; he hadn't forgotten the raft, but he wanted to save time. The wind was with him, carrying his shrill call over the water. He repeated it twice before the cabin door opened and Mrs. Teal stepped to the yard. Young Tom raised his arm, pointing behind him toward his home. Mrs. Teal waved back at him immediately and ran into the house.

Squatted on the bank, young Tom saw the three Teal men come out, lift a boat and carry it to the water; in a moment Mrs. Teal joined them, and the four came over the river. Mrs. Teal had a covered basket in her hand.

She said, "Your mother, Tom?"

"My father's caught under a sapling that fell on him. That made mother sick."

Teal turned on his lank, Indian-dark sons. "Git ahead and help him."

"Oh, Lord, Lord," said Mrs. Teal. "Take the basket, Nate. We've got to go fast. It's going to be unnatural."

Young Tom started after the Teal boys, they running away with a loose and ranging ease. "No," said Teal, "you stay with us. You've had runnin' enough. The boys are a pair of hounds; let 'em go."

They went forward, Mrs. Teal now and then speaking to her-

self with a soft exclamation of impatience. Otherwise there was
no talk. The wind was against them and the rain beat down.
Young Tom opened his mouth to let the great drops loosen his
dry throat, and silently suffered the slow pace. The coming baby
never entered his mind; it was his father lying under the tree
that he thought of with dread, and when the creek began to bend
around the toe of the hills, close by the falls, he ran ahead and
reached the house.

His father had dug himself out from the trap; there was a little
tunnel of earth where he had been. The two boys stood silently
at the fire, and one of them motioned toward the cabin. Young
Tom drew the doorway canvas back from the logs, looking in; his
father had moved the bedstead from the wagon and had set it up
near the cabin's fireplace. His mother was on it, groaning, and his
father knelt at the bedside and held her hands. Young Tom retreated to the fire, watching the Teals come through the trees.
Mrs. Teal seized the basket from her husband and went at once
into the cabin; a moment later his father came out.

John Mercy said to Teal, "It's a good thing to have neighbors.
I'm sorry I can't offer you coffee at this minute." He let his chin
drop and he spread his hands before the fire and gravely watched
it. The sockets of his eyes seemed deep and blackened; his mouth
was a line straight and narrow across his skin.

"My friend," said Teal, "the first winter's always a bad one.
Don't work so hard or you'll be twenty years older by spring." He
turned to the taller of his two sons. "Jack, take Mercy's gun and
go fetch in a deer."

Young Tom heard his mother's sharp cry from the cabin. He
moved away, he stood by the tree and stared at the trench in
which his father had been, and noticed the marks scrubbed into
the soft ground by his father's elbows. He walked along the tree
and gave it a kick with his foot, and continued to the millpond.
Here he squatted, watching the steamy rain mists pack tighter

along the willows of the creek. In the distance, a mile or so, a little timbered butte stood half concealed by the fog, seeming to ride free in the low sky. He tightened his muscles, waiting for the enemy to come single file through the brush, but then he thought of the old savage, so bony and stooped and unclean, who had seized the half loaf of bread, and his picture of a row of glistening copper giants was destroyed. He heard voices by the cabin, and rose and saw Mrs. Teal by the fire. He went back.

Mrs. Teal looked at him with her kindness. "Your mother's all right, Tom. You had a brother, but he wasn't meant to stay. You understand, Tom. It's meant that way and you oughtn't sorrow."

She meant the baby boy was dead. He thought about it and waited to feel like crying, but he hadn't seen this boy and he didn't know anything about him, and didn't know what to cry for. It embarrassed him not to feel sad. He stood with his eyes on the fire.

Teal said to his other son, "That Methodist preacher is probably down at Mission Bottom, Pete. You go home, get the horse and go for him." He walked a little distance onward, speaking in a lower tone to his son. Then the son went on, and Teal turned back to the cabin and got the saw standing by the wall and went over to the fallen log. He called to young Tom, "Now then, let's not be idle men. Puncheons he wanted, wasn't it? We'll just get 'em ready while we wait."

A shot sounded deeper in the forest—one and no more. "There's your meat," said Teal. "You've seen the trout in the creek, ain't you? Mighty fat. Next summer there'll be quail all through those meadow thickets. What you've got to have is a horse for ridin'. Just a plain ten-dollar horse. I know where there's one."

The minister arrived around noon the next day, and out of this wet and empty land the neighbors began to come, riding or walking in from all quarters of the mist-hidden valley, destroying for-

ever young Tom's illusion of wilderness. They came from the
scattered claims along the river, from French Prairie, from the
upper part of the La Creole, from strangely named creeks and
valleys as far as twenty miles away; the yard was filled with men,
and women worked in the cabin and at the fire outside the cabin.
Young Tom stared at strange boys running through the timber,
and resented their trespassing; he heard girls giggling in the
shelter of the wagon. It was a big meeting. A heavy man in buckskins, light of eye and powerfully voiced, strolled through the
crowd and had a word for everyone. People visited and the talk
was of the days of the wagon-train crossing, of land here and land
there, of politics and the Hudson's Bay Company. A group of men
walked along the break of the hill until they reached a knoll a
hundred yards from the cabin. He watched them digging.

In a little while they returned, bringing quietness to the people.
The minister came from the cabin, bareheaded in the rain. Mr.
Teal followed, carrying a small bundle wrapped within a sheet
and covered by a shawl; they went on toward the grave, and
young Tom, every sense sharpened, heard the knocking of a hammer and the calling of a voice. The crowd moved over and his
father walked from the cabin, carrying his mother. Young Tom
saw Caroline alone at the cabin's doorway, crying; he went to her
and got her hand and followed his father.

A little box stood at the grave, the minister by it; he had a book
in his hand which he watched while the rain dripped down his
long face. Young Tom's mother was on her feet, but she wasn't
crying, though all the women around her were. The minister
spoke a long while, it seemed to Tom. He had Caroline's hand
and grew cold, waiting for the minister's words to end. Somebody
said, "Amen," and the minister began a song, all the people
joining.

Looking at his feet, young Tom felt the coldness run up his legs,
and his chest was heavy and he, too, cried. As soon as the song

was done, his father carried his mother back to the house and the crowd returned to the fire. A woman dumped venison steaks into a big kettle on the table, and cups and plates went around and the talk grew brisker than it had been before.

Young Tom said, "Caroline, you go into the wagon." From the corners of his eyes he saw men shoveling dirt into the grave; he thought about the grave and imagined the rains filling it with water, and the shawl and the white sheet growing black in the mud. He went over to the fallen log and sat on it.

He remained there, wholly lost in the forest of his imagination while the round-about neighbors, finished with eating and finished with visiting, started homeward through the dulling day. They went in scattered groups, as they had come, their strong calling running back and forth in the windy rain; and at last only the Teals remained. He saw Caroline and Mary Teal watching him through the front opening of the wagon. He rose and went around to the cabin, hearing the older Teals talking.

Mrs. Teal said, "I'm needed. We'll stay tonight."

Teal looked at his two tall sons. "You had best get at those puncheons. Mercy's legs will trouble him for a while. Tomorrow we are agoin' to knock down some trees for a barn lean-to."

Young Tom quietly drew back the canvas covering of the cabin's doorway. He was troubled about his mother and wanted to see her, and meant to go in. But what he saw suddenly shut him out and brought great embarrassment to him.

His father stood beside the bed, looking down, and young Tom heard him say, "I can't stay here when your heart's not in it. There is no pleasure in this work, and no point in looking ahead to what it'll be someday, if you don't feel it too. Well, you don't. We'll go home in the spring when it's possible to travel. That's what you want, I clearly know."

She was pale and her eyes were stretched perfectly round; her head rolled slightly, her voice was very small. "I couldn't leave now. I've got a baby buried here. It's a mighty hard way to come to love a country . . . to lose something in it. Mercy, put a railing round that grave. I have not been of much use, I know, and it's hurt me to see you work the way you've done. It will be better when I can get up and do what I can do."

John Mercy bent down and kissed his wife, and suddenly in young Tom the embarrassment became intolerable, for this was a thing he had never seen his people do before, and a thing he was to see again only twice so long as they lived. He pulled back and let the canvas fall into place; he thought he heard his father crying. He walked by the big kettle with its remaining chunks of fried venison steak. He took one, eating it like a piece of bread. Caroline and Mary Teal were now at the back end of the wagon, looking at him.

He said, "I know a big cave up on the hill."

Mary Teal came from the wagon, Caroline following; and the three walked into the woods, into the great sea swells of sound poured out by the rolling timber crowns. Mary gave him a sharp sidewise glance and smiled, destroying the strangeness between them and giving him a mighty feeling of comfort. The long, long years were beginning for Tom Mercy, and he was to see that smile so many times again in the course of his life, to be warmed and drawn on by it, to see tears shining through it, and broken thoughts hidden by it. To the last day of his life far out in another century, that smile—real or long after remembered—was his star, but like a star, there was a greater heat within it than he was ever to feel or to know.

SIOUX WAR TRAIL

Warpath

by STANLEY VESTAL

LONG ORPHAN WAS TIRED. INTOLERABLY, INCREDIBLY TIRED. SO TIRED that it seemed impossible to stick on the bare back of his loping pony for even one more jump. His back ached, his head ached, every bone in his long brown body ached from the long, hour-after-hour, day-and-night pounding upon his horse's hard spine. On top of that, his empty belly ached. But far worse than any of these discomforts was the terrible pain in his eyes—the stinging, insistent, cruel pain of eyes which have stared too long into the glare of the sun on the snow-patched plains. But Long Orphan was a Cheyenne. He did not complain. He rode.

He was so tired, so bounded by his own physical misery, that only at long intervals was he aware of other sensations, sensations which had been beating upon his nerves for a day and night. Only when his pony swerved or broke its loping gait did he

85

force his red-rimmed eyes open. Then he would glimpse the plains, and catch sight of his comrades, with buffalo robes belted around them, plunging along at his side. He would see the backs and heads and manes of the stolen ponies just ahead, rising and falling and tossing like the waves of a wind-swept prairie lake.

The rest of the time Long Orphan rode in darkness, where the only sensations were the thud of unshod hoofs, the labored breathing of the ponies, the creak of No Heart's saddle, the smell of sweaty horses, sweaty men, smoke-tanned buckskins, and his own bleeding flesh. This was Long Orphan's first warpath, and it was not what he had expected.

As his name indicated, he was an orphan, and used to hardship and privation. That helped, but his pride helped more. For in spite of his poverty and insignificance, Long Orphan was desperately proud of his ancestry. His grandfather had been a famous warrior. And so he rode. Nobody was going to have the laugh on him. He would not complain or ask for favors. He was no woman!

Besides, Long Orphan knew there was no pity to be expected from his comrades. They were all picked men, seasoned veterans, who resented his presence among them. Long Orphan had no rating as a warrior, no friends of any importance, no relatives to ask him to join a war party. Nobody wanted him along. And so, when he heard that No Heart was going on the warpath against the Crows, Long Orphan had had to volunteer, had had to sneak along behind the party until it was three days' march from camp —too far for the warriors to turn back and take him home again.

When Long Orphan turned up and joined them at last, No Heart was so enraged that he lashed the youngster with his heavy quirt. No Heart wanted only the cream of the warriors on such a dangerous raid. But nothing could turn Long Orphan back. And so No Heart set to work to make the young man's life a burden.

It was the custom to haze a youngster on his first warpath; such treatment was said to make his heart strong. Long Orphan was

prepared for that. But he had not expected malice. And No Heart
was merciless.

It was the custom to douse a lazy man with water if he failed
to turn out at the second call: No Heart doused Long Orphan
while he slept, without any warning whatever. It was the custom
to send a green warrior after water for the others: No Heart sent
Long Orphan after water when there was none within miles of
the line of march. It was usual to have him cook the food of the
leader, to make up his bed: No Heart made Long Orphan do
these things over and over. It was customary for him to carry the
leader's pack: No Heart slipped rocks into his pack to make it
heavy for Long Orphan.

During the long hike up the Yellowstone and over the divide
to the enemy's country, the young man was continually being sent
to some distant hilltop to look for game, or ordered back for miles
to recover some article deliberately dropped along the way. When
the party stopped to sleep, every man who happened to wake up
found some excuse to waken Long Orphan also. And when finally,
that last night, the party neared the Crow camp on the Mussel-
shell, No Heart made Long Orphan stay with the packs, while he
and the others sneaked into the camp just before dawn and captured horses.

Long Orphan was given no chance to steal a pony, no chance
to make a name for himself. He was cheated of the reward of all
his labors. Yet all he craved was a warrior's name—the rating of
a man.

Ever since that dawn Long Orphan had been riding, riding,
riding—one bare-backed, raw-boned bronc after another. For as
fast as one horse was winded, the warriors would rope and mount
another. Even if he had wished to stop and rest, he dared not; No
Heart had seen to that.

No Heart had put his arrow through a sleeping Crow woman,
had scalped her, stripped her, and tied her bloody dress to his

saddle as a trophy. After that, so he told Long Orphan, the Crows were sure to follow. Long Orphan was not to be allowed to quit. No Heart intended to ride him to death.

But Big Tree and the other warriors called a halt. The sun was up, and the whole country behind them was brightly lighted with its rays. Not an enemy was in sight. They had ridden more than a day and a night. Besides, they had not all been lucky as No Heart, who had captured a pony with a saddle on its back; they were tired.

They stopped in the scanty brush along a small stream which flowed into the Yellowstone River from the north. It was an easy day's ride eastward to their home camp on Powder River.

When Long Orphan slipped from his pony's back, he fell down. His legs were like sticks. It was some time before he could stand. But No Heart gave him no chance to rest.

Long Orphan was sent to gather wood, told to make a fire, cook breakfast. He was sent after water, and had to fill the skin only a little at a time from the low water hole. Yet the paunch in which he brought it was emptied before his eyes: No Heart said the water was dirty.

Long Orphan had to gather brush to spread under No Heart's buffalo robe, had to rub down his pony with dry grass while the others sat by the fire, eating, resting and smoking. Last of all he was told to pull sagebrush and throw it on the fire to make a smoke. That smoke was visible for a day's ride in the light of the morning sun. No Heart wanted to signal the folks at home that he was on his way back, victorious. No Heart always made the most of his achievements.

While Long Orphan was busy at these chores, No Heart divided the loot. He himself took the lion's share—ten horses. Other warriors got one, two, three head each. Long Orphan got nothing.

"Why should I give you anything?" No Heart demanded. "You behaved like a woman. You hid in the brush while the rest of

us went into the enemy's camp and stole the ponies. Your bones
would be lying on the prairie if I had not saved your life by
letting you ride some of my horses away from that camp. It is
about time you made yourself useful. Now we warriors are going
to sleep. You go up on that butte and keep watch until sundown."

Long Orphan had had no breakfast, he was staggering with
fatigue. No Heart's command was like a blow on the head. The
tall young man stood silent, swaying, squinting through red eyes
at the leader, at his comrades who watched him without a word.
For the first time he thought he sensed a little sympathy in those
hard brown faces.

Now Long Orphan, according to Cheyenne standards, had been
well brought up. His mother had been the daughter of a famous
man, and the boy had been taught to respect his elders. It was
hard for him to argue with an older man. But now he doubted
that he could carry out that order. His strength and patience
seemed gone. Dully he heard his own voice, like that of another,
mumbling his protest.

"My eyes are sore, Grandfather. I cannot keep good watch. If
you think the Crows are coming after us, why did you make that
smoke?"

No Heart was caught. He had to think fast for an excuse then.
He glared at the young man and began to scold him in a loud
voice.

"I am the leader here, boy. You will do as I say. You are only
a boy, no better than a woman. What do you know about war?
Do you know why I made that smoke signal? To call the Crows!
I want them to come, so that we can have a good fight. Maybe
they will kill you, and then I shall be rid of you. Now go up on
that butte and keep watch. Go quickly, before I lay my quirt on
your lazy back!"

No Heart raised the heavy notched handle of his quirt, and
whirled the double lash around his head. He was furious.

Long Orphan was too tired to resist. Slowly he turned, and dragging his buffalo robe by one corner, walked up the long slope to the rocky hilltop. The men stood silent, watching him go. One or two of them stirred uneasily. Big Tree ventured to protest. He appealed to No Heart.

"My friend, you are too hard on this young man. You know it was never our custom to keep watch. When one sleeps, all sleep. My uncle, who was a leader of warriors, told me that it is the duty of the leader himself to keep watch and protect his men, if necessary. The leader is responsible for the lives of the warriors. Listen to me, my friend. If I were leader and feared surprise, I would not rely on the watchfulness of a worn-out growing boy with sore eyes. That is a duty for a scout."

No Heart laughed. "I do not think the Crows will come so far. How can they? We have all their best ponies. If you are afraid, go and keep watch with Long Orphan. I am going to sleep."

Big Tree replied, "My friend, that was a small village we raided. Maybe there was another Crow camp not far off where they have plenty of ponies."

No Heart did not listen. He rolled up in his robe and closed his eyes. Big Tree said no more. Within three minutes, all the Cheyennes were sound asleep. All but Long Orphan.

Long Orphan sat on the butte, hidden among the rocks there, facing the west, his back to the morning sun. Even with the light at his back, it was impossible to look out over the dry, whitened prairie for more than a few seconds at a time, snatching glimpses of the back trail. But he stuck to his duty, though there was nothing to see.

While the sun was low behind him, it was hard enough. But when it was high in the heavens, the young man was in agony. His vigil was torture. He could only squint at the dazzling landscape for a split second, quickly sweeping the country with smarting, red-rimmed eyes, then shutting them tight for long minutes of rest. And whenever his eyes were closed, he had to fight off sleep.

Cold, hungry, tired, sick with pain, time after time he caught himself reeling. There could be only one end to that kind of thing. Shortly after noon, Long Orphan was snoring.

He dreamed that No Heart was lashing him, flogging him with that heavy quirt. Again and again the heavy double lash fell on the robe wrapped around his body. Long Orphan groaned and stirred, covering his face with his arms to shield himself. Then he felt the stinging lash again—this time on his bare wrist. His eyes flew open. It was no dream. No Heart stood over him, flailing him with his heavy quirt. All around stood the other men, panting from their run up the butte, their faces fierce with anger.

Long Orphan jumped up, jumped back out of reach of the lash. "What is the matter?" he demanded. The whole war party was there, hostile, ready to go for him.

"Plenty," Big Tree growled, his voice hoarse with fury. "While you slept, the Crows came. They have run off our horses. We are all afoot. Look."

Long Orphan squinted after the man's pointing finger. A mile to the westward the prairie was blotched by a dark mass of moving horseflesh. The Crows—a heap of Crows—were riding behind the captured herd. Long Orphan's mouth dropped open in surprise and shame. But No Heart gave him no chance to speak.

"You dog," he barked. "They might have killed us . . . Strip him, men. I'll show him what a Dog Soldier whipping is like."

At his command, the whole party rushed the youngster. One man grabbed him by his long braids, others by his arms. A scalping knife slit his buckskin shirt up the back from tail to neckhole; two others cut away his leggings. They snatched off his quiver, emptied it and broke the arrows. Big Tree cracked the bow over his knee, then snatched the young man's knife from its sheath and hurled it spinning away into the snow.

Before Long Orphan's eyes they slit his buffalo robe into ribbons. And almost before he realized that all this had happened, he found himself suddenly released. Then the air seemed full of flying thongs, as the Dog Soldiers plied the lashes of their notched quirts upon his naked body.

"Run him down the butte," No Heart commanded. "Run him back to our camp so that he can pick up my pack again."

It was death to resist the Dog Soldiers. Long Orphan did not resist. He knew without thinking that he did not want to die—not yet. Not until he had wiped out the disgrace of his offense, not until he had won a name worthy of his grandfather, not until he had got even with No Heart.

Long Orphan covered his face with his arms to save his eyes, and stumbled down the slope to camp. His bare back was laced with blood when he reached it. But even then the malice of No Heart was unsatisfied.

"Put the woman's dress on him, friends," he ordered. "He behaved like a woman, let him dress like one. And I want him to carry my pack."

At that, Long Orphan's eyes flashed, and he clenched his fists. But he controlled himself. He did not want to die—yet. The warriors put the dress over his head, yanked it down upon him. Then they stood back and laughed at the result. The dress was too wide—and too short. It barely reached below the young man's knees. They laughed, and No Heart laughed loudest of all.

"Now, Sister," he commanded, "make up my pack, and let's go. If you stand around barelegged like that, you'll get chilblains."

Long Orphan did not budge. His face was defiant. "I am not going with you. Carry it yourself."

No Heart laughed. That struck him as a good joke.

"Friends, did you hear? She is not going with us. She is going to stay here. Well, Sister, if you stay here, I am afraid you will not live long. There are many Crows in that war party. They have

not forgotten that I killed one of their women. When they have
hidden their ponies in some safe place, they will all come riding
back to fight us. And the first man they will try to kill is the man
who has on their woman's dress."

"Then I will wear it," said Long Orphan. "Is that why you gave
it to me? You want to get rid of it before the enemy gets too
close. You are a brave man. You can kill a woman sleeping, but
when you see her men coming, you are afraid."

No Heart sneered at that. "Friends, our sister is very brave.
She has never seen a battle. She cannot understand that we are
few and afoot, and that the Crows are many and on horseback.
They will ride us down unless we can find a safe place to defend
ourselves."

Then No Heart advanced, raising his quirt. "But nobody is
going to call me coward," he said, beginning to strike at Long
Orphan.

Big Tree interfered. He grabbed the quirt, wrenched it from
No Heart's hands. "My friend," he protested, "if you want to fight,
the Crows are coming. Unless you lead us to a place where we
can defend ourselves, you will soon have more fighting than you
can eat. Are you our leader or only a crazy fool? Leave the boy
alone."

Other warriors grunted agreement; they were in haste to be on
their way. No Heart saw that his rating as a war chief would
suffer if he delayed longer; and his rating was his dearest posses-
sion. Where that was concerned he was stubborn as a mule.
Grumbling to himself, he stooped to make up his pack. He threw
out the stones first.

At that, Long Orphan laughed. That long-legged youth, unarmed, and in that shameful woman's dress, laughed aloud.

"Yes, hurry," he taunted No Heart. "You are their leader. You
are always out in front—when the enemy is after you. Then you

can run faster than anybody. Hurry up now, the Crows will dance over your hair!"

Standing there, easy and empty-handed, Long Orphan laughed again.

One of the warriors echoed the laugh. Perhaps that warrior was jealous of the fame of No Heart. Perhaps the mere novelty of that boy in his silly costume laughing at a war chief amused him. But that warrior's laugh was too much for No Heart. It stung him into action. He stood up, threw down his pack and turned on Long Orphan.

"Let the Crows come," he growled, his dark face set and stubborn. "I am not afraid. I stay here. This is a good place to die."

The warriors, taken by surprise, stood speechless. In that silence, Long Orphan's laugh sounded louder than a rifleshot.

"Show-off," he taunted. "They call you No Heart, but you have a heart—a woman's heart. You talk fire but your words are only smoke. You have weapons. If you really wished to die, you would not hide here in the brush. You would go to meet the enemy!"

Long Orphan had found his tongue at last. He had thrown away his body—all that mattered to him now was his self-respect.

No Heart had never been so insulted in his life. His dark face worked with a fury which made it almost impossible for him to speak. But at last he got out the words: "Like you?"

"Hau—yes," Long Orphan assented, his young face stern and resolved. "I will not die hiding in the brush like a scared woman." He turned and started off after the Crows.

The warriors stood silent, amazed at the young man's courage. They knew, of course, that boys green to war were sometimes bolder than more seasoned warriors. But they had never seen anything to match this. Long Orphan, a boy and unarmed, was starting off to meet an enemy they feared to face. For a time they neither stirred nor spoke.

Then Big Tree took his knife from his sheath and ran after the

young man. When he had caught up with him, he handed him the
knife and said, "When you meet the enemy, you will need a
weapon. We are both Cheyennes." Big Tree's tone was one of
respect.

"*Ah-ho*—thanks," said Long Orphan. Big Tree's friendly offer, his
respectful tone, heartened the young man. He took the knife, and
with it new courage. He was so ashamed of his disgrace, so de-
termined to outdo No Heart, that even without the knife he would
not have faltered. But now, he hoped, he could kill one Crow,
take one scalp, before the enemy killed him. Big Tree's friendship
warmed his heart. Long Orphan trudged away, a strange figure
in his woman's dress. But only No Heart jeered.

"He is a foolish boy—just a foolish boy. He cannot fight. He will
hide from the Crows as soon as he is out of our sight."

But Long Orphan did not head for the brush along the creek.
Instead, he started up the bare slopes of the butte where he had
been stationed to keep watch. He intended to fight and die in
full view of his comrades, so that his fame would outshine No
Heart's for ever after. Straight to the flat top of the butte he
climbed, scrambled over the low broken rimrock, and took his
stand, facing westward, towards the country of the Crows.

The Cheyennes behind him, down below, almost forgot their
own danger in watching him.

Suddenly Long Orphan began to signal to his enemies. They
were coming back, and he wanted them to come straight to him.
He stooped, scooped up a double handful of sand. He tossed it
high into the air, as a buffalo bull paws up the dust before he
charges. The wind caught the sand and spread it into a broad
tawny banner, visible for miles. It was the Indian call to battle.

The Crows were coming for him now. Long Orphan began to
dance and sing on his level hilltop, thus advertising his readiness
to fight them. When the Cheyennes down below saw him making

gestures in the sign language, they knew that the Crows must be coming close.

"Come on—kill me!" he signaled. "I have only this knife!"

The Crows needed no further invitation. As fast as their tired ponies could go up that steep slope, they came yelling and shooting, their leader well out in front. Long Orphan kept right on dancing as they advanced, and for that reason none of their bullets took effect. It was not easy to shoot accurately from the bare back of a pony heaving itself up the slope, when the target was never still for a moment.

Long Orphan watched them come. Far in the lead rode a man in a war bonnet, its long feather mane flying out behind him in the wind. His spotted pony plunged up the long slope, and the sun flashed from the barrel of his rifle. Long Orphan hoped that Crow was brave enough to come to close quarters to fight—where he could use his knife. He did not want to be shot down from a distance like a rabbit.

But the Crow had no intention of risking a stab from the knife of that lone Cheyenne who had already shown such strong courage. Ten paces from the rimrock the Crow reined up his horse. The pony stood quiet. The Crow raised his rifle and took aim.

Long Orphan grasped his knife and ran towards that edge of the level top of the butte. As he ran, he threw his body from side to side, trying to avoid the bullet. But the Crow pulled the trigger before the Cheyenne could reach him.

TCHOW!

White power smoke hid the Crow from sight. Long Orphan saw that smoke—and nothing more. But the Cheyennes watching below saw Long Orphan's head jerk, saw him stop suddenly, spin half round, and stumble down upon the rimrock.

No Heart laughed. "They killed him easy," he sneered. "I told you he could not fight."

The other Cheyennes said nothing. They could hear the Crows

yelling in triumph on the other side of the butte as they dashed up
the hill. On top they could see the victorious Crow in the war bonnet jump off his horse, lay down his rifle and rush scrambling over
the broken rocks toward Long Orphan. The Crow was in haste
to reach the fallen man first, to count the coup and capture the
knife before anyone else could get there. But his haste was his
undoing.

The lariat tied around the spotted pony's neck was fastened at
the other end to the Crow's belt. It was coiled and tucked under
his belt, and paid out as he ran forward. But when the Crow dismounted, his pony turned down the slope, and the rope was not
long enough.

The Crow found himself brought up short before he reached
Long Orphan, and had to stop and haul the pony forward again.
This delay allowed Long Orphan to regain consciousness. And
when the Crow, dragging on the pony's rope, raised his head
above the level of the rimrock, the wind caught the long tail of
his war bonnet and whipped it about his face, blinding him. By
the time the Crow had clawed the tail of his bonnet from his eyes
he found himself confronted by the man he had just shot and
thought was dead.

Still dizzy, his face covered with blood from the scalp wound
which had downed him, Long Orphan towered above the Crow.
Before the astonished Crow could draw his own knife and clamber
to the level of his enemy, Long Orphan grabbed the man's knife
hand and stabbed him twice in the side of the neck. The Crow
went down in a flutter of eagle feathers.

Leaving him wriggling on the rocks, Long Orphan stumbled
down and picked up the rifle. He grinned under the mask of blood.

It was a repeating rifle, and there were still some cartridges in
the magazine. He dropped behind a rock and began shooting at
the Crows coming up the slope. One of them swayed and caught
at the horn of his saddle; the pony of another Crow began to

buck. Long Orphan sighted, grinning, along the shining barrel. It was a good rifle—a better gun than he had ever hoped to own.

Evidently the Crows knew it was a good rifle. Startled as they were by the sudden and unexpected death of their chief, they had not the courage to rush the man on the hilltop, now that he was armed and shooting. They halted, turned and raced down the hill.

Long Orphan kept on shooting at them until the hammer clicked and the magazine was empty. Long Orphan was out of the fight. He went back to the Crow he had killed, took his knife, and scalped him. Then he stood up, facing the Cheyennes in the valley, waved the trophy over his head, and yelled, in mockery of No Heart.

That yell was more than No Heart could stand. He and his men were well hidden in the brush, in no immediate danger. But now he jumped out of his concealment, fired off his rifle, and shouted defiance to the enemy.

At that the Crows, glad enough to leave Long Orphan alone, turned to attack this new challenger. They swept round the butte and scouted up the creek towards No Heart's party. But this time they were in no mood to rush recklessly in against a hidden foe. They dismounted, tied up their ponies in a clump of cottonwood trees, and advanced on foot, trying to drive the Cheyennes into the open. They made use of every bit of cover, and though No Heart's men fought bravely, the Crows kept the Cheyennes on the move.

From the top of the butte Long Orphan watched all this in disgust. Both Cheyennes and Crows had forgotten him. For a while everybody had been watching him, but now No Heart was playing the hero's part. Long Orphan was the spectator. He did not like that. He made up his mind to do something.

Taking his useless rifle, Long Orphan got on the spotted horse and rode down the butte. The only way down—for a horse—was

that up which the Crows had charged. The butte was between
him and the fight along the creek. He had to circle it.

Passing around it, he had to go near the cottonwood trees where
the Crows had left their horses. As he approached, one of the
animals nickered to his own horse. The spotted pony answered,
but nothing followed. Evidently the Crows had left nobody to
guard their mounts. Long Orphan was not much surprised. They
outnumbered the Cheyennes, had them afoot and fighting for
their lives. Besides, now that the Crows had lost their chief, there
was no one with the authority to post a guard. Long Orphan rode
in among the cottonwoods.

There was nobody there—only the horses. Long Orphan licked
his lips. These were all war horses—far better animals than the
ones No Heart had taken from the Crow camp. If he could bring
home such a herd as that, Long Orphan knew his name would be
high among his people. No Heart would be put to shame. It was
worth any risk.

Quickly, Long Orphan rounded up the animals, threw them
out through the trees. He circled back around the butte and
brought the ponies safely down the creek in rear of the fighting
Cheyennes. He found them much farther up the creek than they
had been before. The Crows had been driving them back.

There was a chance that, when they saw the ponies coming,
some Cheyenne might take a shot at Long Orphan. And so he
sang an old war song, a favorite of his grandfather's: "Friends, I
bring you their horses..."

The first man Long Orphan saw was Big Tree, who sat leaning
back against a tree trunk, nursing his wounded knee. Big Tree
saw the young man coming with the horses and covered his mouth
with his hands in sheer astonishment. Then Big Tree laughed
and said, "*Ah-ho*, thanks. Today you have saved my life." Big
Tree called to his comrades, and they all came dodging back

through the brush, eager to mount the horses Long Orphan had brought.

No Heart was sick with chagrin when he saw what the young man had done. He mounted a horse and then said: "Good. Now we can charge them horseback." He wanted to do something brave then, to outdo the boy who had taunted him.

But Big Tree was loud in objection. "No," he said, "let's go home. We have taken these horses and a scalp. We are lucky to get away alive. That is enough for one day. Three good men have been wounded already. Besides, these horses all belong to our friend Long Orphan. If we ride them, we must do as he says. Of course, if anyone wants to stay here and fight on foot, let him do it. What do you say, friend?"

They all looked at Long Orphan, waiting for him to speak. He had become their leader. He glanced at No Heart—the man's face was fixed with a look of furious envy. Long Orphan said, "Let's do as Big Tree says. Let's go home."

When the Cheyennes rode away across the prairie, the Crows ran out of the brush and stood staring after them, amazed, afoot, and two days' ride from home. The Cheyennes laughed and made gestures at the foolish Crows. All but No Heart. There was no laughter in him.

That night in camp the Cheyennes held council. It was agreed that they would all ride home together the next day, timing their arrival about noon, so that the whole camp would see them come in victorious. All the people would be awake and about then, and they would make a good showing. They planned this in advance, for if one or two men slipped away and reached home before the others, the news of their victory would be stale when they got in, and half the fun of the celebration would be lost to them.

Long Orphan was well pleased with this plan, for he was the hero of the expedition. But No Heart left the camp and sat alone on the hillside, smoking and thinking until after the others had gone to bed.

Next morning, before it was light, Long Orphan was up and went out looking for his horses. He expected to find them near the water at that hour, but failed to do so. All the animals seemed to have vanished. He hurried back to tell his comrades. But they pointed to the place where No Heart had slept and to a broad trail of horses moving towards the home camp. No Heart had taken the horses and the scalp, and had gone on ahead. He wanted to steal some of the glory of Long Orphan and make everybody look first at himself.

There was one horse left in the camp of the war party—Big Tree's. For Big Tree had been wounded. He could not walk, and he was taking no chances on being left afoot a second time. He had tied his pony's lariat around his own body before he went to sleep, and No Heart had been afraid he might waken Big Tree if he tried to take that horse along. So Big Tree told Long Orphan to take the horse and go after No Heart. Long Orphan lost no time. He went on the run.

About the middle of the morning, he saw No Heart driving the herd along ahead of him. Quirting his pony on both flanks, Long Orphan quickly came up with the man. He rode up on the right side, like a man about to shoot a buffalo. But Long Orphan did not shoot; he did not say a word. He pushed his horse between No Heart and the horses he had stolen.

No Heart would not give way. He was angry. He turned in his saddle, raised his quirt, and lashed Long Orphan across the face.

Then Long Orphan lost his temper. He was too angry to speak. Instead he lifted the barrel of his rifle suddenly and brought it down across No Heart's head. No Heart dropped from his saddle and lay on the ground without stirring.

"Lie there, dog!" said Long Orphan. "You beat me for disobeying orders. Now it is my turn."

Long Orphan took the horses back to his waiting comrades. When they all passed that way again, later in the day, No Heart still lay where he had fallen. They flung him across a saddle, like a dead man, and packed him into camp. He was still out when they finished the scalp dance next morning.

But nobody seemed to miss No Heart at the scalp dance. Everyone was too busy celebrating the victory of a new warrior with a new name—that long-legged orphan boy who everyone had thought was of no account. The chiefs had thrown his old name away and given him a new title in honor of his brave exploit.

That name was Woman's Dress.

BOZEMAN TRAIL

Crow-Bait Caravan

by LES SAVAGE, JR.

THE PAIR OF MEN STEPPED JUST INSIDE THE DOOR OF THE KAYCEE Freight Company's clapboard office, and there was something ominous in the way the late afternoon sun cast their two shadows across Kaycee Garrett, sitting there with his long legs propped up on the scarred top of the rickety desk. Kaycee turned his head, and when he recognized who it was, his voice was sardonic.

"Well, don't tell me you gents have some freight you want me to haul."

Neither of them answered right away. They sent a swift glance around the room as if to make sure Kaycee was the only one there. And Kaycee couldn't help the sidelong look he sent at his gun and holster, wrapped in the cartridge belt and stuck in a pigeon-hole of the desk.

These men worked in Montana, usually, but they were known well enough down here in Singletree, the Wyoming shipping point for the Montana mines. Glenrock was the smaller of the two, his Holstein calfskin vest hanging from square shoulders, Bisley .44 strapped around square hips, the whole look of him compact and forceful and potent. He had singular, almost colorless eyes that never seemed to focus on any particular object.

The other man was bigger, heavier, slow and deliberate in his movements. The front of his weathered mackinaw coat was spread apart a little by his sizable paunch, and by the gun he wore beneath it. He was known in Singletree as Peso Peters, and Kaycee had always figured that he had been known in other places by other names.

"Bad year for the Bozeman Trail," said Peters, looking finally at Kaycee. "I hear nobody's sending any freight north this season, what with the Sioux, and the cholera epidemic."

"That's what I hear," said Kaycee carefully. "Dudley's last train was wiped out by the cholera up past the Powder."

When he said the name of Dudley, his lips puckered a little as if he'd tasted something bad. For years, a bitter war had been raging between the powerful Dudley Shippers Incorporated and Kaycee's one-horse outfit. Jason Dudley had driven every other shoestring company out of business, but somehow Kaycee had managed to hold on, running just enough freight north on the Bozeman Trail to keep his dilapidated yards going, to pay the feed bill of his crow-bait mules and meet the wages of what few teamsters would whip for him.

Such a long, unequal battle might have made some men discouraged, or bitter. But Kaycee was hard to discourage, and too young for any permanent bitterness. Perhaps his reaction was the sardonic streak that had cropped up in him. It showed now in the dry, unperturbed smile he turned towards Peters.

He was well over six feet tall, Kaycee, and he could have looked awkward but for his eyes. Nobody could look awkward with eyes like that. Their color matched the sunburnt brown of his hair, and they had a terrible shrewdness for such a young man—wary, worldly-wise lights coming and going behind narrowed lids. Peters was watching those eyes, and when he spoke again, his voice had lost its edge of confidence.

"If you were to get a good offer, Kaycee, would you send a train up the Bozeman?" asked the heavy man from Montana.

"I might," said Kaycee. "I might."

"Britten O'Hare will be in soon," said Peters slowly. "She'll want you to take a load of hydraulic equipment to the O'Hare mines north of Virginia City. There's five thousand dollars in it for you if you refuse."

Kaycee took his long legs carefully off the desk and stood up. Deliberately, he took the holstered Paterson five-shot from the pigeon-hole, unwrapping the cartridge belt and lifting the tails of his black frock coat so he could buckle the gun around his lean hips. He looked at Peters' unshaven face with its beetling brows and thick lips and didn't like it, and didn't try to keep the dislike from his voice.

"Who are you fronting for, Peters?"

Glenrock's tone was hollow and flat. "You shouldn't ask that, Kaycee."

"I've done about as bad as any man could in the shipping business," said Kaycee. "But then I've always been particular how I did my business, and who I did it with."

Peters shifted nervous boots on the unpainted floor. He wasn't the kind of a man to enjoy fencing like this, and he said impatiently:

"That much money would buy a lot of new Murphy wagons for you, Kaycee, and you can't keep going much longer on those old Conestogas of yours."

Kaycee had guessed why these men had been sent rather than an ordinary go-between, and he had a good idea what his refusal would bring. He shoved his frock coat back from the bone butt of his Paterson with an elbow, and put his left hand on the back of the chair.

"If your boss had come himself and made the offer as a simple business proposition, I might have considered it. But sending a couple of hombres like you looks to me like a threat. And I don't like to be threatened. It raises my back hair."

Peters had been keeping his impatience down, but it broke over his face now, along with the dull flush of anger. "There's notches on my gun for men who talked like you're talking. It would be unhealthy for you not to take this five thousand."

Kaycee had a certain skill with his Paterson, but he knew he couldn't hope to match these two men, who were paid for what they could do with their guns. His left hand gripped the chair's back tighter, and he set himself to draw, more to focus their attention on his gunhand than anything else. Then he said harshly:

"Whoever sent you here told you to do something if I refused the money. Now either do it, or get out, fast!"

Perhaps Glenrock and Peters had expected it, knowing Kaycee as they did. But for a moment after he spoke, their faces were blank with surprise. Then Peters' mouth twisted with vicious anger, telegraphing what was coming.

"All right, you damn fool," he snarled, and dove for his gun.

Glenrock drew too, no expression on his face, or in his eyes. But Kaycee had seen it coming, and even as he slapped his own leather, knowing both men would be faster, he was swinging that chair up around behind him in a hurtling arc.

All Glenrock's concentration was on beating Kaycee's draw, and he did beat it. But before his thumb had quite eared back the hammer of his .44, the chair slammed into the gun, knocking it from his hand and clear across the room. Peters tried to jerk backward and shoot at the same time, and it marred his aim. The slug he got out went wild. He didn't get out another, because he hadn't stepped back quite far enough, and the leg of the chair slammed across his wrist. Peters' howl of pain was followed by the heavy clang of his gun on the floor.

Kaycee let go of the chair, and it followed its arc on around, crashing up against the wall. He had his gun out by then.

"All right," he said, "you can go now. And if you want your guns back, you'll have to send your boss after them."

The startled anger had fled from Glenrock's face almost before it appeared, and he stood there with his strange eyes not seeming to look at Kaycee. But Peso Peters' face was dark, and his mouth worked a moment before he got his words out.

"I've heard you were a stubborn devil, but I didn't think you were a fool to boot, Garrett. I guess you know what you've started now, don't you? If you take that O'Hare shipment, you won't even leave Singletree alive, much less reach the Bozeman with it."

Kaycee's lips drew back from his teeth in a wolf-snarl. "Get out!"

Glenrock went first, backing through the door. And as Peters followed, the hate in his eyes made it plain to Kaycee just what he could expect when the big deliberate man got another gun.

Britten O'Hare must have passed the two Montana gunmen on her way to the office. She was standing in the door when Kaycee turned from putting the two six-shooters away in his desk drawer.

"Those men looked mad," she said. "What happened?"

"They offered me five thousand dollars not to take your hydraulic equipment up the Bozeman, Miss O'Hare," he said. "And they didn't like it when I refused the offer."

The girl's face took on a pale, confused look. "Why should anyone want to make that kind of an offer?"

He shrugged without answering. The girl had been in Singletree enough times, and they were on speaking terms, Kaycee and Britten O'Hare. But he had never actually seen her up close like this. The whole effect was striking—taffy-blonde hair that hung windblown about her shoulders, framing a face that was highly colored from the outdoors. Ever since her father had died two years before, she had run the O'Hare mines north of Virginia City, and had taken to wearing a man's clothes. On her, somehow, the plaid shirt and slick leather leggins lost all their masculinity. Strapped around her slim waist was one of Sam Colt's new .45's, and it was said she had more skill with it than any girl should rightly possess. Kaycee picked up the smashed chair, soberly taking off the back of it, then setting it on the floor, straightening a leg.

"Won't you sit down?" he said drily.

She looked at it a moment, not sure if he was joking. Then, suddenly, she almost collapsed into it. Her face was strained, and she seemed to be fighting back tears. Kaycee didn't look at her when she spoke, because she affected him more than he liked, and he hated to see women cry anyway.

"I suppose you know I won't be able to get any regular muleskinners," he said. "It's been hard enough for me to get a decent crew in the past, what with Jason Dudley offering higher wages and undercutting my prices and roughing up what few men I'm able to hire. Now, with this cholera on the rampage, and the Sioux threat . . ."

"I've got to get those hydraulic monitors to the mines," she broke in. "Dad borrowed money from the Embar Mining Corporation two years ago, when we weren't getting out enough yellow to run our diggings, and the mortgage is due this September. We've hit a vein that will pay off that mortgage a thousand times, but we have to get the gold out with water. And if I can't get those monitors working in time, Embar will foreclose. Alex Hanson's company hauled the stuff from the Mississippi to here, but they won't take it any farther up the Bozeman. I went to Dudley, and he said he couldn't do it either. You're my last hope."

He would have liked to discuss with her further why anyone should want her shipment stopped, but he could see the strain she had been under, so he shrugged it off.

"I'll see what I can do, Miss O'Hare. You have Hanson's wagon boss pull his train into my yards and unload the equipment from his wagons. I know where I can get some sort of a crew—not the best muleskinners in the world—but at least able to snap a bull-whip."

The Kaycee yards were directly behind his clapboard office—a big open space, crisscrossed with wheel ruts, and a pair of sagging, hiproof barns with a hayrack in between them. Hanson's wagon boss had unloaded the monitors in sections the evening before, and pulled out. Kaycee spent the better part of that same evening rounding up his crew, and the next morning, early, set them to work loading the O'Hare equipment into his own wagons. He was standing beside one of his big, weather-beaten barns when Britten O'Hare cantered in on her taffy-maned palomino. Her spirits seemed to have risen a little, and as she swung easily down beside Kaycee, her smile wasn't quite so strained as it had been the day before.

"About ready to go?" she asked.

He nodded toward the wagons. "Only a few more sections of piping and we'll be set."

The girl turned toward the eight big freighters lined up on one side of the wheel-rutted yard. The smile on her face faded. They were ancient wagons, huge clumsy Conestogas of Santa Fe Trail vintage, swagger-boxes split and paint-peeled, canvas tilts patched and sagging between the hoops. The teams were no better—spavined, stove-up mules standing resignedly in battered hames. A sardonic twist had come into Kaycee's mouth as he saw the expression on her face.

This was what he had been fighting Dudley with for so long—1830 Conestogas against Dudley's bright new Murphy wagons; mules that would collapse if their traces didn't hold them up, against Dudley's sleek fat young animals. And the teamsters—that sardonic twist grew as he saw she had become aware of them.

Sweating over a huge steel nozzle was Blacksnake Brae, riverman, trapper, hunter, muleskinner—and primarily, drunkard. He was a burly, thick-set barrel of a man, ugly and dirty in a soiled red wool shirt and muddy black river boots. His eyes were bloodshot beneath beetling brows, and his black-bearded face was puffy, still flushed with a sullen resentment at having been sobered up for the first time in six weeks. He cast a surly glance at Kaycee, spat disgustedly, and turned back to curse the nozzle into the Conestoga.

Green River Jones and Tomosak, the half-breed son of a squaw man, were levering a long section of pipe into the bed of the next wagon down. Jones was a dried up little whanghide whose greasy tattered elkhides made believable his boast that he didn't change clothes till they rotted off of him. Through the strip of rawhide that supported his frayed blanket leggins were thrust four huge Green River skinning knives.

Backing a pair of wheelers into their traces, one on either side of the tongue, was Sevier, the huge French-Canadian, his cracking bullwhip punctuating a stream of volatile Gallic curses. There was talk of a murder in his past—but if any man could match Blacksnake Brae's skill with a whip, it was Sevier, and Kaycee could overlook the whispers of the Frenchman's unsavory past in favor of his talent with a Missouri bullwhip.

Drunkards, barflies, murderers—the dregs of Singletree. And though the girl was used to her rough miners, used to the brutal, cursing bullwhackers, she couldn't hide the curling of her lips. Her voice held a disappointment, and an irritation.

"You told me none of the regular teamsters would go because of the Indians, and the cholera. But there . . ."

"What did you expect," he asked harshly. "A bunch of parsons?"

This is the best I can offer, and it wasn't any picnic gathering them in."

She glanced at his cut lip, his swelling eye, and for a moment there was apology in her face. Then she turned quickly and mounted her palomino, settling into the silver-mounted Brazos saddle with an ease and grace that would have shamed many a man. She couldn't keep the almost frightened anger from her voice.

"I suppose you did the best you could, but I don't like it. These men don't look any more like muleskinners than a bunch of coyotes would. I've never seen such an ugly bunch."

Kaycee turned his back and walked to his big rawboned mare, tightening the latigo viciously, standing there till his anger faded a little. He shouldn't feel mad, really—she was just under a strain and she couldn't help it. But he'd had one hell of a time getting these men sobered up and whipped into shape, and he was under a strain too.

He was outriding, and he had changed his black frock coat for a heavy mackinaw, his white shirt for a red wool one. The men had hitched up the last team, and by the time he called to them, he had managed to fight down his anger.

"Let's go, you skinners. Sevier, you're on the first wagon. Brae, on the tail. Tomosak, you take the cavayard. We'll try to reach Salt Flats by tonight."

Jason Street was Singletree's main thoroughfare, a broad wheel-rutted way, stretching between the double row of false-front buildings, a plank walk running down each side, sagging hitch-racks standing at the curb. Kaycee headed his train out of town that way, passing the saloon of Rot-gut Farnum, between First and Second, the favorite haunt for most of Dudley's swaggering muleskinners. With Glenrock and Peters still at the back of his mind, Kaycee was expecting trouble before he left town, but he didn't connect it with the crowd of men that had collected in

front of Farnum's. Matt Farrow was standing in the street, a
little in front of the crowd, one of Dudley's unshaven, hickory-
jacketed wagon bosses. As Kaycee's lead wagon rolled by, he
threw back his head and laughed nastily.

"Look at that cussed fool, Kaycee—two trains wiped out by
cholera on the Bozeman, and the Sioux on the warpath, and
Kaycee thinks he'll get to Montana with them Santa Fe relics for
wagons."

"Ah, you beeg *paillard*," shouted Sevier violently. "We could
take these Conestogas to the moon and back with barefoot
teams . . ."

Kaycee spurred his mare up beside Sevier's lead wagon. "Shut
up, Frenchie, and keep on going."

Laughter sifted through the crowd on the sidewalk, and one
of them ran out into the street, poking at a flea-bit mule drawing
the second wagon.

"Look, it's alive," yelled the man.

The laughter grew, and it had an ugly quality. Kaycee held the
anger that flushed his lean-jawed face, tightening the grip on his
reins till his knuckles gleamed white. He had sensed something
deliberate in this gathering, and suddenly he was moved to look
for Glenrock or Peters. But neither of the Montana gunslicks was
to be seen. His horse had passed the crowd, and he wheeled
around, sidling back until he stood between the men on the walk
and his rumbling line of Conestogas.

The batwing doors of Rot-gut Farnum's saloon swung open and
the crowd gave way before Jason Dudley. He wore a gaudy
purple fustian and a furred stove-pipe hat, sideburns running from
beneath it and down the sides of his fat red cheeks. Good food
and rich living had made a big-bellied, pompous man of Dudley,
but beneath the roll of his jowls, his chin still held some of the
ruthless strength it had taken to make such an eminent place for
himself on this wild, raw frontier.

"I always said you were a loco hombre, Kaycee," said Dudley, moving around in front of a hitchrack. "Nobody else would be fool enough to take a train up the Bozeman this year. But then a lot of Sioux pass through Singletree. We'll probably see your hair along about next year, hanging from some buck's scalp belt."

He turned to the crowd, chuckling, and they laughed again, yelling at Kaycee, jeering him. Anger whipped to a froth inside him, Kaycee couldn't help kneeing his horse in close to the pompous Jason Dudley.

"Did you give Glenrock and Peters some new guns, Dudley," he asked, "or were you planning on getting the old ones out of my desk drawer after I left?"

Dudley's face paled, then flooded red with anger. A vein began to pulse in his fat neck, just above his white choke-collar. A couple of hard-faced muleskinners had moved in behind him, big calloused hands hanging above heavy Army Colts. It was unusual to find them armed that way in town. It made Kaycee shove his coat back a little farther from the white bone butt of his Paterson five-shot.

"I know what happened in your office, Kaycee," said Dudley angrily. "Most folks do, by now. And there isn't a man in Singletree fool enough to accuse me of backing a play like that. You'd better not be the exception."

"It seems I've always been the exception when it came to bucking you," said Kaycee. "Only you never came so much out in the open before. Careless of you, Jason, to hire a couple of known gunnies to cut me down right here in town. Or were you in a hurry?"

Choking with rage, Dudley turned half-way around, and the men behind him leaned forward in an eager, waiting way. Matt Farrow's bellowing voice stopped whatever order Dudley would have flung at his teamsters. The wagon boss had spotted Blacksnake Brae riding the tail Conestoga, and he yelled:

"If it ain't the Old Blacksnake himself. Thinks he's a mule-skinner. Thinks he's going to Montanny driving them crow-bait carcasses he calls mules. Don't fall off that seat, Blacksnake."

He threw back his head and laughed in that nasty thundering way. Brae didn't bother to stop his wagon. He jumped from the high seat and landed with short legs spread, bent at the knees, whip uncoiling.

"No stinking Dudley jackass can talk that way without tasting my leather, Matt Farrow," he bellowed.

And before he'd finished yelling, his twenty feet of braided Missouri bullwhip was snarling back of his head. Farrow tried to dodge aside. But Brae's forearm reversed and his snake howled out from behind him, cracking like a gun-shot as it lashed across Farrow's face. The Dudley wagon boss screamed, lurching back against the men behind him, hands pawing at his face.

Before Brae's whip had dropped from Farrow's face, Kaycee's skinners were jumping from their wagons—Green River Jones snaking two of his blades from the thong supporting his leggins, Escalante Baca, the Mexican, grabbing a sawed-off shotgun from the boot beside his seat. It was what the crowd on the sidewalk had been waiting for, and there was a sudden eddying move as they surged into the street, spreading apart. But they had waited an instant too long.

The moment Brae had dropped off his wagon, Kaycee had realized why there were so many of Dudley's men in the crowd, realized they had gathered here by no mere chance. And he had already begun his play before the crowd started to move. As Blacksnake Brae pulled his whip back for a second time, and even before Matt Farrow's scream was dead, Kaycee spurred his mare's flank and drew his gun at the same time.

The horse danced sideways under Kaycee's hard rein and slammed into Brae, knocking him over into the dust with a startled curse. Drowning that curse was the single crashing shot

Kaycee sent above the heads of the crowd. Its stunning detonation dropped a sudden silence over everything.

The two hardcases behind Dudley, who had been in the very act of drawing their guns, didn't draw them. Their faces were turned up to Kaycee, blank with surprise. The other teamsters, just beginning their forward surge to meet Kaycee's crew, halted like a bunch of snubbed horses. Some had one foot on the plank sidewalk and the other in the street. And the only one with a gun unleathered was Kaycee, sitting tall and angry there on his big mare, smoking Paterson Colt commanding the whole scene. He spoke to Brae from the side of his mouth, eyes still on the others.

"Get back to your wagon, Brae. I'm not having any rumpot muleskinner start a fight that would end with my whole crew shot to rags. I'm not giving Jason Dudley that chance."

Brae struggled to his feet, standing there a moment with his face livid, his chest heaving. But Kaycee's own dark face had a harsh, granite look to it, and Brae knew Kaycee well enough to have seen that look before, and to know what it meant.

With a muttered curse, Brae picked up his whip, then turned back to the wagon. Kaycee ordered the rest of his crew back in that same hard, flat voice. Dudley's crowd began to shift. Kaycee sidled his horse toward them.

"Anybody wants a slug through his brisket, just make the wrong move. All right, Sevier, str-i-i-ng out!"

The last was a yell, and the lead wagon lurched into movement, jerking as each span of mules leaned forward against the hames. Kaycee sat his horse there till they were well down the street, meeting Dudley's apoplectic gaze with a sardonic smile. When he finally wheeled his mare to follow, he sat turned in the saddle so that he covered the crowd all the way down Jason Street, knowing what would happen if he put his back to them, knowing this

was only the beginning of the thing that would stalk him all the
way up the Bozeman.

Up past the Salt Flats they rolled, up beyond the Dry Fork of
the Cheyenne, days of creaking wagons and dust, and of constantly muttering men, the threat of cholera putting them under
a terrific strain. Blacksnake Brae was the worst of all. He hadn't
wanted to come in the first place, because of cholera, and Indians,
and because he knew he wouldn't see a drop of liquor between
Singletree and Virginia City. Kaycee had only deepened his resentment by knocking him over back there in Jason Street and
making him lose face to the Dudley men.

The third morning out of Singletree was chill and foggy. The
men rose from their damp sougans in an ugly mood, streaming
out to get their teams from the cavayard, where they browsed in
the blue lupine and stirrup-high wheatgrass. Kaycee followed
them as far as the ring of wagons, listening to the crack of whips,
the violent cursing.

Driving the third wagon was a cocky little old man named Eph
whom Kaycee had found dead drunk in the back room of Rotgut
Farnum's. He was trying, now, to back one of his mules from a
patch of wheatgrass. Nearby, Brae had rounded up his three spans
and was driving them past Eph. The old man whacked his mule
with five feet of bullwhip, shouting in a cracked voice.

"Git outa there, damn 'ee ornery varmint, outa there."

Reacting to the whip with a loud bray, the mule backed right
into Blacksnake's team, kicking and bucking. Brae's mules milled
and crowded into each other excitedly, breaking into a run, scattering. The black-bearded rumpot tried to stop them, cursing,
running this way and that. But they were already gone in half a
dozen different directions.

Blacksnake Brae turned to Eph, snarling. "What the hell are
you trying to do? It took me ten minutes to collect my team and

then you whip your old jackass right smack into the middle of them."

Cursing with rage, he grabbed Eph by the front of his buckskins, holding him there while he smashed him brutally in the face. Kaycee broke into a run for them. Brae had clouted the old man for the third time when Kaycee caught his solid shoulder and spun him around, causing him to release his grip on Eph and let him slide down into the dust.

"That'll do, Brae," he said flatly. "Go get your mules."

"No damn prospector has a right handling a bullwhip anyway," growled Brae. "He scattered my team on purpose. You saw it."

"You know he didn't do it deliberately," said Kaycee. "You've just been aching for a chance to take a swipe at somebody. I guess I didn't make it clear back in Singletree that you aren't going to make any trouble in this crew."

For a moment Brae stood there, hairy hands opening and closing spasmodically. Kaycee could see the haze of rage in his bloodshot eyes. Some of the teamsters had gathered, muttering in a sullen way. They were turned as skittish as a snake-startled horse by the fear of cholera. Brae was their acknowledged leader, the strongest among them, and there would be no telling what they'd do if he blew off the lid now. Knowing that, Kaycee settled himself, muscles tight across his belly, and he spoke in that flat voice again.

"I said—go and get your team hitched up, Brae."

Brae's whole body grew taut as stretched rawhide, and he seemed to gather himself. Kaycee's elbow twitched his mackinaw away from the Paterson buckled around his waist. Brae's own hand curled above his six-gun. But he was no iron slinger, and he knew it. His eyes met Kaycee's for a hard moment. Then he relaxed, and his voice shook with the effort to control his anger.

"All right, Garrett, maybe this ain't just the time."

Kaycee waited for the other men to scatter, then bent to help Eph up. "Did he hurt you much, Eph?"

The old man cackled weakly. "Not much. But he would have done me in sure if you hadn't stopped him. I've seen him in that kind of mood before when he beat men to a pulp. I reckon you're about the only one I ever seen face him down."

"He isn't afraid of me," said Kaycee. "He isn't afraid of anything. And when the time comes, we'll lock horns proper. What was eating that mule of yours, anyway?"

Eph nodded at the animal, standing over by the patch of wheatgrass, its belly bloating, its muzzle frothed—then he pointed to the bunch of blood-red loco weed growing in the grass.

"He's been browsing that loco weed. Makes 'em sicker than a gaunted coachwhip snake with the scours, and nobody can handle 'em for about a week."

"Have to put him in with the sore-back mules," said Kaycee. "Get yourself an extra animal from the cavvy. By the way, didn't Brae say something about your being a prospector?"

"Yeah, I been one in my time."

"Know Montana?"

"Know every gully. Why?" asked Eph.

"I've always thought our cook looked more like a miner than a muleskinner. Maybe you saw him in Montana sometime."

Eph looked toward the wagons. The cook was loading his skillets and kettle into a Conestoga. His chest and shoulders beneath his tight red shirt had the knotted bulky look that comes to a man who has swung a pick for his living.

"Sure," said Eph. "I know Lespards. He used to work for the Embar Mining Corporation."

"Oh," said Kaycee. "And maybe you also know a pair of men by the handles of Glenrock and Peso Peters."

Eph scratched stringy gray hair. "I seem to remember a couple

of triggermen who went by those names. Seems to me they were
on the Embar payroll, too."

"I suppose you know all about Miss O'Hare's diggings?"

"Sure do," said Eph. "Word travels fast when anybody hits a
vein as full of yellow as she did. All she needs to do is get those
monitors working and she'll be able to pay off that mortgage in
a day."

"Tell me one more thing," said Kaycee. "Just who owns the
Embar Mining Corporation—silent partners as well as otherwise?"

Sioux country now, up past Pumpkin Buttes, past the hook turn
in the Powder where it stopped flowing south and curved sharply
west, up where Dudley's last train had been hit by cholera. It was
the girl who woke Kaycee that morning, shaking his shoulder.
Dawn threw a dim light over the circle of swagger-boxed Conestogas. Somewhere a man was groaning.

"The men are sick, Kaycee," said Britten O'Hare. "I don't feel
very well myself . . ."

He was suddenly very wide awake. He stooped out from under
the wagon where he had slept and moved through the mist that
curled across the open space in milky shreds gathering softly
around the group of men by the ashes of the dead campfire. Several of them were lying down, knees drawn up as if in a cramp.
Blacksnake Brae rose from where he had hunkered down beside
Green River Jones.

"He started griping like this about half an hour ago. Me, I got
a belly-ache too."

Garrett looked around. "Where's Lespards?"

"What's Lespards got to do with it?" growled Brae. "This is
cholera. I've seen it before. You get a belly-ache first and then
you cramp up, and finally you get weaker than a drink of water."

Kaycee could see the fear in the men's faces, a growing, animal
fear of the thing that had haunted them from the beginning of

this trip, a thing they couldn't touch or see or fight with their hands. There wasn't much difference between them and a herd of mules just before a stampede. They shifted nervously, sweat bathing pale foreheads, eyes on Brae, waiting. Everything hinged on the stocky, black-haired rumpot now, and he sensed it.

"We're getting out, Garrett," he said. "We aren't staying here any longer. You kept us as long as you can, but you can't make us die like a bunch of rats here with the cholera."

Kaycee's forehead grew damp with sweat. At first he thought it was only a growing excitement at what was coming. Then nausea swept up from his stomach. The fingers of his hands began to curl uncontrollably. And he knew the perspiration wasn't from any excitement.

But this thing between him and Brae had started a long time ago, and he was going to finish it now, whether he had cholera or not!

"Don't be a fool, Brae," snapped Kaycee, his voice strong with the bitter resolve inside him. "If you have the cholera, it won't do any good to slope out now. Chances are you'd never reach Single-tree alive. And if you did, you'd only spread it through the town."

Brae shook out a coil of his twenty-foot whip. "Get out of our way, Garrett."

The men began to move forward, crowding one another, voices raising. Brae shook out another coil. And Kaycee knew whatever he said now didn't matter. They were filled with a reasonless ani-mal fear, and all they could think of was running somewhere, anywhere, away from the cholera.

The whole length of Brae's whip lay on the ground, and his forearm rippled as he tensed his grip. "Get out of the way, Garrett, or I'll whip you out!"

The muscles along Garrett's lean jaw ridged as he ground his teeth shut against the nausea sweeping him, and he spread his legs, and that hard set came into the lines of his face.

Roaring a muleskinner's gargantuan oath, Brae snapped his whip behind his head. The men behind him surged forward, yelling, shouting, grabbing for their guns.

Brae had an incredible swift skill with his blacksnake, and though Garrett had seen it coming, nausea slowed his reflexes. His gun had barely cleared leather when that howling whip crashed across his wrist, knocking the Paterson flying. He grunted with the sudden sharp pain, taking an instinctive step backward. Then they were on him, the whole shouting, swearing bunch of them, Blacksnake Brae's leering, black-whiskered face looming up out of the press, grin triumphant.

The sheer weight of them forced Kaycee to his knees. But he was a big man, and he was hell-mad, and he wasn't finished yet. As the big French-Canadian lurched hard into him, he drove upward, grabbing the man's thick torso and using his momentum to toss him on over his shoulder. With Sevier still flying through the air behind him, Kaycee lunged forward, smashing Escalante Baca full in the face. The Mexican dropped his gun and fell backward, tripping up the wrangler and a couple of others, who stumbled over his body and fell across him.

Even as Kaycee hit Baca, he twisted sideways and caught Brae with his left arm. Then he lunged his shoulder into the shorter man and heaved him backward. Losing his balance, Brae fell among the rushing men, knocking one aside, crashing into another pair and halting them. It stopped their forward surge in that instant, and Kaycee took a swift step back so there was a little cleared space between him and Brae. Already Blacksnake had struggled free of the men, and roaring madly, he brought his whip behind his head again.

The gun-shot crashed loud above the shouts and yells. Brae's hand stopped there behind his head, and a blank look crowded the anger fom his flushed face. Then he brought his hand back around so he could see it.

The bullet had cut the twenty-foot lash neatly from the whip-stock, and all Brae held in his fingers was that foot of braided handle; the rest of the whip lay behind him where it had fallen. Britten O'Hare stood from where she had shot, her new Sam Colt still smoking in her small hand. Her voice had a cool, unshaken sound.

"This fight between you and Kaycee has been building ever since we left Singletree, Brae, and we won't have any peace till it's over. But it's going to be fair—"

They shifted away from Brae, and they wouldn't make any wrong moves, not with anyone who could shoot like that. Britten cast a single glance at Kaycee, and in it was all the plea of a girl who knew her only chance of saving everything she had lay in his beating Blacksnake Brae.

Brae dropped what was left of his whipstock and set himself with a sullen growl, a heavy, broad man with a grizzly-strength in his sloping shoulders beneath the dirty red shirt. Kaycee took a breath, and wondered if Brae was as sick as he. Then he moved forward, bending a little to meet the shock of Brae's rush, stripping off his mackinaw and throwing it aside. And Brae moved forward.

To the sudden scuffle of their boots, and the puff of dust they made, the two men crashed together, bodies meeting with a singular, giving, fleshy thud.

Brae had his knee up as he came. Kaycee took it in the groin, his sick grunt lashing out above the sound of their struggle. Brae bent in and got his thick arms around the taller man. All the skill of a hundred barroom brawls was in his sudden vise-like squeeze, his jerking movement to the side.

Kaycee heard the crack of his ribs, stiffened to the sudden shooting pain through his spine. Then he got his long arms going. Right and left, like pistons shooting out from the breadth of his shoulders, pumping into Brae's face. The shorter man's head snapped back to a left, and his grip around Kaycee's waist was pulled free. His head snapped back again to a right, and he reeled away. Kaycee followed, doubling him over with a jab under the heart, then straightening him with a right that howled in and caught Brae on the jawbone, knocking him over into the dust, flat on his back.

He rolled, though, and seemed to bounce up, dancing away and shaking his black head, roaring curses. Then he wasn't moving away any more, and they locked.

Britten O'Hare stood with her face pale and set, her Colt steady on the crowd. The men spread out, shouting encouragement to Brae, jeering Kaycee, forgetting their fear in the excitement of seeing these two hard men smash each other to pulp.

Brae doubled over suddenly in Kaycee's grasp, butting. The air exploded from Kaycee and he sank down like a deflated balloon. Brae's thick hands were on his face, thumbs seeking his eyes. The burly man's heavy river boot smashed into Kaycee's side. Drawing a choked, ragged breath into his lungs, Kaycee fought upward, jerking his head away from Brae's hands, driving out with a weak left into Brae's belly. Then a stronger right. And he stood erect again, smashing his fists into the shorter man, salty blood in his eyes, agony searing him every time he breathed.

Brae took the blows, grunting thickly to the first, and taking a step backward, grunting to the second and stepping back. The third one put him over on his back.

This time he was a little slower getting up. He shook his head like the stubborn bull he was, and moved in. He ducked a right and shot in with his arms out, taking Kaycee's left jab so he could grapple.

What happened after that was a little too fast for the crowd to follow. Kaycee's long leg snaked behind Brae's knee, and they rolled into the dust. Gagged and blinded, Kaycee couldn't tell whether he was above or below. Finally he heaved up, getting a leg under him, throwing Brae away. His head rocked as Brae's boot caught him across the ear. Then Kaycee was striking out again, following Brae back relentlessly. He caught the man on his jaw with a right. Brae lurched, stopped himself from falling. A left sank into his belly, drawing a wheeze. The right slammed him in the face again, and he sprawled full length on the ground.

Kaycee swayed there above the black-bearded man, shirt ripped off his shoulders and hanging from his belt, blood dripping from his chin. Silence held the crowd as they waited for Brae to get up that third time. It took an eternity for him to rise on his elbow, another to raise himself to a sitting position. He spat some teeth, and some blood. Then he tried to get to his feet, failed miserably, sinking back to his elbow.

He was brutal and vicious and a hopeless drunkard, Blacksnake Brae, but a man. There was no rancor in his voice.

"All right, Kaycee, I guess it's all over now. Not many men can say they whipped Blacksnake Brae. I get awful mad sometimes, but nobody can say I hold a grudge against a man just because he proved he's better'n me."

Kaycee turned to the others, gasping. "Anybody else think they're sloping out?"

There was indecision in the men's faces, and they wouldn't meet Kaycee's burning gaze.

"Then we'll start from scratch again," said Kaycee. "Lespards didn't desert because he was afraid of the cholera, or the Sioux. I figure he'll be back soon, with Jason Dudley and a crew of his teamsters, and some gents named Glenrock and Peso Peters. Maybe Lespards thought you'd desert when the cholera hit, maybe he thought there wouldn't be anybody here when he came back. And maybe he'll be surprised."

The Conestogas stood alone there in the little valley, canvas tilts gleaming in the late afternoon sun, shadows sprawled across the ashes of dead campfires. There was no cavayard browsing in the grass, no sign of men. The whole scene had a certain desolation to it.

The file of dusty horsemen came down the rutted Bozeman Trail from the direction of Singletree, slowing warily as they sighted the Conestogas. Lespards was in the lead, forking a big dun he had stolen from the cavayard.

Dudley must have been waiting with his men somewhere on the backtrail. He sat a stout Morgan, his pompous face dripping sweat, his fustian grayed by dust and bulged at the hip by the six-gun he wore on rare occasions such as this. Matt Farrow was there, too, the Dudley wagon boss, his thick-featured face still bearing the scar of Brae's deadly bullwhip. And Glenrock and Peters riding together, and some twenty Dudley muleskinners, all packing short-guns, all hugging the scabbards of their saddle guns under their left knees. Lespards led on, confidently, and his voice was loud enough to reach the wagons.

"What'd I tell you, not a man in sight! I'll bet they scattered like a bunch of school-ma'ams from a pole-cat when they woke up this morning with a belly-ache and thought it was cholera."

Dudley reined in his Morgan, looking at the circle of Conestogas suspiciously. "I don't know, Lespards, I don't trust that Garrett. Under any other man, those derelicts would have deserted the first day."

"They didn't leave a single horse in the cavvy," said Lespards sullenly. "The whole camp is empty. What else could you ask for? We had rabbit stew last night, and I spiked it with enough loco weed to make a whole cavvy sick for a week. They thought it tasted funny, but I said maybe I put too much seasoning in it, and everybody but me ate some. That loco weed acts just like cholera. And I'm telling you, not even Kaycee Garrett could stop those fools if they thought they had cholera!"

Dudley turned to Farrow. "Have your boys got the axes?"

Farrow nodded. "When we get through smashing those monitors there won't be piping left to pump a drink of water."

"Get your guns out then, and keep your eyes peeled," said Dudley. "I've been fighting Kaycee too long to take any chances."

The soft thud of hoofs was the only sound. A strained line came into the men's bodies, sitting their horses stiffly. Even Lespards shifted uneasily in his saddle. Finally Dudley halted near the wagons, nodding at Farrow. The wagon boss swung from his mount, unstrapping the big double-bitted ax from the whangs on the skirt. The other teamsters followed suit, gathering around him, eyeing the wagons reluctantly.

"Well, damn it, let's go," snarled Farrow, stepping forward.

The two men followed him. The others spread out in twos and threes, each group going toward a wagon. Farrow slowed as he reached the first Conestoga. Then, with an impatient curse, he reached up and grabbed the chain on the tail-gate, raising his boot to swing aboard. . . .

The shout that broke the strained silence came from within the wagon, and it was Kaycee's voice. "Up and at 'em, cuss you. You're a bunch of yellow dogs who wouldn't know guts if they were thrown in your face, but you're going out there now if I have to carry you myself!"

The tail-gate slammed down, catching Farrow full in the face. He sank to the ground with a hoarse sob. And standing there in the rear of the wagon was Kaycee, shoving Escalante Baca the Mexican out in front of him, giving Green River Jones a kick that sent him sprawling from the wagon-bed. Still yelling, Kaycee followed them, throwing himself on the nearest of the teamsters who had come in behind Farrow.

Kaycee had guessed Dudley would come from the backtrail, and had chosen a wagon nearest that approach. All of his crew were sick as dogs, nauseated, cramped. And though he had beaten Brae, though the derelicts had given in to him, Kaycee still couldn't trust them. As his body struck that Dudley teamster, carrying him to the ground, Kaycee still didn't know whether his men would back him, or whether he was alone.

He rose up on his knees, straddling the man's body, clubbing with his Paterson. On the second blow the big teamster collapsed.

Farrow had regained his feet. And as Kaycee rose, he caught sight of the man's blurred figure to the side. The wagon boss had his axe up over his head, already beginning the downward swing that would cleave Kaycee like splitting a rail. Whirling, desperately trying to thumb back his hammer for a shot, Kaycee knew he would never be in time.

Farrow lunged forward, but the axe in his hands dropped down his back instead of arcing over his head into Kaycee. Startled, Kaycee stepped away from the falling body. And as Farrow hit the ground Kaycee saw Britten O'Hare standing in a wagon-opening, with her smoking .45 already aiming at another.

Green River Jones stood where he had landed after being booted from the wagon, and he was standing over a gutted teamster and pulling another skinning knife from the rawhide thong holding up his leggins.

Only then did Dudley and his groups of teamsters begin to recover from their stunned surprise. The whole thing had happened in one blinding flash, and had been so unexpected. But now they were whirling, grabbing for their guns, dropping axes. Dudley wheeled his horse, fumbling beneath his fustian for his six-shooter. Kaycee cast a desperate glance at the other Conestogas. He had planted Brae and the rest of his crew in those wagons. If they failed him now. . . .

Then Brae's roar sounded from the tilt of an ancient wagon. "Come on, you rot-gut boothill muleskinners! Kaycee's our boss now, and I said I didn't hold no grudge against him, and you're going to prove it. Get out there and show those teamsters how real skinners can fight!"

Sevier tumbled over a tail-gate as if he'd been kicked out, and another man followed him the same way. Then Brae leaped out and on top of a hapless Dudley man. The whole circle of wagons erupted then, drunks and barflies and outlaws and even murderers, all sick as dogs, but all following Brae, following Kaycee.

Peso Peters suddenly loomed in front of Kaycee, running for his horse. They saw each other about the same time. Peters raised his gun, hatred twisting his mouth. Kaycee's whole body stiffened as he thumbed back his hammer for a shot from the hip. Then he caught the hammer before it fell because another man had rushed in between him and Peters.

Sevier, the French-Canadian, yelling deep-throated curses and cutting Peso Peters down with a wild slamming volley. A big, red-shirted teamster shot Sevier in the belly before Peters had hit the ground, and the French-Canadian staggered to a halt, bent over, sagged onto his face. Escalante Baca let both barrels go on his sawed-off shot-gun and the red-shirted teamster followed Sevier down with his face blown off.

Kaycee stumbled over Peters' body, and Sevier's body, hunting for Dudley. But the battle had raged in front of the man, hiding him from Kaycee for a moment.

Something pounded into Kaycee's leg. He staggered, throwing a snap shot at the half-seen figure in the dust and smoke, and only after he saw the man go down did he realize he was shot in the leg. He lurched to a knee, trying to rise back up again, seeing Brae where he had risen from the man he'd jumped down on.

A pair of Dudley teamsters came through the smoke, running for their horses. Brae was in their way, and they began shooting fast, still going forward. Brae whirled, his six-shooter bucking from the hip.

But all his skill was with a bullwhip, and he had to empty every shot from his gun before one of these Dudley men went down.

The other kept right on coming, shooting. Brae staggered back, clutching at his side as a slug caught him.

He must have known how much chance he had, facing that blazing six-shooter with his empty iron. Yet he steadied himself and bent forward to meet the man's charge, roaring defiantly in the teeth of hot lead.

Kaycee was on his feet by then. He took a lurching step forward, throwing down on the Dudley teamster charging Brae. His gun bucked in his hand, and the sound was lost in the roar of battle, and he knew he had missed. His second shot was lost, too, in the raging sound, but it struck home. The running man faltered, slid to his knees, flopped over on his face.

Still clutching his side, Brae turned. When he saw Kaycee standing there with the smoking Paterson, a grin split his black beard . . .

Then, on past Brae, Kaycee saw Dudley.

The pompous man hadn't been known to leave the environs of Singletree in years. He must have wanted to stop Britten O'Hare's shipment pretty desperately to come this far north himself. Desperately enough so that if he couldn't smash it, he'd burn it up.

His Morgan was standing nervously by one of the wagons on the far side of the circle. And stooping to light a pile of brush that laid against the wagon wheel was Jason Dudley. Glenrock stood to one side. He had an empty tar bucket in one hand, the bucket that hung on the tailgate of every wagon, filled with a mixture of resin, tar and tallow which the teamsters used to grease their axles. It was inflammable enough, and while the fire it started wouldn't do much damage to the steel piping and nozzles of the monitors, it would certainly burn the dry old wagons to the ground, and keep the girl from getting her equipment to Montana. Kaycee had lost sight of Britten in the smoke and dust, but thought of her helped him to break into a limping run, passing Farrow's body, jumping an outspanned wagon tongue, landing so hard on his wounded leg that he sank to his knees again. He gasped with the agony, fought upward.

This was no pot-shooting at a bunch of wild teamsters who couldn't hit a mule at three paces with a scatter gun. Glenrock made his living by his skill with a gun. And Dudley had always won before.

Knowing that, Kaycee stumbled forward. Flame leaped up the side of the wagon, and Dudley stood. Kaycee brought up his Paterson. But Dudley saw him, and ducked around the wagon, moving incredibly fast for such a bulk. Kaycee's shot hit wooden sideboards where Dudley had been an instant before. Then Dudley was behind the wagon and only Glenrock stood there, settling into a habitual crouch, so sure of his skill that he let Kaycee fire first. He must have known that Kaycee couldn't hit anything, running forward like that with a game leg that made him jerk every time it hit the ground, throwing his aim all off. Kaycee found it out after his third shot.

Then Glenrock fired, and the slug hit Kaycee in the shoulder, and he had to stop anyway. Glenrock's second slug missed him because he had staggered and was falling sideways.

He didn't go clear down, though. He caught himself with his good leg, straightened, holding his Paterson carefully out in front of him. Glenrock might have had his hammer eared back for his third shot, because he was that fast, but he didn't let it drop. Kaycee's big five-shot boomed with a finality. Kaycee saw the dust puff from Glenrock's vest above the heart. Then Glenrock was falling forward.

The fire was licking up the side of the wagon. Kaycee knew once it reached the canvas there would be no stopping it. He stumbled to the Conestoga, kicked dirt at the flames, tore his shirt off and beat at them. He reached up and ripped a piece of canvas from the hoops before it could catch fire. His hands were burned and his chest was blistered when he finally realized the fire was out. His right hand was so bad that he had to put up his left to help hold the gun.

He punched a couple of exploded rimfires out and fumbled two fresh ones from his belt. Then, holding the Paterson in both hands like that, he moved toward the wagon tongue. Dudley's Morgan was still fiddling around on the inside of the circle. Kaycee knew Dudley wouldn't try to get away on foot—he knew this country better than that. He would be waiting, then, on the other side of the Conestoga. The lines in Kaycee's face had taken on that terrible granite harshness. Dudley, now, the man he had been fighting so long and so bitterly, the man who had always won before, in any game he played. . . .

Kaycee crouched over the tongue, waiting for a second at the corner of the high wagon box. Just as he remembered that Dudley could see his legs beneath the bed, there came a small thumping sound around the corner. . . .

He leaped out, turning, hammer carried back under his left thumb, nerves screaming for the release of his booming shot.

He was looking at a small round stone that had bounced off the wagon wheel and was just rolling to a stop. Jason Dudley had thrown it. Knowing how he had been trapped, knowing what was behind him, Kaycee let his body keep right on going, its own momentum carrying it over. Dudley's shot crashed out from back of him, the bullet clipping at the holster on Kaycee's hip, clacking into the wooden side of a Conestoga.

Twisting as he fell, Kaycee was facing Dudley when he hit the ground. His Paterson was still cocked, still held out in two hands like that. It bucked once.

Dudley took the bullet square and went down with all his weight, a big pompous man who had wanted too much out of life and who was dead before he hit the ground. . . .

Kaycee was doing a bad job of trying to rise when the girl's soft arms slipped around him, helping him up.

"I thought I told you to say in the wagons," he said.

"Brae and the others have sent Dudley's teamsters packing and it's all over," she murmured, casting a glance at Dudley. "How in the world did you know Lespards would come back with Dudley?"

"I half-suspected Dudley at first," said Kaycee. "He had good enough reason for not wanting me to go up the Bozeman. If I got through with your stuff, I'd get all the contracts he couldn't meet this year because of the cholera. But when I talked with Eph, I found Dudley had an even bigger iron in the fire than that. Not many people know it, but Jason Dudley is silent partner in the Embar Mining Corporation, owning a controlling share."

The girl saw it then. "And he would much rather have had my mine than the money I'd pay on that mortgage. Then it was Dudley who imported Glenrock and Peters to kill you, and that mess in Jason Street was deliberate, trying to start a riot so he could shoot up your crew."

Kaycee nodded. "Lespards was an ace in the hole. I found him in a saloon and had to sober him up, just like some of the others. But Dudley had planted him. Even when I found out from Eph that Lespards had worked for Embar, and that Dudley owned Embar, I couldn't come right out and accuse Lespards of being a Dudley man until I had more proof. And we've got it now, right inside us. I guess you heard him say what he put in the stew?"

"I'm glad it's loco weed instead of cholera," she said.

"If I didn't have such a big stomach ache, I'd ask you something," he muttered.

"Ask me anyway."

"Have they got a parson in Virginia City?"

She didn't answer. But she didn't have to, because suddenly she was in his arms, taffy hair soft against his burned chest. He forgot the pain of his wounded shoulder, and his leg. Blacksnake

Brae had come into the open space between the wagons, still holding his side, hand blood-soaked. Several others were behind him, all gaping at Kaycee and the girl.

But Kaycee didn't mind that, really. It seemed fitting that they should be present. After all, they were his crew now.

BLACK HILLS TRAIL

Miss Morissa

by MARI SANDOZ

THE WHEELS OF THE STAGECOACH STIRRED UP A LONG TRAIL OF DUST, to sift away eastward like a plume of smoke sprouting from the wide spring prairie. All except one of the passengers were content to be closed in by the heavy side curtains of the coach, even the sunburnt rancher and the naked-faced youth with small dark freckles thick across his cheeks. But the young city woman pulled back the stiff canvas and thrust her head out. She did it with a practicality and foresight that belied the feathered little hat tipped toward her nose. She had asked to change seats so she could look out on the windy side, away from most of the dust. But the wind was strong. The feathers on her hat struggled like agitated yellow birds, and her fashionable bangs that had seemed so duskily black in the shadow were shot with gleaming copper light where the sun ran over them.

With her white skin unprotected by powdering or veil, Morissa Kirk leaned far out to look at the guard carrying a Winchester across his knee, and to watch the driver swing his six fast horses out around the slower travelers. They passed gold seekers, mule freight outfits, and files of canvas-covered wagons drawn by long teams of bulls, the whackers plodding in the dust, their whips snaking out in the afternoon sun, but silently, the wind carrying the sharp, explosive sound away.

As the coach jounced and jolted, a little round-topped trunk tied with other luggage in the rack on top jounced, too, a new pressed-metal trunk that was to have accompanied Morissa Kirk on her wedding journey to Scotland, and was still filled with her trousseau, although her hand was bare of every ring. Beside the small trunk was a doctor's black bag and a chest of surgical instruments, while inside, cradled on Morissa's lap from the rougher bumps, was a case of vials and bottles and other physician's glass.

The coach swung down toward a rugged range of buttes like low, timber-flanked mountains that tapered off to Courthouse and Jail Rocks, standing out together and alone. At their feet the trail turned northwestward, upon the broad North Platte valley of Nebraska, the spreading bottoms grazed so bare that no stock was nearer than the far blue slopes. Morissa could get no glimpse of the river, only a smudging of dust against the ridges beyond, and then gradually a thickening line that reached for miles up and down where the stream must be—a wide, dark gathering like the great buffalo herds that had rested here not ten years ago.

But as the swift coach approached the river, Morissa saw what she had known must be there: at least thirty great circle corrals of covered freight wagons and a far spreading of other vehicles, with tents and bedrolls scattered among them, and knots of men —all jammed together closer and closer toward the new bridge. The crowd was thick as a close-corralled herd, particularly in the one short stretch of trail that was like a street, lined on both sides

by tents and low buildings, mostly log and sod, and little taller
than the bearded, sunburnt, waiting men.

The crowd milled restless as corralled longhorns, too, all waiting for the bridge to carry them over the roily, flooded stream,
release them to hurry toward the Black Hills where gold lay thick
at the grass roots. They had seen the real and shining proof of it
captured in the tiny bottles of yellow dust that were set in the
windows of every depot across the nation—to catch the sun and
the eyes of the gold-hungry, and of all those others eager to live
on, to prey on, them.

It was this rush to the new Eldorado of Deadwood Gulch that
had gathered the great wagon trains of mine machinery and
equipment here, trains of whisky, too, and mahogany bars and
roulette tables, guns, and ammunition, and the finery, the mirrors
and couches for the fancyhouses. It had drawn all the men waiting here, and the curled and tint-cheeked, impatient women.

While still far off the driver on the box of the stagecoach called
out his loud "Yip, yip, yip; yi, yi, yi!"—the signal to get the change
of horses ready for the ride to Deadwood if the bridge was opened
today, otherwise for the return trip to Sidney. And it would be
the return once more, for as they neared the river the passengers
could hear the dull thump of the pile driver and knew that none
of those so eager to go on would cross this afternoon unless he
swam the flood and the quicksand, or took a chance on the French
breed, old Joe Lenway, who had his handwritten sign in all the
outfitting places back down at Sidney:

> I haul you over north river safe
> $2.00 dollar a wagon.

Horsebackers had met the coach a mile out to make a flying
wedge for it past the little rows of shacks and tents to the stage
station that sat beside the river. The galloping escort split the

packed crowd, afoot and horseback, turning each side back upon itself, like treetops bent both ways up a spearhead of wind that was the thundering stage. The horses stopped with snort and clatter of harness, and the driver carried the lines down in his jump from the high box, the guard with his rifle climbing down, the gun still ready. Inside, the passengers stretched stiffly and one after the other stooped out and down into the curious crowd.

"Hey!—a lady-woman, an' a good looker!" a tipsyish youth shouted above the noise as Morissa Kirk was helped off the high step by a station hand. Then she stood alone in her feathered hat and the traveling suit, dusty but still the dark green of a young cedar on a hillside, with sun-darkened faces turned toward her from all around.

After Morissa, the freckled young man came out. He had peered carefully from both coach windows, his hand on his gun, and now he jumped down and slipped away into the crowd, a man or two speaking of him as he went: "Fly Speck, Fly Speck Billy," but keeping the voice down.

A weary crinkle came to Morissa's hazel eyes. Of course—the dark freckles. But she remembered something else now: This must be the highwayman from up around Dakota Territory, a roadagent as Robin, her stepfather, called him. That smooth boy-face hid a thief, a cold-blooded murderer. And yet, well-recognized, he walked free and unchallenged through this public place.

Uneasily the young woman glanced around the rough crowd eyeing her. There were few women beyond those from the saloons, and most of the dusty, wind-burnt men had guns in their holsters or tucked inside the belly band, as Robin called it. Most of the horsebackers seemed to be cowboys, with big hats, coiled lariats at the saddle horn, guns hanging over their leather chaps, gleaming spurs at the boot heels. Morissa managed to push through to her belongings, wondering how she could ever find Robin in all this throng of people, so far beyond anything she

could have imagined. And as she stood there, with nowhere to
go, she finally had to doubt the wisdom of her impulsive, un-
announced journey into this wilderness. There could be no place
here for her, not even a spot to spread a blanket for a night.
Truly none was so bold as the blind mare who would not see.

When the crowd began to drift back to the whisky stores and to
watch the thumping pile driver, Morissa Kirk found the station
keeper.

"Yeh," he admitted, replenishing his cud now that he had the
opportunity, "Yeh, I know Robin Thomas." But Robin was off
across the river there, boss of the graders refilling the new approach to the bridge. Washed out yesterday. Water came roaring
down the old Platte so they couldn't even set pilings.

"Across there's where he's working." The keeper pointed off over
his shoulder with the plug of tobacco he had gnawed, off to the
weathering bridge that stood like some long, low, many-legged
creature, the pile driver at the far end like a lifted head, looking.

As Morissa followed her trunk to the log station building, a
shouting came from the riverbank, followed by a surge of the
crowd down that way. On the far side of the wide rolling Platte,
a wagon broke from the mass of people waiting there also. It
swung around far out, and then headed in toward the river,
turned expertly a little upstream, coming at a good pace—the
momentum to carry it through the quarter mile of flood and
quicksand.

At the shouting the bridge workers all stopped to look, the
piling hammer silent as they relayed a message across. "It's old
Joe Lenway!" the palm-shielded voices called out. "Hold the Sidney coach. Lenway's bringin' a sick man over!"

A murmuring and a movement stirred around Morissa, with
words of uneasiness and protest. The river was too high, after the
sudden thaw in the western mountains and a May blizzard that

had buried the Fort Laramie region last week. Too dangerous, but Joe Lenway would try anything for two dollars.

"Why'n't the man wait a little, so's they can lay planks over the missing spans a the bridge when they gets closer—?" someone demanded.

"Hell, he's probably bad sick—an' the stage don't wait," another answered.

Morissa was being carried along toward the river by the push of the crowd, the yellow feathers of her hat squeezed in between trail-soiled shoulders and dusty beards, but she could see the moving wagon and a man rise up to whip his team into the gray stream. The horses tried to rear sideways at the flood edge, but with firm line and whip old Joe got them in, throwing water high as they went off into the river, still struggling to turn back. Under the fury of the driver's lashes, they settled to the pull, the current boiling up around their bellies, then at their breasts. The wagon swayed and lifted, the end swung downward by the current's force. But the man fought and cursed to hold the horses steady to their upstream turn until they began floundering as in quick-sand, and tried to rear above it, leap its pull. The sudden jerk threw the driver to the dashboard, then, as he recovered himself, the team and the wagon lurched forward together once more and went off into deep water as over a bank, sunk clear under. Joe grabbed the tail of a swimming horse, and behind him a bedroll, no, a man, was washed up on the flood. For a moment the appalled crowd watched a feeble splashing and then the man was gone.

"Save him!" Morissa Kirk cried out, commanding them as though none could see that this must be done, even before the man came up, free of the blankets now and still struggling a little, trying to help himself. But the current was too swift, boiling, turning, rolling, and he was drawn back under almost at once.

By now two riders had broken from the watchers at the far side and spurred downstream. Where the current swept in toward the bank, they sent their horses into the water. When the man reappeared, like a chunk of dark waterlogged piling, and rolling low, their ropes shot out—once, twice, and again. Suddenly a loop caught, the man stopped, swung in an arc against the angry water, and then one of the horses was struggling back against a taut rope, drawing the man in like a bawling calf to the branding fire. At the bank the cowboys carried him out, laid him on dry ground, still and unmoving, while they stood around him, helpless.

Now Morissa Kirk could not restrain herself. Grabbing up her wide skirts she pushed back to the stage station and with her little doctor's bag hanging from her arm she swung herself up on one of the horses at the hitchracks before anyone could stop her. With a knee crooked around the horn like the knob of a lady's sidesaddle, she was off on the rearing, fighting, white-stockinged black, through the crowd and then over the bank into the cold snow water in one splashing leap, the shouts of anger and warning lost behind her.

The horse snorted and began to plunge as he felt the sand moving and alive under his feet, but a sharp cut of the saddle quirt sent him forward in a wild, angry thrusting against the water, and when they hit the edge of the worst quicksand, the most treacherous shift and suck of it, he quieted and forged ahead, a welltrained animal long experienced in such streams. Free in deep water at last, he swam the current with strong, steady strokes, but the flood swirling about Morissa's thighs caught at her skirts, swept them out to balloon in the weight and force of the current, to drag at the horse. Hampered by the pounding bag on her arm she grabbed at the heavy garments, kept drawing them up as she could. But gradually the laboring horse was forced downstream, slowing in his wild push across the current, sinking lower into the water for all her quirting until only his nose was out and it seemed she must kick her skirts off and swim for it herself.

Shouts rose all along the banks and anxious riders plunged in from both sides but suddenly Morissa's horse began to paw for footing again—in quicksand. Yet with the feel of something like bottom, he strengthened and finally they were out on the other side, the crowd pressing close around.

Morissa was soaked, even her yellow feathers hanging wet, but the doctor's bag was still on her arm and as someone grabbed the bit of the horse she slipped off and ran in her pounding skirts. The watchers parted for her, opening the circle around the man still so quiet and remote there on the ground. She stooped over him, felt for his heart under the wet clothing and laid an ear to his breast, but there was no beat, no warmth, nothing of life. Quickly she motioned for space, drew the tongue free, and showed a cowboy how to turn the man, grasp him about the middle and lift up, bringing a gush of dirty water bursting from his mouth and nose. Then, with the man's head turned up sideways on his arm, Morissa knelt over him, lifting, pressing, forcing herself to calm her breath to the slow rhythm as someone brought a buffalo robe and started a litttle fire. When she tired she shook back the hair stringing over her face and gave her place to one of the men while she opened her bag, hoping for something that might help, something to save this man, drowning and sick with a disease of which she knew nothing at all.

By now most of those waiting on the north bank had gathered in close, curious, watching, barely shifting for a man who came pushing through, elbowing his way. The young woman did not notice him or his exclamation when he saw her, but the one word "Morissa!" from Robin Thomas started a wave of low voices that spread clear back. Morissa?—then this must be his stepdaughter, who was a lady doc.

While the young woman fingered her vials and powders, she glanced anxiously at the man on the ground, and the cowboy bending up and down over him. Still no color came, and gradually the watchers began to murmur among themselves. "He's a goner," some were saying. "Sick man dumped in the cold water like that—"

"Yeh, probably same as dead anyway, hurrying him off to Sidney like they was."

"Well, he won't die for nobody tryin'—the poor little bastard!"

The words brought Morissa's head up sharply, her face suddenly dark and flushed. But the speaker was not observing her at all, only the man, and so she hid her foolish anger. Yet she was less confident now, more fearful that in her hurry and her inexperience she might have forgotten something, something that could have been done. The man had no life to swallow anything, no signs of any living that she could see, and so without hope she took over from the cowboy again, knowing that one moment lost could be the fatal one, or one second of faltering in the rhythm.

The young doctor worked until the studied breathing made her dizzy and her arms ached to breaking. But when it seemed that she must give up, a change came, an almost imperceptible change, without a movement or any other indication that she could identify, yet she knew they were winning. Against the excitement of this, she held herself to the steady pressures and finally a tiny bubble rose to linger at the man's gray lips. Tears stung the young woman's eyes but she shook them away, and when there was breathing, shallow and weak, but breathing, she turned the man up and groped for her bag. Somebody pushed a bottle into her hand. Without glancing around she looked at the Old Crow label, licked a test drop spilled on the back of her hand, and nodded. Carefully she gave the man a little swallow and then another, and finally she got him out of his wet clothing and rolled into the warmed buffalo robe beside the fire.

"I been sick couple weeks, I guess, bad sick," the man murmured to the doctor's questions. "I been havin' a gnawin' a long time, inside the belly there, like it had a hole—"

That, and his name, Tom Reeder, was all Morissa discovered

before his voice trailed off into exhaustion and sleep. So she had him carried away toward a tent and when she had time to thank the man who offered the shelter, she realized that it was Robin, still waiting in his long patience. He had let her sob out her relief against his bearded cheek while he stroked her shoulder and held back his rush of questions for a more appropriate time.

But in a moment Morissa remembered her patient and gathered up her awkward, bedraggled skirts to run after him, barely seeing a man who had stopped his horse in her path. The fine bay he was riding was wet to the mane, the rider soaked too from a Platte crossing—a tall, sunburnt man of the region there to stop her, stern, his gray eyes very angry.

"Don't ever do that again, ma'am," he warned. "That Cimarron horse isn't broke for ladies. A wonder you wasn't killed—"

At first Morissa was angry, too, but her manners came back swiftly enough. "Did I take your horse? I'm sorry, but I don't think I've hurt him, Mr.—"

"Polk. Tris Polk."

"Thank you, Mr. Polk. You have a good right to be proud of that splendid animal, so ready for an emergency."

But the man did not rein aside. Instead he stood his stirrups, his palms crossed easily on the saddle horn. "Well, let me tell you something, ma'am," he said. "In these parts taking the poorest crowbait without the owner's permission's a hanging matter—"

"Oh, really?" Morissa inquired, her anger back. "I am sure in these parts, as in all others, letting a man die without attempting succor would be a matter of murder to an enlightened conscience, Mr. Polk."

With this she went around him and his horse, leaving the man free to look after this soft-voiced girl who could muster such fire to go with her courage, and poise too—muddy and bedraggled as she was, with a hat as silly as any that the women of the road-ranches or the Black Hills dance halls might be wearing. But now it clung very unfashionably and slaunchwise to the heavy hair that drooped over the shoulders of the once-handsome green suit.

"I'll try to make arrangements for a plankway to get you back by the bridge—" the man called after the girl, his horse slipping daintily through the crowd behind her.

"Thank you, sir," Morissa Kirk replied, only half turning, hiding the wry smile. "My father is Robin Thomas, boss grader here. He'll see that I am cared for."

Then she hurried on to her patient, the handsome smoky eyes that followed her almost forgotten.

When the full moon rose to silver the boiling flood waters, the pile driver was still working, but in the yellower glow of the lanterns strung up along the tower, as though to guide the hammer that fell with such urgency. Beyond, up toward the ridges against the north, a bonfire lit the sandpits where teams worked at plow and buck scrapers to drag earth down to the new abutment. Understandably Clarke, the builder, wanted to open this toll bridge as soon as possible, before the high water eased off and the more daring and impatient tried to ford the stream. Many of the hungrier gold seekers had planned to risk a crossing in the morning but they hesitated now that they had seen a man come so close to drowning. Even old Joe Lenway, with all his experience, had lost one of Reeder's horses for him—just laid down and died after he got the wagon out half a mile down the river. True, a white woman with feathers on her hat had made it across, but she was on Tris Polk's best saddler, one that had swum the flood waters of every stream from the Red River of Texas past the Yellowstone up north. Besides, this young woman for all her city fripperies seemed to have the daring of an Indian squaw running from the military.

By night Morissa Kirk was settled in Robin's one-room soddy, set beside his wagon corral south of the river. Undismayed by the bare earthen walls inside, almost as though she didn't see them, or the dirt floor and the nail-keg chairs, she had changed her drying suit and brought out her diploma and arranged her medical books and essentials in a big box, pegged up on the sod wall for shelving and cupboard. She hung her clothing and the white hospital jacket behind a blanket above the cot; she unpacked a few of her pretty things from the trunk, too, and set her silver toilet articles and the crystal scent bottles on the bare window sill. She even shook out her China silk and the reception gown of rose and gold brocade, making a steady fussing of it all, giving herself no free moment to think of what lay under the thin ice of her energy all the last week, covered over, shut away.

The rising moon had brought a chill creeping up from the river, carrying the raw smell of cold flood waters with it. Far down the valley and up past the haze-veiled Chimney Rock, and on west, scattered lights were blinking long past the supper cooking— mostly the fires of those who had little interest or money for the inviting doorways near the bridge. Coyotes howled off in the breaks, answered by the dogs in the camp and perhaps a wolf or two, drawn toward this gathering of men and yet afraid; drawn also by the bawling of the beef herds being held along the river, and the occasional low of the quieter work bulls.

In the camp near the bridge there was the thin sawing of the breed fiddlers, the thunder of cowboys galloping in through the moonlight, with their "Yahoos!" and pistol shots. Their horses scattered the cursing crowd from their path, and the dust they raised shimmered in the lantern light from swinging doors and lifted tent flaps.

Although his graders must work through to morning, Robin Thomas felt that no matter how worn by the trip and the day, Morissa should not be left all alone tonight. He asked no questions of her, no explanation, just washed the dust from his long graying hair and beard, buckled on his gun, and took down the lantern. Then, with Morissa neat in a scotch-plaid walking suit only moderately bustled, and a sailor tilted over her bangs, he took her to see the camp, from Clarke's supply and whisky store at one end to the roadranch of Ettier, the Canadian Frenchman, at the other. They followed the light thrown by the lantern around to Etty's place first—a string of weathered sod and log shacks surrounded by a thick sod wall with strategic gun slits for defense. "Old Etty's been around here, on and off, more than twenty years. Stood off outlaw gangs and a few Sioux bucks full of whisky too, although he's married to a Sioux breed—nice woman," Robin said.

Inside the smoke hung thick around the kerosene wall lamps, the low rooms packed, particularly around the bar and the fiddlers. In one Morissa stared at stacks of gold coin glinting in the smoky light, so open and handy for any holdup's taking.

"Yes, it does look easy," Robin admitted, "but I saw a couple in here one night, trying to take it away from Etty. Instead they got that sawed-off shotgun he keeps under the bar, sticking up over it and aimed at the belly. I helped bury one of the robbers."

Between Etty's place and Clarke's were shacks, tents, and open-front shelters with counters rough-sawed from pine in the Wild Cat Mountains. These counters were all that separated the crowd from the whisky and the card sharps or perhaps a beckoning woman, her crib no more than a cot or bunk on stakes sunk into the ground behind a piece of hanging canvas. There were even covered wagons offering the evening's entertainment and necessities, the price a little less because it was three steps up, with the need to duck the head under the wagon bows.

All were busy tonight, particularly where there was gambling, with so many doubly hopeful now that a belt of gold nuggets had been found on Tom Reeder after he was pulled out of the water today, and more yellow dust in the little plank box in his wagon, fortunately chained tight to the wagon bed. Morissa saw the leather pouches of gold it contained—enough to keep the man for life, it seemed. How he got it all, or where, she did not ask, but because the box was carried into the stage station by two men with armed guards riding alongside, all the camp knew what it must contain, and that it was a great deal.

The news of the gold and the nearness of it, the actual sight of such a treasure accumulated somehow by this one puny little man was like the swift warming fire of a placer strike in their midst. Within an hour some had traded their wagons and outfits for saddle horses, tame enough, if possible, to carry a pick and shovel and gold pan. Only half of those who started across the river made it, and one who was washed up on the north bank left his horse to drown in the quicksand. The rest were turned back by the refusal of their horses or their own courage. Some hurried west along the old Overland trail to the rock ford up the river, but that route was a couple days longer, and led up through wild and rugged country full of Indians and outlaws. Besides, tomorrow the native planking of Clarke's bridge would surely thunder to the thousands of impatient hoofs, and so for this one night many spent as though the hot drag of fortune already weighted down their jeans. Some even dropped coins into the hat of the sky pilot outside a whisky saloon, a tall, gaunt, bearded man with the anger of God on his tongue and the fire of another Eldorado burning in his eyes.

The girl held the hem of her skirts out of the dust as Robin Thomas guided her skillfully around the thickest press, past the lurching drunks, the loud-mouthed trouble-seekers whose guns should be taken away before they found it, and the urgently woman-hungry. Several times he stopped to introduce Morissa: "My daughter, Doctor Kirk—" saying it proudly to the handsome, bearded and warm-eyed Henry Clarke of the bridge, and to some Army officers.

"Yes, we're heading for Red Cloud Agency up the trail there," the young lieutenant said. "Reports are that the Sioux warriors have been slipping away north to Crazy Horse—gathering against our troops headed into the Yellowstone country."

"Plenty of them red devils're workin' up around the Black Hills," a freighter standing nearby complained. He had some mules driven off his last trip to Deadwood, and had bullet holes in his wagons to prove the attack. "There's thousands of them hungry bucks no more than a day's ride from here. Claim the bridge's on their land. Probably be burning it some cloudy night."

"Won't be an Indian loose by frost time," the officers promised as they moved jauntily away into the crowd, kept close together by the glowering faces all around them—men who remembered that the miners, even the women, were thrown out of the Black Hills by the troops last year. One word from them could shut out every man here, close up the gold trail and its bridge tight as a jailhouse door.

Robin offered no softening words to all of this. Instead he showed Morissa her first ranch foreman, a man working for Bosler, the rancher and beef contractor charged with defrauding the Indians on government beef deliveries. Bosler had one of the biggest cattle outfits of the West. Claimed a hundred fifty miles of water here, and had the guns to hold it. "But that's the north bank, across the river—"

Morissa glanced over that way in the pale moonlight, but there was no time to consider these things tonight. She met several owners of the big freight outfits and an advance man for an English troupe of singers. They planned to put on some Gilbert and Sullivan for the miners at Deadwood Gulch, if a hall could be found, or some natural outdoor amphitheater. "Anywhere out under God's gentle sky," he said fervently, and received a roar of boisterous laughter, particularly from men who had faced blizzard and dust storm and hail.

Tris Polk came up, too, courteous this time, impersonally complimenting Morissa's riding and her skill with the sick. "—I hear the man is sleeping for the first time in days," he said.

"But it may not mean much. We can only hope," Morissa replied, matching the man's impersonality before the hundreds of people who stopped to watch this second encounter, to listen.

There were only a few women out tonight, mostly around the dances, particularly Etty's big one where the breed fiddlers sawed and stomped, and with Huff Johnson, who had a handsome Junoesque blonde standing beside him at the faro table. She couldn't be lured away even by Tris Polk, it seemed. "But Huff'll have trouble keeping Gilda Ross if Polk really wants her—" Robin predicted.

He pointed out a dozen men who were known as outlaws: holdup men, roadagents, murderers. Fly Speck Billy was still there, but when the young man lifted his hat gravely to Morissa, so recently his fellow traveler, Robin looked at the girl in surprised concern.

She managed to laugh a little. "Oh, water finds it own level very quickly. Or, as you recall Mother saying, 'Short grace for hungry folk.'"

"Or rubbin' your nose in a hog trough don't even make friends of the hogs," Robin answered sourly. Fly Speck was just out of the Ogallala jail because everybody was afraid to testify against a cold-blooded killer. And tonight many others of his kind were here, with the nearest sheriff clear down at Sidney and probably as anxious to stay alive as the next man. Robin had seen too many like Fly Speck since the days he helped grade the Union Pacific to Utah. He wondered what fat cow was drawing these buzzards here tonight. Clarke and the others hired good protection for their property. Sure, such protection was by gunmen too, professional killers picked for their wide reputation, swift as striking rattlers, ready to shoot for the highest bidder. If that happened to be the law, it was lucky.

"—I got my fill of their breed years ago, but Jackie's excited as a kid by them," Robin said with deep concern. "I try to keep him up with my horse herd, helping the guard against Indians and horse thieves. Hard on him but keeps him away from the show-offs around the bridge here."

"Oh, Jackie's only sixteen," Morissa started to comfort. "He'll be all right—he's of your good stock—" but she caught herself, always having to stop her stupid tongue.

Robin seemed not to notice the girl's confusion. "Most of the outlaws here probably seemed good boys at sixteen to their mothers or older sisters," he said, "although I hear Fly Speck and many of the others were already hitting it for the frontier only a jump ahead of the sheriff by then."

Morissa stirred from her sudden weariness to look around again. Over half of those moving through the patches of light and shadow wore heavy cartridge belts, as Robin himself did. Some of the others, the gamblers at least, were certainly armed, too, if less conspicuously. It was a silencing thought, and after a while Robin decided that the girl was finally wearied to sleeping, so he took her back through the pool of light his lantern cast for their feet.

They stopped at the grading corral to look in on Tom Reeder in one of the bowed wagons, sleeping heavily although his small dose of morphia should have done no more than quiet him. As Morissa replenished the fire in the little wagon heater and smoothed the buffalo robe over the man, she wondered how much of this was disease and how much exhaustion and anxiety from guarding his treasure through the long dangers of Deadwood Gulch and the robber-infested trail. But it might be pneumonia developing after the snow water, or only a drug-given respite from a bad conscience.

Robin still seemed uneasy. "Reeder's gold could be what tolled in so many outlaws who're usually more comfortable operating over in Wyoming," he said. "Still, there can't be that much dust in that ditty box of his. If it got out that a haul was coming down, why wasn't that little string of wagons he traveled with held up? It must be something else. I better get back to my outfit—"

But in the little soddy beside the corral gate the father delayed his going and finally settled down on a nail keg for his evening pipe. Morissa sat hunched forward on the cot, worn and pale now for all her sunburn, her hat still on, staring straight before her. For a moment Robin thought of a grouse or a dove, wounded and huddled close as possible to the ground, looking straight ahead, as a man does with blood in his mouth, his staring eyes slowly whitening. But the girl who had pulled herself up from her days as a woods colt on a poor-farm was no dove or even a grouse, no matter what the wounding, nor how surely she had fled to crouch here on the cot beside a wilderness river, here where none except her stepfather knew her, or few were sufficiently whole to see her pain.

"Morissa," Robin said softly, "Morissa, do you want to tell me why you came? Last I knew the wedding was next week—"

A long time the girl made no reply, so still the old cot did not creak. "No—I guess there's nothing to tell," she said at last.

"It wasn't just a lover's quarrel?"

Morissa shook her head, her eyes bleak in the lantern light. "He asked for his ring back," she said. "Couldn't take me into the family, not after what his sister found out—" The girl stopped, her full soft lips quivering for the first time.

"Found out?—about your mother? Oh, I could kill the fool!" Robin exploded, his voice loud as though shouting against a northwest blizzard wind. "No," he added, more moderately, "that wouldn't help. But you know you are welcome here with me, Morissa, to all these poor accommodations. Now get a little sleep. We'll need you tomorrow. There will be man and animal hurt in the tearing hurry tomorrow."

He started out, but turned at the door and slowly unbuckled

his gun. "I better leave this with you. There's no law here for any-body, you know, except what you make."

Reluctantly the girl reached out and took the heavy cartridge belt, holding it away from her as she laid it on the end of the cot, not touching the grip of the revolver that fit so snugly into its worn leather nest.

TEXAS TRAIL

Cowboy Columbus

by WILL C. BROWN

Young Johnny Davis stood on the south bluff of the Red River, staring across at nothing in the Territory dusk, and wondering how Christopher Columbus might have felt if he had shown up at the dock a day late and missed the ship that was going off to discover America.

Cowboy Columbus, he decided, would have been a sad *hombre* and a clabber-headed tamale. Since that fitted his own appraisal of Johnny Davis, in that black moment, he ambled back to the lamp light of the one lonesome shack store on the river. Columbus, he thought, would have retreated to the bar nearest the wharf to fortify his fizzled-out feeling with a slug of whatever passed for firewater in 1492.

In exchange for Johnny's last fifty-cent piece the taciturn old hermit poured out a cracked tumbler of murky corn.

"Hold on to your hat," the old man said, pocketing the half dollar.

"I just missed discovering America," Johnny said moodily, gaz-

155

ing down into the pain-killer. "Too bad. It would have made a nice country."

"I ain't hearing good," the old man said, cupping his ear. "Come again?"

Johnny shook his head and the owner padded back to where he was working at dozing in a rocker.

Since Johnny earlier that evening had drained the proprietor of all the bad news he could take in one night, he sipped on the corn and philosophized to himself on the futility of trying to be a one-man cattle outfit. Working for wages, he concluded, had its desirable points, after all. He had just been too thick-headed to know when he was well off. The information he'd been slapped in the face with like a handful of Red River mud had been bad. It consisted of the news that the big Double Seven trail herd, outbound across the Territory to the Kansas market, had forded the Red the day before and was now well on its way northward. The next jolt for Johnny was the assurance that there was not a herd hand to be hired anywhere on that stretch of Texas shoreline. In fact, he was told, the store man and Johnny himself were the only two human beings anywhere near this jumping-off place.

The front-door hinges complained and Johnny turned.

In a place where there were not supposed to be any other human beings, something very odd was on the loose and such coincidental appendages as two legs apiece called for a quick steadying drag on the corn. Johnny shuddered with the swallow and looked again.

One of them was sleezy-swarthy as a blacksnake on a white rock, and at his gliding heels came a chesty nester with knob nose and muddy boots. They batted eyes at the light and looked about. Nervously, Johnny thought.

Johnny glanced accusingly at the proprietor. The old man shrugged and bent out his palms, as if to say to Johnny that this was all news to him. To the newcomers he said:

"I got corn and that's all. What'll it be, gents?"

They deliberated a heavy half minute. Then the blacksnake hissed, "Corn!"

"Hold on to your hats," the old man said, pouring.

Even in the shadowy light of the one coal oil lamp, Johnny knew that he looked like something washed up with the drift in the last Red River flood. He supposed he had "trail tramp" written all over him. Which would account for the unconcealed suspicion trained on him by the newcomers from out of the night. Not that they looked any better.

The sleezy thin man, with the jumpy snake eyes and black horse-tail sideburns, was something you'd grab a stick for if you saw it crawling on the floor, while his over-larded sidekick with the buttonless vest and frayed rope belt was the standard no-good range type that gave mankind in general a bad name. The only dependable-looking items about them were the Colt sixguns they packed on their flanks.

Speak up and meet your equals, Johnny told himself sourly. *Maybe it'll turn out we're first cousins.*

But the dark one with sharp-edged face and coachwhip eyes made the opening move of sociability. He went over to the one table across the earthen floor, put his glass down, straddled a chair by swinging a leg over the back of it, and gave Johnny a "come-mere" jerk of his head.

Johnny and the fat one moved across together. The three sat a moment in silence, Johnny looking at his drink, wondering how high it would blow the store if he dashed it to the floor, and the two men looking at Johnny. Then they each raised glasses, twisted up faces for the shock to come, tasted, coughed, and leaned back.

The dark one said in oily tones: "My name's Querro."

Knob Nose mopped his mouth with the back of his hand and said, "I'm Jock Baxter."

Johnny said, "I'm Christopher Columbus."

"Did what?" Jock Baxter frowned.

"My friends call me Johnny. Ain't they a crowd here tonight?"

But Querro's next words brought Johnny sharply alert inside.

"We're lookin' for a rider who can help us ford about two hundred head of cattle across the river tonight. You look like a man who might want to make a few dollars. You want a job?"

Inwardly, Johnny stiffened. Outwardly, he grimaced and toyed with the glass.

"Two hundred head? Your herd? You driving to market?"

Jock Baxter stared unpleasantly at Johnny. "Don't ask so damn many questions, friend. Querro ast you, you want a job? Ain't that all you ast him, Querro?"

"Not for cowhand pay!" Johnny retorted. "If you got a slick deal on, let's hear it. You don't ford a herd at night unless there's a damn good reason for risking drowning in the dark."

Querro shot a glance across to Jock that was supposed to convey something. Jock nodded grudgingly.

"He looks all right to me, Jock," Querro murmured. "We got to have help on this."

"First, ast him who he is and what he's doin' here," Jock grunted.

"All right, I'll tell you," Johnny said. "I was supposed to meet the Double Seven herd at the river for a trail drive to Kansas. But I missed 'em. That leaves me high, dry, and willing to listen to propositions." Some inner caution clamped a lid on the rest of it. He would tell them no more than that, he quickly decided. Because, sure as he was facing two of the crawlin'est trail scum in Texas, he was in a crowded corner from here on.

Then he said, "As Jock here says, I ast you the same questions."

"We were just ridin' through," Querro said. Apparently he had decided to lay it on the table with Johnny. It was obvious to Johnny that they had sized up his dirty riding garb to take him for a down-and-outer who would go for anything with money attached. Querro looked about the room and lowered his voice.

"There's a herd of about two hundred longhorns bedded down, a mile south in a grassy draw. Nobody around. We watched for an hour. You noticed any trail riders around here tonight?"

"Not a human." Johnny shook his head.

He had to strain to keep a croaking break out of his voice. What Querro was saying put prickly chills playing on the back of his skull.

"What we figure," Querro said, holding hard to Johnny with the sharp black eyes, "is that the crew went off somewhere to bring up a bigger herd tomorrow. So there they are."

"Nobody around," Jock repeated. "Two hundred head for anybody that can get 'em across the river."

Johnny acted like he was thinking hard.

"It wouldn't be like stealing, would it? It would be like finding mavericks." He tipped a slow wink to Querro.

Jock chortled and slapped Johnny hard on the shoulder.

"This boy is all right!"

"We got the night before us," Querro prompted.

"What about after the fording? What then?"

"We can push 'em all the way to market. Or better, catch up with a big herd somewhere and sell 'em cheap. Then we strike out, back to Texas."

Johnny pulled at his chin and frowned. "They won't ford at night. A cow's not going to swim off in the dark when she can't see."

"Oh-oh!" Jock looked like he'd been punctured with a pig-sticker.

But Johnny said suddenly: "Hell, there'll be a full moon after a while. They'll swim it in good moonlight if we chouse 'em into it fast!"

Jock hit the table with his fist, his spirits restored.

Querro said, "We don't know much about cattle. That's why we need help."

Johnny looked them over. He had to keep his eyes blank, he kept telling himself. Keep from showing what was boiling inside him. But there was something else, too. It was almost too much to hope for. But here it was, put right before him, from out of nowhere. Another boat for Chris Columbus.

"Is it a three-way deal?" He looked straight at Querro.

The swarthy one nodded quickly.

Johnny said, "You agree to a three-way deal, Jocko?"

Jocko apppeared on the verge of balking but he must have caught a warning glance from Querro. He rumbled, "Sure, we'll cut you in. Three-way deal."

Then you can pay me with a forty-five slug and ride off with all the loot, Johnny thought.

He stood up.

"Lead the way. Let's find the damn herd and get 'em moving. It's not going to be easy, a night fording. You'll have to work like all get-out, but it can be done."

As if he had just thought of it, he stopped and confronted Querro. "What if the owner's crew shows up—do we run like hell, or what?"

"We run if there's a lot of them," Querro said tightly. "If only two or three riders come—." He slapped his gun holster.

"I get you." Johnny slapped his holster, too, and Jock slapped Johnny approvingly on the shoulder. "I ast you, Querro, old Jock can pick 'em, can't he?"

Three men and three horses matched guts and stubbornness against two hundred longhorns and a river. It was a mean contest, but men and horses won.

When the last of the bawling, mud-plastered critters scrambled up the north slope in the white moonlight, Johnny rode with numb disbelief. The impossible had been accomplished. He couldn't keep a tight grin off his face. But he shouted directions to Querro and Jock, telling them to keep prodding the cattle upland. And once on the flat, brushy tableland of the Territory, there was no let-up in the drive.

"The more distance we can put between us and the river to-night, the healthier we'll be," Johnny told them.

"You're right about that," Querro agreed.

He and Jock were jubilant over getting away with it. Johnny said the thing to do was to keep the cattle moving north just as long as they could keep on their legs. The three riders rotated positions on flanks and drag through the rest of the night, and all through the following day. When the herd finally slowed and became so unruly that further progress was impossible, the men unsaddled mounts and slept on saddle blankets like the dead. It was hard to get the cattle moving again in early evening, but they were prodded into motion once more. The forced drive kept slogging northward through the night.

At mid-morning next day, Johnny sighted from a low mound the sign he had been looking for. He galloped down and called to Querro and Jock.

When they rode over to him, he said: "Big dust ahead—it's a trail herd. Double Seven forded a couple of days ago and we're catching up with 'em. I've heard of their foreman—he's one that'll go for making some easy money. What about it—do we drive this stuff in and make a sale?"

"How much can we get?" Querro wanted to know.

"They'll likely pay us ten dollars a round for this stuff—they can get twenty in Kansas."

Querro figured it out for Jock. "That'll be two thousand dollars. Split three ways."

"Not bad for two nights' work," Johnny said.

"Then we *vamoose* from here!" Jock beamed agreement.

In mid-afternoon they caught up with the drag riders of the big Double Seven herd. Johnny put spurs to his horse and tore in ahead of the cattle, and was met by a squint-eyed man whose lean face stretched into a slow grin of recognition.

"Where'n hell have you been, Johnny?" demanded Alec Stevens, the Double Seven foreman. "You didn't show up at the river—we wondered what'd happened to you, whether you'd backed out."

Querro and Jock were riding toward the group. Johnny said quickly, "No time for explaining now, Alec. Watch these two jaspers, and you boys kinda keep your hardware handy."

Querro pulled up, showing white teeth all around at the staring half-circle of Double Seven riders.

"You make the trade, eh, Johnny?"

"Yeah," Johnny said. "Lend me eight dollars, will you, Alec?"

The foreman pulled out silver dollars. Johnny rode up and took the money.

"All right, Querro. Here's four dollars for you. Four for Jock. Trail hand's wages for two days. Goodby, boys."

Querro's mouth opened like a river moccasin with its tail caught in a log jam. Jock looked blank. Johnny dropped a hand down to the butt of his gun.

Jock said whiningly, "Four dollars! I don't—!"

"We're being double-crossed!" Querro gritted.

"Ain't that too damn bad," Johnny said.

"What's all this, Johnny?" demanded Alec Stevens.

"This is a stolen herd," Johnny snapped. "These two gents stole it and got me to help 'em ford the river."

"But that stuff's got your Jay Bar brand on it!" Alec said.

"Yeah," Johnny nodded, keeping an eye on Querro and Jock. "But these two partners of mine don't know much about cattle. Me and one Mexican rider got 'em to the river, Alec, to throw in with your herd for the market drive, just like we agreed. Only we got delayed and showed up two days late—after you'd already forded and gone. My Mexican high-tailed it for home and there I was with two hundred longhorns and no way to get 'em forded, much less get caught up with you. Right foolish feeling, it was. Thought I was sunk—my whole ranching venture depended on marketing this stuff." He wiped the sweat off his nose and jerked a nod to Querro and Jock.

"This pair came along like a silver lining. A little rusty and dirty—but silver lining just the same. They'd spotted the cattle where I'd left them. Made me a deal, so we stole the herd and rushed 'em across in the moonlight. You should have seen us, Alec. Damnedest cow thievin' in the history of Texas, I guess."

He grinned then, feeling tired, and just a little sorry for Querro and Jock. Those two, after one last look at the hard-jawed circle of gun-weighted Double Seven men, were already turning their horses south, headed back over the trail, back to the river, probably for eight dollars' worth of corn-drinking to drown their sorrow. They turned back once, to look viciously at Johnny. He raised an arm to wave, and yelled something the other riders did not understand. It sounded like "Much obliged for the boat—I'll tell America I saw you boys!"

To Alec, he merely said, "Let's get on to Kansas!"

CHISHOLM TRAIL

Dry-Trail Showdown

by D. S. HALACY, JR.

Ross Oldham stood in his stirrups, narrowing his eyes against the burning sky to make out the town of Wayneville slanting down the prairie on the near bank of the wide river. The sight of it was a lift, easing some of the bone-weariness that pulled him back down into his saddle.

"There she is," he called to Billy Gannett. "The little metropolis." He grinned and turned his gaze back to the fair-sized cluster of buildings that made the town. Glinting eastward, the tracks of the railroad vanished where prairie met the horizon.

"There's water, you mean," Gannett answered with a dry snort. "And none too soon, either. Them cattle are burnin' up." Dust and tiredness made him look older than his forty years.

Looking back over his shoulder, Oldham watched the moving brown mass that was his herd. Herd, hell. It was everything he had. They were dry, all right. His own mouth felt like cotton. Spring was in the air, but with no rain there wasn't yet a trace of green in the ground. Gannett was right. He had hated to push the longhorns like he had, but it was all they could do.

There had been plenty of water back at Salt Fork. Trapped in the flash flood, nearly a hundred head of bawling cattle had drowned. And along with them went six saddle horses and the cook-wagon. Short of horses, hungry, the seven of them had prodded the remaining nine hundred animals over dry rolling country, feeling the warm wind at their backs and knowing there was no water until they made Wayneville.

Gannett, his right hand man, was all right, along with the other two punchers he'd taken with him from Kansas on his buying spree into Texas. But the three he'd picked up there were ready to take their time and light out. Only Oldham didn't have their time. All he had now was the cattle. And these he still had to push all the way to Nebraska for sale to a feeder.

"What are those cows going to do when they sniff water?" Gannett wondered, mopping at his face with a bandanna.

"It'll be no picnic," Oldham said.

The cattle were mean and edgy and you couldn't blame them. Oldham felt that way himself; dirty, unshaved and tired to death of the drive. But up ahead was rest for them all. They'd hold the cattle by water for two days, and then pick up again, ready for the next leg of the long journey. He'd see Eleanor too, and the thought of the brown-haired girl made him acutely aware of his shabby appearance. He'd have to stop off and see Perry the barber, first.

Oldham had turned twenty-five while they held the longhorns in the Territory, well north of the River. His hair was long and red, and through the powder of trail-dust, sideburns and beard glinted like flecks of copper in the sun. It was a strong face, seldom relaxed in a smile, mainly because there was little to smile at. Since he was ten, Oldham had punched cattle for wages and keep. Except for the brief stint as sheriff. The year that had taught him not to buck money and power. He thought briefly of Slater Collins, wondering what the broad-shouldered Easterner was up to by now. Then he shrugged. It was no concern of his, the issue was closed and he'd keep it so.

This time he wouldn't make the mistake he'd pulled with his first bunch of Texas cattle. The hundred head his sheriff's pay had bought had frozen stiff as cord wood in the sudden blizzard and he'd come out of it with less money than he'd started the year. This time he was playing it smart. The thousand—he caught himself, what was left of the thousand—would go to a feeder in Nebraska. He'd been practically guaranteed twenty a head. That was eighteen thousand. He'd bought sharp and eight would get him square with Horn and Wagner in town, and the ten would buy acreage and the start of a herd of imported cattle, the black Aberdeen-Angus that promised to displace the fading longhorn. There was more to life than pounding leather after cattle. There were things like a home, a wife. The image of Eleanor Finch was bright in his mind again.

The two of them rode down from the slight crest of hill, losing sight of the herd back of them in the shallow basin. Up ahead the trail angled to the right, skirting a mound of brush. The lowering sun splashed from windows in the town ahead, and Oldham began to make out individual houses. He saw the white, steep-roofed one Judge Finch and his daughter lived in. Maybe he'd have dinner with them tonight, and his gnawing stomach welcomed the prospect. Eleanor could cook the way a woman should, and after the months of cow camp grub, the thought was a treat.

"They plowin' fire guards way out here?" Gannett demanded suddenly. His voice startled Oldham; made him look away from the town to where his foreman pointed. Sure enough, there was a wide series of furrows in the sod, crossing the well-worn cow trail just the other side of where it turned to the right. And now that he noticed it, he saw it continued on, bending slightly as it followed a line of scrub oak in the narrow draw ahead.

"Beats me," Oldham said. Unconsciously, he kneed his horse to a trot, eager to see what they were running into. His eyes narrowed, and there was a new stiffness in his body as sudden suspicion kindled in him. He made out the printed signs then, tacked to posts along the furrowed barrier. Posts that carried tight new strands of barbed wire a hundred feet each side of the trail. A minute later he sat his horse, reading the notice printed on the square white paper and stapled to the fresh-planted post.

"Warning," he read it out loud. "Any person or persons driving Texas cattle across this furrow will be arrested and fined five-hundred dollars for violating quarantine." Beneath it someone had scrawled in pencil, "And hung to boot."

"God damn it," Oldham said softly. The warning was signed by Judge Mattheas W. Finch, and Slater Collins, Pres., Farmers Assoc. He knew now what Collins had been doing.

Alongside him, Billy Gannett dropped stiff-legged from his horse and tore the sign from its post, ripping it to shreds. As he seized the post, Oldham shouted at him to quit it.

"You gonna let this stop us?" Gannett flung back angrily. "I'm not afraid of any bunch of nesters. I can take care of six with one hand." His bony fingers dropped to the butt of his Colt as his face tightened with hate.

He couldn't blame Gannett. The man had seen barbed wire cut up the land his cattle had grazed, watched settlers who had once begged cowmen for chips, become his violent enemies. It would have pleased Oldham too, to trample the wire, drive the herd on through. But there was no point in doing it that way.

"I'm not afraid of them, either," he told Gannett. "Least of all Collins. But we'll do it proper." He jerked his head back toward the rise. "Have them hold the herd in the basin. I'll go on into town and square things up. When they know we're not carrying

Spanish Fever there'll be no problem. I'll be back quick as I can."

He stayed until Gannett was halfway up the hill, then he rode through the soft-turned earth around the end of the fence, through the brush draw and back onto the old trail. Now that the fresh shock of it was worn off, the warning wasn't too big a surprise. There had been talk of ticks and fever for a long time, though it was common knowledge that through herds were the menace. The cows Oldham had bought wintered well north of fever country. They were safe, and he'd tell Matt that.

And then he'd tell Collins to go to hell and drive on through to the river. Off towards Bearclaw, the direction the furrow ran, there was no water. The river looped at Wayneville, doubling back to the east for miles. They had to water at Wayneville.

Despite the worry about the warning, it was a tonic to ride into town. It was a quiet time, evening, and the smoke from chimneys rose straight into a graying sky. He passed a dozen shacks on the outskirts, saw kids playing at soldier in scraggling vegetable gardens, heard a woman's strident voice pull them like a magnet to supper.

Across town, visible over the top of the courthouse, was the home of Judge Finch and Eleanor, and near it the place Slater Collins lived in. A sudden panic filled him as he thought of the smooth-voiced Collins and Eleanor. Oldham had been gone the better part of six months, a lot could have happened. The ex-gambler and liquor dealer would likely jump at the chance to marry a girl like her. And yet, in his heart, Oldham couldn't believe Eleanor would do it. Collins, for all his money and position, wasn't the kind she would be attracted to.

A man in a cheap gray suit with high-water pants crossed the road in front of Oldham, looking up curiously at the cowboy riding into the town. He was a stranger to Oldham, a new nester most likely. The town had grown, new farmhouses extending far

up and down the bank of the river. Wayneville had grown, and
so had the fences criss-crossing the country around it.

He passed the Collins Grain and Feed Store, seeing where the
name Nance had been whitewashed over. Collins must own it
outright now. He was moving along. Up ahead the courthouse
looked dim and deserted, but Oldham took the chance, swinging
down in front of the gray painted frame building and dropping
his reins over the rail. There was a trough and the black slupped
noisily. Kicking some of the dust from his feet, he went inside,
boots loud in the empty hall. His shadow long under the light
from the lamp down the hall, he rapped on the door to the Judge's
office. There was no answer, and he could see no light under the
door. He turned to retrace his steps, and a door opened as he
passed. A man with a hook nose under a green eye shade spoke
to him, eyeing him as he did.

"You'll likely find the Judge in the saloon, *cowboy*," he said.
There was an inflection to his voice that Oldham didn't like. Times
had changed a lot, and it was faster all the time. And now this
warning against Texas cattle. Nodding to the man, he went back
outside, pulled into the saddle and rode on down to a saloon on
the corner. Collins had owned it once, but that was before Oldham
had brought him in on the charge of trafficking with reservation
Indians. Now Jack Hoover owned the Lilly Belle, the biggest and
noisiest saloon in town. A two-bit gambler who had never before
had the price of a decent hat. Times changed all right.

The sight of the saloon, and the sound of the piano being
pounded inside, brought Oldham's thirst home to him. Beer would
taste good. Two beers and then a shot of Chapin & Gore's Best.
That made him feel guilty about Billy Gannett back in the basin
the other side of the barbed wire and the furrow. They had
talked about that first drink in the Lilly Belle for the past week.

He could kill two birds with one stone, though. The chances
were good that Matt Finch would be inside, belly pressed to the

bar, a spatted foot tapping time on the rail. The Judge was a hearty man. A jovial soul who loved mankind and his liquor; the latter sometimes too well.

Oldham pushed open the swinging doors, shoving his hat back on his head and smiling his anticipation. He was home, he thought, it was time to celebrate. Back of the bar Big Jim yelled a greeting.

"Ross Oldham! Welcome back, stranger. Thought you'd crossed the Rio Grande and joined the rebels!" A dozen men at the bar turned, some calling greetings.

"No chance," Oldham told the bartender. "Couldn't stay away from the rotgut you put out here." He nodded to Jack Hoover, dealing faro at the table in the back corner. Then he saw the Judge, coming toward him.

"Hello, Matt," Oldham said, smiling. The Judge's hand was soft and fat, the way you'd expect it to be from seeing the man's paunch. But there was a sharp crispness to his attire, from the stove pipe hat on down to the cut-away, the starched shirt. Eleanor saw to that.

"Good to see you, son," Finch said. His florid face made him look all his years, and he was pushing sixty. His eyes were blue, and usually they sparkled with wit and friendliness, but now they seemed troubled. Oldham wondered if the old man was in his cups this early, remembering stories Matt had told him about the wife, also named Eleanor, who had died, and still had the power to make the Judge weep like a child and rail against himself.

"I'll buy you a drink first, Matt," Oldham said, "then I want to ask you a question." He took the Judge's arm, and pushed through the knot of men he knew, seeing them make a place for him at the bar.

"I think I know the question, Ross," the Judge said. "So I'll have that drink."

The bartender produced a bottle and glasses, then the beer for Oldham. The Judge waited for him to down the beer, then lifted his glass of amber liquor, his face serious in the lamplight. Behind them the piano kept up its melodic jangle, and an off-key tenor tried to sing the words.

"Welcome home," the Judge said.

"That's what I want to talk about," Oldham said, and drained the fiery liquid. As he set the glass down, he asked the question.

"What's the whole story on the warning I ran into back at the bend, Matt?"

The Judge set his glass on the polished bartop. Wetting his lips, he answered.

"It's all there on the notice, son," he said. "No more Texas cattle."

"You mean *through* cattle, Matt," Oldham said evenly. His hands pressed flat on the bar. "This herd wintered in safe country. Why do you think I was gone so long?"

"I'm sorry as can be, Ross," the Judge said. "The Association decided against any Texas cattle. We've got all Aberdeen—"

"We?" Oldham asked. "You in the breeding-business now, Judge?"

"I was generalizing," the Judge said. He looked more troubled now, but his voice hadn't risen the way Oldham had let his own. "You know what the Fever can do to these cattle." His tone was almost apologetic now, but Oldham wouldn't be mollified.

"Hell, yes, I know," he retorted. "I aim to raise those black goats myself when I get back from trailherding this bunch to Nebraska. I know about the ticks, give me a little credit, Judge."

The talk around the bar had quieted down, and the piano chorded off into a bare silence, broken only by some talk at the card tables further back. Not wanting the attention he seemed to be getting, Oldham was still unwilling to back down. He was worried plenty, now, that it wasn't as simple as he had told Gannett it would be.

"I got nine-hundred head of two-year-olds, dry as fodder," he said. "I observed your warning down at the Bend, figuring it was aimed at through cattle. But I'm damned if I'm heading west with the herd. They can't make it, Matt." He slammed down his palms, flat and loud on the bar. "Grange or no, I'm driving to water. We'll put back your bob wire, and stick to the trail. No harm will come to your precious Angus."

"Don't do it, Ross," the Judge said. "That warning is there for a purpose. You know I don't back down on my word."

"Yours or Collins'?" Oldham demanded. "Something smells here, Matt, and I think you know what."

"Do I hear my name taken in vain?" The voice was crisp and pleasant behind him, and Oldham turned to face Slater Collins. The man was close, he must have been standing there listening to the last part of the talk between the Judge and Oldham. Collins hadn't changed. The suit he wore was expensive; well-cut coat, tight trousers outside his short, soft boots. His hat was a slightly darker gray than the suit, and as expensive. The white shirt and black string tie were as much a part of him as the squared-off mustache and precise sideburns. The man might have just come in on the train from New York.

"Not in vain, Collins," Oldham said. "You've come up in the world from likkering Injuns. Association President, eh?"

"That's right, Oldham," Collins said easily. He gestured to the bartender for two drinks. Ruck Hutchinson stood behind him, both thumbs tucked into his gun belt, his eyes on Oldham, taking in the single six-gun the cowman wore.

"Hell, Ross," the sheriff said, "you don't need the Colt in Wayneville anymore, or didn't the Judge tell you?"

"From what Matt tells me, I *will* need it," Oldham said. "But don't sweat yourself none. I'm heading out to the basin and drive my herd to water." He said it loud, so they could all hear it. Collins calmly poured a drink for Hutchinson and himself.

"Join me, Judge?" he said genially. "You, Oldham?" His face

was still pleasant, relaxed, but his green eyes were steady on Oldham as he lifted the liquor to thin lips. "First tonight," he said, patting at his mouth with a clean handkerchief.

"Sorry about your cattle, Oldham," he said matter-of-factly. "But we voted on this ban." He shrugged. "You can trail west and then on north. The Association has the area patrolled, and we aim to enforce the law. There's a lot at stake here, thousands of dollars in—"

"I've got a lot at stake, too," Oldham said. "Eighteen-thousand dollars, and that's a lot to me if it isn't much to you. There's no fever in my herd, and I'll be gone in two days. It's that easy. There's no word of your ban in Texas, or I could have swung west way south of here."

Collins smiled disarmingly and shrugged his wide shoulders. He was a good-looking man and he knew it, loving to play to the audience. "My advice to you, Oldham, is to pray for rain."

There was a guffaw from somewhere back of him, and Oldham clenched his fists. Ruck Hutchinson turned away, shielding his face from Oldham so that he could grin. The six-pointed star shone dully on his vest. The same star Oldham had toted not too long ago.

"*You* had better pray for rain, Mr. President," Oldham said harshly. He slapped a handful of silver on the bar. "My cows aren't going to die of thirst, and you can count on that. Give me a bottle, Jim," he told the barman.

As he left the bar with the bottle of liquor, Oldham saw the glance go from Collins to the Sheriff; the quick, guarded nod of the law man. Behind him the Judge called out that he was sorry, but Oldham didn't turn. The piano started as he pushed out the batwing doors into the darkness. It was cooler now, but overhead the stars winked bright, no trace of cloud, and the air was dry of any promise of rain. Quick steps sounded on the boardwalk to his right as he went to his horse.

"Ross Oldham!" someone yelled. "That you?" the man was puff-ing as he came up, a stout middle-aged man, with white hair showing under the black hat. "I heard you was here, Ross. What'll you do about the herd?"

"I'm still thinking," Ross said. This man, Len Wagner, had a right to ask about the herd. He was in it for four-thousand dollars. "Where's Horn?"

"Out running fire guards around the ranch," Wagner said, be-tween gasps. He was too old, too beefy, to run the way he had. "We sent a man to Shawnee looking for you, Ross. This ban is going to raise hell."

"Going to?" Oldham said dryly. "It has already. The country is dry as a bone between here and Salt Fork." He stuffed the bottle of red-eye in his already full saddle bag, then ran a hand through the black's mane.

"Collins says we can pray for rain," Oldham went on. "He's got this place tied up tight."

"And legal, too," Wagner said. He was breathing normally now. "Look, Ross, don't do anything foolhardy. I got two old water wagons, and maybe we can haul enough so the cows can stick it out until you hit the river west of here."

"River?" Oldham asked. "That seep, you mean? If it don't rain, there's nothing for ninety miles and you know it. Good God, man, you have plenty to lose here, too."

"I know that," Wagner said earnestly, "and Horn is hollering like a stuck pig already. This Association is taking over, Ross. You can't fight them."

"It's Collins who did it," Oldham said bitterly. "He pushed the ban for my benefit. He knows it's only through cattle have the Fever."

"Prove he did it," Wagner said. "And while you're at it, prove the cattle wintered in safe country." He had his hat off, running a nervous hand through his white locks as Oldham swung up into the saddle.

"You doubtin' me too, Wagner?" Oldham asked. "Kinda late for that."

"Hell, Ross," the old man said, "you know it ain't that. But face facts. Sure I stand to lose, but I'll lose even more if you pull some bunck. Everybody knows my money is backing you."

"All right," Oldham said. "Bring on your water. My riders are dry, the wagons might hold enough to water them. You got any idea how much nine-hundred longhorns dry as these can put away?" He put spurs to the black, urging him out into the deserted street. Behind him Wagner called something he couldn't make out.

It was a hell of a wind-up to his big plans. The flood at the Fork should have been enough grief for any drive. And now this. The fact that it was Collins made it worse, and yet, like Wagner said, could he prove it? The man was smooth, and he had ideas. Big ideas. Oldham had heard him spout them at the first Farm meetings, when Oldham was still sheriff. Wayneville was the end of the railroad now, but it wouldn't always be that. A through line, farming, cattle shipment. In time the town could be a metropolis. And it was plain to see who would be in the driver's seat when that day came. You could do a lot with money, and Collins had done it shrewdly. The school was something the grangers could thank him for, and even part of the courthouse was built with his money. Bitterly Oldham wondered if Matt went with that.

And now what should he do? Butcher his herd for tallow and hides? Drive them dry to the west? He might make it to water with a couple hundred of the tougher cows. Anyway he did it he'd end up in debt over his head, with two long hard years down the rathole. And what of Eleanor Finch? How long would she wait for a broken-down puncher like him? It would be simple to trample down the guard fence and smash through. And if the Association and the law made a fight of it, he'd at least have Billy Gannett at his side with the oiled six-gun he was itching to use.

He cocked his head then, hearing the clop of hooves back of him. Turning, he tried to make out the rider in the darkness. If it was one of Collins' gunmen, he was pretty cocky about it. The trail angled down a draw and at the bottom, Oldham pulled his horse into a clump of scrub oak, turning him to face the trail he had just left. The horse following him came on, a steady patter of hooves in the dry trail.

Oldham had his gun out, the hammer back when the horse came in sight. There was no point in taking chances. Covering the rider, he called out sharply.

"Get the hands way high, mister!" And as he rode out to grasp the reins he heard the girl cry out in sudden surprise.

"Ross," she called, her voice musical even in her surprise. "Is it you?"

"I'll be damned," Oldham said. "Eleanor!" He slid the gun into its holster, but his hand still held to the bridle of the chestnut mare she rode side-saddle. In the darkness he could barely make out her face, but she was clear in his mind. He wanted to take her in his arms, hold the softness of her to him, but he didn't dare, and his mind was in a turmoil besides. The scent of her perfume came to him strongly, and he remembered other, pleasanter nights when they rode the river bank as far east as the Dells. She was slim as willow in the white dress and her bosom lifted slightly with her breathing. He was glad for the cover of darkness, feeling the growth of beard, the layer of dust that covered him.

At last she spoke. "Dad told me," she said, her voice pitched higher now. "Don't do it, Ross," she said. "Please; if just for me. Don't disregard the ban."

"All right," he said bitterly. "You sound just like everyone else I've talked to tonight. You in the grange too, Eleanor?"

"You know better than that," she said, an edge creeping into her voice. "I don't want to see you hurt, that's all. Believe me, Ross."

"Those longhorns are going to buy a ranch I want you to share with me, Eleanor," he said. It was the first time he had put it that bluntly. He thought they had an understanding, but now he had laid his cards in plain sight. "There's ten-thousand clear for me if I get them to Nebraska on their feet. The only way I know is through Wayneville."

"If you love me, Ross," she said, and his heart jumped, "if you love me you'll not cross the furrow. There's a lot more than ten-thousand dollars here in Wayneville now. The Association—"

"Collins' grangers?" Oldham asked coldly. The thing she had said about him loving her had lost its strength when she mentioned the nester bunch. He had thought she was with him, but it was coming out now. And when he stopped to think on it, why should she fool with him? Collins could offer a lot more. Hadn't Collins let the Judge have the white house for a song, scarcely more than the rent the old man had paid at the boarding house before the Easterner was acquitted? "If you love me—" she had said. Not "I love you." There was a big difference.

"Thanks for the advice, Eleanor," he said. "I'm glad I know how I measure up alongside Collins." He let go of her bridle, pushing her mare back out onto the trail.

"Ross," she said, but there was nothing more, and he heard her cluck to the mare in the darkness and watched her shadow merge with the night. His words had been like gall in his dry throat. Why had he done a thing like that? It had been his imagination, mostly, spurred by fear that she was interested in Collins. She could have meant that his neck was more important to her than the ten-thousand and what it could mean to the two of them. Womanlike, she couldn't know what the herd meant to him.

Still brooding it, he rode on out the trail, coming to the barrier of wire, the furrowed ground. Skirting it, he heard another horse coming from the other way, and recognized Billy Gannett as he came up.

"Damn, Ross," the trail boss said, "I figured you was either liquored up or beat up. What kept you?"

"Here," Oldham told him fishing the bottle out of the saddlebag. "Wet your whistle with this redeye. There's a water chaser coming in one of Wagner's carts. Even he says we'd better not come on into town!"

"The hell," Gannett protested. Uncorking the bottle, he took a long pull, shuddered and stoppered it again. He handed it back, but Oldham told him to keep it.

"You reckon the hides'll bring enough to pay off them Texas riders?" Gannett demanded. "These cows ain't going to reach water if we head west, and you know it." He sounded bitter, defeated. "I say let 'em get a sniff of that river, and let nature take its course. What could the law do about that?"

"I been thinking on it a long time, Billy," Oldham said. "I shot off my mouth good in the Lilly Belle, with Hutchinson and Collins both there. The Judge says we'd better pay heed." He swore as they started toward the basin. "I hate it as bad as you do. I been trying to work out some way. Maybe with those water carts of Wagner's and Horn's, we can water a few head at a time and turn 'em west." There was little conviction to what he said and Gannett snorted loudly in derision.

"You goin' to serve it to 'em in eye-droppers?" he asked. "By God, Ross, we better get us a mattock apiece and get to bustin' sod." Oldham heard him take another pull on the bottle, was about to tell him to go easy and thought better of it. What difference did it make?

The sound of the cattle made him straighten, instinctively spurring the black. The wind was still dry, hot out of the south, but something must have spooked the cattle. The faint snapping of six-guns came down the breeze.

"Hot damn!" Billy Gannett shouted happily. "Now maybe we'll get some action!"

They could hear the herd, feel the pound of thousands of hooves on the hard prairie long before they saw the stampede, and when they did come in sight dimly, Oldham knew it was too late. The longhorns were hellbent for Wayneville, the sound of their bawling overlaid with shots and cries as the punchers sought to stop them. It was a vain attempt, and Oldham shouted a warning back at Gannett, angling off to clear the oncoming mass of cattle.

It was hard in the darkness, but he made out the riders, holding to the right side of the herd, trying to veer them to the left. He and Gannett joined the men, guns blazing, shouting hoarsely. But as they neared the barbed wire blocking the trail, the cattle must have scented the river. The slow curve that had started, broke back to the right, slamming into the wire, the cows behind driving over those who fell, wire-cut and trampled. Flattening the barricade, they plunged on, thirst-crazed, toward the town.

They headed directly for the river, churning across cultivated fields, overturning an outhouse on the edge of town. And then, as fast as it started, it was done, and the cattle fought each other belly-deep into the cool, slow-running river, heads dropped, drinking in the water they had been denied for so long. He was glad for the cattle, but Oldham felt a tightness in his chest as he heard shouting in the town. There would be avenging grangers soon, and with them there would be Collins, and Hutchinson and the Judge. There would be hell to pay now, because they would remember his threat in the Lilly Belle.

"What started it?" Oldham demanded, as the riders bunched around him. There was a man shy, one of the Texans. The thought came to him that maybe they had done it out of anger. They had gotten the drift of how pressed he was, that they might have trouble collecting wages now that the ban was in effect.

"You tell us," a Texan said grimly. "Bob Blaisdell is lying back there with a slug in his neck. Six rannies rode up on us from the south while Bob and two others was night-guarding. They spooked the cows. By God, we couldn't stop them after that. When I get my hands on the skunks who did it—"

It was taking shape in Oldham's mind as he set himself for the knot of riders who came toward them. The whole town was awake now, lamps burning in the windows, and lanterns moving in the streets. He could hear children crying, and realized it was a blessing the cows had kept clear of the town as much as they had. It could have been a lot worse. There was one kind of men who could have done it. The kind whose guns hired out for any job. Just so there was money in it for them. Big money. And there was one man in Wayneville who had that kind of money to spare.

He rode at the head of his outfit, leaving the cows because they wouldn't stir from the river until they were so glutted they couldn't move. He rode, wondering who he would find at the head of the bunch riding out to meet them.

"Collins?" he yelled. "I want to talk to you."

"There he is!" somebody called eagerly. "Take him!" In seconds they were surrounded by jostling, gun-brandishing men. Riding beside Oldham, Billy Gannett got off two shots and was torn from his horse, cursing and struggling, the gun flying into the dirt. Someone grabbed Oldham roughly by the arm, and when he pulled free, something struck him on the back of the head. Reaching for the saddlehorn to catch himself, he felt himself spinning, his head aching terribly. He heard shots and then he hit the ground, flat on his face and didn't remember any more.

He came to slowly, his head and neck a raw ache, one arm stiff from his lying on it. Even before he saw the long, slanting shadows of the bars, he knew he was in the jail, lying on the straw tick pallet that stank of sweat and liquor, his free arm dragging on the dirty floor. He shut his eyes again, pressing them tight together to drive some of the pain from his head. Slowly, he rolled over, eased his numb legs to the floor. Then he sat, head resting on his palms while he tried to clear it. Had he seen Collins? He couldn't remember, he couldn't remember much of anything but the stampede, and asking the Texans what started it. Blaisdell shot, they had said. And what had happened to Billy Gannett, the nervy old gray-haired rancher after they tore him out of his saddle?

Finally he got to his feet, stumbling weakly to hold onto the bars of the cell. The jailer sat with his back to Oldham, writing something at his packing-box desk.

"Hey," Oldham called thickly, his throat dry and tight. "I want to see Judge Finch." The slight effort left his head ringing louder.

The jailer turned, dropping the pen as he saw Oldham standing there, fingers white around the iron rods. A smile creased his pallid face. He was fat, without the softness of the Judge, and his sleeves were rolled up from hairy forearms.

"If you live long enough," he said in the oily voice of a man enjoying himself, "you might do that, cowboy." The man was a stranger to Oldham, not the turnkey he had when he was sheriff. He stood up now and walked halfway across the board floor to the cell. "That was a dumb trick to pull," he said tauntingly. "After spouting so loud in the saloon. The town will take care of you for that."

"I didn't stampede the herd," Oldham said. "One of my own boys was shot by whoever did it. That's why I want to talk to Matt Finch. I've got some rights, even in here."

"Sure you have," the turnkey said, nodding his head so that the fold of flesh at his neck flopped like a turkey wattle. "You want to make a will? Some of these breeders are already looking for a rope

for you. They put that cattle ban on for a purpose. If you
hadn't made such a big noise it wouldn't be so bad." He looked
like a kid watching a dog turpentined.

Oldham's fingers tightened even more on the bars. It was the
first time he had been on the wrong side of them, and he could
remember now the time he brought Collins in, and the threat the
man had made. A touch of panic seized him, but he fought it
down.

"Where's Hutchinson," he asked, his voice steadier now. He
wanted somebody more than this grinning turnkey to talk to.

"He's out helping run your tick herd off the county," the turnkey
said cheerfully. "And the two deputies are chasing down your
riders. What's left of them, that is. That Gannett fellow cashed in
this morning. I hear he had a bad rep, so I guess he only got what
was coming to him."

Oldham shut his eyes, cursing inwardly. The man's only bad-
ness was being a cowman. He remembered poor Gannett's boast
that he could handle six with one hand. There had been a lot
more than six, and now there was nothing for him to worry about
anymore. Maybe men like the old rancher had lived past their
time. Maybe Oldham himself was a relic of something that was
already dead. He wondered about the mention of the rope. Surely
he would be protected until the thing was cleared up. But with
Hutchinson and the deputies out—

He went back to the iron-legged cot, slumping tiredly on it. Au-
tomatically, his hand went to his pocket, reaching for the Durham
tag. The tobacco was gone, and his papers too, and thinking of
Gannett, he didn't want to smoke anyhow. There was a sister Billy
had mentioned back in Missouri, but no one else. It was odd that
the old cattlemen seemed to be the lonely ones. Oldham had no
one, either. No family, that is. And his dreams of Eleanor were
fading now, hopeless.

How did Finch figure in this, he wondered? Was he really

under Collins' thumb? Or was he as honest as Oldham once thought? The girl was Matt's weakness, he wanted the best for her. And maybe in his eyes, Collins was the best. Turning it around, Oldham knew he might have to agree with the old man. What had he, Oldham ever amounted to? And now, he was in jail for violating the cattle ban, damaging property, resisting arrest, and God knew what else. Collins, he thought, would come up with plenty.

Despair was a sick thought in him. The whole drive had been a failure right from the start. Blaisdell dead, Gannett dead, and Gannett was the last real friend he had. His riders fleeing from the law, and the herd at the mercy of the grangers and Collins. It would be like them to slaughter the cattle well clear of the town, and then come back to rub that in. There was the five-hundred dollar fine, and damages they could add up against him.

"How about seeing the Judge?" he yelled at the jailer. "I'm serious, and I know enough about the law to know my rights."

"Yeah," the jailer said, "I heard you used to be the law in this town. Too bad you got on the wrong side of it, Oldham." He blew his nose loudly. "And don't get huffy with me. You'll see the Judge when he gets damn good and ready to see you, and not before." He turned back to his work, laboriously scratching words with the pen.

And then, before Oldham could say the hot words in his mind, he saw the Judge coming toward the door.

"Morning, Jeffers," the Judge told the jailer. "That's all right, don't get up. Finish your work. I just want to talk to Oldham about last night."

The jailer shot an angry glance, and Oldham couldn't help grinning at the man. "I guess he got good and ready," he said. Then his face sobered as he looked at the Judge.

"Hello, Matt," he said. "I was wondering how long I'd be held incommunicado."

"Sorry, Ross," the Judge said. His face was drawn, his eyes shot with red as though he hadn't slept. "I'm mighty sorry. I didn't think you'd do it. Want to give me your side of it?"

"You're damn right," Oldham said. "I hadn't got clear back to the herd when they stampeded. Somebody came shooting in from the south. Killed one of my boys I picked up in Texas. I couldn't stop them." He said the words quickly, bitterly, and as he did, the expression in the Judge's eyes went from resignation to shocked alertness.

"You swear you didn't start 'em?" he demanded. "That they didn't just sniff the water, Ross?" He seemed to want not to believe it, afraid to believe what Oldham was telling him.

"I swear it, Matt," Oldham said. "I don't lie. In spite of all I said in the Lilly Belle I didn't do it. I don't think I would have. Eleanor caught up with me on the trail and asked me not to and—"

"Damn it to hell," the Judge said, his eyes far away. "She was crying when she came back." He tugged at a mustache, his face hard set. Over his shoulder he looked at the jailer, still struggling with his writing.

"Ross," he said, "I like you. I admire you a lot. But you're in a tight. There's not a man in town to believe you. Gannett's dead, you know. I can't buck them all."

"Sure," Oldham said. "I know that. But how bad is it, actually? How do I—"

"They'll ride you out on a rail at the least," the Judge said. "At worst it could be a rope. You know how a mob is, Ross. And Hutchinson's got the guts of a plucked Dominecker." He rubbed tiredly at his eyes and looked up. "Gannett winged Lewiston. He's second to Collins in the Association. But the worst, really, is this Spanish Fever."

"I know I'm wasting my breath, Matt," Oldham said, "but you know that isn't the issue in this case. Time will bear me out on that."

"I won't argue it with you," the Judge said. "I signed that ban; I have to stick by it."

"Why, Matt? Tell me why," Oldham said, staring full into the old man's eyes. "Or is it what I think it is. Is Collins retaining you?"

The Judge swallowed, turning his head to keep from looking at Oldham.

"What do you get, besides the house, Matt?" he went on. It hurt him the way it must hurt the Judge, but he had to know.

"Don't ask me, Ross," the Judge said softly, his face a study in shame. "Think the worst, it's likely true. But don't make me say it. I did it for Eleanor, I wanted her to have some of the things her mother didn't ever get. I'm an old man, Ross, an old drunken fool, but there was this chance, this one way to make it up." He broke off, turning to look at the jailer, bent over his desk. Without a word, he wheeled and walked softly across the floor, easing the gun from his coat pocket as he went. In shocked surprise, Oldham watched as he lifted the gun, brought it down in a vicious slant that landed back of the turnkey's ear! When the Judge turned to come back to the cell, carrying the keys this time, his face had drained of some of the red flush. He looked physically sick.

"You crazy, Matt?" Oldham demanded, looking at the man sagged across the packing box. The Judge had the cell open, was reaching for Oldham, urging him out. It was then that Oldham first heard the noise of many hooves far down the street. The posse was coming back. Or was it a posse? The jailer had mentioned a necktie party, and even Matt had hinted at tar and feathers or worse. And now, after the Judge had buffaloed the jailer, the odds must have been on the side of the rope.

"Get out the back way, Ross," the Judge told him. His face was strained, beads of sweat beginning to run together, coursing down his jowls. He still held the gun by its barrel, and his free hand rummaged in a pocket, coming up with a folded wad of money.

"Take this and get away fast. Head for my place. Eleanor has a fast horse saddled for you—" He was shoving the gun into Oldham's hand, looking nervously at the jailer still slumped unconscious. The noise of riders was closer now, they could hear voices along with the hoof beats.

"Lay me out," the Judge said nervously. "Make it look good for my sake, Ross. I'll claim one of your boys did it and let you out. Then go and go fast. Head for Texas and nobody will bother you."

Holding the gun, Oldham knew how much the Judge was risking by doing it. It would have served the Judge's end to leave Oldham where he was, let the rope settle him for good. That way he would be rid of a suitor he didn't want Eleanor to have; and there would be no embarrassment about his tie-up with Collins. The Judge had sunk quite a ways. He was a weak man with a devil at his back, and another waiting in the handiest bottle. But he hadn't sunk all the way. He couldn't watch an innocent man murdered.

"Thanks, Matt," Oldham said tightly. "I appreciate it. But I'm not clearing out." He thumbed back the hammer on the gun and leveled it at the Judge. "I'm going to see Collins, and you're coming along, Judge. I want to see one more thing. I may leave this town, but it won't be running."

Helpless rage suffused the Judge's big face, and his hands clenched into puffy fists.

"Damn it, Ross," he pleaded, "don't be a bigger fool than I've been. Go while you still can!"

"I'm going, Matt, and you're going with me. Come on, before this toy goes off. Or do you want to stay here and try to explain that away?" He nodded to the jailer. "I don't think you have the guts to knock yourself out."

"You're signing your death warrant, Ross," the Judge said hoarsely as they went out the back door. He pointed to the neat white house that was part of the bribe he was obliged to Collins for.

"Go on. You can still make it. I'll come up with some story to clear myself. For God's sake, go on. There's enough on my conscience now."

The house was close, and as Oldham looked, he saw Eleanor lead a horse from behind the barn. It would take but a few minutes to cut through lots, reach the house and saddle up. There would be confusion at the jail for long enough to let him go, and horses and riders would be worn out, with no desire to ride after him.

But he shook his head. There was more than that to it. He was thinking of the girl, trying to put things together. And he was thinking of the herd he stood to lose and the smooth Easterner who would count it a personal triumph to have Oldham flee. And there was one other thing. An unknown quantity in the Judge beside him. In a minute he would put that to the test.

Jogging up the alley, they came to the back entrance to the Association office. Still holding the gun, he nudged the Judge inside, followed him. They were in a back room, boxes lined the walls, and there was a cot standing beneath the one window in the room. The front door was shut, but in the room beyond, they could hear the hum of voices, and over-riding the others, was the voice Oldham wanted. Collins was in the office.

Silently, Oldham turned the metal knob, let the door open a crack. Holding his breath, he waited. There was no break in the conversation up front. There was an argument going on, and he motioned the Judge to come close to the partially opened door.

"You goin' to pay off or not?" a heavy voice demanded. It was unfamiliar to Oldham and he looked at the Judge questioningly. The old man shook his head, a puzzled look on his face. He was breathing heavily from the jog away from the jail.

"I'm going to pay off," Collins said. "But I want you out of the County by night. You understand? Otherwise I'm going to pay somebody else to run you into the jail for rustling." His voice was heavy with disgust. "Damned idiot. When I want something done I ought to do it myself. Why did you have to kill that Texan?"

"I told you it was him or me, Collins," the thick voice went on, a trace of a whine in it now. "I hate Texans anyhow."

"All right, but remember what I said. Here's your money. Now get out there and mix with that bunch going to the jail. And get out of town as fast as you can. I don't want to see you in Wayneville again."

Oldham looked at the Judge. It couldn't have worked out better than this. He had thought he might have to beat it out of the man, but Collins had tipped his hand, and the Judge had heard it.

"There's your benefactor," he whispered. "Now what, Matt?"

Up front the door slammed, and Oldham eased the one by him wider. Collins was reaching for a gun belt that hung on the wall when Oldham spoke.

"Just turn around," he said. "You've got company. Judge, you stand over there where I can keep an eye on you."

Collins let go of the belt, turning slowly. He swore when he saw Oldham.

"You're being foolish, Oldham," he said drily. "Now you'll have jailbreaking added to everything else. You've really turned into a badman since you gave up the badge, haven't you?"

"Cut the sermon, we heard the pay-off you just made," Oldham said. There was a grim satisfaction in him now, that even the danger of his situation couldn't take away.

"Pay-off?" Collins said. "What pay-off? You must be mad, Oldham. If you had played it smart you'd have got off with a fine. Now you come in here with a trumped up story about a pay-off!"

"He's right, Collins," Matt Finch said wearily. "I'm through. I guess I knew all the time that you were rotten, and not just ambitious. I know it now. You weren't good for the town. What you did was get all the bad going in one direction. Your direction. I didn't think you'd do something like this. Or maybe I just wouldn't let myself think it."

"You're a fool, Matt!" Collins said. His face twisted in anger, losing its suave composure for the first time Oldham could remember since he had arrested the man so long ago. "You're cutting your own throat. When I get through with you, there'll be nothing left but your skin, and I'll nail you to the courthouse."

"There hasn't been anything for too long," the Judge said. "Maybe if I do one more honest thing before I die it will help."

"Use your head, man!" Collins was desperate now. "That mob will be in here before long, and then it'll be your hide along with Oldham. I'll throw you to the dogs. String along and maybe we can forget this. He's got no proof, and he knows it. Think, Matt."

"I have," the Judge said. "All night, every night. Even the bottle doesn't help much anymore. No, I'll testify against you, Collins. And I'll take what's coming to me when it's over."

"Dad!" the girl called from the doorway, and Oldham whirled in surprise, taking his eyes off Collins for a split second. Eleanor Finch's face was flushed and worried-looking as she looked at the three men.

"Keep out of here, Eleanor," Matt Finch yelled. Oldham swung back to cover Collins, but he was too late. The man had ducked back of the Judge, and he had a derringer in his right hand as he pulled Matt toward the rear door.

Eleanor gasped in surprise, frozen in the doorway. There were shouts of anger down the street as the mob stormed the jail to find Oldham gone. In minutes they would be here, piling on him, and there would be no chance to get Collins then. Oldham knew now the man must have ringleaders in the mob, that Hutchinson and his men would back Collins, no matter what.

"Just stand steady, Oldham," Collins yelled. "The law will be here in a minute to take you. Don't budge or I'll let Matt have it."

"No!" Eleanor screamed. Oldham stood, legs spread, the gun cold and useless in stiff fingers, as he watched Matt Finch shielding Collins.

"That's better," Collins said, his tone gloating now. The fear was gone from it and he was a man in control of the situation again. Then the Judge jerked to one side, his move throwing Collins off balance. About to shoot, Oldham held his fire as the man caught hold of the Judge once more, pulled him roughly back. In horror he watched the Judge tear free, turn and grab at the gun in Collins' hand. The derringer snapped, a thin, cracking sound, and a puff of smoke rose even as Eleanor screamed and sprang forward.

Cursing, Collins fired again, as Oldham threw himself in front of the hysterical girl. Something tugged at his left sleeve and his arm went numb. With a yell, Oldham flung himself forward, feet leaving the floor as he dove. He caught a booted foot with his good hand, and Collins crashed against the rear door, falling through into the back room. Oldham heard Eleanor hurrying to help her father, then he was too busy struggling to overpower the easterner to worry about anything else.

The man was powerful, and his fear gave him added strength. A knee slammed against Oldham's head, dazing him, but he got a fist into Collins' stomach, driving the wind out of him as they scrambled to their feet. The front door slammed open then and voices broke in on them.

"There he is!" "Get him and we'll string him up!" And Eleanor's voice, shrill and demanding to be heard over the rest.

"Collins shot my father!" she cried. "Collins is the man you want!"

"She's hysterical," Collins said. He was recovering himself

quickly, now that help was near. "Oldham shot Finch, he was about to shoot me. Take him!"

Still breathing heavily, Oldham leaned back against the doorframe. Was he going to lose out now, after being this close? Eleanor was crying, huddled over Matt Finch. Hutchinson, the puppet sheriff, walked quickly to the Judge. He had both guns drawn, and he glanced hard at Oldham. It could be either way now, it was balanced on a knife edge. The knife edge of Matt Finch. If he were dead, that was the end of it. Eleanor would be discounted, Collins would take over swiftly. If Matt was alive, it was still bad, for the flash of nerve he had shown might wane when the chips were down.

"Collins shot him," Oldham said heavily, his body still heaving from the struggle. "You'll find a derringer ball in Matt." He saw Wagner and Horn both in the crowd, and there were others who had been his friends at one time. Maybe—

"But Oldham pulled the trigger," Collins said harshly. "He's gone too far this time, Ruck. Do like I say—"

"Don't lie," Matt Finch said from the floor. His voice was thin, but it carried above the hum of conversation. "All of you hear me now, in case I don't last for a trial." He wheezed in the sudden silence his words brought, and Oldham stiffened with excitement. Matt hadn't weakened!

"Collins hired Luke Appleby to stampede Oldham's herd. And he planned to take it over for himself after he got rid of Ross."

There were shouts of excited protest, arguing back and forth. Beside Oldham, Collins stirred nervously, wetting his lips. He tried to speak, but the words didn't jell. Hutchinson, kneeling now by Matt Finch, looked uncertainly at his boss and Oldham could see the wavering decision. The sheriff wanted to go on being sheriff, and he knew that whatever else Matt had lost in the years back of him, he still had the friendship of most of the people in

Wayneville. And he knew too that most of those who followed where Collins led so slyly, would rather go their own way, and now the chance was at hand. In that moment, they turned. And Collins knew it, saw his dream slip past him, with the shadow of respectability he had cloaked himself with. With an oath he whirled, bent on leaving the room by the rear door. Oldham put out a foot, grinning as the man crashed heavily to the floor.

Before he could get up, Hutchinson's two deputies, eyes lighting with righteous fury, were on him. They knew too, which side was which in the new shaping of things. From the crowd, a man stepped to Collins' chair, then onto the big desk. It was Lewiston, the vice-president of the Association, the man next to Collins. The man who would take over now. One arm was in a sling, but he held up his good hand for silence, and got it.

"I'm shocked," he said in a resonant voice. He was a politician, Oldham knew, but without the power fever that had sparked Collins. With him holding the reins, the control of the big organization would be spread.

"Shocked as hell," Lewiston went on. "I demand a jury trial, as fast as possible. It looks as though the wrong man was jailed in this mess, and I want to know about it." Shouts of approval echoed him, and Oldham moved through the press about him to Matt Finch and Eleanor. There was a doctor there now, bag open on the floor, and Matt's eyes were opened wide.

"Thanks," Oldham said. He took the Judge's hand and something passed between them. He knew the Judge was thanking him, too. Whatever else he had lost, Matt had his self-respect back, and it shone proud in his eyes.

Eleanor took Oldham's hand in both of hers and there were tears in her eyes.

"Ross," she said softly, and then her throat moved and she didn't go on. He knew then how long the girl would have waited for him, a broken-down puncher and a jailbird to boot. Then a heavy hand pressed on his shoulder, and he looked up at Ruck Hutchinson's stern, worried face.

"Let's go back to the jail," the sheriff said.

The trial didn't take long with Colonel Blackett, from the next district, presiding. It was Matt Finch's testimony that settled Collins. Even the lawyer from St. Louis couldn't help him, and he listened to the sentence with glowering eyes and face full of hate for Oldham and Matt Finch.

Afterward, up at the white house on the hill, with Matt resting easy on the sun porch, they talked it over, Eleanor and Oldham sitting in the swing, hands holding tight and sharing a smile.

"I'm through as a Judge," Matt said with heavy finality.

"We'll need a bookkeeper," Oldham said, "I never was much of a head for figures. Of course, the house on the ranch isn't as nice as this, but—"

It had all worked out. Matt had told in court how Collins had bought him, and in doing it, he probably earned a new respect for his courage. Oldham's four riders, with two more men from Wagner and Horn, were heading on up the trail to Nebraska. There wouldn't be quite ten-thousand, but the five-hundred dollar fine had been waived, and that helped. It would be slow, and it would be different. But the whole country was different now, and he might as well begin to face it.

Billy Gannett was buried in a high corner of the ranch, so he could look out over the land he had loved and help build. That was all Oldham could do for him. That and keep his memory. He leaned closer to Eleanor and felt her squeeze his hand as his lips met hers.

DODGE CITY TRAIL

Wagon-Tongue North

by L. L. FOREMAN

THE TRAIL HERD, STRUNG OUT LIKE A GREAT COLOR-SPLASHED RIBBON, plodded slowly northward. At first glance it looked to be a pretty fair outfit, a Texas outfit far from home, bound for the Kansas railhead and the ready-money cattle buyers. The trails to the north were new and vague, thousand-mile treks across unknown country and through imponderable perils, but there were Texas cowmen who were willing to risk the gamble and able to arrive in middling good shape.

To the trail-wise eye, though, this outfit was a Jonah stumbling to blazes. The pair of men on point up front rode too close together and out of line, causing the lead steers to swerve nervously back and forth. The swing riders hung too far back, allowing the cattle column to bend and bunch up, and the men on flank were practically within speaking distance of those who were supposed to be bringing up the drag.

195

There were two wagons, which for some fool reason rolled ahead of the *remuda.* The herd was made up mostly of two-year-olds, the most skittish age for ornery longhorns, and had evidently kicked up plenty of trouble. These cows hadn't fallen into the trail habit of tramping quietly along at a steady pace. They mingled constantly, restless and wayward, sniffing the air and bawling. It was clear that they had recently popped off and pulled a wild stampede. They were hysterically ready to pop off again, for any reason or none at all.

Furthermore, the outfit had somehow strayed off the northern route and was angling over toward the river where the banks jutted seventy feet high. It was lost.

The signs were plain to Dice Gould, watching from a thinly wooded hill slope. "Damn-fool greeners!" he muttered, and shrugged, absently patting the neck of his grulla horse. The grulla quivered appreciatively, shooting its ears at the long, winding column below.

There was little sympathy in Dice Gould for that unknown, inept outfit down there. Having no weak tolerance of his own mistakes and failures, he gave none to the ignorant errors of others. Life, as he lived it, had toughened him early, made him hard. And failure had lately struck at him, wrecking the careful plans and labor of years, leaving him worse than broke. He stared down at the ill-driven, doomed outfit, with the coldly musing eyes of a man on the make.

Two men rode far ahead of the herd, apparently scouting the route, although they should have been a mile or two farther on. One of them, short and heavily built, wearing a flat-brimmed hat and black coat, and bearded, resembled a solid Mormon elder more than he did a cattleman. The other was tall and thin, coatless, big-hatted and rode with a cowman's effortless ease.

Dice Gould heeled the grulla and rode down to them. In their faces he was amused to see surprise, followed immediately by sharp wariness. Here in the Cherokee Strip, greeners expected trouble and often found it where the rawhides, the old hands, had the *sabe* to get by without a bobble. It was the no-man's-land, haunted by discontented Indians, fugitives on the dodge, cattle-stealing stampeders, and gangs of toll-demanding jayhawkers. A lone rider was a rarity, and therefore suspect. Nobody rode alone through the Strip if he could help it, unless he had sinister connections with the men of the brush.

The two men pulled in, and Dice Gould reined around facing them. They saw him pat the grulla, and their eyes traveled on to the two guns lying snugly in leather-laced holsters along his hips. He was lean and muscular, not overly tall, and about him there was a compact tightness. His clothes were hard-worn, spotted and grimed by campfires, and he was unshaven. Hardness marked his straight, wide mouth. His dark gray eyes, lightened to opaque slate by the contrast of deeply browned skin, regarded them expressionlessly. He cuffed back his stained sombrero. His hair was black.

He said, "Which of you is trail boss?"

The short, bearded man in the black coat motioned toward his tall companion. "Flogger Hood. My name's Matt Swain. I'm the owner. That is," he corrected himself, "part owner. Who're you?"

"Name's Gould." Dice Gould met Flogger Hood's hostile regard. Flogger Hood had green eyes, scanty reddish hair, and a narrow, compressed mouth. A sour-looking man. Dice Gould told him bluntly, "You're off your route, wherever you're headed. An' your trail crew doesn't know up from down. You ever come up the trail before?" It was his way of speaking—sparsely, and to the point. He was impatient of soft words.

Flogger Hood breathed hard through his long nose. "No, I never made the trail before now," he allowed. His voice was deep and growling, oddly at variance with his thinness. "That any concern to you?"

"Not a damn bit," said Dice Gould. "Neither does it hurt me that you had a stampede couple nights ago. But I'm curious to know why you didn't hunt up your missin' cows. You've lost quite a few."

Matt Swain exclaimed astonishedly, "How did you know that? Yes, we've had trouble. The last stampede was the worst. We lost around two hundred head. They ran north. We hope to pick them up along the way, if somebody hasn't stolen them." He shook his iron-gray head worriedly. "If I'd known what this drive was going to be like, I never would have started out. I'm new in cattle."

Dice Gould could well believe it. Matt Swain didn't even sit his saddle like a man of the range. Flogger Hood, though, had the cowman's stamp, and it seemed odd that he should show such fumbling inefficiency in the handling of a trail herd.

Dice remarked, "You'll never come up on your missin' cows, the way you're goin', I'll tell you that."

Flogger Hood glanced aside at Matt Swain. " 'Pears to know all about it, don't he?" he drawled in mock admiration. "Maybe he knows what caused the stampede!"

Matt Swain gave a start, and blurted, "Maybe he does!"

Dice Gould's eyes chilled, glimmering in the sudden dark flare of his face. "If you're hintin' I'm a stampeder," he snapped, "say it plain an' I'll take you apart!"

Flogger Hood's thin nostrils pinched in. "I ain't no gunman, or I'd call you on that!"

"Got fists, haven't you?"

"I sure have!" The trail boss jumped from his horse and rushed at Dice while he was still dismounting. "An' here they are, stampeder!"

His thickened, blue-scarred knuckles were evidence that he was a scrapper. His first blow slammed Dice against the grulla, and the animal reared and knocked him away. He closed in and brought up a knee.

Off balance, the only way for Dice to avoid the knee was to fall back and go down. He landed in gravel, and saw Hood coming at him. Hood took a long stride and bent his right leg for a crippling kick. The man was out to maim him.

Dice rolled over fast, slewed himself half around on the ground, and lunged upward with both feet. One high heel cracked Hood below the knee, the other in the thigh. Hood abruptly fell on his hands and knees, teeth bared in pain. Dice leaped up and hit him as he was rising. He hit him again to straighten him up, and went to work on him.

The leading cattle were coming up, and the two men on point, seeing the fight, came spurring on ahead. Matt Swain shouted angrily at Dice, "Quit it, man, quit it! He's had enough!"

Dice put everything into a last punch. Gasping, bloody-faced, Hood dropped. He had taken a terrific beating in a short time, and wouldn't be good for much for a while.

The two riders reined to a jolting halt, swung down, and advanced belligerently. Dice stepped toward them, his violent mood unslaked, his temper brittle.

"You ducks want trouble? Make your bet, or get back to the cows! It's a hell of a pair o' point riders who go off an' leave the herd to drift!"

They backed up, after a good close look at him, muttering, and remounted and rode back. Matt Swain called after them, "Start bedding 'em down. Hood's hurt and can't go on any farther today."

Dice eyed him bleakly. "It's not a particle to what he aimed to do to me!" Fresh wrath surged in him. "You lost two hundred cows, like a fool! I found 'em, an' came out o' my way lookin' for the trail herd wearing that same road brand. An' what I get for my trouble is hard talk an' a dirty fight! All right! I'm no durn stampeder. But right now, hombre, you're lookin at a mavericker!"

Swain frowned uncertainly. "What d'you mean?"

"I mean," barked Dice impatiently, "that a mavericker hunts

lost or wild cows for cash. Down in the Texas Brasada he gets a dollar a head. Here in the Cherokee Strip he gets a lot better price, things bein' as they are. So—things bein' as they are—my price is five dollars a head. If you want those cows, you owe me a thousand dollars!"

After Swain's indignant snort, Dice could detect and follow his thoughts. A two-year-old was worth ten, twelve, maybe fifteen dollars at the market. Swain was a man of business. He had a head on him.

"I'll make a deal with you, Gould," he said. "I can't spare a thousand dollars now. But if you'll pilot this herd through to where we're going, I'll pay you *two* thousand from the sale. If you fail, you get nothing. Are you a gambler?"

Dice grinned faintly at the question. He had been everything: gambler, gun slinger, mustanger, mavericker, trader, cowman. The proposition attracted him. It meant a fresh stake, a chance to begin building again toward a fortune. A starved and desperate boyhood had instilled in him a hatred of poverty. Hard cash had become his goal. All else was transient and unimportant.

He had come upon the lost cows the previous morning, and knew at a glance that they had stampeded and run a long way. Being longhorns, they had stayed bunched. Weary and sullen, heads low, they bellowed at the river. Before them lay a pear-shaped spit of land jutting into the water, connected to the bank by a flat sliver of earth. But they didn't like the looks of that narrow passage, so they trampled the bank, grumbling at it.

He sized up the situation, his wits and cowman's knowledge immediately at work. There had been heavy rain in the mountains last night. Pretty soon the river would rise, and the peninsula would become an island for a day or two, the narrow neck under water. The solution was simple. The island would make a perfect holding ground. There was grass on it. Longhorns rarely swam unless pushed.

He rode down quietly behind them, suddenly raised a hideous yell, and they made up their minds in a hurry and charged across the narrow neck. He waited there until the river rose and flooded the passage, and then he went looking for their outfit. Any cowman would do as much, free, for another cowman. It was a big country, untamed, lawless, and no man knew when he might need help, himself.

He said to Matt Swain, "I'll take that deal. On condition that I boss the outfit an' no arguments. Sign me a note for two thousand. On the herd. You're bound for Dodge City, I s'pose?"

Swain shook his head, smiling frostily. "No. We have a bonded contract to deliver this herd to the Indian Agent up at Ogallala—and you've just agreed to get us there!"

Dice Gould regarded him solemnly. Ogallala, away up on the Platte, lay hundreds of miles north of Dodge City. It meant crossing the North Canadian, the Cimarron, the Arkansas, going around Dodge, then trailing clear across Kansas up into Nebraska.

"A Jonah outfit on a Jonah trail!" he commented. "No herd has made it there this year so far. I hear those reservation Indians are gettin' mighty hungry for the beef rations that were promised 'em, an' the Agent is scared they'll sharpen their knives for hair. Can't say I blame 'em much."

"That's all the more reason we must get this herd through," said Swain. "Besides, I put up a cash bond to get the contract."

Dice nodded. "So did I. Ogallala was where I was bound, too, with sixteen hundred head I went in debt to buy in Texas. An' my crew was good, which is more'n I can say for yours."

"What happened?"

"Stampeders!" Dice spat the word with all a cowman's hatred. "On Black Bear Creek one night. Must've been a big gang, plenty smart an' organized. We didn't catch much sight of 'em in the dark. First they spooked the *remuda* off. Left most of us afoot. Then they fired the brush an' scattered my cows to hell an' gone.

All we could do was push on to Dodge, an' I went bust payin' off my crew. I guess those stampeders used my horses to round up my cows later, damn 'em! They operate out o' Dodge, I'm pretty sure. I got into a little trouble there, inquirin' around."

He didn't mention it, but his little trouble in Dodge had entailed smacking down a cattle inspector who arrogantly resented being questioned, and putting a bullet through the shoulder of a deputy town marshal who foolishly tried to interfere. The law of Dodge City bore him a grudge for that.

He shrugged. "Well, it's a deal an' I'll stick with your outfit, Swain. But if I get it through safe to Ogallala, I'll sure earn my money!"

Critically, he watched the herd being bedded down, and decided that Swain's crew knew their work but didn't care how they did it. He would durn soon jerk them up on that attitude. The second wagon drew up, and down from it stepped a slight figure wearing a skirt.

"Gossake, who's that?" he demanded.

"My niece, Dinah," Matt Swain told him. "My brother's daughter. He was a cattleman. Died early this spring. I paid off his mortgage, for a half interest in this herd. Dinah owns the rest. My business is farming, and I own a small bank in Illinois."

Dice closed his eyes. "An Illinois farm-banker an' a gal! A gal with a trail-herd outfit! What next, oh, Lawd!"

"As half owner, Dinah is entitled to—"

"Entitled to be stared at, like any gal a thousand miles from the next one! No wonder your trail hands prance so gay back with the wagons! By golly, I'll put a stop to that! Hey, you leanin'-to-hell Arbuckle pilgrims—"

The herd traveled slowly up the long trail with the grass, losing no weight. The outfit had picked up the two hundred head off the island, and crossed the South Fork of the Canadian. Two night stampedes had been halted. The cattle were as spooky as wild deer, and as hard to handle.

Swain's trail hands, driven and bullied relentlessly by Dice, rode in good order now. But they were resentful, hostile, and talked a lot with Flogger Hood. After savage fights with four of them, Dice had convinced them that he was boss. They hadn't accepted him, though. They were secretive, and it was obvious that they still looked on Flogger Hood as their leader.

Dice took to sleeping apart from the crew, an hour at a time, lightly, with a horse ready saddled for him to jump on in case of sudden emergency. He grew gaunt and more taciturn, his eyes sunken and sharp. His clothes were giving out and he was in rags, but every day he cleaned and reloaded his guns, one at a time, the other ready at hand. There was a lot that was wrong with this outfit. He didn't trust it. It was a Jonah.

"My uncle has told me about you," Dinah Swain remarked to him. She rode alongside him on a buckskin mare. She wore tight riding-pants.

Dice didn't approve of those pants. He didn't like the way the trail hands looked at her. It was an ugly, scrubby crew. He guessed that they had been hired on Flogger Hood's say-so.

She was young and more than pretty, a fair-haired girl with eyes much like his own, dark gray and controlled, often expressionless.

Dice said curtly, "Your uncle doesn't know much good about me."

"Maybe there isn't much good to know."

"Could be."

A rider came back from on scout. He was Tanker Todd, a bleary old boozer, but Dice trusted him more than he did any of the others. Todd shouted, "North Canadian ahead! She's high. I guess we wait till she goes down, to cross over."

"I guess we don't!" Dice said. "Can't afford the time. Cut out that big yellow steer an' take him up front to lead. He don't mind water, I notice."

They had the herd strung out, the yellow steer in the lead, getting to the Canadian. After drinking, though, the yellow steer balked at crossing and the herd began crowding up dangerously on the bank. Half a herd could be lost that way in flood water, the rear cattle pushing those in front, then the whole bunch winding up tightly in a mad, threshing panic in the river, forcing the center cows under.

The yellow steer, thrust onward, roared its frightened protests, scaring the rest of the nervous brutes.

Hood shouted maliciously above the bawling racket. "There goes your herd, Swain! I'd never have tried this, was I boss! I got more sense!"

Dice stripped hurriedly to his pants. He handed his guns and clothes to Dinah Swain, and plunged his horse into the water. Quitting the horse, dodging hoofs and horns, he climbed aboard the yellow steer and kicked and punched him into going on. Once in deeper water the steer swam strongly to the north bank. Those already in the river came churning after him, losing some of their senseless fear, and the herd lined out across without much further trouble.

Dropping off the steer and ducking out of the way of the rest, Dice swam downstream, recovered his horse, and rode back up the south bank to where the crew was guiding the herd over the crossing. Not all the hands were needed for that task. Some were needed on the north side. But Flogger Hood appeared to be giving the orders.

As soon as Dice showed up, Matt Swain, red-faced and worried, blared at him, "You damn near played hell with the whole herd!"

Dice's temper snapped. He was half naked, soaking wet and cold, and what he had done had been to risk his life to prevent a pile-up.

"Why, blazes burn your hoeman's fool hide!" he rasped. "Don't talk that way to me, or I'll plow you down! Get over on the other side an' line those cows out as they come, before they drift all over the territory! Take Hood an' a couple more o' your juniper pilgrims with you—I sure don't need 'em here!"

Swain cooled off and started over, followed sullenly by Hood and a couple of the crew. Dice found Dinah Swain beside him, and he took his clothes and guns from her.

She scanned him curiously. "That was a crazily reckless thing you did. You could have got gored, kicked, or swamped under."

"You're a better cowman than your fool uncle. No *sabe* there."

"That's true. I really don't know him very well. But why did you do it?"

He shrugged into his shirt, belted his guns on, donned his wreck of a hat. "We've got to get the wagons ready to float over— Huh? Well, I got two thousand dollars in this herd, for one thing."

"You're earning it!"

"Yeah. But it's a stake an' I need it."

She said quietly, "Money means a good deal to me, too. All I have is tied up in this herd. Poverty is all I'm afraid of. For a girl, it means the loss of independence, even more than it does to a man."

She was silent for a moment. Then she observed, "If those Ogallala Sioux Indians get too hungry, there'll be an uprising. A lot of people—homesteaders and others—will suffer by it. So will the Sioux, themselves, after the soldiers round them up. I've been thinking of that. Have you?"

"No," he disclaimed curtly. "I just don't like to be broke, is all. I've been there!" He raised his voice in a harsh yell at the crew. "Push 'em easy there, you Arbuckles! Lawd, what a trail outfit!" He heeled his horse down closer to the river and hailed, "Line 'em north, Swain!" and he added dryly, "You 'member which way is north?"

Swimming the river on his horse, Matt Swain looked back and nodded. Their idea of establishing north, Dice had learned, was to set the tongue of the chuck wagon aimed at the North Star in the evening, and draw a point from it the next morning. Helluva system. Somebody was always likely to sit on the wagon tongue and jiggle it, brush against it, kick it out of kilter—and next morning north was northeast, northwest, any old direction. It could go toward explaining how the outfit had strayed so far off the route when Dice came upon it.

True, the trails of previous herds were visible. Swain maintained that he had purposely swung away from them in order to avoid going through Dodge. But he had veered off much too soon into untracked country, as Hood and the others should have known. And there was no good explanation of why the herd should have had so many stampedes that it was ready to take off in fright at the twitter of a bird in the brush at sundown.

They crossed the wild old Canadian, not a head lost. But there Matt Swain ended his inept venture in cattle.

Dinah Swain saw it, and called out urgently, pointing. Dice looked in time to see Matt Swain go under. Swain and Hood and two trail hands were swimming their horses over on the upstream side of the crossing herd. Swain was nearest to the splashing column. Something either startled his horse, or else the current caught him off guard, for he drifted clumsily right into the ruck of cattle. A horseman in the water was nowhere near as authoritative as a horseman tall in the saddle on solid ground, and Matt Swain promptly disappeared when an enterprising steer got the notion to climb onto the saddle with him. The horse came up without him, kicking, nearly causing a deadly mill in midstream.

They fished him out, a quarter mile down the river. A steer had hoofed him over the eyes and knocked him out, and it was the air trapped under his coat that finally floated him to the surface. He was dead.

Nobody had a Bible. They dug him a decent grave, though, and laid stones over it against coyotes. Dice said, when it was done, "He was a good man, I guess, where he came from. Just didn't know how to ride a river. God have mercy on him. Amen. Let's get after the cows!"

Dinah Swain said to him that night, after the herd was bedded down and the cook's fires lighted, "You're hard and callous. It wasn't his fault that he was a poor rider."

She wasn't pretending to be broken up by her uncle's death. She was too honest for that. Dice guessed that she and Matt Swain had not hit it off any too well.

"I didn't mean it was," he responded, getting hot coffee for her from the huge, blackened pot. "I only spoke my mind. Now I'll speak it to you. He's gone, which makes you full owner, I guess. But let's get this straight. I boss your outfit through to Ogallala, an' collect two thousand dollars. Boss, y' hear? That means if I tell you to get to your wagon, you hop into it, *pronto!* Next crossin' is at Black Bear Creek."

She flushed, raising her chin. "Where you lost your herd, I hear!"

He nodded. "Right. I don't figure to lose this one. Those starvin' Sioux—" he cut himself off. "Lady, I'm a tired an' busy man. Just you don't bother me!"

In the mid-morning sunshine seven men, well mounted and heavily armed, waited on the trail. One of them, a fair-haired giant with protruding blue eyes, evidently the leader, held a hand raised in command for the Swain outfit to halt and parley.

Dice, who had started ahead to scout out the trail, came up to them. He didn't care for their looks, and asked bluntly, "Well?"

The big, fair-haired man ran a searching survey over him. "I'm Wyatt Wrangel," he announced. His voice was that of a man of some education, and his manner conveyed a cool expectation of respect. "My ranch is close by. We're here to inspect and cut your herd for any strays of mine you may have picked up."

Such a request was reasonable. But this was a demand. Wyatt Wrangel motioned toward one of his armed men, a dark, lean man who fingered his rope and gazed at the oncoming herd. "My range boss, Lariat Sanga. He'll handle it. Who're you?"

Dice hunched over in his saddle. "I'm Dice Gould. That's the Swain herd comin' up. I'm trail boss—an' I'll see you in hell before you booger round with the outfit! The herd's too spooky to chouse round. Kindly get off the trail, Mr. Wrangler!"

"Wrangel," corrected the blond giant, and glanced at his range boss. The armed squad quietly spread out. "We cut!"

Lariat Sanga gazed with chill thoughtfulness at Dice, and loosened his coiled rope. He waited until the leading steers came up abreast, and fastened his eyes on the big yellow steer, which had decided that it was the king-pin since crossing the Canadian. Flogger Hood, arriving with the point riders, exchanged a look with Wyatt Wrangel, and dropped back.

"One of ours, that, I'd say," murmured Lariat Sanga. "Let's get a look at it." His rope snaked out.

To cut a herd without permission was arrogant insult. To rope a lead steer was infinitely worse. It could fluster even a placid and trail-broken herd. Cows, creatures of habit, got used to following the same leaders, and didn't like change.

Dice acted fast. His rope sailed out and slapped across Sanga's, spoiling the throw. While the big yellow steer tramped untroubledly by, Dice said, "Don't try that again, hombre!"

He was one against seven, and he glanced around to see if his crew was coming up to help out. In any kind of outfit all hands stuck by the top screw in time of trouble, regardless of personal and private opinion. But Flogger Hood and his picked pals were hanging back, obviously opposed to mixing in. There was scant difference between their expressions and those of the Wrangel squad. Their stares, fixed on him, contained much the same look of coldly hostile expectancy. They were like willing witnesses to a prepared and thoroughly approved execution.

It flashed through Dice's mind that Hood had been alongside Swain, when Swain's horse lunged off on that crazy tangent and got snarled up among the swimming cattle. The reaching jab of a sharpened and locked spur rowel could have accomplished that. Hood wore wired spurs, with rowels the size of silver dollars.

And it came to him bleakly that he was alone, trapped, nobody here to back him up—except Dinah Swain, riding toward him on the lope, a rifle swinging in her right hand. The girl screamed, "Watch out!"

He jerked around, and saw Lariat Sanga's grease-slicked raw-hide *riata* loop whisperingly at him.

It was a straight throw, a hungry loop intended to snub fast, yank Dice off his saddle, and drag him to shreds over rocks and and through brush. Dice had seen it done, in lariat duels below the Rio Grande. Such fights were deadly, more often fatal than most six-gun scraps, the loser ending as a battered and lifeless hulk at the end of a rope.

He was riding the grulla. He flattened over, the saddle horn punching his chest, and dug in his heels. The horse leaped like a scalded cat, and the braided rawhide slapped Dice's back and slid off its flank. Dice reined around, glaring.

Unperturbed by his first miss, Sanga deftly whipped up his forty-foot line, smiling. By his nickname, Lariat, he had evidently earned title as a wizard with his fine *riata*. His eyes, glitteringly confident, mutely challenged Dice to a duel. He was out to have sport and to display his skill. In his hands the *riata* became a living, writhing thing.

Dice carried a short *maguey* rope, hard-twisted, made of the tough fiber of century plants. Sanga must have taken note of that, for his smile deepened. Top ropers scorned the *maguey*. Too stiff. But Dice had worked his a lot in the Texas brush, where a long rope wasn't much good, and it had become supple and smooth with long use. He rode at Sanga. He lacked Sanga's forty-foot reach, and needed to get in closer.

They watched, Wyatt Wrangel's armed squad and the Swain crew. And Dinah. She uttered no sound now. Her face was white. She held the rifle across her saddle.

Sanga darted his horse aside, neck-reined it around, and twirled a loop, still smiling. He rode superbly, gracefully, with a Spanish flair, insolently contemptuous. The rawhide *riata* flicked, the loop whining softly through its thin bone *honda*. The loop was a neat and tricky *mangana de cabra,* a curling figure 8 to snag Dice's head or, failing, the head of the grulla. Dice dodged it by inches, but his own loop went to pot. Sanga laughed aloud, circling his horse and winding up again.

The next lightning toss was a hoolihan. Dice rode right into it, hitting the grulla's head down with his fist, lowering his own. He used his left fist, letting go of the reins, his right hand busy with the short *maguey*. His knees and heels commanded the grulla to spin around, scattering sand in a tight turn, and he rode again at Sanga, whose *riata* was still out and dragging.

Sanga slung his horse around to get out of range, but he was too late. The *maguey* settled over him, snapped his arms and body. He hadn't time to pull up and attempt to free himself. His horse ran on, and the rope plucked him off and slammed him to the ground.

The grulla, being a good cow horse, halted at once, bracing its legs and keeping the rope taut, waiting for Dice to tie and brand the caught critter. Dice touched him on, dragging Sanga, who cursed and closed his eyes fatalistically. For Sanga to free his arms from the rope, if he could do it, meant its slipping up around his neck. It was a doubtful choice between that and being towed over the rocks. So Sanga waited for the Wrangel squad to pitch in.

But it was Dinah who called, "Hold it, Dice! Hold it!"

They all looked at her. The Wrangel squad, starting forward, paused. She held the rifle now in both hands, and was gazing north past them. Dice followed the direction of her eyes. His baleful, savage anger abruptly lost its edge. He loosened the rope on Sanga, and said to Wrangel:

"Take him away! Gal, go easy with that rifle! Put it down!"

Wrangel gave the nod. His armed squad, sliding uneasy glances up the trail, helped Lariat Sanga to his feet. One of them had caught his horse. They got him into his saddle, and rode off into the brush east of the trail.

Wrangel called back tonelessly, "See you later, Gould—maybe!"

"Maybe!" replied Dice, and went on surveying the mob of riders who had suddenly and silently showed up on the trail.

He counted over sixty of them. They were cloaked in shabby blankets, and their ponies were small and scrawny, but the sight of them had been sufficient to send Wrangel and his gunmen home. They sat their ponies in careless disorder, and the only bright color about them was in the few dyed eagle feathers here and there. The danger was in their strong, hard faces.

These silent, coppery apparitions were men who paid homage to nobody, willingly. Self-reliant, quick to grin or scowl, as capable of cruelty as of tenderness. As sensitive as any Spanish grandees. Gods of the earth, in their own opinion. Fighting men. No weapons were visible among them, but the ragged blankets could conceal much.

This was Cherokee country. Yet these men were not Cherokees. They traveled without women and children and *travois*. A bad sign. They looked hungry, and they were far from home. Hungry Indians were unpredictable. Their broad and elemental sense of justice could set the spark to a swift, berserk rage. Memories of better days were a constant prod to dark discontent.

Dice said again, "Easy with that rifle, gal! If I was them I wouldn't like it pointed at me. I'd be inclined to do somethin' about it!"

He handed her his guns, and rode forward, unarmed. He had known and traded with a good many Indians, and got along with them. There was in him a good deal of their forthright view of things, as well as a grimly dry humor that they could appreciate.

He picked out the leader, an ancient hawk of a man, tall and cavernous-eyed, and raised a hand to him in respectful greeting. Pulling out his tobacco sack, he offered it, not condescendingly, but as a common courtesy generally expected as a prelude to friendly parley.

The sunken black eyes regarded him impassively. Slowly, a thin brown hand emerged from under the blanket, acknowledged the greeting but ignored the tobacco—a blunt intimation that a congenial understanding was not to be easily bought. Dice knew then that these men had come through tough times and were out of patience, suspicious, on the prod.

From the wrinkled lips came one harsh word: *"Wohaw!"*

This was not begging, but a demand. They wanted beef, good red meat to roast on sticks and to put into their stomachs, for strength. Men's food. They were starving for it.

And Dice, who had defied Wrangel's demand, compromised with this one, recognizing the desperate need behind it. He pointed to a silver ring on the old chief's hand, then toward the cattle, and spread two fingers and went into rapid sign language. Two fat steers for the silver ring. Or nothing. He was not to be cowed and preyed upon, by anybody.

The cavernous black eyes kindled understandingly. Here was a man of dignity and self-respect. The silver ring, a cheap thing, came off, was surrendered, and Dice, taking it, yelled, "Cut out two fat steers for my friends!"

Dinah said to him later, "You make pretty free with my cattle! That ring isn't worth five dollars. You gave in to them!"

"I sure did," he assented, gazing at the ring on his finger. "I got rooked on the deal. But, y' see, they were hungry. If I'd given 'em the beef for nothin' they'd figure this was a poor kind of outfit. If I hadn't, they'd have made trouble. So I made a trade an' off they went, satisfied. Seems simple to me!"

She was irritated by his casual assumption of superior wisdom. "The cows were mine!" she insisted.

His gaze turned stony. "Heck, you care more about money than even I do!" he drawled. "All right, take the price of 'em out o' my two thousand dollars. Maybe you should charge up what I eat, too, while you're about it!"

He rode off and left her with that insult, and didn't see her shamed flush, her small white teeth biting her lower lip, and the tears starting in her eyes. In his mind sprang the thought that they were too much alike, he and she, ever to get along well together. He cursed the visions that made his scant hours of sleep restless. Dammit, he was getting as bad as Hood's crew, prancing around her like bewitched fools. The hell with all that. She just happened to be the only female in a male world, and any fool knew the harm a woman could wreak in an outfit going up the long trail. He decided to stay away from her, henceforth.

Toward sundown a lone rider showed up, a knotty little man, compactly built, with blue-gray eyes and graying hair. He looked hard and capable. His name, he said, was Thad Veck.

"I'm from Ogallala," he told Dice crisply, and flashed a small badge. "United States marshal."

Dice stiffened warily. "You've come quite a way. Business?"

Veck nodded. "A band of Ogallala Sioux have jumped the reservation and headed south. We don't know what they're up to. They might be scouting, getting set for a big uprising. If it comes, God help the settlers in the Stinking Water country, south of the Platte! They'll be wiped out before any help can reach 'em. Those folks have had it tough enough already, fighting a big cattleman who wants that country for himself. Man named Wrangel."

Dice quirked an eyebrow. "Wyatt Wrangel?"

"Yeah. All respect to cattlemen, but some of 'em think they ought to own the world. Especially Wrangel." Veck spat, and shrugged. "It's a mess. These Sioux bucks, they're led by Wambli-gi—he's old as the hills, but he's still a fighter and they think a lot of him. The agent didn't want to call the troops out after 'em, for fear of starting a fight. So he called on me. My job's to track 'em down and persuade 'em to go back home. Seen anything of 'em?"

Without waiting for a reply, the lawman, staring at Dice's right hand, exclaimed, "That's Wambli-gi's ring! Where is he?"

"Eatin' beef with his folks, somewhere down the trail," Dice answered. "I didn't know they were Sioux from the Ogallala reservation. That's where we're bound with this herd."

"I sure hope you get through all right," Veck assured him earnestly. "Nothing else will convince the Sioux that they're not being deliberately swindled out of their beef rations. You know how it is. Starving men can't think straight. It's a pretty desperate situation up there. If old Wambli-gi knew where you're headed, I bet he and his band would turn right around and ride guard with you all the way. I'll tell him, and talk him into catching up with you. Where'll you camp tonight? At Black Bear Creek?"

"Not on your life!" said Dice. "I lost one herd there. We've been held up an' delayed today. No, I figure to push on over, if I have to do it in the dark. I don't like that brushy bit o' country!"

Veck nodded. "You're wise. More'n one herd this year has been lost there. Well, it's an early moon tonight, so you can trail late. Good luck to you." He reined his horse around, halted, and said gravely, "I'm hoping to God you get this herd to Ogallala! If you don't, there'll be hell to pay! Those Sioux are starving. And when a hungry Sioux takes it in his head to set out—brother, he's a flaming, scrappy, loco wampus! I know the Sioux. My mother was one. My father was a mountain man, a trapper. He married her."

Abruptly, the lawman heeled his horse and rode south.

In the moonlight the slowly moving herd resembled a ghostly army of monsters, horns and eyes shining. Dinah, riding up forward, demanded of Dice, "Are you thinking of crossing the creek this late?" Then Flogger Hood came up and asked much the same question.

Dice was more worried than he cared to show. Trailing this fractious, spooky herd by moonlight was risky. He wouldn't have attempted it, except that he considered it a far lesser risk than making camp here in the tangled oak and buckthorn wilderness of the Black Bear Creek country. Along here was where his herd had vanished in the most complete stampede that he had ever witnessed. He hoped to get through with this one, by pushing on without a halt into the open country north of the creek.

But he could feel the crazy temper of these cattle. Their eyes had begun glaring and burning as soon as the sun went down. The stampede devils were in them. Anything could set them off. So he answered curtly, "We cross the creek tonight, yeah. It's just ahead. An' we keep goin' as long as there's enough moon."

Flogger Hood nodded, averting his eyes. "That's what we figured," he muttered, and dropped back.

Dinah said, "You're taking chances with my herd, Mr. Gould!"

"Yeah," Dice agreed. "Got to." A sudden wrath rose in him. He turned and looked at her. "After I get your durned Jonah outfit past Dodge, it's all yours an' you can keep that two thousand dollars! *Sabe, senorita?* I'm finding out that there are some things I won't do for money—an' one of 'em is to go on workin' for a lady boss who doesn't trust my judgment! You an' I don't get along!"

She trembled suddenly and put a hand to her eyes. "We don't

seem to, do we?" she whispered. "I'm sorry. I—I'll go back to the wagon."

He was immediately regretful, but could find nothing to say, and he watched her ride toward the rear. She looked small and forlorn, and he swung around and started after her. Hood delayed him with a question about the creek.

"It's an easy crossin', no water to speak of," Dice told him. "Don't let 'em stall there, if you can help it."

Old Tanker Todd drew alongside Dice. "I prospect trouble, Gould!" he muttered. "Keep your eyes open, an' watch out for the gal!" He rode off quickly, with a parting nod.

Dice gazed after him, frowning, and touched up his horse to overtake Dinah, who was out of sight in the rear. He was riding down the line, trying to locate her in the moonlight, when disaster struck the herd.

The first sign of it was a bobbing glow of fire that rapidly brightened, coming up behind the drag and the *remuda*. As instantly as if an electric current had been shot through it, the whole herd jumped and ran. The trail became a deafening chute of plunging, bellowing steers, horns clacking and eyes redly glaring. Billowing dust thickened, darkening the moonlight and adding to their wild panic. Somewhere in the mad chaos men were shooting and yelling.

Dice made one attempt to break up the stampede. Riding hard and yelling, he charged at the hurtling mass of cattle, seeking to turn some of them. It was as useless as trying to ride through an avalanche. They wouldn't bend, break, or side-jump. They were going too fast. Two riders passed on the lope, and he got an impression that they were laughing, although he couldn't be sure.

The last of the panicked swarm thundered by, a tangled confusion in the blinding dust, while down the trail burned an overturned and wrecked wagon. Numbed, Dice stared at the blaze. It had all happened so suddenly, and with such devastating finality, that he could hardly yet believe it. "Whole outfit—gone to hell!" he mumbled, and went looking for Dinah.

He came upon her a little way off the trail, hatless, leaning dazedly against her horse, which shivered nervously. She had a cut on her forehead and a smear of blood on her face. He dismounted and steadied her, helping her into her saddle.

"You're hurt," he said, as she swayed against him.

She held her head. "I hit a low branch in the dark. Two of the men were after me. Somebody set fire to my wagon and let the team bolt right into the *remuda*. Is everything—gone?"

He nodded heavily. "Cows, horses, an' crew—everything! I'm the man who said he'd get your outfit through. Two herds I've lost here. Two! Now you're as broke as I am. We're both wiped out. If yours was a Jonah outfit, I was a Jonah boss! Licked!"

She leaned down to him from her saddle, unsteadily. "Licked, heck!" she said fiercely. "Us? Dice Gould and Dinah Swain licked by brush-skulking stampeders and a worthless trail crew? Not yet! They must have some method of keeping the herd together, and taking it to where they want it. We're going after them!"

He looked into her face, and drew a breath. Her eyes were blazing. He asked, "Are you thinkin' o' those starvin' Sioux an' what'll happen if they don't get some beef soon?"

"Yes," she answered. "The money doesn't seem very important to me now."

He nodded in full understanding. "Nor to me. We appear to be gettin' to know each other better. Or maybe we've both changed some, now we're busted together. Short time back you jumped on me for takin' a chance with your herd. Now I've lost it, an' you haven't said a word o' blame."

"The blame belongs to my uncle, for hiring Hood and his bunch. No man could do more than you have done, Dice."

"Thank you, Dinah." It was the first time that they had called each other by their first names. "Okay, let's go."

The torn-up trail wore a strange and almost unearthly look, silent and deserted as it now was, after the wild tumult of the stampede. Here and there a steer's trampled corpse bulked motionless on the ground, and they passed one of the horses of the *remuda,* dead of a broken neck. Dinah shivered a little at the grim relics of her trail herd, and Dice swore behind closed lips.

They reached the creek. The crossing was shallow. Trail drivers of previous years had cut down the banks here, and their herds had worn them smooth. But on either side of the crossing, the banks were steep, darkly overhung with brush.

Dice rode on over to the north bank and studied the ground, frowning. No fresh tracks were visible there, as they were on the south bank. Returning, his searching attention was caught by a pair of pale objects under the bank, on the west side of the crossing, and he dismounted and examined them. They were large squares of tarpaulin, fastened to pole frames and fringed with streamers of white cloth. Dinah joined him, and he pointed to them.

"Stampeders' equipment!" he explained to her bleakly. "First they set fire to your wagon an' started the stampede. Others were posted here to stop the herd from crossin' over an' scatterin' out. They did it with the help o' these things, flappin' 'em as the cows showed up. Only one way left for the cows to run—they bent here an' tore east along the creek. The high banks would keep 'em from scatterin'. You were dead right. These hombres have got things worked out. An' Hood an' the crew were in on it, shootin' an' yellin' to stop any break off the trail into the brush. Pretty smart, these—"

A slight sound like a groan whirled him around, a gun out and and his free arm pushing Dinah behind him. He rapped, "Show y'self, quick, or I shoot!"

The groan was repeated, followed by the hoarse voice of old

Tanker Todd. "No need to shoot me—it's already done! I can't move."

They discovered the broken-down old cowpuncher in a clump of thorn-brush, where he evidently had crashed after being shot. Dice hauled him out. "Who did it?"

Tanker Todd breathed noisily. "Flogger. He suspicioned I was gettin' too friendly with you an' the gal. Gunned me an' rid off with the others. I knew the big stompede was due here. Tried to give you word, didn't I? Flogger'd said somethin' about the gal. I didn't like it. Stealin' cows is one thing, but—"

"You were all in on it, huh? From the first?"

"Sure. That's why we played hell with the herd, comin' up. To get the critters good an' spooky an' ready to run. Flogger's been up the trail plenty times, an' knows the tricks. Main idee was to bust the outfit an' see it never reached Ogallala."

"Whose idea's that?"

"Wrangel's. He's big boss. Flogger figured to whittle off some o' the herd for hisself before we got this far. You stopped that an' whipped him. He ain't forgive you. Then we got a whisper late last night that not far ahead Wrangel would be on hand with a squad to settle you. It was Sanga's job. But that missed, too. You're a tough duck to kill, Gould—dam'f you're— Hey, I guess I'm dyin'!"

"I guess you are, Tanker," Dice agreed, and drew Dinah aside. "I'm settin' out now to trail after the herd," he told her.

"*We are setting out!*" she corrected him. "As tired as those cattle are, they won't run too far tonight no matter how they're pushed. Until the breeze died, I thought I could still hear the rumble of them. The breeze came from the east."

"You stay behind! Don't know what I might run into."

"Would it be safe for me here?"

He rubbed his jaw. "Maybe not. How 'bout ridin' on up to Dodge, though?"

"Nice safe ride for a lone young lady!" she commented. Her

eyes suddenly blazed again. "We're going together! Don't try to stop me! Don't try to treat me like a child!"

He gazed at her and grinned slowly, for the moment forgetful of catastrophe. "What a girl! A lady one minute, an' a wildcat the next!" His grin faded, and he went on gazing at her. Then he drew her to him and kissed her. Releasing her at last, he said gruffly, "Sorry. May never get to kiss you again. Seemed like a good thing to do."

"Yes," she said. "Yes, Dice."

He went back to Tanker Todd, but the man was dead. So he and Dinah mounted their horses and rode east along the creek, the moon high over them.

The moon was half down when they sat peering out over a valley that, narrow at the west mouth emptying toward Black Bear Creek, appeared to widen eastward against a flat horizon. It looked peaceful. A stream wound around small islands of trees, cattle thickly dotted the grass, and far in the distance a speck of light indicated a ranch house.

It was, as Dinah commented, good cow country. Dice surveyed it for a long time, and remarked, "Good cow-thief country! See how it seems to be shaped like a funnel? They can run a herd into the little end, out o' the creek, and turn 'em loose here. The cows paw around some, o' course, but after a while they settle down an' graze. They don't even need riders, any more'n they would in a pen, an' I don't see any. Then, maybe weeks after, riders can start workin' 'em gentle up the valley, out the big end onto open range. By next year, bills o' sale can be cooked up, or brands altered, an' on they go to Dodge or wherever. By then the real owner is way back home, tryin' to figure how to pay off his debts!"

"Like you?"

"No. Right now I'm tryin' to figure how to get back a herd for a young lady wildcat. By the way, there's more than your herd here. You didn't own that many head." Dice got off and tested his cinch. "I aim to ride on along these hills, then prowl down for a look at those cows on east yonder. This time you stay back, for you can't do me any good there!"

"All right," she assented reasonably. But if you're not back in an hour I'm coming after you."

He got back to her in less than the hour. His eyes gleamed, and his voice was thin and tinny when he spoke.

"Those cows up ahead o' yours are mine!" He stared hungrily into the valley. "Both our herds! Right down there! An' I don't know a thing I can do about it! Need a big crew to move 'em out. A fightin' crew. Lot o' men up there at the ranch house. I could see 'em shiftin' back an' forth against the light. For all I know, they could be readyin' to come an' work these cows east to some range where nobody would ever find 'em."

Dinah said, "We can go on up to Dodge and raise the law."

Dice barked a short laugh. "I show my face in Dodge, an' the law will raise itself! I left there on the high lope!"

"Then I'll go!" she declared. "It's best for you to stay, anyway, and keep track of the cattle in case they're moved."

He was dubious, and worried for her. "It's a long way for you to go alone."

"I'm going!"

When she used that tone there wasn't much that one could do. She used it, he noticed, when insisting upon doing her share. A man couldn't get all bowed up over that.

"Well, here, take one o' my guns, then. I'll see you back to the trail. Take care o' y'self, hear?"

"You too."

They rode quietly back the way they had come, to Black Bear Creek. Both knew that the chance of ever recovering their herds was slim. This was the Cherokee Strip, far outside the bailiwick of Dodge City law. And although the lawmen of that beef-shipping Babylon were tough, there weren't anywhere near enough of them to go against Wrangel's organized army of six-gun scrappers and stampeders.

They didn't talk of that.

In the brush-hung blackness of the creek Dinah uttered a stifled scream. "Dice! Watch out!" Even in her terror she could think of warning him first.

Dice had fallen behind to watch the rear. Glaring, nerves tingling, he slapped out his gun and spurred to her side. "What's—"

He didn't finish his sharp query, suddenly aware that he and she were surrounded by cloaked and silent horsemen whose eyes shone from dark, indistinguishable faces. Then the crisp voice of Thad Veck rapped at him, "That you, Gould? Take it easy!"

The knotty little U. S. Marshal pushed forward out of the surrounding mob. "What happened to your herd?"

Dice holstered his gun. The silent horsemen were only Wambligi's band. "Stampeded!" he replied tersely. "An the crew gone with it!"

Veck blew a harsh breath. "Damn! Guessed so. Saw the signs as we came up. Any idea where? Evenin', ma'am."

"On Wrangel's so-called ranch, just east o' here. My crew is in his pay, I found."

"Wyatt Wrangel! Phooh! He's a powerful big man. Him?"

"Yeah, him!" Dice growled. "Why not? There's some who get big that way. You told me he's tryin' to get the Stinkin' Water country cleared of settlers, to get it for himself. A Sioux uprisin' would clear the settlers off for him, an' after soldiers settled with the Sioux, Wrangel would move in! You told me the Sioux are ready to rise because they're starvin'. It's Wrangel who's starvin' 'em. Dodge City herds get through. Ogallala-bound beef don't. For land, Wrangel's willin' to sacrifice the lives o' hundreds o' settlers an' their families—to say nothin' o' the Sioux an' soldiers who'll die fightin' later! He oughta be skinned an' scalped!"

"Maybe you're right, but don't talk that way," said Veck uneasily, glancing around at the blanketed men. "Some of 'em *sabe* English better'n you think. But look. I've promised 'em beef for Ogallala. I've got to make good on it. What'll we do?"

Dice motioned toward Dinah. "She was goin' up to Dodge, to raise the law. Didn't look too promisin'."

"Not much prospect there," Veck allowed, "but maybe I could do better. I'll try it. I'll go alone, though. These fellows—well, Dodge would think it was a raid or something!"

Dice had a thought. He said, "I bet my old crew is still there. An' I bet they're broke by now. You look up Rory Rostam. He was my *segundo*. Tell him I said to round the boys up an' come back here with you. You can swear 'em in as deputies or such."

"It's an idea," Veck allowed, swinging onto his horse.

Dice watched him depart, and said to Dinah, "Not a chance there! Only a dozen in my old crew. Couldn't handle the Wrangel bunch, though they'd sure try, an' get themselves wiped out. Veck wouldn't consider usin' these Sioux folks. Scared they might make it a scalp hunt. Can't say I'd blame 'em. Veck's half a Sioux, an' the other half's white, which makes him cautious. Me, I'm a Texan an' I'll take a chance! Ho, Wambli-gi!"

The hawk-faced Wambli-gi came forward to him, nodding, full of beef, giving proper respect to a man who would trade generously but who would not be robbed. A few minutes later Dinah stood by while they exchanged rapid sign language, guttural exclamations, and an occasionally recognizable word.

"What are you up to?" Dinah asked.

"We're goin' after our cows!" Dice drawled blandly. "My friend, here, is all for the idea! He's got a good, sound *sabe* o' the situation—"

In the moonless darkness before morning they trooped eastward across the hills overlooking the valley, avoiding the sky line. The cattle had not yet been moved, but riders could be seen strung out across the narrow end, waiting for daylight and the signal to start. Wrangel's riders, those, and probably some of Flogger Hood's men.

Dice threw up a hand for a halt. After a brief consultation Dice and Wambli-gi and a few others proceeded on toward the lighted ranch house, while the rest filed furtively down into the valley.

Dice said to Dinah. "I shouldn't have let you come. There'll be some trouble, maybe more'n we can handle."

"How could you have stopped me?"

"Wambli-gi knows," he responded. "He keeps a quirt for his women when they don't behave!"

"I'm not your woman!" she flashed.

"That's true," he agreed regretfully. "Quiet, now. Here's the house ahead. We got to see to it that whoever's inside stays there till the boys get those cows headed back toward the creek."

She was frightened. Her eyes, that could blaze so fiercely, showed it. She whispered, "You're mad, Dice! The whole thing is impossible! You can't do it with Indians!"

"No?" His hard brown fingers clamped around her wrist. "No?" In the darkness his face, gaunted by work-strain and loss of sleep, had a good deal of the hawklike cast of Wambli-gi, the gray eyes glimmering with something more than cool recklessness. "I can try!"

"If you fail—" she began, and broke off, aware of the futility now of words, realizing that he was a desperate and dangerous man.

He muttered somberly, "My folks were killed when I was a kid, after they moved over into New Mexico. I wasn't there. Some white outlaws bushwhacked a band o' Mescalero 'Paches an' took their horses. Sold 'em to my dad, who didn't know they were stolen. The 'Paches soon learned where their horses were. They put on paint an' set out. A stranger, who was passin' through, got wind of it, an' rode to warn my folks. He got killed along with 'em."

"I—think I understand, Dice."

"Yeah. Puts a kind o' debt on me, what that stranger tried to do. I'm thinkin' o' the Stinkin' Water settlers, an' what could happen. An' their kids. It's no-way easy on a kid to be left alone an' adrift. I didn't find it so."

The little party drew up, all eyes fixed on the lighted house ahead. Dice eased down from his horse. "You stay here," he ordered, speaking not only to Dinah, but to Wambli-gi and his half-dozen young men. It had occurred to him that a clash was best avoided, if possible, between the old warrior's party and Wrangel's bunch. The law in general was intolerant of any Indian attempt to redress wrongs by force. If an all-out fight flared up, the Sioux would be blindly condemned for it, and nobody could predict what that might lead to.

Wambli-gi argued hotly, snorting, eyes flashing, as indignant as an old colonel deprived of his command. Dice stuck fast by his decision. The habit of blaming the Indian was pretty deeply implanted in the mind of authority. Some excited and prejudiced fool behind a desk, hundreds of miles away, would probably demand wholesale arrests and punishment, and in the end the guilt of the Wrangel outfit would be lost in the smoke.

At last Wambli-gi jerked his chin in the Indian shrug and turned his back, furious. On foot, Dice prowled alone to the house. There was no separate bunkhouse that he could see, from which he guessed that this was not the ranch headquarters but a glorified kind of line-camp cabin, built to accommodate a large and permanent crew, likely one of several. It was an indication of the size of Wrangel's operations. No doubt Wrangel owned a town house in Dodge, played politics, and knew the right people.

Moving steadily closer, Dice listened to voices. The house was a long single-storey with a low porch and few windows. The door leading out onto the porch hung open. He toed lightly onto the porch and to the door, and looked in.

The room was barely furnished with bunks, a long table, benches, and a couple of hanging lamps. There was another door at the far side, also open to let in air. Another, closed, evidently led into the kitchen, for a clatter of tinware sounded behind it. Three men were seated at the table—Wrangel, Sanga, and Hood. Sanga's face bore the marks of its contact with the ground, in the lariat duel, and Hood hadn't lost the scars of his beating. Both men were glowering down at the table, while Wrangel did the talking.

Wrangel was saying in his dispassionate tone, "You should never have let him come back up here, Hood. This is the second herd he's lost. He made trouble enough over the first one. We don't know what he'll do now. I don't like his being on the loose. You should have settled him, Hood!"

Flogger Hood fingered his long nose, scowling sourly, and grumbled, "How? He's a tough nut. I tried him out!"

Wrangel's protruding blue eyes flicked him contemptuously. "You had the crew with you—and you ask me how? And you, Sanga, getting tricky with your rope, when you should have shot him! A fine pair! He certainly put his mark on you both! I shall expect you to take some of the men and hunt him down while I'm gone."

"You going up to Ogallala?" Sanga queried.

"Hardly at this time! Things are coming to a head there, and I prefer to keep my hair!" The giant smiled, removing his hat and brushing his thick yellow hair back with his hand. "When those Sioux we saw on the trail get back, and tell their folks not to expect any beef—"

In the act of stroking his hair, he raised his eyes and saw Dice at the open front door. He gave a start, released a gusty breath, and quickly recovered himself.

"Well, hello there, Gould!" he greeted him. "We were just now talking about you."

"I heard you. Sit tight, Sanga! An' you, Hood!" Over his leveled gun Dice raked a glare over them. "All hands on the table where I can see 'em!"

Wrangel's eyes bulged angrily, but his voice remained emotionless. "What do you want here, Gould?"

"Cattle!" said Dice. "All those in the valley!" He held his sharpest attention on Sanga, as being the fastest of the three. The lariat master, defeated on his own proud field, showed by his tense stillness the alert thirst in him to seize the first chance to even the score.

Wrangel murmured, "You'll need riders for that, Gould."

"I've got riders. Sixty of 'em! An' every one a scrapper!"

"Ah!" Wrangel nodded. "The Sioux, eh! I don't hear them."

"You will!" Dice promised. "Any minute now you'll hear 'em start the run—an' your crew down the valley sure better climb out fast or get four thousand cows right in their laps! This time they'll know what the wrong end of a stampede's like! I'm holdin' you here till it's rollin'!" he ended, but as he said it he knew it couldn't be done without disarming them.

They were watching him, weighing their chances. Wrangel, dropping the mask of bland control, leaned far back, resting only his fingertips on the edge of the table, his glance whipping from Sanga to Hood and back again. Hood kept blinking his green eyes at the covering gun, like a gambler meditating a bet and figuring the percentages. Lariat Sanga didn't move or change expression, but a muscle of his left cheek quivered.

Dice paced toward them, toward Sanga first, who was nearest and most needed to have his fangs drawn. Sanga still didn't move, still watched him. Their chill stares locked.

The kitchen door banged open. The cook came backing through, balancing in both hands a tray loaded with a pot of coffee, mugs, half a haunch of beef, and a loaf of bread. He was a hulking big man, wearing a gun. The bread knife was shoved under his belt. He turned around with his load, started toward the table, then goggled at Dice and nearly let go of the tray.

Dice had to back-step quickly to get him covered along with the other three. "All right, set that on the table," he said. "An' sit down."

The cook hesitated and came slowly forward. His hairline and eyebrows hadn't much more than a crease dividing them, and he didn't look bright. Gazing inquiringly into Wrangel's face, he slid the tray onto the table. Stolidly, he grasped the loaf, drew the bread knife from his belt—and with astonishing speed he flung it at Dice and dug at his holster.

Dice dodged and fired. The knife ripped through his tattered shirt and gashed him. He shot the cook. But the cook, too dumb to know better than to obey Wrangel's mute command, had served his purpose. The lid was off. Two benches crashed over, and suddenly the three men were no longer at the table. Their chance had come.

Sanga darted behind the stumbling cook and fired around the hulking figure, first from one side, then the other. Dice nailed him on the second try, but to do it he had to give Wrangel and Hood the instant they needed to get their guns to bear on him.

They had him. He saw that Sanga and the cook were out of the fight, rocking aside through the trailing smoke. There wasn't time to do the same for Wrangel and Hood, both lining their sights on him, both putting the last pressure on their triggers. He slashed his gun around to get off a snap shot that might rattle their aim, hoping for not much more.

It was a gun at the open front door that roared before his, and Flogger Hood's bullet went wild a split-second later. Hit and grimacing savagely, Hood fell against Wrangel and brought his gun barrel up again, this time pointing it at the door. Dice tripped his hammer down fast and stopped him, for it was Dinah at the door, Dice's other gun smoking in her hand. Wrangel shoved Hood off and dived out through the rear door with his yellow hair flying.

A gathering bedlam of noise swelled up from the valley. It began with wild, high-pitched yells, soon drowned out by the booming rumble of running cattle.

"There they go!" Dinah said faintly, and handed Dice his gun. Her hand shook, and she kept her eyes away from dead Flogger Hood.

Wambli-gi came stalking through the back door, looking smug and nodding cheerfully to Dinah.

"You two," growled Dice, "sure take a lot o' notice o' my orders!" He eyed Wambli-gi suspiciously. It seemed to him that he had heard a slight scuffle out back. "Let's get out o' here! I don't feel too good, somehow—"

The two herds traveled as one, beating up clouds of dust in the sun, forging steadily north toward the Arkansas River where it would skirt west around Dodge City and head on up through Kansas. The point riders kept just the right distance apart, the men on swing and flank were evenly spaced, and those back in the drag kept the tail-enders humping right along. They knew their business. They were Dice's old trail hands. And along both sides of the great herd rode Wambli-gi's young men, singing interminably.

Thad Veck and the trail hands had met the herd north of the Cimarron. Rory Rostam and the others greeted Dice boisterously, eyed Dinah admiringly, and were inclined to hang around and get better acquainted with her, until Dice roared:

"Hey, you Dodge-broke saloon sinners, we got cows for Ogallala! Get to work, or I'll sic my Sioux pals on you! It's been a tough ol' trek!"

"You sure look it!"

Thad Veck said later to Dice, "Wambli-gi here, has sent a couple of his boys on to Ogallala to let 'em know you're comin'."

Dice nodded. *"Bueno."* He and Dinah were riding ahead together. He wished that Veck and Wambli-gi would drop back and leave them alone, but there they were, right behind.

He glanced aside at Dinah and caught her eye. "We—uh—seem to be gettin' to know each other better right along, don't we?" he observed, low-voiced for only her to hear.

She inclined her head gravely. "Yes, don't we?"

He stared for a minute, and glanced at her again. "By the time we get to Ogallala we ought to be gettin' along pretty good."

She met his eyes again. "Yes, Dice. I'm—" she flushed—"sure we will."

He twisted from his little finger the silver ring that he had traded from Wambli-gi. This, he thought, was a heck of a way to have to do it. But there was no privacy around a trail outfit. He extended the ring to her.

"This is yours."

"Thank you, Dice." She held out her left hand, palm down, and he slipped it on her finger.

He figured it was just between them. But behind them old Wambli-gi, a shrewd observer, grunted approval, and soon wheeled his pony around and rode back to his young men. There would be a big feast and dance after the herd was delivered.

Veck, though, less perceptive, pushed his horse on up alongside Dice and remarked thoughtfully, "Look here, Gould, you pulled a whizzer on me, and you know it! You talked me into going to Dodge, and soon's my back was turned you took these Sioux boys on a raid! You haven't yet explained just how you got your cows back. Was there a fight?"

"There was," Dice admitted. "But I kept 'em out of it. They didn't fire a shot at anybody. I give you my oath on it."

"H'm!" Veck grunted. "Well, I'm glad of that. I believe you. I'll tell the Indian agent, or anybody else who asks me, that they all behaved themselves very nicely." He turned his horse to ride back, and paused.

"But look!" he said, raising a knotty finger. "Old Wambli-gi has got a new scalp at his belt—a yellow one—that he better keep out of sight!"

GOODNIGHT-LOVING TRAIL

Maverick Factory

by NOEL M. LOOMIS

HODGE SNYDER CANTERED FORWARD ON HIS BIG BLAZE-FACED BAY.
His foreman, Rush Manso, saw him coming, and pulled his rangy
grullo around to wait for him. The horse cropped at the buffalo
grass while Rush leaned back against the cantle, studying Hodge
with gray eyes. "Whyn't you come up the other side of the herd,"
Rush asked, "and stay out of the dirt?"

Hodge looked back at the trail herd—three thousand steers,
some cows, and a few bulls—that wound like a long snake's trail
back into the middle of the heavy dust cloud. Hodge shook his
head wearily. "Take a chance on spooking a mixed herd? Not me.
We had enough trouble getting 'em strung out after Vogel's
outfit choused 'em up last night." He yawned. "Three nights in a
row without sleep—and mostly on account of Vogel." He shook

his head hard and forced his red-rimmed eyes open. "Anyway, the boys on the drag have been eating dirt all morning. Who am I to be fussy?"

Rush was a tall, skinny fellow who seemed all bones and angles. He crossed his arms on the flat saddlehorn, and his long bones seemed to run together and relax. "Well, it's good dirt—the best in southeastern Colorado."

"There'll be more before we get to Cheyenne," said Hodge. He looked worried. Hodge always looked a little worried. He was a big man with light brown hair and an odd scar like a worry crease that ran straight across the bridge of his nose.

"How're they coming back there?" asked Rush, pulling the grullo's head up out of the grass.

"Not so good," said Hodge. "When we got straightened out this morning we found four cows with burned feet."

"Burned?"

"Seared with a running-iron," Hodge said shortly.

Rush tried to whistle through his dust-covered lips. "Then Vogel *was* running a maverick factory back along the Apishapa."

"He was," Hodge said positively. "Every one of them cows had a heavy bag, but no calf. Vogel took the calves and burned the cow's feet so they couldn't follow."

"What are you doing with 'em now?"

"We wrapped their feet in rawhide, and we're doing the best we can."

The front end of the herd was spreading out. Rush pushed the grullo in a little closer to keep them together and moving forward.

"It's going to be a long day," said Hodge. "I should have watched my own beef instead of chasing cow thieves with the vigilantes."

"It was the right move," said Rush. "Vogel's gang has got to be broken up before we can stop cattle stealing in this country."

Hodge was riding alongside. He scraped his dry lips with the back of a hairy hand. "Wish we'd got Vogel himself."

Rush caught the eye of the man riding the left point. He threw his arm in a circle and pumped his fist a couple of times toward the north. The point-rider moved in toward the herd a little.

Rush said, over his shoulder. "You'll get another crack at Vogel. There'll be grass along the Apishapa next spring, and you'll be bringing another bunch of cows up from the Concho."

"Maybe." Hodge hazed back a big one-horned steer that came trotting forward out of the dust, head high. "Only one thing," he said. "I wish they hadn't hung them two men of Vogel's to that light-pole in Pueblo."

Rush turned halfway around in the saddle. "I thought it was providential," he said. "There ain't no piñon in the country tall enough to hang a man from."

The scar on Hodge's nose became a definite worry line. "Thelma is coming in to Pueblo in the morning, and that pair of buzzard bait is the first thing she'll see." He took a deep breath. "She might get an idea the West is uncivilized."

"Proves what I said all along," said Rush. "You should have sold out, taken your traps back to Kansas City, and gone into business with Thelma's old man."

"Who—me?" Hodge asked indignantly.

"But," Rush went on, "as long as you didn't do that, and as long as you went and fixed it up for her to come out here with you, mebbe you better have some faith in her. Women ain't like cows, you know. They got sense— Hi, you! Get back in line, there, you one-horned, mouse-colored maverick!" He yelled back at Hodge as he pushed the steer into line. "That's the critter that led the stampede last night."

Hodge nodded absently.

What *would* Thelma, with her fine manners and her fancy clothes, think of this country? To Hodge and to Rush and to ten thousand others, it was God's real country—but would Thelma see it that way?

Hodge rode out ahead to check the trail. He should have told Thelma more about what it was really like in Colorado Territory. He should have told her about the drought and parched grass along the Apishapa; the long, dusty trail days ahead on the way to new grass; the maverick factory, and men like Vogel.

But he hadn't. Like a moon-eyed calf, he hadn't been able to think about anything but Thelma since the day he'd gone in to K.C. with his last trainload of beef. He had seen her there at the stockyards with her father, sitting side-saddle, just outside the dust around the cowpens, looking as fresh and untouched as a sunflower loaded with dew on a summer morning.

Somehow he had supposed she was used to being around cows and the dirt they kicked up and the smell they made, their incessant lowing and bawling and blatting. But now it seemed plain that he had assumed too much. Thelma had never been closer to the cattle country than the unloading pens. But by the time he'd found that out, he'd been like a dry steer headed for water; all he worried about was getting her to say yes.

But now, in front of the herd and out of the dust, he saw things a little more clearly. Maybe the dust fogged a man's mind as well as his eyes. He remembered, now, little things Thelma had done and said. Any fool who could swing a barn-sized loop would have known she was persnickety as an Eastern buggy-horse.

A man who's spent his life in the cow country should have known that—but in Kansas City he was like an old mossyhorn that'd been dug out of the black chaparral for the first time. He hadn't seen an unattached white woman in four years, and there *she* was, sitting very straight and proud. Her hair was a dark red in the sun, and on top of it was perched a small white hat with two deep blue ribbons hanging down her back. The ribbons were the color of her eyes, which were blue and shining and laughing as she talked to her father and the brand inspectors and commission men gathered around her.

Then she saw Hodge staring openly at her. She looked over the size of him, and gradually worked her way to his eyes, and then for an instant her eyes were still shining but not laughing, as if she had just caught her breath. She didn't smile at him as she had been smiling at the others, but turned away hurriedly. She had smiled later, but it was a private smile and meant for nobody else but him. It wasn't a gay smile like the ones she had been throwing around the loading pens, but a quiet smile that said, "I'm yours, Hodge. I'll go with you always."

Pulling out through the deep sagebrush around a butte that stuck out like a giant bear's paw, Hodge watched the country ahead, but his mind wasn't on it. The worry crease deepened between his eyes. Thelma had been game, but he should have had sense enough to tell her what to expect. It wasn't until he got back into the cow country that he began to see things. There was a girl who had lived all her life in the cities, and always had servants, and even a boy to saddle her horse. Why hadn't he told her that out in this country a woman would have to saddle her own horse? He shook his head. He was as nervous as that one-horned steer.

They crossed the Arkansas and bedded down the herd a couple of miles beyond, along in the middle of the afternoon. It was hot, and they put the herd on high ground. Hodge turned the blaze-faced bay into the remuda. He picked out a big smoky horse for himself, and a smaller calico for Thelma.

"We ain't got a side-saddle," Rush reminded him.

"I'll buy one in Pueblo," said Hodge.

"I'm going out after a couple of stray buffalo I saw back there along the river," Rush said. He added slyly, "Reckon you'll need any help in Pueblo?"

"When I needed help," Hodge said morosely, "was in Kansas City before I talked her into marrying me."

"It'd have been easier," said Rush, "if you had brung her on out here before you had time to think about it. But no, you had to build a new house and all—and now look what happened. The house sets back there on the Apishapa, but there ain't no grass for the critters, and you're on the move, and she'll have to set up housekeeping in a covered wagon on a drive."

Hodge's jaw worked. "It's bad enough," he said, "without you driving me around the snubbing post."

Rush straightened. He seemed at last to feel pity. "Where'll we meet you?"

"I'll pick you up some time in the morning," Hodge said, and swung the smoky horse toward Pueblo. "Watch that one-horned steer," he called back. "That son will try to spook again along toward morning."

"I'll watch," said Rush. "So long."

"So long."

In Pueblo, Hodge went to the barber shop and had a bath and got shaved. Then he went out and had a drink. He said to the bartender, "Why don't they cut down those two from that light-pole?"

The bartender was a short, heavy man, with skin the color of old leather and dyed black hair parted in the middle. "I hear the vigilantes wanted to leave 'em there for a warning," he said, wiping up a ring of whisky on the bar.

Hodge looked at the bartender without seeing him. "Vogel doesn't know how to take a hint," he said heavily. He emptied the small glass and cracked it down on the bar. "Better make it two," he said. "There's a lot of dust between here and Cheyenne."

He threw out a goose, then half turned and watched the bodies swaying from the pole. He said uneasily, "It wouldn't be quite so noticeable if the wind wasn't blowing so hard." He killed his drink and looked again from under his big eyebrows. He felt ashamed to be looking. "The one on this side keeps twisting and untwisting," he said.

The bartender sprayed change from the gold eagle in a semi-circle on the bar. "Good thing the wind does blow," he said. "It keeps the buzzards from settling down."

"It's right where the stage comes in," Hodge muttered.

"No use working yourself into a state over a couple of cow thieves," the bartender said.

Hodge bought a side-saddle for the paint, and left both horses at the livery stable. He used a broom on his boots. They were pretty wrinkled around the ankles and beginning to wear through, but they were comfortable, and he thought he'd wait until he got the herd to Wyoming before he spread himself.

He bought a red wool shirt, and when he got that on, and installed a beaded white buckskin vest he'd bought from an Oglala up in Nebraska a couple of years before, he began to feel pretty dressed up. The big brim of his old hat was getting a little floppy, but it would still keep the rain from running down onto his clothes. He filled the pockets of his vest with sack tobacco and papers and matches, keeping one eye on the time. Then he went to the Drovers Hotel to wait for the stage.

It was midafternoon when the Concord rumbled in from the east. The driver, a man with a huge mustache and an embroidered silk waistcoat and a red taffeta muffler, pulled the six horses to a stop. The brakeman took over the reins and wrapped them around the post, while the driver stepped down grandly and headed for the saloon.

The side door of the coach opened, and Thelma appeared. The afternoon sun made her hair richly red, as he had remembered it, but this time she was wearing a light blue hat with white ribbons. She gathered her gray taffeta skirts under her and stepped down into Hodge's arms. He held her for a moment, and neither of them could say anything.

"Your baggage, Mrs. Snyder." The brakeman handed down a bonnet-trunk. Then he saw Hodge holding her. "You're Hodge Snyder, ain't you? Gimme a hand with this zinc-top?"

They carried her luggage to the hotel porch. "We might have to leave some of your stuff here for a little while," Hodge said uneasily.

Her slim, cool hand was inside his arm. She looked up at him. "Is something wrong, Hodge?"

"Grass dried up in the valley," he said shortly, "and we had to move a herd north. You could have stayed on the ranch, but it would be kind of lonely, and there's still a few wild Indians now and then—"

"Of course, I'll go with you," she said. "When do we start?"

"We've already started. When the grass begins to dry up, you can't wait." He pointed. "The herd is over there, just south of the road you come in on. We'll catch up to them in the morning." He steered her into the hotel. "We'll have supper here, and you can get freshened up a little when we go to our room."

He felt the reassuring pressure of her slim, strong fingers. "Don't be scared," she said. "We've been married months, you know."

Hodge said, "Me scared?"

They were in the room then. He said, "I'll open the window. It'll be warm in here."

She had taken off her hat and put the hatpins through it. Now her blue eyes shone as she said, "I'll help you."

The window came up suddenly, and Thelma shrieked. "What's that?" she cried.

Hodge swore at himself. The two cattle thieves swung from the crossarm of the light-pole, right across the street from their room, silhouetted by the setting sun. The right one was turning and twisting.

Hodge stammered. "I—"

"Are those *men?*"

"They stole cattle," Hodge said defensively.

"Your cattle?"

He looked away, pulling in his lips between his teeth.

"Then you helped hang them?" she insisted.

"I—well—it was the vigilantes."

She looked again at the swinging figures and shuddered. "Isn't that murder?" she asked finally.

Hodge was miserable. "Some might think so—if they didn't know how it is out here."

"You never told me it was like this," she said accusingly.

He couldn't answer. This was what he had been afraid of.

She sat down on the bed. Her ivory face was pale. She didn't look at Hodge.

Finally he picked up his hat. "I've got to see about some supplies," he said clumsily, and lumbered out.

He went down the street to the bar and had two quick ones. The bartender looked at him curiously. "Your wife come in this afternoon?"

Hodge nodded, staring into his glass.

The bartender was twisting a corkscrew into a fresh bottle. "She going with you in the morning?"

"Yes, I reckon."

"I hear," the bartender said after a pause, "that Vogel is some put out because you short-handed him."

Hodge glanced at the man, then studied his glass. He looked around him. The saloon was filling up. Hodge shifted his six-shooter belt a little.

"You hear any talk about him heading off my drive?"

"Can't say that I have, but if Vogel was mad at me I'd be ready for anything."

Hodge stared at him. He bought a bottle of whisky and took it with him to the hotel. He sat down in a corner of the lobby and swung out the cylinder on his pistol. There were five cartridges in it, and one empty chamber for the hammer. He swung the cylinder back into place and shoved the pistol into its holster.

Then he started in on the bottle. He thought of Thelma's fine clothes and the lovely picture she made, and with every drink he felt more and more that he had played the fool by bringing her out to Colorado without telling her what it would be like. His guilt settled on him, and he didn't have the nerve to face her. . . .

They rode out the next morning. Vogel's men were still swinging from the pole, but Thelma said nothing. Hodge looked straight ahead.

Thelma rode the side-saddle easily, and they caught up with the herd about the middle of the morning. At first it was a long, rolling dust cloud, then presently they passed the cook's wagon, which was eating dirt as usual. Hodge led Thelma around the west side and out of the dust. He caught up with the drags. "How're the sore-footed cows coming?" he asked.

"We got two in the wagon there—the wagon you brought for you and the missus. The third one is getting along pretty good. The other one we shot."

Thelma spoke up. "What's the matter with their feet?"

"Those men you saw—or some of their bunch—used a hot iron on the cow's feet to keep them from following their calves," Hodge said gruffly.

Thelma swallowed hard.

"And that ain't all," said a hard voice behind them.

Hodge turned. Rush was riding up, with a small calf over the grullo's withers. Rush had fire in his eyes. He took hold of the calf's nose and its lower jaw and pulled its mouth open. "See that?"

Hodge glanced. He knew what to expect. But Thelma moved closer. "What happened to it?" she asked.

"This one here," Rush said, "got its tongue split with a bowie knife."

Thelma gasped. Rush rode up to the wagon where Thelma was supposed to start housekeeping, and lowered the calf inside the tailboard with the two sick cows.

Thelma pulled up beside Hodge. "I don't understand," she said.

Hodge pulled his floppy hatbrim down harder. "It's like this," he said. "A calf is always branded with the brand of its mother —but only at roundup time, in the spring or in the fall. In the meantime, any calf that gets separated permanently from its mother becomes a maverick—an unbranded critter, and anybody who tosses a rope around its neck can throw his own brand on it. Generally a calf will run with its mother till roundup time, but if men like Vogel get into a herd and cut the calves' tongues so they can't suck, and burn the mothers' feet so they can't follow the calves, pretty soon you've got a bunch of mavericks. That's why we call it a maverick factory. Vogel and his men keep an eye on the calves, and as soon as the calves leave their mothers for good, they cut them out of the herd and brand them."

"And that's legal?" Thelma asked.

Hodge pulled his hatbrim still lower. "Not exactly legal, but it doesn't leave any evidence. When there's no mother to claim her own calf, anybody who finds that calf has a right to brand it."

"In other words," said Thelma, "you've always depended on the presence of the mother as proof of ownership."

"That's it," he said.

They rode on to the point. This was Rush's day on the windward side, but he didn't relieve the point-man right away. He pulled alongside Hodge and said in a low voice, "You see that party up ahead?"

Hodge nodded, his heavy hatbrim flopping.

"They're aiming to cut our trail," said Rush.

Hodge took a slow breath. "You think so?"

"They been up there by that clump of piñons for the last half hour. Now they're riding out to meet us."

Hodge shifted his gunbelt.

"You better check that thing," Rush said under his breath. "You used it the other night."

Hodge looked at Thelma. She was studying the riders far ahead. Hodge said quietly to Rush, "I checked it last night. You stay with the point—and keep the herd moving." He rode the big smoky horse out ahead. Thelma pulled up alongside him, and he glanced at her.

"You better stay back with Rush," he said.

"If there's going to be trouble," she said, "I want to be with you."

He looked closer at her then, and for the first time he saw her red eyes. He felt bewildered.

"All right," he said, "if you've got to come, you've got to come. But this may not be nice."

She did not answer, but spurred the calico pony alongside the smoky.

The riders were coming diagonally to intersect the path of the herd. There were five of them, and one wore a white hat. That would be Vogel, Hodge knew.

Hodge picked up his pace, but Thelma held her place at his left rear. He looked back. Rush was thirty feet behind him. Hodge turned back to the front. There wasn't any use of all of them getting killed, but he might have known Rush wouldn't hang back.

The leader of the five men cut Hodge's trail. He was a gaunt man with black hat and long, drooping mustaches. Hodge pulled up to the gaunt man's right, so his pistol-hand would not be hidden. The gaunt man said in a Yankee nasal voice, "I'm Beeson. One-eyed Turtle brand. Are you Hodge Snyder?"

"I am." Hodge's quick glance found the five men all well heeled.

Beeson's sharp eyes looked over Hodge's shoulder. "Them your cattle?"

"They are."

Rush pulled in at Hodge's side. Three men moved up around Beeson. Vogel, a dark-skinned, slick hombre in his big white hat, stayed back.

"You aiming to go north?"

"Straight north to Colorado City and Cheyenne."

Beeson's eyes settled on the crease across the bridge of Hodge's nose. "I've got a lot of stuff ahead of you."

"That's all right," said Hodge. "You can look for your brand after we get through you—long as you don't chouse up the herd."

But the gaunt man didn't move. "They're Texas cattle, aren't they?"

Hodge nodded, watching Vogel.

The gaunt man's voice became unexpectedly loud. "Don't trail your critters through my range," he said. "I don't aim to have three or four thousand head come down with Texas fever."

Hodge leaned hard on his saddlehorn with both hands. He fastened his eyes on Beeson. "There's no Texas fever in these cattle," he said. "They wintered on the Apishapa."

Beeson's eyes narrowed. "That ain't what I heard. I heard these cattle came straight from the Concho country."

"You wanta see the papers?"

"I don't trust no papers," Beeson said. "I got good, graded-up American cattle on my range, and I don't aim to have it contaminated by any Texas critters."

"The papers will show—"

"You could forge the papers. I meant what I said. You ain't driving them Texas cattle over my range."

Hodge began to tighten up. "How long you been here, Beeson?"

"Three months."

"You know that man behind you in the white hat?"

"He warned me about these cattle. That makes him a friend of mine."

Hodge raised up in his saddle and found Vogel's eyes. "He's a horse thief," he said harshly.

Vogel shrugged. He was waiting, Hodge knew, for Beeson to do his killing.

Beeson's voice was high. "You got pointers back there. Start riding in a circle."

Hodge stared at him. "I told you these cattle are clean. We're comin' through, Beeson."

The gaunt man started to reach for his pistol.

"Leave it be!" Hodge ordered, and Beeson's mouth dropped open as he stared into the muzzle of Hodge's big .44. The three men around him stopped in the act of drawing.

Rush's calm voice came from Hodge's right. "Control yourselves, gents. It's mighty unhealthy, reaching for hardware sudden-like."

"Now," said Hodge, "ride out one at a time, with your hands up, and don't make any quick moves. You, Beeson—you better go first!"

The gaunt man's thin lips were in a tight line. He moved his horse forward without lowering his hands. Hodge reached for his pistol, but froze as Vogel said sharply, "Drop those irons in the dirt, you two!"

Hodge stared for an instant. Vogel had maneuvered himself into a spot where he was covering both Hodge and Rush with two pistols. Hodge hesitated, but he had no choice. From where he was, he couldn't get a decent shot at Vogel. His jaws were hard together, and his grip on the butt of the .44 began to loosen.

But a woman's voice came from his left. "Drop those pistols, Mr. Vogel."

For an instant Hodge didn't comprehend. Then he saw that

Thelma, almost hidden by his own body, was pointing the muzzle of a nickel-plated derringer at Vogel.

That could end only one way. Hodge whomped the big smoky in both ribs and charged into Vogel's face. He scattered Beeson's men, and before Vogel could get a good shot, Hodge was in the clear.

Vogel's right pistol roared, and Hodge caught a slug in the thigh. Then his .44 exploded. For an instant Vogel looked surprised. He shot again, but it went into the dirt. He tried to raise his hand. Hodge fired again. Vogel seemed to hesitate, and Hodge poured lead into him until Vogel fell stiffly sidewise out of the saddle. He hit the ground headfirst. His legs pulled up once and then he rolled over, dead.

Hodge turned his horse. Rush was covering Beeson and his men. Hodge loaded his pistol while he talked to Beeson. "This here Vogel was running a maverick factory down below the Arkansas," he told Beeson. "You want me to take you back to Pueblo to prove it?"

Beeson looked at Vogel's body. Beeson's mustaches drooped lower. He looked back up as Hodge swung the cylinder into place. "I reckon I'll take your word for it," Beeson said, staring at the pistol, "if you let me see your bill of sale."

Hodge fished a wad of papers out of his pocket with his left hand. He kept the .44 in his right. He separated the papers with his thumb and two fingers, and held one out to Beeson. "Here's a bill of sale on twenty-eight hundred and six steers that came from South Texas last summer. The cows and bulls are Colorado stock. That satisfy you?"

Beeson looked at the papers. Hodge's herd was drawing close now. The air was filling with dust and the bawling of thirsty cattle. Beeson folded the papers and handed them back. "Maybe we got taken in by a slick talker."

"That's the way it looks from here," Hodge said flatly.

Beeson sounded weary. "All right."

"You satisfied?" asked Hodge.

"I'm satisfied. Go ahead." He gestured to the north with a thin hand. "But if your cattle leave any fever," he said harshly "you can figure on seeing me again."

Hodge grinned. "We'll figure on that," he said, and chucked his pistol in the holster.

Beeson and his men rode off slowly. Beeson glanced curiously at Vogel's body, but he looked up and saw Hodge watching him, and did not stop.

The herd was pulling up on them. Hodge rode out ahead. Then he turned to Thelma, his eyes narrowed. "Where in thundering blazes did you get that shiny little piece of hardware?" he asked.

She looked up at him, smiling in amusement. "You didn't tell me about Colorado yourself," she said, "so I read about it in the Kansas Pacific guidebook. It said most people in Colorado go armed by custom, so I bought this pistol in Kansas City. It isn't very big, but the man said it would be effective at close range. Besides, Father didn't think a pistol like yours would look good on me."

Hodge stared at her. The laughter in her blue eyes was melting him like butter in the sun. He moved the smoky toward her. Then he remembered the herd behind them. It could wait. There'd be a lot of trails for him and Thelma.

Rush had pulled into place on the point and sent his relief man back to the swing. Thelma pulled closer to Hodge. "You're a strange man," she said. "Last night you were afraid of a woman who weighs less than a hundred and twenty pounds, but today you pulled a pistol on four men at once, and then you rode square into a killer."

Hodge licked the dust from his dry lips. "Well, I—"

Rush rode up. "You want somebody to bury him?" he asked.

Hodge nodded.

"I'm glad you shot him," Thelma said, and shuddered. "It saved hanging him."

Hodge looked at her. She was crying. He wondered if she was going to faint. He started to put his arm around her, and then he felt the wound in his thigh. His right boot was full of blood. He leaned over, and things went suddenly black. . . .

When he woke up he was in the wagon along with the two sore-footed cows and the split-tongued calf. He raised his head. The leg of his pants had been split and his thigh bandaged. The wagon was jerking along over the buffalo grass. He realized that his head was on Thelma's lap and her cool hand was on his forehead. Rush rode up from somewhere and looked in the back end of the wagon. "Like I always said," he told Hodge, "if things get out of hand you better count on the woman."

Hodge looked up into Thelma's face. He noted the little valleys of dust alongside her nose. "I'm counting," he said to her, "but you better let me have that little cannon before it hurts somebody."

"You are in no position to be disarming a defenseless woman," she said.

Hodge looked at her eyes; they were very tender. He took a deep breath and relaxed. "Anyway, I'm no maverick," he said. "You've got your brand on me for good."

Trail Song

by BENNETT FOSTER

Come along boys and listen to my tale,
I'll tell you of my troubles on the old
Chisholm Trail,
Co-ma ti yi you-pe, you-pe ya, you-pe ya,
Co-ma ti yi you-pe, you-pe ya.

CHISHOLM TRAIL, WESTERN TRAIL, ANY TRAIL—IT MADE NO DIFFERence to Dan McKee. Dan couldn't recollect the day he was too young to follow after cattle; he couldn't recall the time he wasn't with a wagon.

Dan thought he was someplace around twenty-one or two; he didn't know for sure. He reckoned his folks were dead, but he wasn't certain. Once he rode clear to East Texas to see some people named McKee but it turned out they were no kin. Dan's idea was to stand on his own feet and look the boss and every other straight in the eye. He wasn't the only kithless, kinless man in Texas.

In the spring of '82 Dan went north with Sam Cashmole's trail outfit. When Dan hired on in Sanantone he and the boss had a talk.

"I figure," Cashmole said, "that any man who can't put enough strays in the herd to make three times his wages ain't worth his salt. That's the way I figure."

"That used to be so," Dan said, "but there's a trail cutter at

Doan's Crossing and another up by the Nations. You can't take
no strays through them. They pare a herd down to its road brand."

"I know that," Cashmole agreed, "but we ain't goin' by Doans
or the Nations. We're goin' north of Fort Sumner and through
Trinchera Pass over the old Goodnight route. There's lots of little
ranchos that way and them Mexicans never had nerve enough to
cut a herd. Unless we have real bad luck we ought to do all right.
Want to gamble?"

"I reckon," Dan agreed.

Cashmole's trail crew received their cattle in Kendall county.
They burned the Hackamore road brand across the noses of the
big, many-colored steers, and when the count had been agreed
on and a settlement made, the men who had tendered the cattle
gave them a full day's help to start. After that it was up to the trail
outfit. They went northwest through the mesquite and every night
for the first week double guards were put around the cattle and
half the remuda was hobbled and guarded, too. Then, with the
steers shaken down to trailing, they entered a more open country
and precautions were relaxed.

Dan McKee and Church Fynas rode the points. The two of
them spread their bed together and stood last guard together. In
the morning, when the cattle left the bedground, Dan and Church
were on hand to drift them in the right direction. On the drive,
they bent the leaders according to Cashmole's orders, and when
native cattle tried to join up, it was Dan and Church who loped
out and threw them off. Behind those two the others rode in
swing and drag, pinching the herd down to size, sacking up the
corners, bringing up the rear. The cook drove the wagon, off to
right or left as the wind indicated, keeping out of the dust, and
the horse wrangler brought the remuda along. There were twelve
men, a hundred horses, two thousand cattle and a wagon moving
across the plains and for awhile they were scrupulously honest.

The wrangler kid got homesick.

"When I get home," the wrangler said, "I'm goin' to sleep a month. My maw's got the best feather beds in Texas and I'm goin' to lay down on about two of 'em an' get up when I'm ready."

"You're gettin' the idea, kid," said Dan McKee. "Trail hands learn to do their sleepin' in the winter."

"An' this water," the wrangler kid continued, "ain't fit to drink. Nothin' but alkali. I had the belly cramps all day. Down home we got a spring and a spring-house where maw keeps the milk and butter. The water's just as sweet!"

Supper was long done and the fire was dying. The first guard men were circling the cattle and Sam Cashmole had ridden out to prowl around the herd and see how it was resting. Church Fynas sat up on his bed.

"My folks have got a spring-house on their place," Church said. "We put the buttermilk there to cool after we've churned. There ain't nothin' better than fresh, cold butttermilk with little specks of butter floatin' in it."

Across the fire Ben Sparn and Steve Youngalls paused in their pitch game. "We had a dug well," Steve said. "Thirty foot deep and the water cold as ice. I could have used some of that today."

"Branch water." Ben Sparn spoke thoughtfully. "A creek run right through our place. Us kids swum in it."

"We'll drink water out of cow tracks this trip," said Dan McKee, "and like it, too. This water ain't so bad."

"Eggs," said the wrangler kid, his thoughts passing from drink to food. "I ain't ate a egg in I don't know when. Maw used to fry me half a dozen and dish 'em up with home cured ham."

"Come out of it, kid!" Dan ordered. "Do you want to get the cook down on you? You hired out for a tough hand; if you're homesick, why did you take the job?"

"Blamed if I know," the wrangler kid answered, his candid eyes on Dan. "Wasn't you ever homesick."

"I guess not," said Dan, and laughed.

Next night, fifteen miles along the way, Dan McKee sat down beside the wrangler kid. "Get the cook to give you some soda an' mix it with tallow," he advised. "Take a little of that and this alkali water won't gripe you so bad. Whereabouts do you live, kid?"

"Up by New Braunfels. We got a farm."

"Tell me about it." Dan rolled a cigarette and smoked and listened while the wrangler kid talked.

> *Last night I was on guard and the leaders broke the ranks,*
> *I hit my horse down the shoulders and I spurred him in*
>   *the flanks!*
> *The wind began to blow and the rain began to fall,*
> *Hit looked, by grab, like we was goin' to lose 'em all!*

North of Yellowhouse, a brisk and businesslike man, carrying authority for the CV and other brands, met the Hackamore herd. Sam Cashmole made him welcome, fed him at the wagon, and proffered a horse. The stranger needed no horse for he led a spare and, after dinner, worked the herd, bunched and held for his convenience. The trail cutter was complimentary when he had finished.

"As clean a bunch as I've worked this year," he announced. "You must of been extra careful, Cashmole."

"We've tried to be," Sam Cashmole answered piously. "Better stay the night with us."

The trail cutter spoke his thanks but refused the offer. When he was gone, Cashmole addressed the crew. "Tomorrow," he said, "we'll be out of Goodnight's country. I wouldn't want to start anything with that old man around. Two-three days and we'll be across the line. After that you can turn loose your wolf."

Next day the route led straight west and so for two days following, then curved north again. Now, when native cattle appeared, curious and eager to join the marching ranks of steers, Dan and Church rode out as usual. Some they drove off, but others—cattle that offered contrast in neither size nor sex—they added to the herd. Not many; just a few. Any trail herd was bound to collect some strays and if Sam Cashmole's Hackamores arrived at market with more than ordinary—why then, who would question them?"

"Just don't be greedy, boys," Cashmole advised. "There ain't no use in bein' reckless."

The Hackamore herd passed well north of Fort Sumner and, reaching the Pecos, followed up the stream. Then, leaving the river, they entered upon a broad and grass-grown plain, flanked on either side by broken country. So far the march had been uneventful, the steers handling like well drilled troops; but now, daily, storm clouds appeared to north and west and were eyed apprehensively.

"Makin' bag," Dan McKee stated. "It wouldn't surprise me none if the boss didn't call a rain guard tonight."

Sam Cashmole called the rain guard, splitting the crew in half. As part of the second guard, Dan and Church turned in but not to sleep. They watched lightning flicker along the horizon and heard the thunder roll. Big raindrops splatted down, the wind blew steadily and, suddenly, the rain was a torrent.

"Here's hell!" Dan shouted above the wind. "Come on!"

They fought their way to their night horses, mounted and started to the cattle. Before they reached the herd, they knew that it was moving.

A figure loomed up beside Dan and Ben Sparn's voice came to him. "They ain't runnin'. They just got up an' walked away. We couldn't hold 'em."

"Stay with 'em!" Dan called and, turning with the wind, went with the cattle. He was ahead of them; he planned to stay ahead.

Toward morning, the rain thinned, then ceased. The dawn crept over the hills like a dripping veil. As the light grew, Dan saw that he was in broken country, and when the sun came up, a clean and new-washed world lay all about him. He stopped his night horse on a ridge and took his bearings.

Behind him the flats showed in the sun, dotted here and there with clumps of cattle; to right and left the ridges fell away and before him was a valley. A stream ran down it to the east, limpid and silvery between cottonwoods, a hay meadow glistened with its wetness and there were other fields, smaller and planted in rows. From a house, hidden by rising land, a thread of smoke rose up and, down below apiece, were six big steers.

Dan McKee was wet and cold but did not notice his discomfort. He drank it in, the fields, the stream, the rolling, grass-grown ridges. Here, so his cowman's eyes remarked, was cattle land. Hay from the vega to feed the winter horses, breaks and cedars for protection and grass over all outdoors. He rode on down.

The house with the smoking chimney was in a fold of ground. There were cottonwoods for shade, a well with curb and pulley, a monstrous woodpile and a set of pole corrals. As Dan arrived a man stepped out and a woman peered from the door. A boy came from the pens toward the woodpile and Dan drew rein, speaking his greeting gravely and in Spanish. He was, he said, looking for cattle that had drifted during the night.

The grizzled man listened, nodding his head in understanding. He had seen a few cattle, doubtless his visitor had seen them too. Coffee was ready and an invitation was issued. Dan got down and tied his horse; the boy had carried in an armload of wood and the scent of frying meat was almost more than a hungry man could bear. Dan gave his name and the grizzled man shook hands and tipped his hat politely. He was Blas Aragon, he said and, shivering in the cold and damp, Dan followed him.

The house was adobe, its walls full two feet thick. A girl, kneeling at the hearth, sprang up as the men entered. Blas spoke the introductions naming his wife, Duvina, his daughter, Filepita, his son, Jaime. Coffee steamed in a cup, the meat was crisp fried steak and there were hot tortillas. Filepita—"Fia" her brother called her—waited on Dan McKee. Her hair was black as a midnight sky, long lashes shielded her dark eyes, her cheeks were flushed, her mouth was a full-lipped, red-ripe menace. About eighteen, Dan judged. It was hard to tell.

'Fia had a question. Had Senor McKee seen a steer, a gray steer, three years old, branded with a Spanish A and with white horns, black tipped?

Dan shook his head and Blas Aragon laughed. The steer was 'Fia's pet, he said, she had raised it from a calf after the cow died. El Topo, the mole, she called the steer.

"He will eat tortillas from my hand," 'Fia added, "tamales, too, the husks and all. *Por favor, Senor,* if you see El Topo will you drive him back? He stays about the house. Sometimes he wanders, but never before has he stayed away so long."

Gravely, Dan promised that should he see El Topo he would turn him back. Then, having spoken thanks for food and warmth, he mounted and rode. On the slope he collected the six steers, all Hackamores and, farther on among the ridges, found eight head more. Driving these, he reached the flats and met Church Fynas with another drive.

"I got a dozen," Church reported. "We were ahead of 'em, Dan. I think we got the ones that went the farthest."

"I think you're right," Dan agreed. "What's that you got?" He pointed to a gray steer, its white horns black tipped.

"That's a stray." Church grinned all across his beard-stubbled face. "Got a little Spanish A on him and not another mark. Ain't he a dandy? Looks like a mouse."

"More like a mole." Dan returned Church's grin. "El Topo. Let's take 'em on. We got to change horses and work them little pockets out."

They took their drive on. To north and south they saw other
cattle and west of them was a band of horses.

"The kid's got the remuda anyhow," Church said. "He didn't
lose 'em. Looks like he was headed for the wagon."

By mid-morning the Hackamore crew had help in gathering
their scattered steers. A man named Linder, accompanied by four
riders, arrived at the wagon. Cross VL was Linder's brand and he
ran on the flats, between the broken countries. Steadily, on fresh
horses, the Hackamores and Cross VLs pushed cattle into a herd.
By evening time Sam Cashmole estimated that he had most of
his steers.

"And some of your stuff, too, of course," he said to Linder.
"We'll make a circle in the morning, then work the herd and get
yours out. We got some strays with us, naturally, but we know
them." He looked at Linder narrowly.

"I ain't interested in nothin' but Cross VLs," Linder announced.
"What strays you got are your business. I wouldn't mind if you
picked up every cow in the Trementina."

"The Trementina?" Dan McKee queried.

"The country over east," Linder said, impatiently. "Nothin' but
Mexicans. Them and me don't get along too good."

"Have they been stealin' from you?" Cashmole asked.

"I just moved in here," Linder answered, "an' they ain't had a
chance. I rode over there an' told 'em if I had any trouble I
wouldn't send for no sheriff." His face was grim. "Closest sheriff's
at Raton anyhow an' that's a hundred miles. I told 'em . . ."

Dan McKee turned away. It was an old story he had heard
before. Little men held down a country; then somebody—somebody bigger and tougher than they were—brought in cattle. Dan
knew how the story ended. Linder would run his bluff and after
a time the breaks as well as the flats would be Cross VL.

That night, when Dan took his guard, the man he relieved
spoke a warning. "There's a gray steer hangin' out on the east

side of the herd. I had to turn him back four times. Better look out for him."

"I will," Dan promised.

Stray in the herd and the boss said to kill it,
So I shot him in the rump with the handle of a skillet.

The herd was worked next morning. Before noon, Linder declared himself satisfied and the Hackamores moved on. That night, when they bedded, El Topo took station at the south side of the herd and Church Fynas, noticing this, pitched a loop over the steer's head and tied him to a bush.

"You were just a little too anxious last night," Church said. "I'll tie you till we're out of your country."

At two o'clock, taking the last guard, Dan saw El Topo standing there with the rope around his neck. El Topo was looking south.

As the Hackamores moved on north the gray steer became one of the characters of the herd. He was gentle as a dog and had no fear of men, either on foot or horseback. Once, when wagon and herd were close, the steer wandered over and begged so plainly that the cook passed out a piece of bacon rind. El Topo chewed and slobbered rolling his eyes in ecstasy, and after that the first guard always roped him and tied him up. If they didn't he would haunt the wagon for awhile and then drift unobtrusively southward until caught and driven back.

"That gray steer," Church said, "is sure a homelover. He's in the drags all day and every night he's on the south side, lookin' back. He's homesick, I guess."

"Yes," said Dan, "he's homesick. I've been noticin'."

"You talk like you was sorry for him," the wrangler commented. "Wasn't you ribbin' me about bein' homesick awhile back? Didn't you ask me why I'd hired on if I was homesick?" With time the kid wrangler had grown bolder.

"You're a man," Dan said. "You could make up your own mind. El Topo never had a choice; we just brought him along."

That was the way Dan thought about it. El Topo had been given no choice and Dan felt sorry for the steer. And there was another way he felt; a way he could not describe. On last guard, in the lonesome morning hours, Dan saw El Topo yearning for the south and, as he rode his slow circle about the herd, it seemed to Dan that he could see the valley, too. There was the limpid stream between the cottonwoods, the rain-jeweled meadow, sparkling in the morning sun, the thread of smoke from the hidden house. Sometimes it seemed to Dan that he could smell the coffee and the frying meat, could hear the grave and courteous voice of Blas Aragon; could see 'Fia's eyes, anxious and dark beneath dark lashes, and her red lips forming a request.

Por favor, senor . . .

Then, when he looked at El Topo, Dan McKee felt like a dog, a sneaking, sheep killing dog.

The Hackamore trail herd crossed the Ratons and, two days north of Trinchera pass, Ben Sparn's horse fell with him. Ben had to ride the wagon for awhile and Dan took his place on first guard. Steve Youngalls, also on first guard, roped El Topo and staked him out. Dan, circling the cattle, saw the gray steer and stopped. El Topo was looking off toward the south through the dusk and, after a long minute, Dan rode up, removed the stake rope and coiled it. He went on and, meeting Steve, passed over the coil.

"You won't need this," Dan said gruffly.

Continuing his circle, Dan came to the spot where the gray steer had been. El Topo was gone and, the next morning, Dan spoke to Church.

"I turned El Topo loose last night," he announced awkwardly. "Seemed like he wanted to go home extra bad."

Church Fynas was Dan's friend. "Oh?" Church said.

"Yes," said Dan. "I'll settle with you for the steer when Sam pays off. An' Church—I'd just as soon you didn't say nothin' about it to the wrangler."

We hit Caldwell and we hit her on the fly,
We bedded down the cattle on a hill close by.

Sam Cashmole sold out in Pueblo. All the cattle, Hackamores and strays, too, went to one buyer, a man who supplied beef to the mines. Sam sold the wagon, the wagon mules and the remuda, making a clean sweep, and then paid off his hands. Each man had three month's wages coming as well as a prorata share in the strays and, with money in their pockets, they went to town. There were baths to take, shaves and haircuts to acquire; their clothing was worn out and, besides these necessities, Pueblo offered liquor, gambling and women. Dan and Church walked into the first saloon.

"I want to pay you for that gray steer," Dan said. "Sam got thirty-six dollars a round for the cattle. Here's what I owe you."

Church took the money, knowing better than to offer objection. "I wonder if that steer got home," he said. "Be kind of funny to find out, wouldn't it?"

"Yes, it would," Dan agreed and then, "You know, Church—I think I'll go an' see."

"Ride back all that ways?" Church was incredulous. "You're crazy, Dan. We're goin' home on the cars."

Steve Youngalls, Ben Sparn and the kid wrangler came into the saloon. They were gaudy in cheap new suits, their faces shown from close and recent shaving, they were feeling their liquor. They hailed Dan and Church boisterously, decreeing drinks for all.

"Where's Dan?" the kid wrangler demanded after a time. "I want to buy him a drink. Where is he? He was here a minute ago."

I'm on my best horse an' I'm goin' at a run,
I'm the quickest shootin' cowboy that ever pulled a gun!

Dan McKee rode south on a horse bought in Pueblo. He led a pack horse and his eyes were fixed on the horizon beyond which lay the Ratons. He rode eagerly, covering in hours those distances which had taken days on the drive north, and when he was below Trinchera pass he looked at every cowtrack, wondering if El Topo had made it.

Nearing the end of the trail, Dan slowed down. He reached the flats below the Trementina in mid-afternoon and could have completed his journey before sunset but an odd fancy held him. He wanted to crown the ridge and again in the morning sun look down upon the valley. Dan made camp, boiled coffee, and waited.

With false dawn he was up and saddling. When the morning wind blew chill, he entered the broken country and, as the sun came up, stopped on the ridge. The Trementina spread before him, the rolling grass-land, the limpid stream, it's cottonwoods yellow now that frost had come, the hay vega, still green, the little fields. Dan saw a thread of smoke against the eastern sky and rode on down.

A gray steer stood by the well at Blas Aragon's house. El Topo! Dan reined in and the steer looked at him inquiringly. Blas came to the door; there was recognition in his eyes and he spoke a greeting, bidding Dan dismount. Jaime came and led the horses away as Blas and Dan walked to the house. At the door, Blas paused and stepped aside.

¡Pas! he said. *Mi casa es suyo.*

It was an old word, spoken in courtesy. "Enter. My house is yours." Dan went in. Duvina was pouring coffee and 'Fia sprang up from beside the hearth. It was just as Dan remembered.

He spoke to Duvina. To 'Fia he said, "Your pet came home."

"Two weeks ago," 'Fia answered.

Jaime came in. He had put the horses in the pen, he said. Blas seated his guest and food was brought.

All the way south Dan McKee had ridden in anticipation, eager and expectant, of what he did not know. On the ridge, in the sunrise, it had bubbled in him, rising like heady wine. Now, when fulfillment should have come, the buoyancy was gone. Why, Dan wondered. Why?

He looked about him and in blank eyes read the answer. On his first visit he had been a stranger but he was welcome. Now he was not a stranger but the welcome was gone. That was why. Blas might say, "my house is yours", Jaime might care for the horses, Duvina might cook and 'Fia place food at his hand but these things were obligations to a guest. They did not want him. Why? Because of El Topo? Dan did not know.

The meal ended and Dan gave thanks for the food and arose. Outside the house there was a bench and above it, from the roof, thrifty Duvina had hung long curls of squash and melon to sundry. Dan sat on the bench and rolled a cigarette but his host refused tobacco; talk also. To Dan's conversational gambits Blas replied in monosyllables, closing each opening. The wind freed leaves from the cottonwoods and they fell in a golden shower. Dan McKee ground out his cigarette and stood up. He was, he said, just passing through; he was grateful and now he would ride on. Blas murmured polite and insincere objections and Dan went to the corrals.

Jaime had unsaddled and unpacked. Dan caught his bed horse and packed; he caught the other horse and saddled. He was a fool, he told himself; he didn't know what had brought him back to this country or what he had expected to find. Whatever it was, he surely hadn't found it. Anyhow he had his horses and his saddle and his bed; he had money in his pocket and a gun on his hip and what more did a man need? Or want, either? Dan tied his latigo with a final jerk.

Horses stopped, hidden from him by the house, and he heard men talking. Collecting reins and lead rope, Dan started for the gate. The voices lifted in anger and he let the horses go. When Dan rounded the corner of the house he saw Linder, a Cross VL rider that he recognized, and Blas Aragon.

"I told you I'd be over after that steer!" Linder's voice was loud and his face was red. "That's a Hackamore stray. I seen it when we helped 'em gather cattle!"

Any pretext, any little thing, seized on and magnified to make trouble. That was the way it was done. Bully and quarrel, push and shove, kill sometimes; crowd the other man and drive him out. Dan remembered Linder's words to Sam Cashmole. This was a chapter in the same old story and—relief flooded Dan—it was an explanation as well. The Aragons didn't know about El Topo; their coldness to Dan had been a reflection from their difficulties with the Cross VL. Dan had stepped into the backwash of resentment that Linder had aroused; it wasn't Dan the Aragons disliked, it was all *gringos*.

Blas stood with his back toward the house, facing the Cross VL men. He wasn't giving an inch; he didn't act a bit scared. Dan moved along the wall, getting into position. It was the same old story but this time there would be an added entry. Linder nor the rider nor Blas saw him arrive.

"Hello, Linder," Dan said.

He leaned against the wall, negligent, lounging, his thumb tucked into his belt, the picture of a man at ease. His voice was soft but his eyes were not, and from the way he stood and the way he looked, plain as plain, Dan was siding Blas Aragon. Three faces turned toward him and everybody stood still and kept still.

"Up kind of early, ain't you?" Dan continued.

Linder grunted like a man hit low. "Hello, McKee."

Dan pushed off from the wall. "That steer you're talkin' about belongs to Aragon," he said. "We picked it up by mistake. I've

come a considerable out of my way to see that it got home. It's
the girl's pet."

"Well," Linder said awkwardly, "I didn't know that. I was just
tryin' to do you fellers a favor." Confronted by one of his own
breed, a tougher member of the clan, Linder backed down.

The time to crowd a man was when you had him running. Dan
moved up beside Blas. "It looks to me," he drawled, "like maybe
you was tryin' to steal a steer. That's how it looks to me." Linder
had come to start trouble; Dan dumped trouble in his lap and
waited.

Now was the time. It started now or not at all. Dan watched
Linder and saw no trouble there. Linder looked away. He was
going to take it and Dan gave him a way out.

"Of course a man can be mistaken," he said.

"That's right." Linder spoke quickly with relief. "Anybody can
make a mistake. I didn't know about the steer."

"But you know now," Dan said. "Was there anything you
wanted to tell Aragon? He don't talk English much. Maybe I
could tell him for you."

"No," Linder answered. "No, there wasn't. We got to be goin'.
Come on, Pete."

The Cross VL men rode upvalley, climbed a ridge and were
gone. Dan moved, turning toward the corrals. Blas caught his
arm, protesting, stopping him.

"No! You are not to go! I will not let you go!"

'Fia and Jaime came from the house. From the door Duvina
urged her husband to bring their guest. 'Fia caught Dan's hand
and held it and El Topo, loafing around the corner of the house,
stopped and lifted his nose toward a dangling strip of melon.

¡Por favor! Blas said, his voice warm and urgent. ¡Pase! ¡Pase,
amigo!

Dan looked as Blas, reading the friendship written on his face.
He looked at Duvina and in her eyes there was a welcome and

a pleading. They needed him. Blas and Duvina needed Dan McKee. Dan realized their need and knew its cause. While Dan McKee dwelt in the Trementina it was safe, secure from Linder and all his kind. While Dan McKee was there the waters of the stream would flow undisturbed, the sun would shine, the rain would fall and, through sunshine, wind and rain, Blas and Duvina, 'Fia and Jaime, would move in peace and unafraid. And why? Because of Dan McKee.

Dan looked at 'Fia, 'Fia with night-black hair and eyes that were quickly hidden by long lashes and, suddenly, it was there again, the eager, buoyant effervescence that lifted up his heart. Why?

El Topo stretched his neck, pulled down a strip of melon and stood munching it, the yellow rind dangling from his mouth. He looked for all the world like some big, overgrown boy, enjoying stolen sweets. Like a boy, Dan laughed, not at El Topo but at the answer to his question. El Topo had come home to stay—and so had Dan McKee!

> *With my knees in the saddle and my seat in the sky,*
> *I'll quit punchin' cows in the sweet bye an' bye.*
> *Co-ma ti yi you-pe you-pe ya.*

TRAIL'S END

Weep No More, My Lady!

by NORMAN A. FOX

THEY CROSSED THE WIDE, MUDDY ARKANSAS RIVER IN LATE AFTERnoon, and bedded two thousand longhorns on the flats beyond the north bank; then they turned their faces toward Dodge City, five miles to the east, every man of them. This was what they had waited for; this was trail's end; and across all the thundering miles up out of Texas and through the Indian Nations and into Kansas, on days of dust and nights of storm, through monotony and weariness and heat and danger, they had talked of this. They stepped up into saddles when the work was done, all but those who'd volunteered to hold the herd; and they came to Dodge in the time-honored manner of Texas trail men, crowding their horses at a high gallop up Second Avenue, and not even reining down in the plaza, where teeming humanity split a path for them, and glassed-in kerosene lamps spread their brilliance.

Sam Travis rode up front—the right of gray hair and twenty

years of saddle-whacking for the Twin-T; and Deef Bicknell rode
at his one hand and Sid Kendrick at the other; and the rest of the
crew, five of them, were strung out behind, with Jody McClain
eating the dust, just as he'd done all the miles out of Texas. Jody
was as bug-eyed as any pilgrim tonight. They'd told him that
Dodge was a hell-roaring town, but Jody hadn't supposed you
could actually hear it roar. Yet there was a low, muttering tone to
it, incessant and passively ominous, and it made Jody's spine
tingle. They didn't have anything like this in the Ohio farm
country, where he'd been reared; nor in the Texas Panhandle
where' he'd gone to be a cowboy. It was wine in your blood to
be eighteen and trail-weary and seeing Dodge City for the first
time. It made you forget that you were still being weighed in a
balance, and might be found wanting.

The Old Man had come on ahead, taking the wagon across the
toll bridge; and he was waiting for them at the Wright House.
When they put up their horses at a hitchrail and trooped into the
hotel, he was there, freshly barbered but looking no less grim than
always, a big block of a man, eagle-beaked and lion-maned. It
soured the wine of excitement in Jody, just seeing him. They said
in Texas that Flint Maxwell had drunk the juice of the cactus and
cut his teeth on a branding iron, and that he had no heart in
him; but they also said that the Old Man asked no hand to do a
chore that he himself would shirk.

He gave his crew an unsmiling look and opened his iron cash-
box. "You've all got wages coming," he said. "You'll want to draw
some tonight. Just remember we may be loading those longhorns
onto stock-cars tomorrow if I find our cattle-buyer this evening,
so leave a drop or two in the saloons. . . . Sam—"

Sam Travis wanted sixty dollars, and there wasn't a one of them
but knew how he would spend it; for each man has his weakness,
and Sam's was cards. They got their money, one by one, and Jody
was last; and when he stood before the Old Man his thought was:

This is it. Now he'll tell me whether he's keeping me on or not.

The Old Man looked at him as thoughtfully as he might have eyed a steer that needed to be cut into the culls, and Jody was conscious of his clothes, worn threadbare by the trail, and of his body, too lean for the length of it, knowing that he must look altogether gawky and inept. The Old Man dropped his eyes to his tally-book. "You've got three months' pay coming, McClain," he said. "How much of it do you want?"

Jody said, "Fifty dollars," wondering if his breathlessness told in his words; and then the high giddiness went out of this moment with a sobering thought: *He isn't paying me off in full, but that doesn't prove he's keeping me. He needs me tomorrow for the loading, that's all. Probably he'll hand me my walking papers then.*

The Old Man counted out the money, then fished in his vest for a small envelope. "This is for you too, McClain," he said. "The desk-clerk gave it to me when I first came in. A message from a friend of yours, he said."

Jody took the envelope and saw his name upon it, and was conscious of the stares of all of them. There was a smell of perfume about the envelope, and the handwriting was feminine, and that could let a man in for a great deal of hoorawing. He tore the envelope open, took out a note which said:

I hope you remember me. George Henderson who used to run the mercantile back home was in Dodge awhile ago, and your name happened to come up, and he told me that your folks had said you were working for the Twin-T in Texas. The word was going around this afternoon that Twin-T was hitting town. I'd like very much to see you. Could you meet me in front of the Opera House at ten?

The name *Crystal Alva* was signed to it, and Jody remembered only because it was such an odd name and apt to stick with a man; but even then it took a moment to conjure up a picture, and that picture was misty and dim, and he himself was in it, small and brown and bare-footed and linsey-clad, and she was there too, calico and legs and pigtails, and he was carrying her school-books and making enthusiastic talk of a frog he had captured.

He tucked the note away and said to all of them: "An old friend from where I used to live."

Jody went with the others, after they'd checked their guns at the hotel according to the law of Dodge. Bunched and noisy, they strode along a plank walk where wooden awnings made a continuous canopy, and water barrels stood spaced intermittently in case of fire. There was just time to get barbered before ten o'clock. Front Street had as many barbershops as it had saloons. Jody got out of a chair ahead of any of the rest, because he didn't need much of a shave, and he gave them a wave and slipped to the street and had no trouble finding the Dodge Opera House because it was three stories, the tallest building in town. Its front was dark tonight, for there was no show; and he stood hesitating, peering, when she moved from the shadows.

She said: "You're Jody?"

She was taller than he'd expected her to be, and these five years since he'd seen Ohio had turned her into a woman; yet simple arithmetic made her no more than eighteen. She wore something dark and shapeless—a cloak, he guessed, and a foofaraw bonnet with a curling white plume atop it. She'd become a looker; you could tell that. But it was her voice that had changed most; it had become brittle, and somehow it scared him. He said, fumblingly: "Howdy, Crystal," and wondered if he was supposed to shake hands. A pause became long and awkward, and he said, with a growing desperation: "Were my folks well when you left? I haven't been much of a hand at writing."

"It's four years since I was home," she said.

He remembered her own folks then, a futile pair, bowed with

much toiling, and defeated constantly by stubborn acres, and he supposed he should ask about them. He said: "Could we go some place where we could talk?"

She drew in a long, hard breath, and her voice trembled and then came with a rush. "Jody," she said, "there's a cattle train heading east at midnight. I could buy a caboose passage if I had the money. Likely you think I'm nervy for asking, but could you lend me a hundred dollars? I could send it back to you later, or pay it to your folks. I want to go home, Jody. Ma—Ma's sick."

Just like that.

A coldness gathered in him, nameless and belligerent, for he was facing a stranger who had made an outlandish request. He saw, too, that she was wearing paint and powder, too much of it, and he wondered why she should seem so much older than he, when that wasn't so. He said: "I haven't a hundred dollars, Crystal."

She came closer, pressing against him and putting her hands on his shoulders, so that he smelled the perfume she wore, the same perfume she'd put on the note; he fought against its headiness. She said: "Please, Jody! You could get the money!"

He wanted to slap her, and he couldn't have told why; and oddly he wanted, too, to put his arms around her, the way a man does around anybody who needs comforting. Yet they had never been sweethearts, really, and there was nothing in this mad moment that was made of love. Maybe it was homesickness that had him by the throat; maybe there was a ghost in her face, the ghost of another girl she'd once been; anyhow, the smell of hay was in his nostrils again, and the remembrance of truck-patches and paling fences, and hound dogs, and a frog kept alive in a fruit-jar, made a blur in his mind. He stepped back from her and said gruffly: "Wait here. I'll see if I can get you the money."

He was halfway to the Wright House, before he remembered that drawing another fifty dollars might mean that Flint Maxwell would ask him questions; and because there could be no sensible answers to those questions, he turned instead toward the Long Branch Saloon, recalling all the trail talk Sam Travis had made of the place. He came into the biggest room he had ever seen, a noisy, smoke-layered room awash with light from oil chandeliers heavy with dangling cut glass; and he skirted a bar he'd heard was the longest in the world, eyeing the keno layout and the crowded gaming tables until he found the one where Sam Travis sat with several professional gentlemen of the green cloth. He stood behind Travis silently until a hand was dealt and played, and then he said with careful courtesy: "A minute with you, Sam?"

Travis nodded and forced a way to the bar and ordered drinks; and Jody knew then how it had been with Crystal when she'd made her request, for his own voice trembled when he said: "I'd like the loan of fifty dollars, Sam."

Travis bunched his white, bushy eyebrows and smiled with an old man's wisdom. "That friend of yours, kid, from your old stamping-grounds?"

"A girl I used to know," Jody confessed. "She needs money to go home."

"You could draw it from the Old Man. You've got it earned."

"You don't want to trust me for it, Sam?"

Travis fingered his whisky glass, and he said then: "I've had my eye on you, kid. Lemme see, it was spring when you rode to the Twin-T asking for work, and lookin' like you'd had a hard winter. Flint put you on for this drive north, and said he'd talk about a steady job after that. The Twin-T is a hard outfit, kid, but it pays better than most, and it keeps its men, good times and lean, if they measure up. I ought to know. You want to stay on with the Twin-T, kid?"

"I reckon I proved that on the trail."

Travis nodded. " You ate the dust of the drag, and you never kicked. You took the middle watch night after night, the one that busts up a man's sleep. You rustled wood for the coosie without anybody asking you. Yes, kid, I think I savvy how bad you want to be a regular hand. But the trail's one thing, and the town's another. How you behave yourself tonight is gonna count with the Old Man. Mind you, none of us are spying for him. But he'll know. He'll be down at the tracks dickering with the cattle-buyer and mindin' his own business; but just the same, he'll know every move any of us makes. This is part of your test, kid."

Anger stirring in him, Jody said: "Doesn't a man have any private life when he rides for the Twin-T?"

"Sure," Travis said. "But before he's proved himself, his private life can tell a heap about him. You wouldn't be making a fool out of yourself, kid?"

Jody turned away from the bar. "Thanks for the drink, Sam."

"Just a minute," Travis said, and began peeling bills from a roll. "There's some in Dodge who fancy themselves poker-players who are already sadder and wiser. Here's the fifty, kid. Pay it back when you please. The spiel was free."

Jody took the money and stood staring at it, and then he raised his eyes to Sam's and said again: "Thanks, Sam. I appreciate the spiel as much as the fifty. How's a man to know when he's making a fool of himself?"

"I never learned that," Sam said. . . .

Jody went out to the street, tucking the fifty Sam had given him in beside the fifty he'd drawn. He went hurrying toward the Opera House; and because it came to him that he was hurrying to pass over that money before he changed his mind, he moved all the faster. You could tell yourself she was a girl you had known once, and that made a claim. You could remember that she must have been desperate, to ask for the loan; and you could remember that her mother was sick and needed her; but once suspicion had got an edge to it, you thought of a lot of other things too, and mostly you didn't want to be played for a fool. Not only because of what the Old Man would think if he knew, but because of what you would think of yourself afterward.

But when Jody reached the Opera House, she was gone.

The man who stood waiting had the frostiest eyes Jody had ever seen; there was about him a cool implacability that was more evident than the badge he wore. But the badge was there, plain to see, which made him a marshal of Dodge, one of that formidable lineage that had included Wyatt Earp and the Mastersons and Mysterious Dave Mather. He said: "Looking for somebody, cowboy?"

"A girl," Jody said. "She was going to wait for me here."

"I sent her along where she belongs," the marshal said. "South of the Santa Fe tracks. I've got no quarrel with the way any woman makes her living, but she's Rolle Durango's woman, and that puts her in a class by herself. We like to see you Texas men have a good time, son, but we wouldn't want you swindled. I'm not asking you what her game was. Just consider yourself lucky, cowboy."

Jody's voice turned brittle. "Where is she?" he asked. "I've got to find her."

Pity took the frost out of the marshal's eyes. "At a place called the Sedalia House, cowboy."

And that was how Jody came to Hell's Half Acre, that nether world south of the Santa Fe tracks, crossing the line of demarcation to the dim and ugly section where Dodge peace officers, by common consent, let lawlessness run rampant so long as it was confined to that one part of town. Jody knew about the district; he'd heard of it in campfire talk and in the long watches when the nighthawks had spoken of Dodge. The marshal had told him everything when he'd said where he'd sent Crystal. And now Jody had to see the girl again, but not to give her the money she'd wanted.

He inquired twice of passers-by before he found the Sedalia House, a gloomy frame structure that must have been standing when Dodge had been known as Buffalo City. He came into a hall so dark that he had to grope for the stairs, and these led him upward to another hall, dimly lighted and flanked by many doors. Somewhere in the building a man cursed drunkenly until high, shrill laughter drowned out the sound. Three of the doors opened, and Crystal looked from one of them, her eyes wide with astonishment as she recognized Jody. She hastily drew him into her room.

"The marshal!" she cried with sudden understanding. "He told you I'd be here!"

Jody didn't answer, merely stood looking at her, a hot, terrible anger buzzing in his ears. She's discarded her cloak and bonnet, and he saw that her dress showed her silk-stockinged legs and fell low in the front; and he saw that her hair, which he'd remembered as yellow in those long-ago days, had acquired a reddish tinge that must have come out of a dye-bottle. He stared beyond her at the room; there was a rickety bureau and a chair, and the bed. He said then: "You didn't ask me how I'd been getting along since I left home, Crystal. I reckon you didn't give a hoot. A truck-patch wasn't my idea of what I wanted, and I ran away to Texas when I was thirteen to be a cowboy. I rode for every rag-tail outfit along the Pecos, and then I got a chance to sign on with the Twin-T. It's a big outfit, Crystal, and I'd like to stay with it. But a man has to measure up, for that."

She took a step away from him, her gaze hard and suspicious, and she said: "If this is the start of a sermon, I've heard too many of them. What is it you're trying to say?"

"Just that I almost risked my chances of keeping my job to give you a hand, because I thought you were telling me the truth. How many other fools have furnished a hundred dollars for train-fare home?"

The hardness went out of her face, and it turned white beneath the paint. "You think I was lying to you?"

"And why not? What's there at home for you?"

"Escape from this," she said, and her arm moved, sweeping the room, and she began to weep then, silently, putting her hands to her face while her shoulders shook. Her voice muffled, she said: "I did lie to you about Ma being sick, Jody. That wasn't why I wanted to be on that train at midnight."

He stared at her, feeling wretched, and wishing he hadn't been quite so harsh. He never had known what to do with a crying woman, but he couldn't bring himself to touch her, to comfort her. Not now. Yet not because of this place and her being in it; there'd been a time down in Texas when he'd been broke and hungry, and he'd thought of walking into a crossroads store with a gun in his hand; and he might have done it, only he'd stopped at a ranch first, and they'd fed him. He took the hundred dollars from his pocket and laid it on the bed, and he said: "All I want is your promise that I'm the last man who'll walk through that door."

He said it without looking at her, without waiting for an answer, and he closed the door softly behind him as he quit the room.

He met a man on the stairs, almost colliding with him in the gloom; and the fellow said in a soft voice: "Sorry, cowboy." Jody grunted and would have moved on, but the man said: "Got a match?" Jody found one, and the man brushed it against the wall and touched the flame to a small evil-smelling cigar. He was a lean and catlike man, wearing the black cut-away coat of a gambler, and a flowered waistcoat with a watch-chain of nuggets strung across it, and a beaver hat tipped at the proper rakish angle. His skin was olive and flawless, and he had a whisper of a mustache above thin, over-red lips. He said, "Thanks, cowboy," and moved on upward.

Jody came out of the Sedalia feeling like a man who has toiled in a boghole extricating a calf from the mire, and who stands at

last on firm, clean ground. He paused on the edge of the plank
walk and drew in the night air, and he turned and looked back
then, seeing the lighted rectangles that were the windows of the
Sedalia, and marking the one that was hers. And while he stood
watching, a silhouette moved against the drawn shade, the silhouette of a man wearing a tall beaver tipped at the proper
rakish angle. A shadowy arm rose and nudged back the hat; and
Crystal was suddenly silhouetted there too, and the two silhou-
ettes blended and became one in an embrace.

Afterward Jody didn't remember turning back and climbing
the stairs again. In anger that left him weak and sickened, he
found himself before the door of her room; he kicked it open and
stepped inside. They were still standing by the window, still em-
bracing, that catlike man and Crystal, the girl's arms about the
man's neck, the man whispering to her in what might have been
Spanish. They both became aware of Jody at the same time, and
the catlike man whirled, pushing Crystal away from him and
leaving his arms clear, and he said in that soft way of his:
"Trouble, cowboy?"

Crystal cried sharply, agonizedly: "Rolle! Don't!"

It came to Jody now that indecision had ridden him ever since
he'd entered Dodge City, that each new event of the night had
left him with a choice to make and a doubt as to how to make it.
But he knew what he wanted to do now, and how to do it, and
there was a joy in the knowledge as he came at the catlike man as
a longhorn charges an unhorsed rider. *So this is Rolle Durango,* he
thought. The fellow flicked a hand under the tail of his coat, and
when the hand reappeared it had a derringer in it. Jody grabbed
him by the wrist and twisted hard, and the tiny gun went skidding
on the floor. Durango tried to bite him, but Jody turned him
around and fastened one hand at the collar and the other at
the seat of his pants, and he danced the man across the room and

through the open door and shoved him at the stairs. Durango fetched up at the bottom of the steps with quite a clatter. *I hope I broke his fool neck,* Jody thought. But Durango scrambled to his feet, hissing and swearing. The outer door banged; he was gone.

Jody turned toward Crystal. "The money?" he said. "Where is it? Hand it over!"

Her hand fluttered toward the low-cut front of her dress. "You think—" she began.

"I *know* he's your man and the pair of you work together! I think he was waiting on the stairs because he heard my voice in this room, and didn't dare come in till you had me fleeced. I think he came here now for his cut."

His eyes must have given her the measure of his anger. Her hand dipped into the front of her dress, and she extended the roll of bills. He leafed through this and tucked the money into his trouser pocket.

As he turned toward the door again, afraid to trust himself to further words, she cried: "Wait, Jody!"

His voice became a lash. "How many times do you think you can make a fool of me in one night?"

She said: "Jody, will you do this: Will you *take* me to the train? Will you buy me passage and pay over the money with your own hand? Will you watch that train till it pulls out, so you can be sure in your mind that I'm on it? Would *that* convince you that I mean what I said? Or would you be afraid that I was working with the train crew, too, and that they'd let me off at the first stop with a share of the money given back to me?"

He stood baffled, feeling her desperation like a living, scorching thing, yet not understanding, not able to make sense out of this new request of hers, suspicion still strong and sharp in him. She said breathlessly: "I suppose I can't expect you to believe anything I'd say to you. But will you take one more chance? *Will you put me aboard that train?*"

"Get your things ready," he said.

He didn't want to think. He was afraid to think, for fear that thinking might show him the means by which she was once again using him. He wanted to believe in her, in spite of everything, no matter how fantastic that might be now. He paced the room nervously, and was glad to be able to busy his hands by helping her with the telescope straps. She got her cloak around her and donned the plumed bonnet she'd worn at the Opera House, and he lifted the telescope and got her by the arm and they started for the stairs.

When they stepped out on the planking, Crystal pressed something bulky and hard into Jody's hand, and he stared in surprise; it was a six-shooter. She must have got it out of a bureau drawer, he realized. She said: "Take it. And keep it handy. A man doesn't do what you did to Rolle Durango and get away with it. I know him too well for that. His sneak gun's still up there on the floor, but he carries a forty-five in a shoulder holster, too. Watch yourself."

She crowded close against him; and on impulse, he put his free arm around her, still keeping the gun in his hand. To the north of the tracks the lights of Dodge's brighter world cast a sulphurous glow against the night sky, but down here Hell's Half Acre was like a shadowy limbo; even the sullen ominous roar of the town was muted by distance. There was an intangible threat in the night, something weird beyond Crystal's warning and the mute reminder of the gun in his hand, something that kept Jody's eyes alert, probing every shadow, peering into the slots between buildings. And so they came through tangled streets until they were among the many white-washed shipping pens below the tracks, came without incident or challenge; but there seemed to be acres of these corrals, and Jody's high-heeled boots were hurting him long before he heard the chuffing of an engine on a siding and knew they were nearing the tracks.

It was almost midnight, he judged. The sky was overcast; and the stars, the cowboy's clock, were distant and hooded. *Have to hurry, or we'll miss the train,* he thought; but when he increased their pace, he found that Crystal, who'd been breathing heavily, was now, strangely, breathing more easily, and some of the tenseness seemed to be gone from her shoulders beneath his arm.

Then an orange ribbon of flame unfurled from the vicinity of one of the shipping pens, the bullet sighing past Jody's ear, and he lowered his free arm and tugged at Crystal awkwardly, edging her behind him; and that was impulse too. He let the telescope drop to the ground, and he shifted the six-shooter from his left hand to his right and fired blindly at the spot of darkness from which the gun-flame had come. The gun bucked hard against the heel of his hand. He shifted sidewise as he fired, and he felt a bullet pluck at his sleeve; but when he fired again, a man coughed and moved out from the distant shadows mincingly, and seemed to peer about as though searching for someone before he fell on his face.

Jody advanced cautiously, then touched the sprawled figure with the toe of his boot and saw the beaver where it had fallen and rolled a full pace away. He was sick then, a violence of stomach beyond denial, for he'd never used a gun in anger before tonight. As he came back to where Crystal stood waiting, men were shouting yonder, and there was a stampede of boots as they came running, drawn by the shots. Jody said, "He's dead, Crystal," and kept his eyes away from her face. "I'm sorry," he said then. "He's dead, and he must have meant something to you."

He wondered if she'd cry and hoped she wouldn't; her face, when he looked at her, was a ghastly mask. She said tonelessly: "He knew every rotten scheme there was for making a dollar, and for some of them he needed a woman. He trained me well, but the idea to get a hundred dollars out of you was my own idea. Yes, he meant something to me—something I wanted to fight against when he wasn't around. But whenever he whistled, I came; and it would always have been that way as long as I was near enough to hear him whistle. Even tonight, when you'd given me the money and left the room and I knew I was free, I melted because he took me into his arms. You see, Jody, it was *him* I've been trying to run away from. But there wasn't any way I could tell you and make you understand."

Even now he wasn't sure that he understood. He took the money from his pocket and thrust it into her hand. "Hurry now, or you'll miss the train," he said. "I'll stay to do the talking. Here come men now with questions to ask. Good-by, Crystal. Good-by —and good luck."

She stood on tiptoe and kissed him, straining hard against him, and then she grasped the telescope and went fleeing toward the tracks. A dozen men were suddenly around Jody, and some were looking at the body of Durango, and some were talking, a babble of voices; and one of these men was Flint Maxwell. Jody thought despairingly: *Of all the men in Kansas, he'd have to be here at a time like this!* It didn't even make sense, the Old man being here, until Jody remembered that doubtless he'd been dickering about cattle-cars.

The Old Man said, "McClain!" a vast disbelief in his voice. "Just what is this?"

Jody told him, told him all of it, and while he was talking, he heard the whistle of the departing train. There were a dozen men listening, but Jody talked only to the Old Man, for it was as if the world had now narrowed down to the two of them. At the end Maxwell said: "Do I get this right? She was a childhood sweetheart?"

"No," Jody said. "Just a girl I knew, long ago."

"You didn't owe her anything?"

"Not a thing," Jody said. "I didn't owe her a thing." And then, knowing what was inevitable and remembering that a man had a right to his pride, he said: "My private horse is out with the Twin-T remuda. I'll get him tomorrow. You'll be paying me off, I reckon."

The Old Man's face had nothing of softness in it, but he said, "Eh?" like a man recalled from something remembered. He frowned. "I do the hiring for the Twin-T," he said. "Likewise I do the firing. When I want to pay you off, I'll let you know. You can do me a favor now by getting into town and rounding up the crew. We've got cattle to load, come dawn."

Jody stared. "Sure," he said. "Sure, Mr. Maxwell." And he went running, because he needed the wisdom of Sam Travis now as he'd never needed it before. . . .

They were up into saddles, the bunch of them, and beyond Dodge they headed west, letting their horses run unchecked to where the herd was bedded. Sam Travis should have been riding up front—the right of gray hair and twenty years of saddle-whacking for the Twin-T—but he'd dropped back beside Jody; and Jody had talked then, telling him how it was, all of it.

Travis said: "Quit your frettin'. You're a hand now, kid. Otherwise he'd have paid you off instead of sending you after the rest of us."

"But he knows the truth!" Jody exclaimed. "He knows I gave her the money for no other reason than because I happen to be a soft-hearted, soft-headed fool!"

"I wonder," Sam Travis said softly. "What does a man like Flint Maxwell use for tallying when he measures another man? Would there have to be more to it than just being able to do the chores? Do you reckon that any *real* man would have to have it in him to be a grand fool just once in his life? You reckon that the

Old Man might have made just as big a fool of himself at some time in his life, and was maybe remembering that tonight?"

"Sam!" Jody ejaculated. "You had a hunch all along that it might work out like this! You knew him better than anybody!"

Sam Travis smiled in the darkness. "Just the same, you owe me fifty bucks, kid," he said. "Don't be forgetting that. It's no more than fair. Every man should have to pay for his own experience."

Lynch Mob at Cimarron Crossing

by THOMAS THOMPSON

DRUM ROLLS OF RAIN RATTLED ACROSS THE WOODEN AWNINGS OF Cimarron Crossing's false-fronted buildings and the sound beat against Deputy Marshal Clint Bentley's ears like echoes of the gun fight that had set off the trouble. He stood by the window and looked out at the Kansas town, a tall Texan with anger in the set of his shoulders and worry in his eyes, a grown man who was suddenly conscious of the fact that he was only twenty-one years old and looked younger. Behind him, the wounded man on the cot drew air sharply through his teeth, a quick protest against pain, and Clint Bentley cursed.

Without turning, he said, "What the devil gets into them, Brick? The Civil War's been over fifteen years. Do they want to start it up again?"

The man on the cot didn't answer, but the kid in the jail cell down the hall started laughing shrilly. "They'll start it, all right, rebel," he said. "And when they do, I know where to get me another Texan. I'm looking at him now."

Bentley turned swiftly, taut nerves driving his anger. "I should have pistol-whipped you until you couldn't talk, Mathers," he said. "Keep pushing me and I'll do it yet."

Marshal Brick Dillingham shifted his weight on the cot the doctor had set up for him here in the office. The marshal's left leg was mangled by the stray bullet he caught when he rushed into the saloon to try to stop the shooting. He was an old man who looked as if the constant Southwest Kansas winds had dried all the juices from his body. His face was gray, his lips pulled tight with pain.

He said, "Take it easy, Clint."

"It'll be Tony Coford that starts it," Clint said hotly. "Why not let me bring him in?"

"You got no charge against Tony Coford," Brick said. "You couldn't hold him. You throw him in jail, you'll make a hero out of him, and that's the last thing you want to do."

In his cell, Bud Mathers laughed softly, a swaggering eighteen-year-old with a practiced sneer. He had just shot a man and he liked the feel of it. It showed in his eyes, in the mirthless savageness of his grin. He pressed his lean face against the bars of his cell door and called to the young deputy, his voice taunting, "You're so anxious to lock everybody up, rebel, why don't you start with your brother-in-law? Johnny Tarbell was in on it."

Clint started toward the cell and Marshal Brick Dillingham stopped him. "Johnny didn't have a gun, Clint. Neither did Tony Coford. If they had of, I'd 'a' had you bring them in."

"You didn't say Johnny was with them," Clint accused.

"I didn't think I had to say it, Clint," Brick said quietly. "Johnny always is with them lately, ain't he?"

A new tiredness tugged at Clint Bentley's shoulders. He had been married six months and he had done everything he could to make friends with Betty's sixteen-year-old brother, but he had failed. Moody, resentful, caged by his age, Johnny Tarbell was following the pattern and advice of Tony Coford and Bud Mathers straight down the line.

He turned back to the window and looked out at the soaked town, and he could see the river, running wide and brown. Yellow mouths of foam lipped at seal-black tree stumps that turned soddenly in the flood. Three Dodge City-bound Texas trail herds had piled up there, waiting for the flood to subside, and fifty or more Texan riders had been thinking of the warmth of the town and a drink and the sound of a woman's laugh. It could have been as simple as that. Four Texans had ridden into town today, not looking for trouble, and one of them had got a bullet in his chest just because an eighteen-year-old kid had to prove he was tough. And now Tony Coford and the rest of Bud Mathers' friends wanted to push it further.

"You have any trouble taking the guns off those other two?" Brick asked.

Clint shook his head. "They're all right, Brick. I knew both of them down in Texas. That kid Bud Mathers shot is a friend of theirs, that's all. They're just waiting to see if he's gonna live or die."

"They won't wait long," Bud Mathers said from his cell. "Tony will get a gang together. He'll drag those two Texans out of town on the end of a rope."

"If that kid dies, you'll get a rope, Mathers; don't forget that," Clint said.

"If I'm here," Mathers said.

Clint stared out the window, and across the street he could see the two Texas men, friends of Prentice, the wounded youth. The two were waiting, their faces set in an angry worry that was straining toward the breaking point. The two men wore yellow slickers and they stood on either side of the door of the doctor's office, unmindful of the rain that fell straight down in heavy leaden drops.

Clint turned suddenly, a desperation in his voice. "Shag Holliver knows about it by now, Brick," he said. "The other one rode on back to camp. Those are Shag's men, they told me that, and I know how Shag is."

"Shag Holliver's like your very own father," Bud Mathers mocked. "Took you in and raised you up all sweet and purty."

"Shut up, Mathers," Clint said. "Shut up or so help me ——"

"What, Texas boy?" Mathers said.

"I got a notion to go across and give the guns back to those two," Clint said. "I got a notion to give 'em their guns and let 'em find Tony Coford and the rest, and clean this rat's nest out."

"And Johnny Tarbell?" Brick asked quietly. Brick kept his voice down, hoping Bud Mathers wouldn't hear, but Mathers heard. He started to laugh wildly.

"I don't know, Brick," Clint Bentley said, and now he looked old for his age.

Brick was right. He was always right. He had experience in such things. Johnny wasn't one of them yet; he hadn't had a chance to prove his toughness. But running those two Texans out of town would give him his chance.

There was a kindness in Brick Dillingham, a streak of the senti- mental that let him sense a man's doubts. "Quit blaming yourself, Clint," Brick said softly. "The town had a head start on you before you ever met Johnny."

Clint supposed that was so, but admitting that truth was no solution. Cimarron Crossing was a small place, taking its seasonal life from the Dodge City trail that passed a mile upstream from here. The town had started as one saloon on the south bank of the river and then, as the trail herds increased, so did the town, and now it was caught in its own growth, not big enough to sup- port its own population. Older men could move away and find a start someplace else; the really young didn't care. But there were the in-between, the sixteen- and seventeen-year-old, hot-blooded kids straining to break down the final barrier to manhood, herding together to share their own miseries. A very few found jobs; some ran away—from home, they thought, but really from themselves. And some, if they could prove themselves tough enough, found a restless sort of security in the hero worship they lavished on Tony Coford and Bud Mathers; and sixteen-year-old Johnny Tarbell was one of these.

The druggist from next door came in to sit a while with Brick, and Clint said, "I might as well go eat while I got a chance. Can I bring you anything, Brick?"

"If I know your wife, she'll have something fixed for me," Brick said, and Clint grinned, just as he always did when anyone mentioned Betty. She was a world of her own, a place where everything was good and right. And maybe that was why he hated toughs like Tony Coford and his gang, Clint thought. Sooner or later, if you let them go, they invaded the private world of people like Betty.

Bud Mathers, from his cell, said, "Why don't you let me go home in your place, rebel? Maybe Betty would enjoy finding out what it's like to have a real man come home to her."

Clint turned and walked swiftly over to the cell door. Bud Mathers moved back, but he wasn't quick enough. Clint reached through the bars and gripped Mathers' shirt, and he jerked the youth forward, slamming his face against the bars. He saw the blood start from Mathers' nose, the quick fear in Mathers' eyes, and Clint let him go, disgusted with the fear he had seen, angry with himself for letting his temper get away.

Bud Mathers retreated to the back of the cell and he stood there, cursing vilely, now that he was safe. Clint went outside and stood a moment to let the rain lash his face, finding a savage satisfaction in it. In front of the doctor's office the two Texans in yellow slickers looked up briefly, their eyes following the young deputy. They knew he was the only law in this town tonight, and they knew he was inexperienced law, just as Tony Coford knew it.

He hurried down the darkening street and the reflections of scattered lights wavered through the dusk and settled on puddles that were black as blood. It was only a few doors to the house where he and Betty lived, and he went up the path and onto the porch. Betty opened the door before he even knocked, and he felt the shock of the gun fight and the trouble in the town leave him in one swift wash of affection. He swept her into his arms and kissed her thoroughly, and the water from his hat ran down her neck and she didn't care. She was small and her hair was as black as night, her eyes a smoky blue, and she had to stand on tiptoe to kiss him back.

"Brick's all right," Clint said, knowing that was what she wanted to hear. "He won't walk for a while, but he's all right."

"The cowboy?"

"I don't know, Betty," he said. "Doc's doing all he can, you know that."

She put her arms around him and clung to him fiercely, just for a moment, her face against his chest. "Clint, sometimes I'm scared," she said. "I promised you I wouldn't be, and I try not to be, but sometimes I can't help it."

I know, he thought. *Sometimes I'm scared myself.* "It'll be all right," he said.

"There's so much talk," she said. "People keep remembering that Shag Holliver's men shot up Prairie City." She bit her lip and looked up, her eyes pleading. "Clint, he wouldn't try it here, would he? Not with you here?"

He looked at her, hoping she couldn't see that that was his own worry. He said, "I'll tell you what. If Shag Holliver gets any ideas like that, I'll come right out and advise him against it."

He made himself grin and he slapped his open palms against her hip, making the whole thing not even worth talking about, let alone worth worrying about. She had worries of her own with Johnny; Clint didn't want to add the burden of his job to her shoulders.

"I want to meet Shag, Clint," she said. "I know he's proud of you and I want him to know me."

"Maybe you wouldn't like him," he said, his grin genuine now. "He's rough and tough and big as a barn, and he can't even say his own name without cussin' about it."

"I'd like him," she said. "I'd love him. I love every single person in the world who was ever nice to you and I hate every single person who was ever mean to you."

"You got a heap of hatin' and lovin' on your hands," he said. "Do I get my supper or not?"

"You get your supper," she said. "And while you eat I've got some soup and a pot of coffee to take down to Brick."

"I'll take it when I go," he said. "No sense you getting out in that rain."

"Oh, pooh!" she said. "When did a little rain ever hurt anybody? I want to see Brick. Besides," she said, tilting her head, "if I'm real nice to Brick maybe he'll talk the council into giving my husband a raise."

"Betty," he said, "you're downright wicked."

She came and kissed his ear and nuzzled his cheek. "You ought to know," she murmured.

He sat down to eat and he heard the front door close behind her when she left, and he was immediately more lonely than he had ever been in his life. There for a few moments his job and the trouble had been vague and unreal, like unpleasant thoughts to put aside, but now they were back and he was alone with them, and when the showdown came between the Texans and Bud Mathers' friends, Clint Bentley would still be alone, for he belonged to neither faction and yet he belonged to both. Shag Holliver, the trail driver, had given Clint a chance at a decent life. Johnny Tarbell, who tonight would try to earn his right to be Tony Coford's new henchman, was Betty's brother. He became conscious of the thick perspiration gathering on his forehead and he wiped it away with his sleeve.

The voice from the kitchen's back door said, "What's the matter, rebel? Your nerves bad?"

Clint looked up, forcing his grin, and Johnny Tarbell was slouched there in the doorway between the kitchen and the back porch, his shoulder jammed against the door frame. He was a handsome kid, with a lot of Betty's good features, but none of her good humor, and at times, when he didn't know anyone was watching him, he looked young and a little afraid. He looked sure of himself now, standing there with a match dangling from the corner of his mouth and the thumb of his left hand hooked in his heavily studded belt. Tony Coford wore a belt like that, and so did Bud Mathers and several of the others. It was like a uniform to them, a tie to hold them together, to prove they belonged. It was a wicked weapon in a fight.

There was no use beating around the bush with Johnny. Clint had tried it. Clint said, "I want you to stay out of it, Johnny. It'll get you no place fast."

The kid spit the match from the corner of his mouth.

"Johnny, listen," Clint said, and now he was pleading, and he hadn't intended to plead. He wanted to get up and slap the smirk off Johnny Tarbell's face, but he couldn't look at the kid without seeing Betty, without realizing that Betty had been both a sister and mother to this boy, doing the best she could. There was perspiration on Clint's forehead again, and he couldn't help it. "I know what I'm talking about, Johnny," he said. "I tried it myself when I was sixteen. I know how it feels—like you're standing in a tub of molasses and the world keeps turning without you—but Tony Coford isn't the answer, Johnny, believe me." His words were rushing and he was remembering himself, tangled up with another Tony Coford, another time, another place, but they were all the same. Shag Holliver had made Clint see that, and it had been the turning point in Clint's life, and now he had a law badge on his vest and a woman like Betty to love him.

Johnny said, "You through?"

"I've told you," Clint said. "Stay out of it."

"It's funny," Johnny said. "I came to tell you the same thing."

For a moment Johnny stood there, and the look in his eyes was more than a teenager's natural rebellion against authority. It was a challenge. And suddenly Clint knew how Johnny was to win his place. If he backed down a Texan, that would prove he was tough. If the Texan was a lawman, that would be better. And if the lawman was Johnny Tarbell's own brother-in-law, that would be as high as you could get. That would be Tony Coford's new right-hand man.

Clint looked at the boy, seeing no hardened savageness such as he had seen in Bud Mathers, seeing rather an excitement, a drive, a soul-tearing need to prove himself.

Clint said, "All right, Johnny. You've told me. I'll watch my back and you watch yours."

There was a flicker of doubt in Johnny Tarbell's eyes, almost an opening, and then he closed it off. He turned and went out through the back door, and Clint sat there. In time he got his hat and went outside into the rain. He didn't put on his slicker. He wanted his gun handy.

He wasn't going to stop at the marshal's office because he didn't want to see Betty. By now Betty would know Shag Holliver was coming. Brick Dillingham didn't lie about such things. He walked straight down the street, noticing only that the two Texans in yellow slickers were still by the doctor's door. Prentice wasn't dead yet, then.

He was just even with the marshal's office when he looked up toward the north end where the saloons and dance halls were, and saw the crowd start down the street toward him. Tony Coford had spread his poison and found his supporters. This was to Tony Coford's liking—a gang behind him and two unarmed Texans to fight.

There were twenty-five or thirty in that mob, Clint judged, but that didn't mean much. Talking trouble and facing it were two different things, and whisky courage would wash off fast in this downpour. They kept walking straight down the street, tramping through the mud, a dark moving body of men, and Clint tried to visualize them as individuals, deciding in his mind almost exactly who would be there. The two Texans in front of the doctor's office had seen the mob now. They knew what it meant.

"Give us our guns, marshal!" one of the Texans called. "Just give us our guns and let 'em come!"

"You two keep out of it," Clint said.

One of the Texans said, "Clint! What's the matter with you? Have you gone that Damnyankee? You ain't gonna let us stand here and be murdered, are you? Give us our guns!" The Texan's face was drawn and white, his lips pulled away from his teeth.

"You fool!" the other man shouted. "Look up the street there!"

"That's my job," Clint said. "Not yours."

The man cursed helplessly.

The sound of the mob was lifting above the pelt of the rain now, and Clint moved back to the middle of the street. He was soaked to the skin, but he was strangely warm, and he could feel his heart beating heavily. He could make out faces; now, and he recognized most of them. Half of them were too drunk to be dangerous; some of them would run. There wouldn't be more than half a dozen guns among them, probably, but one gun in the hands of a crazy kid trying to prove himself was one gun too many. He saw Tony Coford, then, walking in the front ranks, swaggering, sure, and Johnny Tarbell was right beside him. Johnny was packing his heavy, studded belt in his hand.

The mob stopped, no more than fifteen feet away, and now the voice of one Texan rose high and wild, like the sound of the storm, "You can't whip all of Texas! We'll keep comin' and keep comin'! We'll take this town apart, board for board and nail for nail, and we'll throw it in the river and watch it wash away!"

Someone in the back of the mob yelled, "There they are! Let's get 'em! I got a rope here! Somebody get a horse and we'll drag 'em!"

"Get Clint Bentley too!" another yelled. "He's a Texan!"

"Get Bentley, and then we'll bust down his jail and get Bud Mathers out! Bud wouldn't want to miss any of this!"

"Get the three Texans first, and then we'll get Bud out!" Tony Coford yelled.

The light from the marshal's office spilled across Tony Coford's young face, lean, wolfish. He had prominent teeth and a receding chin and straw-colored hair. Clint kept watching Johnny, flushed with excitement, a kid who was suddenly a part of things, belonging, wanted.

"Listen to me!" Clint yelled. "Are you fools enough to get tangled up in Bud Mather's trouble? If that boy in the doctor's office dies Bud Mathers will hang for murder! What the devil did Bud Mathers ever do for you? These two men here don't want trouble! They haven't even got guns! What the devil you gonna gain by getting the town shot up? Some of you will get killed! You're bound to! Are you that tired of living?"

A dozen at least started moving out of the mob and over toward the sidewalks. They had come along for the walk in deference to the free drinks they had had, and nothing more. They had never had any intention of getting mixed up in it.

Tony Coford said, "You gonna listen to this Texan? You heard what that one on the porch said, didn't you? You gonna stand by and see this town torn apart, board for board?"

There was a drunken babbling and shouted threats, and then a quick, startled silence. A dozen riders had come out of a side street directly at Clint Bentley's back, and Shag Holliver, the trail boss, was riding out in front, a brute of a man with heavily lined features and iron-gray hair and a rifle across his pommel. The riders reined up tight and the mob split in two, half of it holding ground, half hitting for cover, and now it was even, twelve men against twelve, and Clint Bentley was in the middle.

Clint heard Shag Holliver's voice, and without turning, Clint said, "Don't start anything, Mr. Holliver."

"Don't give me orders, boy," Shag Holliver said. His voice was deep-throated, solid like the man. "One of my men was shot. I come to see about it. If I don't like what I find, there won't be no town here, come tomorow."

Clint looked at the rain-slick faces of the mob backing Tony Coford. Half of them were young, no older than Johnny Tarbell, and suddenly they weren't so sure. But Tony Coford was still there, the leader, and as long as Tony stayed, they'd stay. Coford pulled back his coat and Clint saw the gun thrust in the gang leader's waistband. And Johnny was there, breathing heavily, holding his belt. Clint Bentley started moving forward, straight toward Tony Coford.

"This was your idea, Tony," Clint said quietly. "No use all your friends getting killed. Let's make it between you and me."

"Don't try to shove me around, rebel," Tony said.

There was the faintest hint of indecision in his voice. His hand fumbled at the gun he had thrust under his studded belt, and he took two steps back. Clint Bentley kept moving forward. He started to laugh then, softly, and when he was sure, he deliberately dropped his own gun back into its holster. The gang of kids stared, not sure what the gesture meant, and they started to split off, leaving Tony Coford and Johnny Tarbell there alone.

"I been practicing my draw, Tony," Clint Bentley said. "I'm gettin' pretty good at it. You want to see how good, Tony?" He kept walking forward, and now he was no more than two feet away and he could see the bulge of Tony Coford's eyes. "Go for your gun, Tony," Clint said. "Give me an excuse to kill you."

"You're crazy!" Tony Coford said. "You got stakeout guns. You talked them Texans into backing you up!"

"What do you care, Tony?" Clint asked. "You're real tough. You're the toughest kid in town. You wanted to fight the Texans anyway, didn't you? Try me first; then go after the Texans."

"Stay away from me!" Coford said. "Stay away from me or I'll get yuh!"

"No, you won't, Tony," Clint said. "You know why? Because you're a coward. A dirty, yellow, rotten, two-bit coward."

He reached out suddenly and slapped Coford hard across the face with his left hand. He saw Johnny move in, start to swing the belt, and at that instant Clint half turned and drove his elbow into the pit of Johnny Tarbell's stomach. He saw Johnny sit down hard in the mud of the street, heard him get sick, and now he was following through on Tony Coford, swarming in at him, smashing at his face with his fists.

As if from a distance, Clint heard Shag Holliver's bellow, "Stay out of it, all of you! The first one makes a move, my man or anybody else, I'll cut him down!"

Clint had a grip on Tony Coford's wrist. He jerked him around savagely and tripped him, and Coford fell full length in the mud. Clint fell on him. He grabbed a handful of the long hair on the back of Tony's head and he rubbed the kid's face in the mud. Tony struggled, but the fight was going out of him fast. Clint hit him hard; then roughly, he managed to unfasten Coford's heavy belt, and he yanked it off, tearing belt loops with it.

Panting, his breath choking in his lungs, Clint dragged the slimy figure of Tony Coford across his knee and started laying the heavy belt across the tight, water-soaked jeans. In time he heard Coford's sobs, and he let him up, blubbering, holding him a moment by the shirt front, and then he shoved him away.

"You ain't even worth putting in jail, Coford," he said.

The kids were standing there staring. Clint turned his back on them and walked straight toward Shag Holliver and his riders.

"Toss down that gun, Mr. Holliver," Clint said. "Tell the rest of your men to do the same. We got a law against guns in town here."

"I don't give my gun to nobody, Bentley," Shag Holliver said. "You ought to know that."

"Don't make me take it away from you, Mr. Holliver," Clint Bentley said. "I think a lot of you. Don't make me do it."

Shag Holliver hesitated a long moment, and Clint saw him fighting with his pride, a man who backed down from no one. Then, slowly, a grin started spreading across the cattleman's rugged features.

"What the hell?" he said. "It's the way I learned you, ain't it?" He tossed down his rifle. "Shuck your irons, boys," he said across his shoulder. "Looks like this wolf pup of mine growed up man-size."

A dozen bewildered kids stood there, looking at Tony Coford, watching the Texans throw down their guns. They looked at Clint Bentley, and before he asked, three of them took guns from their waistbands and dropped them in the street.

Tony Coford made one last, desperate grab to hold his place in this town, "Get Clint Bentley! He can't whip all of us! The Texans won't stop us!"

One by one, they turned and walked away from Tony Coford, and Johnny Tarbell stood there, looking first at Tony, then at Clint, and then he, too, walked away. The doctor came out of his office, wiping sweat from his moon face, and Clint saw the defeat on the old man's features and didn't have to ask.

"You got a murder charge against Bud Mathers, marshal," the doctor said. "I did the best I could." He looked at the Texans, his eyes pleading. "Honest, boys," he said, "I did the best I could."

There was a long silence, and then Shag Holliver said, roughly, "It's all a man can do."

Clint looked at Johnny Tarbell, standing there on the sidewalk, his face white and drawn. Johnny was thinking about Bud Mathers, Clint knew, swinging at the end of a rope, and maybe he was thinking of how he had wanted to take Bud Mathers' place.

Clint said, "You'll be needing another hand, won't you, Holliver?"

"Yeah," Shag Holliver said slowly. "I will. You know of or

Clint didn't make any show of affection toward Johnn wouldn't be the thing to do. He said, "Johnny Tarbell there my brother-in-law. He'll make you a good hand."

Clint could see Shag Holliver glaring down at him, bi was a certain understanding softness in the cattleman's e hint of memory, maybe.

"You think he's tough enough to ride with my outfit?" asked.

"He's tough, Mr. Holliver," Clint Bentley said. "He's tough i the right way."

He turned and walked across to the marshal's office, leaving Shag Holliver and Johnny Tarbell to work it out themselves, remembering a time just five years back when Clint himself had gone to work for the fabulous Texan. A lot of things had happened in the past five years; a lot would happen in the next five, he supposed, but it wasn't something a man worried about.

He went into the office, and Betty ran into his arms and she started to cry, but sometimes a woman's crying, if it's the right kind, is a beautiful thing to hear. In his cell, Bud Mathers lay on his back and stared at the ceiling.